Istralla

CITADEL FIRSTLIGHT

FOREST

THE VAST SEA

DREAM
BY THE
SHADOWS

DREAM BY THE SHADOWS

LOGAN KARLIE

Christy Ottaviano Books
LITTLE, BROWN AND COMPANY
New York   Boston

Copyright © 2023, 2025 by Logan Karlie
Maps copyright © 2025 by Virginia Allyn
Cover art copyright © 2025 by Andrew Davis
Cover design by Karina Granda. Cover copyright © 2025 by Hachette Book Group, Inc.
Interior design by Carla Weise.

Christy Ottaviano Books
Hachette Book Group
1290 Avenue of the Americas, New York, NY 10104
Visit us at LBYR.com

Originally published in hardcover and paperback in 2023 by the author
First Little, Brown Edition: August 2025

Christy Ottaviano Books is an imprint of Little, Brown and Company. The Christy Ottaviano Books name and logo are registered trademarks of Hachette Book Group, Inc.

The publisher is not responsible for websites (or their content) that are not owned by the publisher.

Little, Brown and Company books may be purchased in bulk for business, educational, or promotional use. For information, please contact your local bookseller or the Hachette Book Group Special Markets Department at special.markets@hbgusa.com.

Library of Congress Cataloging-in-Publication Data

Names: Karlie, Logan, author.
Title: Dream by the shadows / Logan Karlie.
Description: First Little, Brown edition. | New York : Little, Brown and Company, 2025. | Audience term: Teenagers | Audience: Ages 14 to 99. | Summary: In a kingdom plagued with a deadly curse spread by dreaming, eighteen-year-old Esmer has the ability to enter the dream realm where she falls in love with the wicked Shadow Bringer.
Identifiers: LCCN 2024048797 | ISBN 9780316587747 (deluxe) | ISBN 9780316588157 (standard) | ISBN 9780316587761 (ebook)
Subjects: CYAC: Blessing and cursing—Fiction. | Dreams—Fiction. | Love-hate relationships—Fiction. | Fantasy. | LCGFT: Romance fiction. | Fantasy fiction. | Novels.
Classification: LCC PZ7.1.K36427 Dr 2025 | DDC [Fic]—dc23
LC record available at https://lccn.loc.gov/2024048797

ISBNs: 978-0-316-58774-7 (deluxe), 978-0-316-58815-7 (standard), 978-0-316-58776-1 (ebook)

Printed in Indiana, USA

LSC-C

Printing 1, 2025

This is for the dreamers.
Dance with your nightmares and emerge victorious.

PART ONE

In Shadows Deep,
We Wander

In the Kingdom of Noctis, to dream was to die.

Dreams weren't golden reveries, decadent celebrations, or flights with soft, outstretched wings into a sea of clouds. Dreams were death, decay, rot. A wicked haze of illusion in the hands of a devil. But I, either bravely or foolishly, was unafraid of what I couldn't see. And it was all because of *him*.

The Shadow Bringer.

For years, he had been a phantom in my head. A menace under the floorboards. A ghost in the cellar. A creature who haunted others, lurking in the shadows of every dream but never daring to hurt me. The Shadow Bringer and the fantasies he ruled over had been a temptation. A promise of adventure in the darkest, loneliest of nights.

Until my sister died.

"If you follow Eden's path, you'll become a monster, too," my mother warned, cradling my face in her too-cold fingers. "Remember this day and what happens when the elixir isn't taken. To dream is to die." Her thumbnail was chipped; I tried not to flinch as it scratched my cheek. "Eden's soul is with the Maker. Spare no tears for the demon lying in the coffin."

The demon.

But what did a demon look like? Feeling nauseated, I peered down at Eden's body, trying desperately to convince myself that my sister's soul was, in fact, somewhere else. That the thin body in my sister's coffin wasn't actually *her.* There were no flowers in her tangled dark hair. They didn't blanket her in white, nor did they try to conceal the fading shadows under her eyes. Her coffin was a crude box of splintered wood, her burial clothes dirty and torn. There was blood in places I couldn't help staring at—under her nails, seeping from the corners of her mouth, and lining the edges of her bare feet. Her lips were upturned in the parody of a smile, her unfeeling hands clasped in the mockery of a prayer.

Villagers from Norhavellis surrounded us, eyes bright with both curiosity and condemnation.

"Corrupt," they damned.

"The Shadow Bringer killed her," they hissed.

"So young. Just fifteen."

"Poor thing."

"What a shame."

Mother steered my little brother and me away from the growing mob, shielding us from the worst of the comments. Her face was a pale, emotionless mask, but her hand trembled atop my shoulder. Villagers often maligned her as too rigid, even heartless. But where they saw something hollow and unfeeling, I saw strength. While her tears had dried hours ago, my father's had not. Right by Eden's coffin, Father sank to his knees, tears streaming into his unkempt beard.

"My girl," he wept, clawing his fingers into the ground. He tore up pieces of grass, crushed them between his hands, and threw them senselessly into the wind. "Maker save us."

Elliot looked up at me, lower lip quivering.

"It's going to be okay," I whispered, giving my brother's hand a reassuring squeeze. "I promise."

It's not going to be okay. It's never going to be okay again.

Still, he nodded solemnly, believing me.

Before Eden's coffin was lowered into the late-spring ground, the Light Legion commenced their questioning.

"When did the shadows first appear?" a sharp-tongued legionnaire asked. His golden armor, adorned with a sweeping crimson cape, was a bright mark against a lifeless sea of gray. He wore a metal mask, as the other legionnaires did, and only his eyes and close-cropped hair could be seen. "And how long was she afflicted?"

"The shadows first appeared last week," Mother answered simply. "From what we gather, she was afflicted for less than ten days."

I bit my tongue. Eden had carried the marks for over a *month*. She had convinced us she wasn't sleeping well and simply covered them with a bit of pressed powder. By the time the Light Legion arrived, the marks were ink black under eyes bright with malice.

"What crimes were committed?"

"She took a dress from the tailor." Then Mother added, mouth in a tight line, "It was promptly returned, however."

"Is that all?"

"Yes, that is all."

Eden had stolen a dress, but she'd also destroyed our remaining elixir vials, slammed a pillow over my mouth while I was sleeping, wandered Norhavellis in the depths of the night, and been caught eating a rat from our cellar. She'd been imprisoned shortly after that, locked in the village's makeshift holding cell with vermin blood still dribbling from her chin.

The legionnaire continued with more troublesome questions. Questions my mother and father stumbled over.

"You had enough supply, didn't you? Why was she the only Corrupt in Norhavellis this season?"

Mother's hands twisted in her lap. "I don't know."

"Was she not given the elixir?"

"She was given *plenty*," answered Father this time, voice cracking with despair. "We gave her everything we had."

"Well, then—"

"Will this affect our status as Absolvers?" Mother asked sharply.

"No," the legionnaire said simply, much to the visible relief of my parents. "You will still be allowed to distribute elixir on behalf of the Light Bringer. It is clear you strove to uphold your sacred duty; you will not be punished for this tragedy."

A deep rumble halted the legionnaire's interrogation. A storm, quickly approaching, cast a dim shadow upon his golden armor. And as the rain began to fall, the sickening feeling in my stomach turned into something else. Something angry and foul.

Rain fell harder, seeping into our clothes and chilling our bones.

And Eden was swiftly buried in her box of splintered wood.

Later that night, I crawled into my bed and finally allowed myself to feel. I bit down on my sleeve, letting my anguish run fast and deep. It had been my idea—not Eden's—to dream.

Only once, I had begged.

Eden had considered my request seriously, sipping from her mug of steaming apple cider as she glanced at the vial of amber liquid in my hands. "They check the vials every day," she whispered. "They'll know we didn't take it."

"We can pour it out the window."

Eden shook her head, her smooth braids like snakes upon her night-gown. "The snow would stain," she said, ever logical. Ever perfect. "And they'd hear the window opening."

"Down the floorboards, then," I insisted. "There's that crack, over there—"

"If we missed, they'd smell it on the wood," Eden interrupted. "Not to mention that's a waste of perfectly good elixir."

I rolled my eyes. "They have more. They *always* have more."

A loud, drawn-out squeak from the stairs made us freeze. I swapped the vial of elixir for my own mug of cider, taking a hasty sip even as it burned my tongue.

Another squeak. Another footstep.

Eden stared at me in horror.

"Eden? Esmer?" called a soft, hopeful voice. "Are you still awake?"

"Elliot," I said in a huff, rising to peer down the rickety stairs leading to our bedroom. Sure enough, there stood our five-year-old brother, holding a book and smiling sheepishly. His large brown eyes, a mirror in color to his messy curls, were luminous even in the dim candlelight. People always told me that I looked more like him than I did Eden. Our eyes were fiercer, our hair less tamed, our builds a bit taller and ganglier. Eden, on the other hand, was all smooth, silky hair and delicate features—something that boys from the village were starting to notice. "Go back downstairs."

"I wanted to read some stories together," he said with a shrug. "If you were still awake and all."

"More Dream Weaver stories?"

He nodded, squeezing the book to his chest. "Uh-huh. Was thinking the one where Nephthys saves the sea dragon from a nightmare. Or when Lelantos teaches dreamers how to fly."

"Those are lovely stories," Eden chimed in. "You should—"

"Have *Mother* read them with you," I finished, giving Eden a pointed look.

Elliot frowned. "She didn't want to."

"Father, then."

"He's busy."

"Well, we were just about to go to sleep." To make my point, I sat back in bed. Unfortunately, I moved a bit too erratically, and the cider sloshed over the edge of the cup, burning my hand. "Ouch," I grumbled, pressing the affected skin to my mouth. "Elliot, just—okay, *fine*. Come here."

Elliot plopped into my bed, jabbing me with cold feet and a skinny elbow as he opened the book he was carrying. It was in quite the deplorable state, pages velvet soft and spine crumbling from years of enjoyment. My bed was too small to properly fit three, but I made room for Eden, too, cocooning us all in my least scratchy blanket. Winter always found its way into our bedroom, clawing up from under the floorboards or squeezing its frosted body through the walls. I fought against the urge to shiver, wishing that I could turn the pages of the book without stiff, clumsy fingers.

"Oh, she's my favorite," Eden noted, peering at an illustration of a silver-haired woman dressed in a gown of silk and starlight. "Theia, Weaver of the Future," she said reverently, pronouncing the Weaver's name with careful respect. "She's beautiful."

"I suppose," I said with a sigh, then flipped past Xander, Weaver of the Present, to a man with long ink black hair adorned with a crown of bones. "But Somnus is far more interesting."

Eden scoffed. "What can the Weaver of the Past do? Theia would give us dreams of our *futures*. That's what counts the most."

"Like what we'll have for dinner tomorrow," Elliot chimed in.

Eden's mouth quirked up in a grin. "Or who our friends will be."

"Or our enemies," I added.

"Who we'll love. Who we'll marry," Eden suggested.

"How we'll die," I countered.

The thought hung heavy between us.

But only for a moment.

Elliot made an impatient sound. "Hurry up; I want to read the stories."

Eden laughed, the sound as clear and sweet as a silver bell. We were similar in some ways, but different in the ways that counted. Where she was graceful, I stumbled. Where she was smart, I was dull. Where she was kind, I was selfish. Her goodness came naturally, and it couldn't be replicated. Not even by her thirteen-year-old sister.

Eden flipped to the next page. A warrior, glistening with the flames of a thousand suns at his back, stared up at us, defiant and taunting. Fenrir, the Fire Weaver. The next page held Nephthys, the Water Weaver, her dark blue hair crowned with shining jewels.

"I wonder what it'd be like to dream," Elliot said. "Do you think I'd be able to visit Nephthys's castle by the sea? I want to see what a purple sky looks like, too. I bet it'd be strange, and one of the Weavers could teach us, like they used to, and—"

"Is that all you want? To see castles and purple skies?" I teased, pulling the blanket tighter around our shoulders. "Think of what you could do. Or *be*. If we dreamed, we could learn to fly across those purple skies. Travel across the Dream Realm in a blink if we wanted."

"That would be amazing."

"It would be, wouldn't it?" Eden said, thumbing her jaw. "I sometimes wonder what it would be like, too."

I flipped the page this time, past Ceres, the Earth Weaver, in her emerald forest and Lelantos, the Air Weaver, on his mountain, to a masked man wrapped in gold, sunlight spinning from his hands. His radiance filled his page with bright, shimmering waves, washing over those who worshipped at his feet. Mithras Atrelle Tethebrum, our sovereign and holy Light Bringer.

"The Light Bringer!" Elliot exclaimed with a toothy grin.

The next page depicted the seven Dream Weavers in battle against the Shadow Bringer. It was the final confrontation before the Weavers disappeared and Corruption slid over Noctis like a black cloud, leaving the Light Bringer to carry on alone. The artwork exploded violently with shadows, blood, and demonic beings devouring dreamers' souls. The Shadow Bringer sat hunched in the middle of the page, teeth sharp and dripping with gore as he tore apart a Weaver with his claws. Black horns sprang from his skull-like face, framing hideous red eyes.

"I don't like this page very much," Elliot grumbled, squirming deeper into the blanket. "What about the one where—"

A noise sounded from below, much like the heavy creak of boots on a wooden floor.

Father.

"It's bedtime, Elliot," Father called. "Leave your sisters be."

Elliot sighed dramatically, plodding downstairs to the room he shared with our parents. As the door shut behind him, wind snapped against our sole window, rattling the glass. An omen, maybe. But if it was, we missed it.

Or decided to forget.

"We should go to bed," Eden whispered, reaching for her vial of elixir. "I'm cold."

I bit the inside of my mouth. It was now or maybe never.

"What if we didn't take it—just once?" I made a face at the vial in her hands. "We'll say a prayer to the Weavers. They could hear and protect us." I barreled on, knowing if I stopped talking, I'd lose the courage to continue. "If it's scary, we won't do it again. We can take the elixir like we always do."

Eden bit her thumb, considering. "Is it truly worth it, though? We could see a demon."

"Then we will do what we've been taught. Run and force ourselves awake before the demon can touch us." I threw off my blanket, a wicked plan forming. "Let's pour the elixir in our cider. The color will hide it perfectly."

"Only once?"

"Only once," I agreed. "Think of what we'll see in the Dream Realm, what we'll *do*."

But *once* became a word forgotten.

At first the dreams were beautiful, bursting with adventure and wonder. The visions made us feel alive, as if we had a purpose beyond our desolate village in the middle of the woods. They gave us nights to cherish after dull, chore-filled days and our mother's tedious rules. But one day, for Eden, the dreams weren't any of those things. They weren't beautiful, lovely, or safe. They became what we were warned against: dark and festering with the Shadow Bringer's demons.

Her Corruption came quickly.

Too quickly to prevent.

Alone after her funeral, I stifled a scream into my pillow, sobs racking my chest. I was selfish. Horrible. *Unforgivable*. The Shadow Bringer hadn't been real—not truly—until he was.

And by then it was too late.

Five Years Later

As a child, I thought Norhavellis felt like home.

The moment our daily chores were finished, Eden and I would run, flush faced and laughing, through the shadows of the Visstill Forest and into the friendly and predictably safe arms of our village. We'd lay a blanket in the grass under some tree or another, fresh bread with a dollop of honey in hand, and simply watch for travelers on their way to Noctis's seaside capital of Istralla.

We didn't often have visitors, but those we encountered were always interesting. Merchants with their goods—we liked to imagine they carried treasure fit for the Light Bringer himself—tucked away in heavy trunks; legionnaires with their profiles—we liked to imagine they were handsome—covered by their golden masks; or even the rare traveling troupe on its way to perform at Istralla's theater. It was a feast for our imaginations. We'd lie back on our elbows and daydream, wondering what it would be like to travel the kingdom ourselves. Sometimes this mental exercise proved difficult; what opportunities, if any, truly awaited us? But we fantasized, anyway.

In my memories, Norhavellis is sweet smelling and gentle, not harsh and cloying like a dead thing left to molder in the rain. But that memory faded, and I was left with only the weight of the present.

I pulled my cloak tighter, the dark red velvet heavy on my shoulders despite its tattered edges. The hood hung low, casting shadows on my face and shielding me from the chill in the air, but it couldn't protect me from the foul stench that enveloped Norhavellis. It was more than just a scent; it was decay of the mind, body, and spirit. My village was filled with filthy buildings, broken people, and the threat of Corruption that loomed like a storm, ready to burst and drown us all.

A grim transformation, indeed.

I knocked on the chipped door of a small cottage, careful to make as little sound as possible.

"I don't think she's home," Elliot whispered, shifting on his feet and narrowly avoiding the thin string of bells staked low to the ground. It was early evening, so his boyish face was more shadowed than usual. "Maybe we should just come back tomorrow morning. It's getting dark."

I thumbed the vials of elixir in my pocket, reassuring myself that they were still there. Elliot and I wore full-length cloaks that partially hid our hair and faces. If we were recognized while distributing the final dregs of elixir on behalf of our Absolver parents, we'd be swarmed by demon-fearing Norhavellians. Typically, the villagers would accept the elixir that we held, bartering their animals, their crop, and their services for extra vials. But lately, they demanded more. *Questioned* more.

Because Corruption was spreading in droves, regardless of how much elixir was consumed.

"Let's give her a minute," I whispered back. "Maybe she's just—"

Behind the door came the sound of sliding chains and a rattling lock. The door creaked back on its hinges, revealing a blond woman, eyes sunken and thin hair brittle, and her two young children. She was Margaret, the blacksmith's wife, but it took a moment for the recognition to set in. Never before had she looked so miserable or disheveled.

"You came," Margaret squeaked, aimlessly caressing both her skirt and her children's misshapen hair. The twins were young—perhaps only three or four. "I didn't know if you'd come. The village can be a dangerous place at night."

I swallowed uncomfortably. Of course it was. Locks on doors, warning bells threaded, dogs on guard, and hollow-faced men and women sitting on their dark porches with crossbows in hand. Anything to keep their last elixir vials from being stolen.

"What do you think—aren't the twins getting so big?" Margaret asked, peering down at her children. "Say hello, Matthew. Say hello, Isabelle." Matthew's face was a blank slate as he looked up at his mother; his lips mouthed *hello*, but the sound didn't come. Isabelle simply buried her face within her mother's skirts, whimpering softly. Elliot mouthed *hello*, too, and gave a little wave, but the children didn't react. Margaret straightened, smiling nervously. "We were just on our way to the holding cells."

"In that case, we won't keep you. Here," I said, offering her one of the slim vials in my pocket. "It will be enough for one week, even when shared. Just a small mouthful is fine."

One week. Just enough to last them until the Light Legion came with their seasonal redistribution, which would be any day now. I smiled politely before turning around, intending to step off her porch as quickly as possible and return home for dinner. Elliot and I had been rushing around Norhavellis all afternoon, and our stomachs were pathetically empty.

But the woman grabbed my sleeve, holding me back.

"One more vial," Margaret pleaded. "I know you have more. Just one more."

"You have enough elixir to last until the restock," I said slowly. "The rest of the vials belong to other Norhavellian children." She knew this. *Everyone* knew this. "There will be more in just a few days' time."

"Maybe even earlier," Elliot added brightly. "The Light Legion will be here any day now."

"The extra vial isn't for us," Margaret snapped. "It's for my husband."

Isaac, her blacksmith husband, had been discovered to be Corrupt last month after bludgeoning his friend to death with an iron rod. The poor man's face had been unrecognizable afterward.

"Wasn't Isaac found to be..." I let the statement trail off, uneasy with where the conversation was headed.

"Corrupt, yes," Margaret answered coolly, letting go of my sleeve and waving her hand as if the implication were a pesky insect at her throat. "I know what he's done. What he looks like. But what if more elixir can reverse his condition? Maybe it can stop his dreams as it does ours."

"We don't give elixir to the Corrupt," I said flatly. What she was asking was impossible. Corruption had no cure; it would be a waste of a vial.

"If you won't grant me an extra vial, I will give Isaac ours," she threatened. Her children shuffled their feet, peering up at us fearfully. "He needs it more than we do."

Her demand was clearly a threat, but one we couldn't appease without drawing attention to ourselves. Not to mention that her children would be at risk for Corruption if she gave away their vial.

"You may give him one-half of a standard vial," I finally said, hoping that I sounded authoritative. "No more. And you must keep the first vial for you and your children." I wiped my hands on the sides of my skirt, irritated at their growing clamminess. Margaret tapped her foot, eager for me to hand her the extra vial, but I made no move to give it to her. "We'll also accompany you to the holding cells to ensure you're following protocol."

Margaret agreed to this, and she hastily bundled her children in soft woolen sweaters to ward against the late-summer air before we all headed out to see Isaac.

The holding cells were in a quiet part of the village, near the very woods that wrapped around our property. The cells used to be in the center of town, but as Corruption worsened, it was quickly discovered that no one wanted to hear their demon-infested loved ones screaming for release. The new structure was built on the outskirts, surrounded by thick, gnarled trees and stationed with an ever-rotating patrol of guards. And then, every season, the Light Legion would come to purify the Corrupt and bury them in simple graves.

I put what I hoped was a reassuring hand on Elliot's shoulder, knowing that the contents of the holding cells were never pleasant. A few years ago, there had been only one cell. Now there were at least two dozen.

And tonight they were full.

We followed the guards—a small handful of men—down a dimly lit hallway. The Corrupt either slept in unnatural angles, stood stock-still with violence in their eyes, or appeared eerily calm both in character and countenance. All had shadows under their lashes; all seemed distinctly *other*. Isaac was in the last cell, and when we reached him, the guards left us alone.

Isaac was chained to the wall, but he had enough leeway to slowly slide to the bars. Margaret greeted him warmly, brushing the ratty, sweat-slicked hair from his forehead. As though he was still her husband and not a demon. A cloudy substance dripped from Isaac's eyes, mingling with a thick, fleshy fixative that covered the upper half of his face, making the skin appear fractured in several places.

"I try to conceal the shadows so that he doesn't scare the children," Margaret whispered, pulling a brush and a small tincture of flesh-colored putty from her skirt pockets. Concealment, because elixir would be futile. Corruption had no cure, just as the shadows on his face couldn't be scrubbed off. "Would you mind keeping the twins company until I'm done?"

Elliot immediately sat with the children, entertaining them with a tale of Lelantos, the Air Weaver. It was a delightful story, but it twisted an unseen knife in some soft, vulnerable part of me. Before Eden's death five years ago, I had enjoyed reading about the Weavers. It had seemed possible that they would one day return from their centuries-long absence, making everything right and true. That they'd save the world from Corruption and rid us of the Shadow Bringer and his demons.

It was difficult not to flinch as Elliot finished the story.

I didn't want to hear a tale from our kingdom's perfect past. Not when the present was dark, twisted, and haunted by the ghost of what it used to be. What it was *meant* to be.

"And then the mountain bursts like an egg," Elliot continued, throwing his arms open dramatically. "Lelantos flies from the rock, reborn with wings, and saves the dreamers!" He jumped to his feet and pretended to fly around the cramped hall. Once he'd made a few passes, he knelt in front of the twins, an intense expression on his face. "The end."

The children broke into giggles, forcing a dry, rattling laugh to crawl out of Isaac's throat. I smiled politely, struggling to focus on the twins' joy and not the shadows marking lines into their father's skin. And who was laughing? Isaac, or the demon within him? Margaret worked quickly, blending the concealment onto his face until the shadows were hidden, but the effort felt futile. The concealment would last just long enough to uphold part of his dignity before the Light Legion purified his soul, and that was perhaps the cruelest part of all. Although Isaac's soul would be saved by the Light Bringer, his Corrupt body, like Eden's, would still need to be sacrificed. He was destined to die.

Because once a demon claimed its victim, nothing could be done. It would feed on its host, slowly and delightedly, one dream after another, until the afflicted mind rotted and its body bore signs of decay. It might take months if one was strong enough to resist, but few ever did. Most fell into Corruption within a week.

Once Margaret was done, she motioned her children over to their father. They shared a few quick words and an embrace through the bars—one that made my stomach churn with discomfort—and Isaac was handed the half vial of elixir. He rolled it in his rough fingers, sniffed the substance, and recoiled violently.

He won't drink it. Waste of a vial.

Isaac leveled his gaze at me. As if the demon inside him heard.

Afterward, when we were safely outside the holding cells, Margaret gave Elliot's and my hands a meaningful squeeze. "Thank you," she said sincerely. She shot a nervous glance behind us, adding conspiratorially, "I have hope for Isaac's soul. I have hope for my children's, too."

Night descended at a crawl.

Dinner was fragrant and hearty: rosemary, butter, and goat cheese melting around a stew of rabbit and potatoes. It was a sickening contrast to the bile churning in my stomach. There were simply too many villagers with the beginnings of shadows leaking into their cheeks and fingernails.

"How was your visit to the village?" Father asked, reaching into his bowl to pluck out a stray rabbit bone.

"It went as expected," I responded politely, ever striving to be the dutiful daughter. Elliot frowned, chewing the inside of his cheek. It had gone as expected, except for Isaac. *Waste of a vial.* "We distributed the rest of the vials. Will there be more to give tomorrow?"

Father snorted at this. "Yes, but the supply is nearly empty. Scarcely a week's worth, if that." He gnawed on the bone absentmindedly, snapping it in two and using the pointy end to clean his teeth. His dark brown beard nearly covered his mouth, so the steady flash of teeth, bone, and rabbit sinew was more unsettling than it should have been. "Our own supply is dwindling, too. Be mindful with your rations tonight."

I closed my eyes, momentarily losing myself. Isaac, along with the other Norhavellian Corrupt, would soon be cleansed and buried by the Light Bringer. Their souls would be saved from wandering eternally in the dark, unable to find their way back to the Maker's light.

I clenched my hands together. Thumbed away imaginary dirt.

The Light Bringer was exalted across the kingdom for his ability to purify souls, but it only worked if the Corrupt was alive. If a

Corrupt died before they were cleansed, their human soul would perish, and the demon would be free to be reborn in the dreams and skin of another.

Wind rustled through the house, forcing the old wood to creak and groan, and I couldn't help picturing a demon leering at us through the kitchen windows. It would probably crawl in, sink its claws into my shoulders, and *smile*, knowing I was as monstrous and revolting as it was. Forcing Eden to dream was an unforgivable mistake. One I'd never escape.

"When will the Light Bringer come?" Elliot asked, stuffing his face with a heaping spoonful of stew. "This is very good, Mother. Thank you."

"Shouldn't be long. And you're very welcome, Elliot," Mother said, adding a pinch of salt and a handful of dried plums to the remaining mixture. Her eyes were bloodshot, and her long hair, so dark it almost looked black, was scraped back into a bun. My hair was almost identical to hers, except I preferred to wear mine loose and unbound. "Why aren't you eating, Esmer? Have some bread."

I took her offering wordlessly, but I didn't have the stomach to eat it.

"We have a surprise for you both," Mother continued, lowering herself into the chair next to mine.

Elliot and I shared an uneasy glance. Our lives were about survival, not frivolity. Surprises simply did not happen.

"We're leaving for the capital tomorrow," Father announced, "to start a new life in Istralla."

Elliot gasped. The bread dropped from my hands, falling to the floor.

"What?" The question spilled from my lips before I could stop it.

"I know it seems sudden," Mother said, exhaling heavily. She brushed a strand of hair from my eyes with cold, thin fingers. "Your Father and I can't stand to be among this madness any longer. We must claim a different future for ourselves. One where you and Elliot can have the lives you deserve."

16

"We've never been able to leave," I said carefully, ignoring the sudden thrill that slid through my veins.

The Light Legion came only to restock our elixir supply and purify—or hunt, if they escaped—our Corrupt, but as elixir distributors, our family was the last line of defense against Corruption. We couldn't just leave. To leave Norhavellis meant abandoning it.

Even though I deeply, *desperately* wanted to do just that.

I was sick of the constant despair. It clung to every interaction, scraping at the edges like a starved wolf. But as the kingdom-anointed Absolvers, we had a duty to uphold; an entire village relied on us to fairly distribute their lifesaving elixir each season.

"We can afford it now," Mother said, smiling. "We'll have a cottage by the sea and whatever else you desire. Your very own rooms, perhaps."

"Who will manage the elixir in our absence?"

Mother shook her head. Shadows from the candlelight danced across her face, carving out its most hollow parts. "There's no need to worry about that. I'm sure the Light Legion will manage to find a new set of willing Absolvers."

Wind threaded through the walls again, breathing out in a long, meandering sigh. A rattle sounded from the front of the house as it passed, almost as if someone were tapping lightly at the door.

"Now, finish your dinner and start packing," Mother said brightly, spooning another serving into my bowl. "This will be the last meal we share in this house. Tomorrow, our new life begins."

Father snapped another rabbit bone in half, smiling broadly at what remained of his family, and the wind quieted, silent and still as if a heavy shroud had settled over our roof and fallen like a veil down each wall.

Shadows touched my skin, fine as silk.

They slipped behind my eyelids, wrapped their soft hands around my neck, and slid like a lover's fingers through the length of my dark hair. Tonight they felt relentless. Needy. *Hungry.* I breathed in, guiltily relishing the familiar pull, and breathed out, letting my breath tumble through the air in a silent scream. It didn't matter that I took the elixir—they came regardless. The short visions. The glimpses of dreams.

A beautiful man silhouetted against a raging, endless sea.

A flash of silver, rot, and ruin.

A castle of writhing, living darkness.

The pull on my skin dwindled, dissolving like smoke, just as the fog in my ears faded into Elliot's snores and the buzz of an insect under our dresser. I groaned in disgust, fully awake and aware of my traitorous body, and settled back into my pillows. Pressing my palms into my eyes, I focused on their weight instead of something rising sickly sour from the pit of my stomach. I had allowed the dreams to coax me under. Willingly let them twist and seduce me like a fool.

And maybe I was.

Because, at this rate, the Shadow Bringer would surely devour my soul by sunrise.

One more Corrupt to the holding cells.

A traitorous girl with a monstrous heart.

Good for her to die so that her family might finally be free.

I turned to my side, dragging my hands down my face as I tried to quiet the voices of every Norhavellian who would surely condemn me if they knew the truth of what I'd done to Eden. Elliot slept heavily in the bed next to mine, chest rising and falling at rhythmic intervals. His face was mostly relaxed—though an eyebrow was slightly scrunched—and the threadbare leg of Chester the cow, his favorite keepsake from toddlerhood, peeked out from underneath an elbow. Lumpy wool stuffing threatened to spill from Chester's seams, and his once-bright button eyes were now a bit dull, but Elliot still treasured him.

Crskkk. Crskkk.

I stilled.

A misshapen form scraped at our half-open window, clawing at the glass in jagged swipes. I jolted out of bed, stubbing my toe on a wooden board.

"*Maker*, that hurt," I grumbled.

I took a deep breath, trying to snap free from my negative thoughts. I needed to ground myself in reality, not lose myself in another fantasy. The shadow was merely a branch. A *branch*, for Maker's sake.

"Esmer?"

Elliot peered at me through the shadows. His hair, as dark and wild as mine probably looked, curled around his ears in a disheveled halo. He appeared small and possibly too warm under his heap of blankets, but the pile helped him feel safe, veiled from the prying eyes of monsters and humans alike.

"Sorry, Elliot. I didn't mean to wake you."

"It's all right. Better you than a demon," he said half-heartedly, trying his best to lighten the mood and defuse our fears. He pulled at his blankets, positioning them strategically around his slim shoulders as he let out a yawn. "But now you owe me a chocolate. Maybe even two."

My mouth lifted into a smile. "I'm sure Istralla will have plenty of chocolate for us."

"We'll have chocolate every day," he said, returning my grin. We both knew we didn't have the gold needed for regular indulgences, but it was fun to bask in the possibility. Decadent confections, clothes that weren't thinning from too much wear, a comfortable home by the sea, fresh seafood, bottles of elixir—it seemed like an unreachable dream. A beautiful, unreachable dream. His smile faltered as his attention shifted to our window, where a leafy branch was still scuffling against the glass. "Need to keep that shut. Don't want birds flying in and taking my eyes."

"That's a strange thing to say. Are you having dreams, too?" I instinctively bit down on my tongue. He couldn't know I was having dreams. *No one* could know.

Elliot squinted at me. For a moment, I thought he registered my confession.

"No, I'm not having dreams. Though it's nice of you to worry about me," he said with another yawn, covertly pulling Chester into a hug. "I'm going back to sleep. Busy day tomorrow. Especially if chocolate is to be involved."

"Are you certain you're fine?"

"I'm certain," he mumbled, reaching for the elixir at his nightstand. He tilted it to his mouth, but no liquid came out. "Hmm. Thought I had some left."

"Here." I handed him my vial, which still contained a dreg of the amber liquid. "I should check on Father first and see if he needs anything. He's probably still sitting on the porch and watching the woods."

"You think he'll be out there all night?"

I nodded. "He always keeps watch when the season is drawing to a close." I wrapped my dark red cloak around my shoulders, covering my nightgown, and tied it loosely under my chin. It was a modest, plain garment despite its velvet fabric—as were all my clothes—but it would provide some comfort against the midnight chill. "Be glad it's only for one more night."

"The Corrupt really are getting bad. You don't think..." He paused, chewing his lip. "You really think we'll be able to leave? Won't the villagers be mad? What if a Corrupt finds us before we can—"

"No," I said firmly. Convincingly. "They can't hurt us. Not with Father watching."

"Good. Father's brave." Elliot settled into his blankets, content. "And so are you."

The unexpected praise landed like a rock in my chest. I wasn't worthy of it.

"I don't know about that," I said, swallowing the rising lump in my throat. "If anyone's brave, it's you."

Elliot laughed, pulling Chester under his chin. "Maybe you're right. Because you don't like bugs, I guess. Fish, too. You hate fish eyes. And baths. You must *really* hate those, because you always smell like—"

"Since I'm clearly so flawed," I began sarcastically, gesturing to the dim clearing beyond our window, "perhaps *you* should be helping Father instead of me."

I expected Elliot to laugh or make another joke. Instead, he started to get up.

"Oh no, I was just kidding," I said quickly, watching as Elliot's face fell. The lump in my throat was becoming harder to ignore. If I stayed much longer, I'd succumb to it. "Keep warm in bed. I'll be back soon."

"All right," he said. But he wasn't looking at me; his gaze had fallen to his feet.

"Promise me."

"I promise," Elliot answered, crawling back into bed. "You're the brave one, after all."

"Sure," I mumbled.

I left our room before he could see me cry.

Nothing about me was brave or admirable. A single tear slid down my face. I hastily wiped it away, willing the lump in my chest to shatter like an egg. If Elliot knew what I'd done to Eden, would he still look at me the same?

Downstairs, I noted that our home was heavy with darkness. It roved through the air like a coat of thick, oily paint, spilling into the kitchen, the gathering room, and the hallway to both the apothecary and my parents' bedroom. It curled around the furniture in wide, suffocating sweeps, turning our haphazardly packed trunks into wide-shouldered monsters that seemed to grow larger the second I looked away from them. Even the paintings appeared distorted; human subjects were suddenly headless or gape mouthed and screaming, and landscapes displayed pitch-black water and murk where forests should have been.

Focus, Esmer.

Boots. I needed to find my boots. They should have been just around the corner, but everything was indiscernible in this lighting. I reached forward, grasping for what I thought were my boots, but the dark shadow, once boot-like in shape, shifted away as if it were nothing but dust.

I turned another corner, but I was too hasty; my toe caught an uneven floorboard. My knees smacked against the ground, a corner of the wood snagging my nightgown and pressing a razor-sharp line into my skin. I hissed in pain, cursing lowly enough that my parents wouldn't hear. I probed the wound, flinching when my fingers met something wet through a tear in the gown.

A dark, low chuckle sounded just behind my neck.

I spun around, heart racing, but there was no one there. I strained, listening intently for another laugh, but nothing came. Just silence and the sound of my own racing heart as I quickly found my boots, laced them tight, and headed outside.

Father was sitting on the porch in his favorite rocking chair, taut and straight-backed even while dozing. The wind was strong, coaxing the chair to sway and ringing the string of bells tied around our property. It was a miracle the chair had lasted through the years, splintered as it was. I always thought it strange that the most trivial objects could last for decades while the people who owned them never had the same luxury. They grew sick, frail, and old while an object remained perpetually itself. Broken and faded, maybe, but never dead or dying.

I leaned against the house, considering. Father looked exhausted. He reminded me of a cracked, overburdened glass, leaking water when no one else was around. Maybe it was the row of torches circling our property, flickering under the strength of the wind and casting the lines in his face with deep shadows.

Shadows like the markings of a Corrupt.

Like Eden's eyes—

I shook my head. No, there was my father. Warm brown eyes were underneath his lids. And though his expression was wretched and weak, he would wake with a smile, the smile he tried his best to give despite the burden of his labor and his duty as our shield. A wool blanket was fixed around his shoulders, and a small elixir vial stuck out of his shirt pocket—items of care left by Mother at some point in the night. Calloused hands rested atop the crossbow in his lap, and his work boots were filthy from walking the property to light the torches and scrutinize any late-night visitors.

Visitors desperate for our last elixir vials.

I moved to wake him, knowing he'd be upset at sleeping so heavily, but reconsidered. I had helped him before, during long nights such as these. Elliot had, too. I could wake him later, after I'd finished. I shivered, crossing my arms to ward off the chill in the air. Besides, it wasn't as if I had much more time left *to* help. If my recent visions meant I was close to Corruption, my time was short. Splintered. Blurry. It was impossible to be useful if my mind was half-rotted by a demon.

I scanned the surrounding clearing, noting the weak torchlight. The flames ran precariously low, struggling to fight against the encroaching dark. I quietly gathered the materials I needed into a bucket, its handle as worn and dented as the rocking chair, and positioned myself by the nearest torch. The flame surged to life under my care, smoldering, glowing, then rising to take a breath. It pierced into the night, defying the wind as its light filled the air.

I took a breath, too. Tried to squeeze all the darkness from my lungs.

Out of habit, my fingers threaded through the rising smoke. The warmth felt wonderful—cleansing, even. I eagerly stretched out my hands, closing my eyes as the smoke lapped against them.

Esmer.

Esmer.

Esmer.

"Father?" I called out.

But Father didn't move. The voice was inside my head.

I swore, hands shaking as I relit the next three torches. Maybe a demon had finally curled itself around my mind, sinking its claws nice and deep as it waited to claim territory upon my soul. I swore again, muttering under my breath. Maybe it would be better if I just—

"It's me," called a tentative voice. Elliot was standing in the middle of the clearing, smiling sheepishly. Rather than wear a sweater or a cloak of his own, he had wrapped himself in a blanket. "Thought you looked lonely out here, but it turns out you can talk with yourself just fine."

The voice hadn't been inside my head. It had been Elliot all along.

I lunged for him, pretending to be upset, but he made a quick, dance-like spin, avoiding my hands as the blanket swished around his ankles. "This is how you repay me for helping, huh? Sort of rude if you ask me."

"If you ask *me*, I never requested your help," I said, lighting the next torch. It wouldn't take long to finish, but I secretly welcomed his company. "But if you want to be useful, you can carry this bucket. I also need to check the bells."

A hand darted out from underneath his blanket, snatched the bucket, and pulled it to his side. "Fine by me. Once Father's back, though, I'm going to bed."

"Once he's back?"

"Really hoping my bed isn't cold now. Don't know when we'll—"

"Elliot," I said, grounding him. "What did you mean by 'once Father's back'?"

"Oh. Um, he wasn't in his chair when I came out." Elliot tilted his head to the side, eyebrows creased in growing worry. "I figured he was taking a break while you finished with the torches."

I squinted at the porch.

Sure enough, the empty rocking chair was creaking softly in the wind, knocking into the crossbow and quiver that sat discarded on the ground in front of it.

Why didn't I hear him leave?

It was unusual for him to desert his post, especially if he saw that we were outside, but I didn't voice my concerns. Maybe he just needed a glass of water. Or a quick trip to the washroom.

Still, I took the crossbow and quiver as a precaution, slinging them across my back.

We made quick work of the remaining torches, saving the farthest for last. I watched the smoke as it rose, threading through the lower branches of an oak tree, and threw my arm around Elliot's blanketed shoulders. It was going to be okay.

I was okay.

We'd check the perimeter for any missing bells or cut strings, then we'd head back inside—

A high, clear sound rang through the trees, warbling like a distorted wind chime.

Fear doused my skin in an icy chill, instantly raising the hair on my arms and neck. Another bell chimed. Then another. *Another.* The bells were designed as a precaution against any wandering Corrupt; they did not chime without reason. In the dim torchlight, it was impossible to see who—or what—was creeping toward our house, but it shuffled heavily in the dark forest, carelessly snapping twigs.

"We need to get Father," Elliot started, horrified.

"There's no time," I hissed. I took a deep breath, numb to the weight of the crossbow as I prepared to cock it. With shaky hands, I quickly grabbed a bolt and affixed it to the crossbow's groove, ensuring it fit snugly against the string. Then, with a smooth motion, I drew the string back with a click. "Stay with me. Don't move."

A movement caught my eye, a flicker of darkness darting between the trees. I raised the crossbow, sighting along its length with steady determination. As I aimed, my senses sharpened, attuned to the subtle sounds in the forest. The whisper of leaves rustling in the nighttime breeze, the distant cry of a bird—then it all faded into the background as my focus narrowed to a single point.

There.

With a flick of my thumb, I released the safety.

A surge of anticipation coursed through my veins, my heart a frenzied, clawing thing as I aligned my sights. I held my breath, finger hovering over the trigger.

"It's coming," Elliot gasped. "Esmer, it's *coming!*"

The dark figure surged out of the trees with a growl.

I squeezed the trigger, feeling the release of the string beneath my touch. The bolt leapt from the crossbow with a fierce twang, slicing through the air with deadly precision. It struck true, embedding itself into the figure with a satisfying *thud*. The figure halted, swaying as if it were drunk, then fell to its knees with a cry of pain. It made another sound, this time heart-stopping in its familiarity. I knew that voice.

I'd known it from the moment I was born.

"M-mother?" I gasped, dropping the crossbow. It slammed heavily against my hip, still attached by its leather strap, but I scarcely felt it. "No."

My mother clutched the grass, steadying herself against the tremors moving through her body. The bolt had struck her soundly in her shoulder. Blood wept from the wound in a dark stream, nearly black in the torchlight.

"I didn't know," I choked out, numbly reaching for her. "I thought you were a—"

I froze, noticing the discoloration on her knuckles. The bloody rabbit clenched haphazardly between her fingers. The feral curve to her back. The missing shoes. And then, when she looked up, the two smears of shadow staining the skin under her eyes. Corruption.

"Oh, Esmer. How pathetic of you to act like you care," Mother growled, lips peeling back in a savage grin. Her teeth were red, stained bright by a cut splitting her lip. "You may be beautiful, but you're rotten on the inside. Such a mockery of your sister. What a shame."

Elliot shouted from somewhere behind me, his voice a strange, piercing warning.

I stood with a stumble. "Elliot, *run!* Get Father. This isn't Mother."

Mother shook her trembling limbs into stillness. "Oh, if you had just kept sleeping," she said in a voice that was hers, and wasn't. A demon's voice, rattling like bones over gravel, layered over her softer timbre. "But you had to go outside, didn't you? Had to meddle where it wasn't needed. I was just gathering some provisions for our trip tomorrow." I spun around, making to sprint for the house, but Mother was faster. She dropped the rabbit and grabbed my face, squeezing her fingers around my throat before I could even register the movement.

"I've come for you and your softhearted brother. I was going to take my time—savor your Corruption—but it's too late for that," the demon inside her snarled, its voice darkening. As she dug her nails into my skin, blood pooled from her fingers and slid down my neck. "I'd have one more babe to hunt, but she's already dead."

She pinned me to the damp, rot-smelling ground as I screamed, clawing at her face, kicking at her shins, but it was useless, *useless.*

"Let her *go!*" Elliot sobbed, slamming his bucket hard into the side of her head.

Mother's bloodshot eyes widened. I expected her to fall over—any ordinary person would have been knocked unconscious by the blow. But she merely stood up, spat some blood from her mouth, and snatched the blanket that had fallen from Elliot's shoulders.

"Oh, Elliot. I would have saved you for last."

Mother threw Elliot to the ground, easily overpowering him despite the injury to her shoulder, and pulled the blanket tight over his mouth and nose. I staggered to the nearest torch, head spinning and legs threatening to give out. Elliot was going to *die*, and this demon—this *animal* within my mother—would kill me next without hesitation.

But first she'd kill Elliot.

I heaved the torch from the dirt, fighting to stay conscious even as my vision blurred. A troubling decision was rapidly forming in my mind, desperate to sink its claws in before fear took over and rendered me useless.

"Your mother and father damned your village," the demon inside her growled, stuffing part of the blanket into Elliot's mouth and wrenching his arm away when he tried to pull it free. "Damned you, too. They made a desperate bargain for your safety, but I overcame. We always overcome."

But first she'd kill Elliot.

The sound I made was unlike anything I'd ever heard: raw grief and primal terror. It propelled me forward as I raised the torch and swung it hard at Mother's face. I hit her again, this time lighting her cloak on fire. She immediately fell to the side, rolling in the dirt as she fought to remove her cloak, but the fire was quicker.

"Esmer," Mother moaned, this time sounding more like herself. She knelt while the flames crawled higher. "*No.* Did I...? What am I...?"

Elliot sobbed in my arms, utterly horrified. I needed to get him inside. I needed to get Father, and—

"Elena!" Father screamed, half running, half sliding into Mother. He hissed in pain as he threw her cloak aside, stomping it into the ground until the flames were nothing but smoke.

"Esmer's a vile girl," the demon inside Mother condemned, its voice breaking and stumbling into cries as smoke curled around her ears. She clung to Father's arms, glaring at me. "She tried to kill me, Galen. I fear we've raised a monster. She's Corrupt—"

"You're the one who's Corrupt," I gasped, taking deep breaths and trying not to pass out. I dug my feet into the ground, desperate for sensation to return to my body. "Father, just—just look at her."

"Stop talking," Father snapped. "Enough."

"But she's right," Elliot cried. "Mother hurt us. She's not herself."

"*Just. Stop. Talking.*"

"But—"

"Give me the crossbow," Father commanded coldly, holding out his hand.

For I had already aimed the next bolt at Mother's heart.

"Get up," I said shakily to my mother, defiant. "You're both going to walk to the cellar and wait there until the Light Bringer can assess you. It's protocol."

"Give me the crossbow, Esmer," Father commanded again. The hint of something *other* lingered in the underbelly of his words, making my skin crawl. "You don't know what you're doing."

"If you don't start moving, I will shoot this bolt through her heart. I won't let her demon hurt Elliot again."

"You're—"

"*I'll do it!*" I screamed, switching my aim from her heart to Father's. "Go *now!*"

My hands shook violently as I directed them into the cellar, its weathered entrance like the dark, gaping maw of some terrible beast. I ignored the wildflowers that peeked through the stone and shouldered the door shut behind them, quickly wrapping chains over the lock to secure it firmly in place.

Elliot, hysterical, ran to the village to get help, and I dropped to my knees, retching into the grass.

Dawn was hours away, and the stars should have been bright and sparkling.

But darkness, leaking in through the trees, swallowed them all.

4

For the second time that night, elixir sat sour and wrong on my tongue.

Sleep taunted me, toyed with me, wrapped its hands around my eyes and *called* to me; still, I couldn't settle. Unease descended in a horrible black cloud, splintering my mind into pieces. Several villagers stood watch over the cellar, ensuring that my parents would remain in place until morning. I should have been sleeping. Resting. Getting my energy back so I could continue protecting Elliot.

I shuddered and sat up, again reaching for the elixir vial. I would take a longer drink and count backward from a thousand. A hundred thousand, even. I would bar Mother's demon-infested body and Isaac's leaking eyes from my mind. But when the glass grazed my lips, only a small rivulet of liquid trickled out.

I stared in disbelief at the empty vial.

Disgusted with myself, I stormed downstairs to our family's personal elixir reserve. I didn't have a choice; if the tonic wasn't taken immediately before sleep, my soul might drift into the realm of demons. But this was another reason the average family—the average *person*, even—struggled to maintain an elixir supply. A stomach tight with hunger, fear, or discontent made sleep difficult, but most couldn't afford to waste more than one or two mouthfuls per day.

I searched the dark recesses of our kitchen shelves, expecting to graze the smooth glass of elixir vials, but I felt nothing but dust and shadows.

Norhavellis's remaining supply, tucked away in our makeshift apothecary, silently beckoned.

Darkness pushed into the apothecary, bloating the walls with thick shadow, and plants cascaded from the ceiling, pressing against curtain-drawn windows. They felt serpentine, more akin to slimy, writhing beasts than harmless vegetation. I quickly searched for a spare vial, ignoring the sensation that something was watching me, lurking just beyond my vision. Once I found what I was looking for—a small portion of elixir, suitable for a few mouthfuls—I hurried upstairs, drank from the vial, and settled under my blankets, fully prepared for an unremarkable night of demon-free sleep.

But before I knew it, I was dreaming.

No—*falling.*

My body hurtled down a dark abyss as I succumbed to sleep, limbs flailing.

Then I slammed into a hill, unable to stop sliding. My hands clenched around wet, slimy things. Cold mud. Decaying leaves. I was a doll, a stone—useless, *useless*—slamming into branches and the sharp undersides of tree roots. By the time I stopped moving, I didn't recognize the gasping, pitiful breaths that stumbled out of me.

Slowly, I opened my eyes.

Trees swayed overhead, glistening softly in the twilight. Still reeling, I absently noted the wet soil between my fingers. The papery leaves as they pressed against the back of my head. I sat up, gently stretching out my joints. I must have been delivering elixir parcels with Mother and Father. I must have fallen from the cart as we made our rounds. Yes, that was it. *They must be so worried.*

Entirely forgetting I was in a dream, I noticed the whisper of a melody—the only indication of any life beyond trees, mud, and a rapidly darkening sky. The song was beautiful—simple and carefree. It reminded me of a day when Eden and I were finally allowed to go into Norhavellis by ourselves. We were on a mission to collect a certain herb, but the job itself didn't matter. We spent that whole morning pretending to be warriors, sparring with branches and dancing through the tall grass as if nothing could ever hurt us. I sang along to the tune, making up words as I went. Time lost itself as I walked, but I continued to sing, deep in my thoughts and my made-up song, until I heard the crunch of quick footsteps moving through the leaves. I had only an instant to grab a fallen branch to use as a weapon, its tip curved and sharp.

A group of masked men materialized from the brush, covered in oily fur and the stench of unwashed flesh. They slunk around me, silent except for muffled panting. Saliva oozed from between their cracked lips, sliding into their fur. Their costumes were terrifyingly intricate; there were no seams in the material.

Performers from Istralla, then.

My palms felt hot around my makeshift weapon. Performers or not, humans shouldn't ever look like this. It was unnatural.

A mimicry of life.

"What do you want?" I asked, my voice uncontrollably shrill. "My father and mother are the Absolvers of Norhavellis. They're somewhere near...." I didn't know where to look. They were everywhere, forcing me backward. Where were their eyes? "Get away from me—get *away!*"

One performer stalked forward, growling out puffs of air from slits in the mask's nose. I lurched backward and tripped, collapsing to the ground. They were wretched. Absolutely *wretched.* My head was burning. White dots sparked like fire across my vision. I shut my eyes tight.

Then I realized. Remembered.

I was *asleep.* I was *asleep,* and this was a *dream.*

My eyes flew open. These men weren't performers. They were demons, grinning at me with maniacal glee.

Dragging myself to my feet and picking a direction at random, I ran for my life.

Do everything in your power to escape the demons.

Do not fight the demons. You cannot win.

If all else fails, surprise or harm your body enough to force yourself into consciousness.

The voices of my parents rang through my head, echoing each rule and every deadly warning just as the trees shifted around me, branches gleaming like iridescent fish scales as they opened to a wide, crescent-shaped expanse dotted with blue flowers. Overhead, a purple sky dusted with silver-bright constellations slowly began to darken.

Beautiful.

I nearly laughed. No one had told me that damnation could be *beautiful.*

"Girl."

I stiffened. They'd found me.

"Girl," repeated the demon, voice jagged and strained, like rusted metal groaning in the wind. "You do not reek of demon flesh, and yet here you are. Perhaps you desire what we seek. Perhaps we are one and the same."

"I don't desire what you seek," I snapped furiously, wielding my branch like an ill-suited sword. My stomach churned at the thought of Eden and Mother being stalked by these creatures before succumbing to Corruption. "I am nothing like you."

One of the monsters, filthy and grotesque, stepped into the clearing. It looked as though it had recently clawed its way from the depths of hell, digging through layer upon layer of earth until it had finally broken free. Thick cords of gray hair wilted from its scalp, hanging at crooked angles, and mud dripped stringlike from its body. A tattered piece of embroidered cloth clung to its shoulders, trailing into the grass behind it, and its eyes matched the state of its hair, gray and sagging.

"Look around," the figure said, stilling itself. "Do you see? See, and you will be free."

The demons surrounded me, forming a loose circle within the glistening trees.

Terror clogged my throat. What did I see? I saw demons. I saw ugliness. I saw filth.

But I also saw a crescent-shaped glade bursting with shimmering trees and flowers. I scanned the space again, finally settling on something in the distance that was murky and irregular.

"You have found it," the creature sighed.

The massive shape of *something* unfurled before me like the husk of some newly discovered creature. Its form slipped in and out of focus, sometimes taking shape, other times whisking away into the air as though it were nothing.

Breathe. I needed to breathe.

I took a lungful of perfumed air, willing my mind to clear, then I examined my hands, staring until the skin sharpened. Once I was satisfied with the clarity of my fingers, I took a final breath, steadying myself. A castle loomed overhead, casting shadows across the landscape. It was a Goliath of lofty spires, obsidian walls, and sculptural work that was beyond what my mind could understand. Stars dappled the expanse of dark purple sky just above it, reflecting in the stained glass arches of the upper floors and illuminating walls that were either partially broken or fully caved in. I could feel the power the castle held; so deep within the gilded woods, it seemed to foretell a presence that waited in silken, shadowed corners and *watched*.

When I finally tore my eyes away, I was alone.

The demons were gone.

I walked through the castle's sprawling courtyard, unable to keep from admiring its uncanny beauty. Lush floral arrangements bloomed from sapphire vases, dipping into starry water that poured from stone fountains. I ran a hand along a vase, alarmed that it felt so real. I could touch the surface, glossy and dark, and feel the twilight air upon the glass.

Instinctively, I reached for the castle doors.

Knock.

Knock.

Knock.

The castle doors quivered in time with the echoing knocks, rippling as their smooth surface suddenly changed into thousands of meticulously detailed sculptures. I tried to examine the images, but they escaped me, flitting from my vision like spinning grains of dust.

The shadows stained everything. I couldn't see.

I can't see.

I woke in a panic, kicking at the blankets knotted around my legs. The layers of bedding felt like arms, legs, fingers. Barely suppressing a scream, I stumbled to my mirror.

Breath lodged in my throat as I examined my hands in the early-morning light, too terrified to begin the inspection with my face. The earliest sign of Corruption was bruised skin under the eyes. Delaying the inevitable was pointless. Still, I searched every finger for purple skin clinging to my nails. Then my wrists, the inner crooks of my elbows, and the sore skin of my neck.

I forced myself to meet the eyes in my reflection.

Dark, sleep-tangled hair; arched eyebrows framing bloodshot eyes; lips raw and red from biting them in my sleep. But the skin under my eyes was clear.

Clear.

I took the elixir vial from my nightstand and examined it. It didn't taste, smell, or look any different, but how else had I been able to dream so vividly and for so long? Was something wrong with the elixir, or was there something wrong with *me*? I clutched my throat, the ghost of my mother's fingertips bruising my skin.

I crumbled, knees hitting the floorboards.

"What's wrong?" Elliot cried, scrambling from his bed. He knelt by me on the floor, peering up at me with exhausted, red-rimmed eyes. Eyes *no* child should have.

"Woke up nauseous, is all," I offered weakly, wrapping my arms around his shoulders and pressing my chin to the top of his head. "Thought I was going to be sick."

"Please don't lie to me," he begged. "I know something isn't right."

I hesitated a moment too long, unable to wield the right words in response.

"That's...," he began, squinting at the vial still in my hands, "village-marked."

"It is," I said, slowly turning the vial around in my hands. Sure enough, *Norhavellis* was written in Mother's scrawl down the side. It didn't taste or smell any different, but what about the elixir inside? The glass was tinted, obscuring the full effect of the liquid's coloring, but it appeared slightly paler than usual. Surely I was just imagining things; surely it was *me* who was wrong. "My vial ran out last night, but our personal supply was empty. I would have asked Mother or Father..." I trailed off, barely suppressing a sob at the back of my throat.

I couldn't lose it now. I *wouldn't* lose it in front of Elliot. He needed me to be the strong older sister, as Eden had been to me. Stronger than I was capable of being, perhaps.

"Oh. Right," Elliot said matter-of-factly. Then his face bunched up, contorting into grief as he let out a hopeless cry. "What's going to happen to us? If Mother and Father are both Corrupt, what happens to us?"

"I don't know," I said softly, trying to make sense of what our future would be. My chest felt tight at the idea of forging ahead without our parents to guide us. "But I don't think we can stay in Norhavellis anymore. We need to make a new path for ourselves. Maybe travel to Istralla with the provisions Mother and Father put together."

Elliot squeezed his stuffed cow to his chest, considering this possibility. "Maybe we can."

Maybe we can.

The Light Legion arrived in Norhavellis that afternoon.

By the time they surveyed the Corrupts' holding cells in the village, the sky was growing dark and the air had chilled, creeping in from the depths of the lengthening shadows. They emerged from the Visstill, the sprawling, shadow-drenched forest that separated Norhavellis from Istralla, dressed in their golden finery and led by our holy Light Bringer. The revered Lord Mithras was, as usual, a sight to behold.

The Light Bringer's clothing was immaculate, interwoven with layers of ivory and gold, and his cloak, as brightly hued as his horse's white hide, swept across his back in a brilliant drape. A gilded mask, far more ornate than those of his legion's, partially hid his face, leaving only his mouth, tan jaw, and golden hair exposed. The Kingdom of Noctis's immortal ruler and Maker-blessed savior—the lord who fought tirelessly to save his people from the Shadow Bringer's desperate clutches.

He was so radiant and good that it made my chest ache.

With a quick gesture, he motioned for the torches to be lit, and the flames—redder than usual—sparked crimson light into the space. Some legionnaires entered our storehouse, dragging out medical supplies and burlap bags filled with seed; others ransacked our home, pulling out vials of elixir, books, papers. They burned some items and packed others away.

Mother and Father stood in chains between two legionnaires, looking pale and sickly. They hadn't been allowed to change into new clothes, and the crossbow bolt was still embedded in Mother's shoulder. Elliot and I were ordered to stand near our parents as the Light Legion searched our property, but I couldn't bear to even look at them. Instead, I focused on holding Elliot's hand and striving to appear like the strong, virtuous daughter everyone expected.

Virtuous, despite my visions of shadow.

Virtuous, besides forcing Eden to dream.

"We confiscated your elixir supply," the Light Bringer began, his voice radiating warmth and power. It felt like honey sliding over a gilded throne, decadent but with a bite of strength underneath. "It is a pity—truly—that someone in your station could host such wickedness." He shook his head again, slowly circling Mother and Father. "To think that Absolvers would stoop to such depravity. Tonight, you will stand trial and be purified." He paused on Elliot, then settled his gaze on me. "And your fates are yet to be decided."

I wondered if he could tell I was having dreams. The dream from the night before, filled with hideous demons and starlit castles, felt like an inky stain marring my skin in its wake. I wouldn't have been surprised if he could see it.

"So, we've been found at last," Father said in a low, resigned voice, looking at the ground. "Please forgive us, my lord."

Mother spat at the Light Bringer's shining foot. Legionnaires immediately wrenched her away from him.

"What is the meaning of this?" the demon inside Mother shrieked. "You dare harass an innocent family?"

The Light Bringer shook his head. "Lower and unveil them."

"No!" Mother howled.

Legionnaires brought over a trough of sloshing river water and dropped it with a heavy *thump* atop the grass. They then knotted their fingers in my parents' hair and shoved their heads under the surface.

Mother and Father thrashed. Violently.

The men worked meticulously, washing and peeling away their skin. Only no—it was not skin at all.

It was *concealment*.

The dark stains of shadow under my mother's eyes were also in the hollows of her cheekbones and at the corners of her pale lips. My father's were more subtle: small black threads intertwined with the wrinkles on his face, dipping below his beard and disappearing across his throat. Both displayed the damning signs of Corruption. And both had been hiding it.

Faintly, my ears registered a sharp, sickening buzz.

A painful memory of Eden's eyes swam in front of me. Dark lines webbed from her irises, settling under her eyes and dripping down her cheeks. She reached for me, screaming, *screaming*—

Elliot grabbed on to my cloak, the dark red fabric quivering underneath his fingers, and I held him by the shoulders, wishing I could shield him from it all. Wishing he didn't have to see any of this—*experience* any of this—in his lifetime. But this was his life.

This was *my* life.

"Galen and Elena Havenfall, you are hereby charged with high larceny against your kingdom and sovereign, attempted escape from prosecution, and the murder of the innocent people under your care." The Light Bringer held an elixir vial between gloved fingers and let it splash to the ground. Everything about it was off—its color was too pale, its form too thin, its smell too faint. "Watering down elixir is an unforgivable sin. How many villagers have fallen into Corruption because of it? Likely every Norhavellian Corrupt in recent years. Perhaps even your eldest daughter, if I recall."

Anger and shame burned in my stomach. Anger at the accusations. Shame at the sea of bitter, disgusted faces. Anger at not knowing, and shame at what little I did. Elliot's face, now red and tear streaked, was tucked tightly into my side.

"We only did it to protect our children," Father began, shadowmarked eyes welling with tears of his own. He sounded like himself, which meant the demon vying for control over his body was subdued. This was normal in the early stages of Corruption; only in the most heated moments did the Corrupt's nature begin to twist. "We did no harm to our eldest," Father continued, just as Mother's eyes slid to me, cold and accusing. As if the demon inside her knew the truth. I shuddered, feeling her condemnation as if it were a brand against my skin. "We did no harm to *any* child of ours."

"And yet you harmed many others." The Light Bringer's eyes turned cold. "Explain yourselves."

Mother's body shook. Slowly, her eyes changed, and she appeared lucid. "It began the winter after our eldest daughter died. Our youngest became very sick," Mother rasped. "I'm certain Esmer and Elliot remember."

Of course I remembered. I remembered Elliot, eyes sunken and dull, skin paper-thin and stretched tight over his bones. I remembered looking at the dry, cinnamon-dusted strings of apples Mother used for decoration and being hungry enough that I contemplated eating them. I remembered the dark. I remembered the stench of despair. Of missing Eden and her comforting, steady presence so much that it made everything else seem bleaker in comparison.

"Oh, Elliot. Esmer." She craned her neck so that she could see us, and a hard lump lodged itself in my throat. She looked almost like herself, but the shadows were undeniable. "We tried our best."

"The cost of his medicine broke us. We no longer could afford it," Father added. "Not without sacrifice. And the elixir supply was down to its last vials, with all of winter ahead of us." His eyes dropped in shame. "We kept the purest elixir for our children, and we diluted the rest of the village's supply. We traded the excess for favors, food, and for a neighboring healer to visit us weekly."

"How long did you do this?" They didn't answer the Light Bringer right away, and horror flooded me. "A month? A season?" The Light Bringer's attention flicked to Elliot. "Your son appears to be in good health."

"You have to understand—"

"That winter was five years ago."

"We know," the demon inside Mother growled, shoving itself back into her body. "We are aware."

"W-we started saving more elixir just for ourselves. We intended to do it only for a little while, but we couldn't risk losing one of them, not again."

The realization was like a knife into my chest. They'd done it because of Eden's death. They'd done it because of *me*.

"You are admitting to tampering with the Maker-given supply for *five years*," the Light Bringer roared. "I should refuse your right to purification. Perhaps eternal damnation would be sentence enough."

"We love our children, my lord."

"Lord, lord, lord," Mother mocked. "He is not our lord. He is only Mithras."

"We just wanted them to be happy and safe," my father pleaded.

"What you wish for does not matter. Lest that *wish* would speak of Maker-given goodness." The Light Bringer's masked face was impassive, but wisps of fury lurked in his eyes and settled in his mouth. He motioned for Mother and Father to be yanked up by their bindings, tightening the rope enough that they wouldn't be able to run. "Say your goodbyes. You will not get another."

"I don't want to say goodbye," Elliot whispered hoarsely, tears sliding down his face. "I don't even want to look at them. They're not—they're not Mother and Father anymore."

My stomach churned, sick with guilt.

They had watered down the elixir to save us. Just two parents wanting to keep their surviving children safe in the only way they knew how. If Eden hadn't become Corrupt—if she hadn't died—then they likely wouldn't have been driven to such desperate measures. They would have found another way.

"We don't need to say goodbye," I said stiffly, answering for the both of us.

The Light Bringer inclined his head, eyes softening slightly. "I understand." He nodded to the nearest two legionnaires. "Escort them inside and guard the entrance." To the rest of the Light Legion, he said, "Make camp in this clearing. At dawn, I will purify the Norhavellian Corrupt and right the wrongs of these demon-cursed sinners."

Light from the torches and darkness from the encroaching night, mingling with the smell of woodsmoke, billowed through the sky as Mother and Father shouted at our backs.

"Forgive us."

"Forgive us."

"Forgive us."

I made the mistake of looking back. I wasn't sure if I was looking at my parents or the demons within them, but desperate, guilt-ridden words clawed up my throat—words I couldn't say without risking suspicion. I shoved the sensation aside, unwilling to confront it, trying instead to focus on Elliot and failing at that, too. My head was throbbing, spinning, heavy.

Forgive me.

Forgive me.

Forgive me.

The Light Legion had ransacked our room. Paper, clothes, and blankets lay strewn about the chipped wooden floorboards, and a smell—a smell of something other, something not of our family—seeped through the space. Elliot rushed to his bed and curled against the wall, sobbing into his pillow. Two men stationed themselves in the stairwell, positioning their bodies so that they could see both inside the room and downstairs into the foyer. Their faces, partially covered by masks, lacked emotion or even a single distinguishing feature.

"Are we supposed to sleep now?" I asked, feeling strange. My head spun with something resembling amusement. Everything felt false. A distant, crazed vision never meant to last. "We will need elixir first."

The legionnaires didn't respond. Their golden masks cast such dark shadows over their eyes.

"Even if our parents are Corrupt, Elliot and I require it." Words spun around in my mind, forming aimless, murky sentences—sentences I didn't wish to bring into existence. And that word—*Corrupt*—tasted like bile on my tongue. "The Light Bringer said that our fate wasn't decided. We need the elixir. As is proper."

More silence. They did not so much as twitch.

"You must allow it, or else..." Or else what? I'd throw them in the imaginary dungeons of Norhavellis? Cook them into a stew? Banish them from our property with the pointy end of a spade? *Control yourself.* "I will get it myself from downstairs."

The shorter legionnaire leered at me. His beady eyes shone in the faint candlelight as he handed me a vial from the pack he wore underneath his crimson cape. "Aren't you an irritating one?"

I ground my teeth.

Control yourself, Esmer.

The taller legionnaire clicked his tongue. "Deduct that from the seasonal ration they'll get tomorrow."

Dark thoughts, once nameless and without force, rose to meet me. *Tomorrow.* The Light Bringer would cleanse Mother's and Father's souls, but the process would destroy their mortal bodies. It was what happened to all Corrupt. Left unchecked, the Corrupt would commit unspeakable, violent crimes against their friends and neighbors. Against their families, too.

But where would Elliot and I go? How would we survive in the village our parents betrayed? The bitter truth laid itself bare: We had nowhere to go.

I sat next to my brother, wrapping my arms around his slight shoulders. He leaned away from me, burying his face in his hands. I stroked his hair, settling into what I hoped was a calming rhythm. Eden used to comfort me in a similar way, brushing or braiding my hair if I was ever uneasy, but I never fully appreciated the gesture. After her death, I vowed not to make the same mistake again.

"They should've just let me die," Elliot warbled, voice cracking as his hands balled into fists.

"Don't *ever* say that," I said fiercely. "Look at me."

His large brown eyes, utterly heartbroken, met mine.

"None of this is your fault. None of this will ever be your fault," I said, squeezing him tight. "It's the Shadow Bringer's fault. He's the one who caused Corruption in the first place."

Elliot buried his face in his hands again. "I know it's not my fault.

I know. But we've been giving them bad elixir. I thought we were doing good things. Instead, we've been *killing* our neighbors. And now Mother and Father are going to die, too."

"They may look like Mother and Father, but it isn't truly them," I whispered. "Our real mother and father will be dancing with the Maker soon. Their souls will finally be set free."

The woman and man who thrashed under the water, gasping for air as they nearly drowned, were puppets filled by their respective demons. But in the presence of the Light Bringer, their souls would travel somewhere else; the Light Bringer would walk into their dreams and free their souls so that they could bask in the Maker's light.

That's what we'd been taught, at least.

But then there was me.

Were demons not roiling under my skin, waiting to take over my soul? They'd found me last night; perhaps they'd find me again. I held Elliot tighter. This time he didn't resist, and he sank against me, sobbing into his elbow.

"I love you," he whispered.

"I love you, too, Elliot," I whispered back.

I'll keep him safe for you, Eden.

A desperate plea to a sister who couldn't hear me, but I made the vow regardless.

I couldn't keep Mother and Father safe, but I'll protect Elliot with all I have left.

Elliot found Chester, placing him between us on the pillow. And that's how we fell asleep—tired, scared, and more alone than ever before.

My back was freezing. Still, I clenched my eyes shut. The day could wait.

Yes, it can wait.

But a wind, damp and bitter, wound its way into my dress, demanding otherwise. I tugged on the hem, tucking it around my feet, and settled miserably against the pillows behind me. No, not pillows.

A *wall*.

My eyes flew open.

I was leaning against an impossibly beautiful castle, its obsidian walls gleaming from a star-flecked sky the color of a dark amethyst. I clawed at my chest, probing the unfamiliar material with too-cold fingers. Black silk draped from my shoulders, narrowing to tighter sleeves across my forearms. The fabric continued across my chest, coming to a stop just below my jaw and flowing long and full around my legs. An ornate metal belt, shaped to perfectly conform to my waist, wrapped around my stomach to sit perched atop my hips, and dark tights hugged my legs like a second skin, meandering down my legs to meet knee-high leather boots. It wasn't practical, but it was beautiful. Something I'd dreamed up, surely.

Dreaming. I'm dreaming.

My heart thudded violently in my chest. Even after I'd taken the legionnaire's vial of elixir, the Dream Realm had found me once again. The carvings on the castle doors, previously blurry, were clear this time: Flowers spiraled into delicate willow tree branches, a young boy rode a cloud shaped like a chariot, and a king and queen happily conversed with winged dreamers.

But the more I looked, the more I didn't want to see.

The flowers began to burn, shadows bubbled from beneath the willow branches, and the figures' smiles twisted into gaping screams. The boy's cloud spun into a surging tempest of shadow, eating him alive. I cried out in surprise, wheeling back from the carvings, but I had nowhere to go. Dozens of demons, ugly messes of haphazard body parts, were lurching—or crawling—toward me from the castle's courtyard, trapping me.

"You can see, you can see!" the first demon cried. It was the one with the tattered cape and wilting gray hair. "Horror, beauty, dreams, life. Oh, but what will you do now? Let us in—let us be with him. Set us free!"

Shadows fell from the grooves in the carvings, forming into grotesque monsters. They rippled on the surface of the iron doors, moving so quickly that it was difficult to distinguish one from the other. Hooked claws, serrated horns, lips peeled back into malicious grins—I could feel their hatred as they poured out. Hundreds of eyes glared at me, seething with malice. It didn't look as if they had the power to break free, undulating against the doors as they were, but I didn't want to find out, either.

The demons were moving more quickly now, stumbling every few paces with their uneven gaits.

"Stay away from me!" I shrieked, edging closer to the monster-infested castle doors.

"Must you stare with such disgust?" The first demon held out its arms, showing off its gray, wrinkled flesh.

"It is because you *are* disgusting," I hissed. I couldn't believe it. I was conversing with a demon, and a deranged one at that. "All demons are disgusting."

"Cruel girl. My mortal body died during—what do you call it?" It paused, looking at the demons behind it as if they were supposed to know what it was talking about. "Forgive me. It's been some time since I walked the true earth or exchanged words with a human. Does your kind acknowledge you by a name? Or shall I just call you 'girl'?"

"You will not trick me, demon. I've heard many tales of your deception."

"Well, if you wish to be closed-minded, so be it. Makes it easier for me." It tossed the cloth that trailed from its shoulders and bent at the waist, mimicking an aristocratic bow. It stood again, a smile upon its cracked lips. The light of the stars, looming over the castle's many spires, glowed in its eyes. "Open the castle or I will devour you."

"Open it yourself and stay away from me!" I shrieked again. "I won't help you."

The demon held up its gray, claw-tipped hands. "It won't open for these hands, girl. The doors flinch and scream and hide—just as you do."

"If only we had wings," groaned a demon with spines protruding from its back.

"If only," agreed the gray-haired demon. "But alas."

Then they started walking, steadily closing the gap between us.

Esmer.

Esmer.

Esmer.

It was as though someone—or *something*—inside the castle was tugging on a single invisible thread fixed tightly around my rib cage and needed me to go beyond the gates of shadows and monsters. The call didn't feel evil, exactly, but it reeked of hatred and despair.

It felt achingly familiar.

I stretched my hand toward the castle doors, bracing myself in case the monstrous carvings decided to bite it off. But as soon as I reached their snapping jaws, the creatures slid away, leaving just enough room on the metal for two carved handles inlaid with onyx stones.

Behind me, the demons began running, nearly to the base of the castle stairs.

"Let us in!" they shrieked. "Lead us to him!"

As soon as my fingertips grazed the handles, the doors swung inward, sliding quickly and quietly against a marble floor. The creatures decorating the doors stilled, shifting their eyes to the abysmal darkness that coaxed from within. It felt similar to standing atop a precipice and staring into the eyes of a mysterious immortal beast that was clearly staring back. But there was no time to ponder.

Move, Esmer.

The demons were climbing the stairs, so I hurried into the castle, flinching as the doors crashed shut behind me. Fortunately, the doors were silent and unmoving once closed; they wouldn't let the demons in.

"Hello?" I ventured softly.

In response, a snarl sounded in the distance. The noise hovered in the musty air, raising the hairs on the back of my neck. Inching forward, I finally ran into something solid—a corner. Not a door, but not a demon, at least. I pressed myself against the stone, legs threatening to give out, but the growl echoed again, low and guttural. Unhurried, even.

As if it knew I couldn't escape.

I shivered as my eyes adjusted to the darkness. The vestibule was cavernous, adorned with opulent furniture and sprawling, gold-framed paintings and mirrors. And the colors—the colors within the space, slowly emerging—were unlike any I'd seen before in Norhavellis: indigo like the sweeping night sky, emerald like a forest floor at dusk, burgundy like a bruised plum left to settle in red wine.

I gritted my teeth, attempting to muster some courage. I needed to fight. Whatever came, I *had* to fight. If I didn't resist the demons intent on Corrupting me, I'd be just like Mother and Father, festering in a dark room until the Light Bringer came to purge the shadows from my soul.

And Elliot would be left alone in a world that preferred him rotting in an unmarked grave.

But the vestibule, even with its sumptuous decor, was more like a moonlit cavern than a castle, and as I searched for a weapon—preferably something extra sharp for whatever it was that wished to devour me—I found nothing of use. Apparently, the lord of this miserable castle never thought to invest in a weapon rack.

I was deliberating over a small table, wondering if I could use it as a shield, when a sudden wind ignited a series of hidden candelabras set deep into the walls. As they burst alive, their ghostly flames appeared in every gilded mirror, casting the paintings in an uncanny glow. Light filled the space, toward where it grazed—but didn't quite reach—a haze of darkness atop a staircase cut in the center of the room. The stairs towered higher than the vestibule's massive ceiling, winding away into the upper floors.

Then, in a rush, the haze disappeared.

Shadows poured down the stairs in thick tendrils, revealing a wide crack splitting the upper floors. Just beyond the hole, circling the castle in a suffocating sweep, came a horde of winged demons. They dipped and dove in front of an armored figure, growing nearer and nearer as if they wanted very much to be seen. The man raised his gauntlet-covered hands as if in greeting—and then a wild tempest of pitch-black shadow surged from him toward the mob of demons, sweeping out of the castle and into the sky. As the shadows swept around the demons' bodies, they were silent.

Silent as if he had sated them.

A strangled sound of fear slipped from my throat. The figure turned, noticing me at last.

He was a serpent poised to strike, a powerful demon sculpted from the shadows themselves. Ornate black armor clung to his body as if molded to him, marked by epaulettes carved to resemble feathers or scales and a cape that fell like fog past his feet. His face was fully covered; a pair of horns, protruding from intricate metal panels, curled up from a draconic helm, and a caged structure was set over his cruel mouth and pale jaw. Save for his mouth, his eyes, and a sweep of moon-white hair that fell just above his shoulders, every inch of his skin was covered, even down to the clawed gauntlets that stretched across his hands. He took a step forward, moving as if he were a ghost. His cape trailed behind him, hovering like a shroud of thick smoke.

He was painted differently in the history books, more monster than man. I was used to seeing him with red eyes, a bloody mouth, and a hideous, beast-like body. He was always devouring souls, fighting Weavers, or dripping with gore. But even though he looked different, I recognized who stood in front of me. He was a plague that ripped apart families, destroyed souls, and isolated humanity from their dreams. A nightmare who had ruined my life.

The Shadow Bringer.

Shadows sparked from his clawed gauntlets, rushing forward as a current of snakes. They swept around my body before I could react, enclosing my rib cage with their cold, slippery forms. Once I was fully bound, the Shadow Bringer strode down the stairs, leading with pointed, armored boots.

"You aren't of the demons or the darkness," he said, voice dripping with contempt. "Therefore, you must be of my enemy."

I thrashed and bit my tongue, focusing on the pain.

"Wake up," I cried out, biting down harder. "Wake *up*." I flinched, surprised at how real the bite felt. The metallic tang of blood, warm as any human blood would be, pooled in my mouth.

As he loomed over me, the metal scales atop his shoulders—carved to look like feathers—gleamed. They cascaded down his back, settling atop the thick material of his cape, and jointed talons, made of the same carved metal, encased each of his fingers.

"Which Weaver sent you here to kill me?" he asked sharply.

When I didn't respond, he clenched his fists. The snakes obeyed, squeezing my chest and binding my arms.

"Speak," the Shadow Bringer snarled, materializing a light-eating black sword from his palm and ghosting it across my neck. "If you refuse to respond, I will draw the answer out in other ways."

"Please let me go," I whispered hoarsely, fear making my throat as dry as parchment. "No Weaver commands me."

He scowled, and the snakes tightened in turn, constricting my lungs with their shrinking bodies.

"Lies won't serve you here," he warned, pressing the blade into the hollow of my throat. My skin buzzed where the metal touched me. "Especially pathetic ones."

"I'm not lying," I gasped.

"You *reek* of lies," he spat, sneering down at me with utter disgust. "The Weavers and their pets never change."

"Please," I begged, desperate for absolution. He pressed harder, forcing a cry from my lips. Maker, it *hurt*. "Have mercy."

"You take me for a fool, whimpering like you deserve my mercy."

"I *do* deserve your mercy. You took everything from me." Fear was beginning to ebb into despair. This monster stole Eden's life. My mother and father, too. My future—my world. "You won't have me, too."

His eyes, resembling twin silver pools, flashed violently.

"I can—and will—have you. In this place, I can kill whatever and whomever I please. Particularly if you serve one of them."

I gritted my teeth, thrashing hard against the snakes, but they did not relent.

"Every trespasser must pay the price," he continued. "The darkness will become you, just as it has done with me. It will consume you, drain you of your light, and leave you cold and empty." He held his mouth over my ear, smiling cruelly. The desire to bite him hard and make him bleed was overwhelming, but no skin was exposed for me to even try. "But since I'm feeling charitable," he added, this time with a stab of sarcasm, "perhaps we can strike a deal. If you want my mercy, you must first set me free."

Set him *free*?

He urged the snakes backward, dragging me toward the castle doors.

"Open them," he commanded, his voice an icy tempest of barely contained rage. "Let me out."

Impatiently, he grabbed my wrist from the snare of snakes and closed my fingers around the handle. With his hand over mine, the doors would not budge. He growled in frustration, trying again. Still nothing. The doors would not move.

"These doors must be the answer," he said angrily, dropping my hand. He paced back and forth, cursing and muttering to himself. "The balcony, the windows, the cracks in the walls—they all lead not to freedom but intolerable pain. What am I *missing*? If she can't free me, then what else—"

"Why do you need me to free you?" I choked out, scarcely believing what was happening. By some miracle, this beast was imprisoned in his own castle. The Weaver histories said nothing of the sort. "What's stopping you from leaving of your own accord?"

"Again with the mockery," he snapped, mouth curling in rage. It was clear he wanted to hurt me, but something was holding him back. "You know the Weavers imprisoned me here for five centuries. Unlock this Maker-forsaken door, and I will *mercifully* give you a sixty-second lead to crawl back to them. Then I will tear each Weaver apart limb by limb."

I shuddered in disgust, wondering why the Weavers had imprisoned the Shadow Bringer but not killed him. His imprisonment hadn't helped anything; Corruption still tore across Noctis. Perhaps he couldn't be killed. Or perhaps the Shadow Bringer's demon army had chased the Weavers away before they could.

He urged me to try again, this time without his hand over mine. Slowly, the doors shifted open.

He made a hoarse, surprised sound—

And then I released my grip on the doors, letting them shut with a loud, satisfying *bang*.

"Never, *demon*," I spat. My voice shook in terror. I'd never forgive myself if I let him out, even if it meant I had to forfeit my life. "If the

Weavers trapped you here for five centuries, then I hope you rot for one hundred more."

"You're all the same," he said, yanking my chin up and forcing me to look at him. Blood slipped from my lips, trickling from my injured tongue. "To you, I'm just a monster unworthy of living. A monster who isn't any different from the demons that roam this land."

"You *aren't* any different," I insisted, meeting his hate-filled stare with my own. His clawed hand felt cold, biting into my neck and making me forget the snakes at my ribs. "You're everything the Light Bringer teaches us to hate and fear."

The great hall went completely still, save for the flickering candle-light and my erratic breathing.

"You follow the Light Bringer." A statement. Not a question.

"He is my holy sovereign." The snakes loosened, slipping off my shoulders. "Of course I do."

He brought his caged mouth close to mine. His breath was cool, his eyes now devoid of feeling as he pulled my hands into his. "If you follow Mithras," he began darkly, bringing my fingers up to touch the blood dripping from my chin, "then why do you bleed shadow instead of light?"

I glanced down at my fingers, shivering as I noted a hazy smear of black. The inkiness lingered on my skin, smokelike, before disappearing into the air. I wiped my mouth again, only for a new smudge to appear.

A thread tugged at my rib cage, calling me back to consciousness.

The pain clawed, burned, *demanded*, muffling the Shadow Bringer's voice and dimming his features.

I don't understand. Help me understand—

Then the shadows exploded, bursting outward in a riot of all-consuming black.

7

I woke up to someone shaking my shoulders. Fingers, small and desperate, digging, digging—

"Get up, Esmer!" Elliot screamed, eyes wild and face contorted with anguish. Tears slid down his cheeks, running into his mouth. "Please get up, *please!*"

For a moment, I was unable to comprehend. *Refused* to comprehend. Then the shouts—the shrieks—rose in a hellish chorus, giving me no other option but to face reality straight in its horrible face.

"They're trying to kill us. We need to hide," Elliot insisted, grabbing me by the arm and pulling me up.

As my feet found the floor, I faintly registered a numbness shifting over my limbs. I wanted to hide. I wanted to do nothing *but* hide. But it was too late for that. Whether Eden heard me or not, I'd made a promise to her: to protect Elliot with all I had left. To keep him safe no matter the cost—even if I'd just dreamed of the Shadow Bringer himself.

"Elliot, who is trying to kill us? The Light Legion?"

"No, the village," he wailed. "The entire *village.*"

The tendons in my knees felt liquid, weak, but I moved toward the windowsill, anyway. The sun was hours from lifting over the horizon, but it was not darkness that met my eyes. Torchlight, dancing fiendishly across our property, stabbed at the night air. The Visstill was alive with glints of metal and crazed, hate-filled eyes. Dozens of eyes, hollow and feral. And they were moving in a frenzied mob toward our home.

They were gathering in front of our *home.*

"I saw—I saw—" Elliot shuddered, his small shoulders curling inward. "I think Mother and Father are dead. When you didn't wake up, I thought you might be dead, too."

"Elliot—"

"I think they're dead," he howled again. "And I don't want you to die, too!"

Elliot's beautiful, innocent face made my stomach roil. Thick lashes clumped together with tears. Eyes a soft, warm brown, now somber with grief. Dark hair curling over his ears and neck, now knotted with tangles. I reached out to hold him, to put my arms around him and will the world away, when a crash resonated from below.

A masked legionnaire stumbled up the stairs into our room, clamoring on his hands and knees as something grabbed at his foot from behind. He glanced wildly at Elliot and me as he struggled, kicking again and again—but whatever it was at the foot of our stairs began to pull, dragging him down.

"A little help would be nice!" the legionnaire yelled, throwing another violent kick at a Corrupt that resembled a local farmer. The young man's golden armor was streaked with blood, and his cape, now trailing along our floor, left behind darker marks of red. "A knife, a hammer"—he paused to take another kick, groaning with effort—"a chair, a vase—*something!*"

Elliot and I ran frantically around the room, seizing the first objects we saw. Elliot threw a quilt, which tangled around the Corrupt's body, and I flung a landscape that Eden had painted, which ricocheted through the air before it slammed against the monster's sneering face. The Corrupt fell back, howling, and landed in a heap of unnatural angles at the bottom of the stairs.

The legionnaire jumped to his feet, immediately wincing. "Ah, that stings," he hissed, clutching a wound in his side. "Though I do have my legs back, thanks to your valiant"—he glanced at the lifeless heap at the bottom of the stairs—"blanket and art throwing. Interesting technique."

"Th-thank you, sir," Elliot mumbled.

"On a more serious note, do you have any family or friends in the next village?" He pulled off his mask, wiping the sweat from his brow with a swipe of his forearm, his brown skin glistening in the dim light. He was young—and handsome. Wounded and smeared with blood and dirt, but hardly a few years older than me. He didn't put the mask back on. Instead, he clipped it to a holster at his side. "Half of Norhavellis has succumbed to Corruption. It's too dangerous for you to remain here any longer."

"Silas, where are you?" called a frantic voice. "Silas—oh." A masked young woman, clad in Light Legion armor, appeared at the bottom of the stairs, nearly tripping over the Corrupt's body. "I thought this one had you for certain. How fortunate you aren't dead." She glanced between Elliot and me, pulling off her mask and placing it at her side to take a better look. Her kohl-ringed eyes, framed by waves of dark red hair, were curious and slightly judgmental. "Ah, the two Havenfall siblings. Are these your rescuers?"

"It's great to see you, too, Mila," Silas responded. "And yes, they are."

I drew myself up to my full height, sending the woman the most imposing gaze I could muster—not unlike the one the Shadow Bringer had given me. "We saved your comrade's life, so you will take us with you to Istralla."

"Now, what would the Light Bringer think about that?" Mila asked, clearly perplexed. "You'll need weapons first. Knives? An axe, perhaps." She hopped over the Corrupt and bounded up the stairs. Once in our room, she looked around, frowning at what she saw. "But you're not fighters at all, are you? Especially *you*, little boy," she said, gesturing absently at Elliot, who made a face back at her. "What should we do with them, Silas? Can't have them running around with wooden spoons."

The Corrupt at the bottom of the stairs shuddered and groaned.

Silas and Mila shared a pointed look.

"Mila," Silas urged, a hard edge to his voice, and they descended the stairs once again.

Mila pulled a line of cording from around her hip, artfully tying knots around the Corrupt's wrists and ankles. "There, there. Help me move him so he can be purified later."

Silas grunted in agreement.

I shuddered and turned to Elliot, who looked just as aghast as I felt. We didn't say what we were both thinking: that Mother and Father would be sharing the fate of this Corrupt. Their souls would be spared by the Light Bringer, but the demons inside them would be destroyed. Along with their mortal bodies.

If they weren't already dead.

A loud crash resonated from below. If more Corrupt were breaking into our home, we had nothing to defend ourselves with and nowhere to go.

"Elliot, come on!" I urged, shoving our window open and clambering to the roof.

Outside, the clanging of metal on metal muffled what little sound we made, so we carefully moved to a quieter, darker side of our house. Silas and Mila chased after us, capes catching in the jagged texture of the wooden shingles. They crouched forward, balancing against the uneven surface, just as three Corrupt grabbed the edge of the roof, reaching for our feet.

Elliot screamed, yanking me back by the hand.

The Corrupt pulled themselves up until their elbows were pinned to the roof, feet kicking against the side of the house for leverage. They grinned at us—the three of them—and let out a chorus of gleeful snarls.

"Esmer, Elliot! How wonderful that you're still alive," one rasped. It was Norhavellis's baker. Edgar. His dripping mustache leaked a dark substance, and his eyes no longer reflected the kind, warm man who'd always made magic with sparse ingredients, bringing light into Norhavellis where there was scarce any to begin with.

I recoiled, horrified, as I recognized the faces of the others: Muriel, Edgar's wife, and Anna, their child. Their brawn and the unnatural resonance to their voices must have come from the demons within them. The demons that now *were* them.

"Yes, better for us that they're not already dead!" Anna bellowed, clambering over the edge before the rest. She was a slim girl near Elliot's age. If Norhavellis had the luxury of a schoolhouse, they'd be in the same year. Tears wet her cheeks, reflecting in the torchlight, and she headed straight for us, eyes aflame. "You ruined us."

"That's not true," Elliot insisted. "We always tried to help."

"Traitor!" Anna screamed, lunging with a snarl and throwing herself at Elliot before I could react.

Mila sprang from behind, flipping the girl to the roof with a practiced sweep of her boot. Anna leapt back up—far too quickly—and rolled under Mila's foot, diving for Elliot again. But Mila was quick, too. She knotted a fist in the girl's cloak and flung her away in one fluid, forceful movement, leaving her sprawled on her spine and sliding backward down the roof. Edgar and Muriel grabbed for Anna's flailing limbs, still struggling to worm their own bodies over the edge.

"Let go a' me! Let go!" Anna shrieked.

But the more they grabbed, the more Anna lurched backward. She slid off the edge, dragging Edgar and Muriel with her. After they hit the ground, they did not move.

"Th-they sounded almost—almost *themselves*," Elliot sobbed.

"We need to get to the Light Bringer," Mila said, grasping us by the elbows and ushering us back to our open window. "We're not safe up here."

Reluctantly, I let her guide me. There was nothing else we could do. Elliot and I didn't have a chance, not against the red rage of the Corrupt or the cold precision of the Light Legion. We moved quickly through our home, pausing only to step over the fallen Corrupt at the foot of our stairs, and followed Silas and Mila as they took us outside again.

The Light Bringer, along with a few of his more ornamented followers, stood apart from the fray. He held a large scepter in his armored hand, and he wove it through the air, chanting as smoke billowed from its crevices. Undulating smoke coiled against my tired skin, freely drifting, rippling, encircling.

The purification ritual.

It was the scent of fertile earth, of mud soft from a rainstorm. It was dried, sweet leaves on a warm forest floor. It was security and comfort and dreams. The feel of limitless promise and ancient secrets.

Music thrummed out with the smoke as it spread, led by the Light Bringer and the people around him. Voices blended with the low hum of accompanying flutes, and the melody rose in strength with the smoke, growing stronger and more brilliant with every passing moment. Corrupt began to fall, dropping their weapons and going silent. The smoke and the music seeped through cracks in my skin, and I exhaled, scarcely conscious.

Then I collapsed backward into the mist-drenched grass.

I crashed into bone-numbing water.

It rushed over my head in a wave, burying me, and for a moment, I was stunned into stillness, suspended and floating.

Incredible.

Light and darkness mingled around me, casting an endless array of luminous shapes across my arms, and the gleam of something iridescent floated through it all, rotating and spinning like a thousand moving stars. It swept over my skin and danced along the lines of my dress, nearly making me forget who I was and where I was supposed to be. A familiar melody hummed in the distance, drifting faintly, ever so faintly, through the water. It repeated twice before threading into nothingness.

And as the sound faded, so did the light.

I clawed to the surface, crying out for breath the moment my mouth met air.

"You," a familiar voice snarled.

The Shadow Bringer stood at the edge of the water, hatred radiating from every inch of his tall, shadow-wrapped frame. He was wearing the same attire from the previous dream; intricate black armor covered him from foot to throat, and a horned helm with a caged lower jaw hid all his features except for his mouth, eyes, and silver-white hair. A dark cape was affixed to his shoulders, sometimes appearing corporeal, sometimes appearing as though its threads were hewn from shadow. Above us, stained glass windows arched into an unfathomably tall ceiling, twining with vines, crumbling stone, and an expansive collection of candelabras.

"Why am I back here?" I cried, more to myself than to him.

I couldn't decide if I should swim to the edge—where he was—or remain where I was, suspended in a bottomless pit of icy water. I was also wearing the same attire from the previous dream, and while the dress was beautiful, it was painfully difficult to swim in. Realistically, I'd probably drown before I made it to the edge.

If dreamers *could* drown, that is.

"A foolish question, considering you're the one trespassing. A second time, no less," the Shadow Bringer said, fixing me with a stare as frigid as the water. He clasped his metal-encased hands together, drawing a stream of billowing, inky darkness from somewhere within himself. It draped across his shoulders in a languid pile, likely waiting for his orders to capture me or maim me in some way.

"I won't let you escape so easily this time. Your unconscious mind is prone to wandering into forbidden places, and I intend to find out *why*." His silver eyes narrowed.

The shadows rushed from his shoulders, rampaging in fierce, erratic loops over my head. A few separated, springing out from the cloud like a swarm of serpents, and rustled around in my hair, prodding and pulling. I screamed, clawing at them, but they fell against my neck regardless, pricking at the skin with a depraved eagerness. Dark, smokelike blood appeared from the injury they caused, rising in the air to mingle with the rest of the shadows.

The Shadow Bringer crossed his arms, looking oddly perplexed.

"Strange. I'd expected to draw his hideous stain, but there is still only darkness in your blood."

"I am not *stained*, you bastard."

A shadow slipped beneath the water, pinching my side with a deft clip of what felt eerily similar to teeth. I blindly swiped at it, horrified, and watched as the entire swarm released itself from me, nestling back into place at his side.

"You're a fitting counterpart to your Light Bringer," the Shadow Bringer said disdainfully, brandishing *Light Bringer* as if it was a terrible insult. "Weak, deceptive, and unwilling to wield your power when it matters most."

As he considered this, the shadows atop his shoulders roiled in unison. It bore a slight—very, *very* slight—resemblance to laughter. But whatever it was, laughter or amusement or something else entirely, was gone before it could solidify, replaced instead by the Shadow Bringer's overpowering scowl. The shadows quieted. "Still, this is an unforgivable breach," he continued, deadly serious. "Come closer, dreamer. If you follow me and open the castle doors, I will consider showing you mercy. But only after I am freed and not a breath before."

"Never," I spat without hesitation.

"Then I will send you back to Mithras in pieces. Or you can help me. Your choice."

Cold water continued to lap against me, swirling my dress into tangles. I kicked against the clinging folds, aiming to untangle the fabric from my legs, all the while fighting to keep my expression neutral. If the Shadow Bringer knew I was struggling, he'd likely use it against me. I had no doubt he'd force me underwater to suffocate in the murky, swirling liquid.

A strange, frantic understanding prodded at me.

Dream Weaver tales, along with other histories told within our kingdom, declared that the Shadow Bringer *prevailed* all those centuries ago, suffocating the Dream Realm with demons and Corruption. That he freely reigned, commanding his monstrous armies with a bloody fist and gnashing teeth. And yet here he was, trapped in his own castle and desperate for release. I wondered if the Light Bringer knew this. Because if the Shadow Bringer was vulnerable, I needed to stay alive long enough to tell him.

The Shadow Bringer noticed something in my expression—something distracting. He tilted his head. "You're unable to swim. How unusual. Especially for a dreamer."

"Don't mock me, demon." I sucked in an angry breath, indeed struggling to remain above the water.

He bared his teeth. "Careful."

Something grabbed my flailing ankle, *hard*, and pulled me under.

At first, I thought it was him—that he manifested some ugly, clawing menace again for the sheer purpose of punishing me. But as I twisted, thrashing and choking, I saw what was squeezing my ankle so roughly that it was close to snapping.

The thing had golden eyes, a ruined, gaping mouth, and vaguely human features—but it wasn't human at all.

A monster.

A *demon*.

It peered at me through the water, its too-wide mouth snapping open and shut. I fought hard, kicking a heel into the demon's bony neck. The cloth of my dress danced out of its claw, tumbling through the water like a frightened animal, and the demon gurgled out a piercing screech so full of madness that its entire body quaked.

I surged to the surface and took a deep breath.

Then it grabbed my ankle with both claws, dragging me under a second time.

My arms moved in ways I wasn't conscious of—jerking, swirling, reaching—and my lungs filled with a brutal, suffocating flame. I was dying. I was going to die. And it felt so *real*. This was a dream, but the fire burning my lungs and breaking my ankle was *real*.

The thing fixed its yellowed eyes on me again.

Was *this* what it felt like to fall into Corruption? To be taken, ruined from within?

The water shifted into darker and colder hues as we dropped, clouding my vision and settling over the scarred face of my captor. Its yellow-gold eyes were incredibly swollen, bulging out of its skin, giving the impression of a giant, misshapen river fish.

The claws at my ankle slipped, sinking deep into my boot and pulling it off.

Now. I had to move *now*.

Again, I tore my way to the surface, hating myself for being so damnably *useless* at swimming. My shin knocked against something—another demon? No, a ledge—and I stepped on it, not caring that my left ankle was shrieking, likely broken.

The Shadow Bringer stood with his arms crossed, unbothered by my struggles.

"Will you come with me now?"

"No."

His upper lip curled in disgust. "I don't think you understand. The castle doors only started to open when my hand wasn't forcing yours. If you agree to come willingly, I will save you."

"I said no, demon."

"Then I have no further use for you," he said, pinning me with dead, empty eyes. "But perhaps the demons do."

He turned without another word, cape billowing out from behind him, and left the cavern. The demon, still clawing my discarded boot, broke through the surface behind me, along with several more of its kind. All humanlike but marked by horrific, deformed additions. Additions that made them other.

At that moment, something snapped within me.

A tautness behind my eyes, connecting me to something outside the cavern—connecting me to the Shadow Bringer. A rush of power interwoven with pain, anguish, and a few final, pathetic shreds of courage poured through me, raging in my mind like a feral sea. It felt familiar and yet unfamiliar. It felt overwhelming and yet *not enough*. It felt like a blanket of soft silk. It felt like a squeezing cage of iron. It felt uncomfortable.

It felt *glorious.*

For a moment, the rush made me forget my bleeding, injured ankle. It made me forget my grief—grief at Eden's death and Elliot's despair. Grief at seeing Mother and Father, shadow marked and hated. Grief at seeing Corrupt Norhavellians fighting and dying. Grief at imagining my future—my *lack* of future. Grief because of my weakness. Grief because of my world.

Then the shadows burst in.

They churned around me, spinning and rotating as a furious whirl-wind, flashing and sparking like daggers of obsidian. The shadows were more powerful, more demanding, than the languid pile that had draped itself over the Shadow Bringer's shoulders.

The shadows fell upon the demons in a fury.

I could scarcely see, scarcely *breathe* as the dark ripped skin, forced itself down throats, wrenched heads into the water—until it finally moved into a towering cage of impenetrable black, pinning the demons to the grotto's glistening walls. The demons—or what few left that could move—prodded weakly against the smothering shadows. One by one the monsters stilled, and the roaring power faded like smoke forced away by the wind.

Feeling equal parts horrified and delirious, I wanted to cry.

I wanted to laugh.

Of course I'd have some sort of demented, evil power in the Dream Realm. I'd tried to be the dutiful daughter after Eden's death, but duty couldn't mask what had been festering within me.

A crashing noise echoed from somewhere behind me.

The Shadow Bringer had returned.

He swept into the room as if he was death embodied, blood leak-ing from his mouth and marring his pale skin. It slid down the column of what was exposed of his throat, pooling at the top of his armor. His blood was identical to mine: filled with shadows that rose like smoke and stained like ink.

"How dare you?" the Shadow Bringer gasped, materializing a dark blade from his palm and charging into the water after me. "How *dare* you?"

I staggered backward, now immune to the pain in my ankle. I tried to fling up shadows over and around me for protection, but the darkness fluttered, sputtering, and was extinguished entirely, releasing the demons into the water.

"You think you're entitled to my power?" He grabbed the cloth at the front of my collarbone, roughly twisting it in a taloned hand. He jutted his blade under my chin as the cold water swirled around us, pooling at our hips. "You think you can control it—control *me*?"

I pulled at his hand, trying to weaken his grip, but the metal on his gauntlets was impossibly sharp. Touching him was like grabbing a rose by its thorns or a snake by its fangs. My gaze dropped to his mouth. His lips, ever so slightly, were trembling. My chest heaved against our hands, feeling close to bursting.

"This wretched power belongs to me alone. I have *always* been the only one."

For a moment, we just stared at each other. The Shadow Bringer's tone and stance were filled with hatred, but his eyes, a dim shade of gray, appeared hopeless. Miserable and without any light or soul.

"Enough of this," he said.

And then he made to separate my head from my body.

Deep in the Shadow Bringer's dungeon, I leaned against my cell's bed, trying to ignore how revolting it felt against my skin.

Earlier, I hadn't wanted to be anywhere near the bed, let alone actually touch the thing. It was a skeletal, flimsy monstrosity draped with blankets and pillows that felt more like cobweb than cloth. Still, a paltry frame with thin bedding was far better than the ground. I learned that lesson quickly enough, finding that the crack at the bottom of my door was just large enough to watch slinking, shadowy things pass by. Things that paused at the door. Scratched at it. Whispered fragments of sentences in hollow voices.

"Let us out," one had pleaded.

I'd ignored it and turned away from the door, shivering.

The Shadow Bringer despised me. Wanted me *gone*. He had made that clear enough when he nearly beheaded me—his blade had vanished into shadow right before it met my throat—and he made it clearer still when he dragged me down a candlelit hall, conjured a dungeon out of thin air just for me, and stalked away to some other Maker-forsaken part of his castle.

Two days had passed, but I felt no hunger or thirst. Over time, my chilled skin had dried, and my wet, tattered dress had restitched itself. My ankle had also healed at some point—though when, exactly, I didn't remember—and it no longer hurt. Strangely, as a part of this nightmare, the inside of my cell reset itself each night, arranging its innards in some unholy, endless cycle. My room's singular candle never fully melted; if I broke something, it was fixed the next morning; and if I tried to remember what I'd done the day before, the memories felt foggier and foggier. There was nothing to do. Nothing to see. But the worst part was this: When I slept, I no longer woke up in Norhavellis. I just kept waking up in this Maker-forsaken *dungeon*.

I slumped against the wall, a cold slant of stone, and cursed every inch of the leaking, miserable room and the bastard who ruled over it. I cursed until my mind was raw and fraying.

"Let us out," a demon moaned at the door.

"I won't!" I yelled back.

I tried everything to escape. I called the shadowed power back to my palms, but it ignored me. I bargained with the demons in the hall, but they had no understanding of what I was asking. I tried sleeping, willing myself back into reality with every shred of my soul, but I couldn't focus, couldn't *think*.

"Let us out," repeated the demon.

This castle was hell. Not a living nightmare, but hell itself.

No wonder the Shadow Bringer is a raving lunatic.

I stifled a scream into my elbow, crying out until my throat was raw.

On the third day, the demons grew silent. And in their absence came the shadows.

The Shadow Bringer didn't say a word, but I could feel him. He stood out of sight from the crack under the door, but his shadows crawled in regardless, slinking along the floor and touching my ankles as though they were the muzzle of a lonely dog.

I lurched to my feet.

"How long do you plan to leave me rotting? Until I am so old and resentful that my hair turns white like yours?"

The questions leapt out, angry and bitter, before I could stop them.

My cell door disappeared; in its place stood the Shadow Bringer, emanating a halo of darkness. It slid along the lines of his body, spilling chaotically into the hall and my cell as if he couldn't control the shadows very well. Either that, or he didn't care to control them.

"Until you free me," he answered. His voice was rich and melodic, a smooth mask over his cold rage. "Break my curse, and you will never encounter this place again."

"It sounds like you're still asking me to release you from your castle. A castle that conveniently keeps you isolated from the rest of the Dream Realm."

"I am not asking," he began, stepping into the cell as his shadows hissed around me. "I am commanding."

"Well, then..." I paused.

"Then?" he parroted, his lip curling.

"I shall execute your command...never."

His silver eyes narrowed. A whisper of that cold fury was back. My stomach dropped, clenching in fear. I had been too bold. Too careless.

"Please don't hurt me," I choked out. This was the Shadow Bringer, for Maker's sake. He'd rip my soul from my bones and use them to pick his teeth. "Please spare my soul, I'll—"

"Just your soul? Not your family's, your friends', your lover's? How selfish to beg for yours alone."

I swallowed. A lover's?

I further considered his provocation. It *was* selfish of me to think only of myself. Elliot's soul, and the broken souls of my Corrupt parents, were far more deserving. And then there was Eden. My beautiful, perfect sister who had loved me with all her heart. Who had trusted me until the very end, indulging in my obsession with dreams even though it meant she'd lie in a coffin before her sixteenth birthday. The Light Bringer had purified her, reuniting her soul with the Maker in heaven, but perhaps the Shadow Bringer still had his claws around it. Around her.

"Not just mine," I began carefully, wary of placing targets on my family members. "There are four others."

"And what would you give for their safety?" he asked, coiling his shadows around the floor. They slowly began to rise, mimicking the snakes that previously bound me. "Would you let your kingdom's villain roam free?"

This gave me pause. I didn't know what it would mean for the Dream Realm if he was released. Another idea flashed through my mind. Frantic and half-formed, but an idea nonetheless.

The Light Bringer.

If I found a way to warn Lord Mithras, perhaps he could travel with his legion into this dream and kill the Shadow Bringer while he was still contained. If *I* could find and enter his castle, surely the Light Bringer could, too.

I just needed to keep the Shadow Bringer captive long enough for our savior to arrive.

"Perhaps I would set you free," I finally conceded, taking a step forward. I needed him to trust me, to believe that I wanted to set him free. At least until I could lure a legion of predators into his den. I almost smiled at the idea of it. Lord Mithras, radiant in his power, would burn the Shadow Bringer down to a pile of iron and ash. "But first I need to go home to Norhavellis. How much time has passed? Does dream time correlate with reality?"

"If there is a correlation, this castle confounds it. When you wake up, it's possible one hour will have passed. Or perhaps one year." He stalked forward, leaning over me. *Maker*, he was tall. "But that shouldn't matter, because I will not grant you the gift of 'going home.' This room anchors you; you shall remain contained in this castle until you free me."

His snakes jumped forward, bodies rushing to encircle me. I flinched, and they slammed to a stop before they could even touch my dress, spinning instead to face the Shadow Bringer with wide-mouthed screams before dissolving and falling like rain upon the floor.

The Shadow Bringer's eyes went wide behind his horned mask.

"What are you?" he murmured, almost as if he didn't intend to be heard.

Before I could answer, he spun on his heels and slammed a newly conjured door into place. I slid to the ground, despair crawling up my throat like an unwelcome sickness, and cried myself to sleep.

I woke up slowly, eyes already swimming with unshed tears. An image of my brother arose in my head: Elliot curled up in his blanket burrow, hiding from the world and all its monsters under a heap of warm cotton and wool. How he'd tuck Chester the cow into the crook of his elbow. His tufted brown fur was always knotted, his button eyes dull from age. I tried to imagine Eden, but it wasn't as easy. My memories were muddled and foggy: a glimpse of her hair, a single chime of her laugh, a graze of her warm hug. I tried to reach for them, but they kept fading away. It was like grasping for dozens of small, slippery fish as they tumbled down a waterfall.

I pressed my face into my palms and tried not to hyperventilate.

No, no, no.

I willed my tears to stay where they were—in my head, not running rampant down my face. But they escaped regardless, falling in long, meandering lines down my cold skin.

Curse it all.

After a time, I opened my eyes. It simply hurt too much to keep imagining. Although the memories I could salvage were comforting, they were false. I looked around my cell, noting the dim light, the dirty ground, the stuffed cow in the corner—

A stuffed cow slouched against the corner of my cell, its button eyes staring upward.

I nearly fell out of the bed.

"Chester," I whispered. The name felt odd on my tongue. Gingerly,

I picked him up, thumbing the knots in his fur. "What are you doing here? Where is Elliot?"

Other things appeared. A wooden chair, scuffed and peeling where Eden had painted flowers on it years ago. The bookshelf from my room. A favorite linen dress, a hand-me-down from Eden, its cloth soft and practical despite its fraying edges. A plant-filled wall from Mother's apothecary. Elliot's favorite book of Dream Weaver tales. The beamed ceiling from our kitchen. Our front door, its window bright with morning light. In seconds, my cell doubled, tripled in size, unfurling and shifting. It was a creature growing into its second set of skin.

The more I saw, the more I felt, and the more I remembered.

The space shifted with my thoughts, readjusting and rearranging its innards until it more closely resembled what I knew to be home. Gone was my cell in the Shadow Bringer's castle. This was *home*.

"Elliot?" I called. "Mother? Father?"

I ran from room to room, frantically searching—but found only silence. It looked like home, but there was no one there to fill it. Outside, I collapsed, scarcely feeling the whisper of grass upon my bare legs.

No longer was I wearing the dark, high-necked dress with billowing sleeves. I was barefoot in one of my favorite cotton nightgowns, and the sensation was glorious. The morning light pressed its warmth into my neck; birds soared overhead; woodsmoke mingled with pine and lilac bushes; trees swayed in the breeze—but it was still lacking. All of it, lacking.

Where is everyone?

At the familiar clinking of pointed boots and taloned gauntlets, I turned around.

There was the cause of my despair, descending the wooden steps of my family's front porch. His white hair, horned helmet, and black armor were a stark contrast against the vibrant color around him; he looked unfit for such an ordinary setting.

"What have you done?" he asked. Despite how odd he looked on my family's property, his eyes were curious, mesmerized by the earth, the trees, and the cloud-covered sky.

Memories of the last few days rose up, cold and terrible. I hated his castle. I hated *him*.

The ground suddenly cleaved apart at his feet, almost as if I had *caused* it, sending him sprawling face-first into the grass. I tensed, expecting him to rise in a fit of rage, but he merely rolled to his side, picked a wildflower, and spun it between clawed fingers.

"What you've accomplished goes against the laws of my castle." He tore his eyes from the flower, dropping it. "How did you do this?"

I crossed my arms, distrusting the hint of genuine wonder in his question. "I'm not telling you that."

Something misshapen and dark formed behind his back: wings.

Two wide, velvet-black *wings* unfurled from him in a burst of feather and shadow. He glanced back at them, surprise briefly registering on his face, before taking a powerful leap into the sky. Within a few beats, he had disappeared into the mist beyond the clearing, leaving gusting, swirling patterns in the air behind him.

"What in the *Maker*?" I gasped.

The wake he left ruffled my dress, and I felt every sensation sharpen: the tickle of grass beneath my feet, the cool spot of mud pressing into my heel, and the edge of a stone touching my toe. Small lifelike sensations. Memories of my childhood flashed before me, too. Lying in the sun with Eden, searching for shapes in the clouds with Elliot, all three of us running barefoot on prickly midsummer grass as we played tag or some other jaunty, mindless game before dinner.

After some time, the Shadow Bringer reappeared through the mist. He fell from the sky, not pausing to catch his balance, and collapsed hard into the grass. He ripped off one of the metal gloves that armored his hands, trembling as he did so, and clutched at the ground with long, white-knuckled fingers.

It was more unsettling, perhaps, than when he'd nearly beheaded me.

"Little," I heard him murmur. He placed his helmed brow against the tangle of grass at his knees, pausing to draw in a deep breath, then rose to his knees again, still grasping the ground. "Your world is so little."

"I don't have much of a say in the matter," I responded, eyeing him warily from where I sat. "My parents are Absolvers. We have a duty to the people of Norhavellis. It's the only place I've ever been."

"So this is truly all you know? You crafted this dream based on your reality, but your reality is limited. A town—no, a village—infested with ruin and rot. That is Norhavellis? And then, five miles at most beyond that, an uneven perimeter around your home. That's all?"

He paused to look up at the sky, almost as if he was uncertain about saying anything else. But then, as quickly as he had descended into that strange pit of sorrow and contemplation, he shifted, jolting upright as if branded by fire.

"There must be more. If you're bound to the Light Bringer as one of his followers, there must be more." He stormed over to me, his lifeless eyes now burning. "Give me your arm."

I made to move away, to scramble across the porch into my house, but the dream was starting to blur, its colors melding into smeared pools of pastel. I stumbled to my feet, swaying as he grabbed me by the wrist.

"You will *not* wake up now," he snarled, forcing me back into focus. "Let me see what you know. Show me your world."

10

Trees shook as the violet sky darkened into a bloodied plum.

Wind tangled my hair and hissed past my ears as sparks caught the side of my face, falling like dust around us, and I looked on, numb, as my home erupted into flames. Shadows of people, donning the garb of the Light Legion, marched from the depths of the Visstill, eyes haunted and faces hollow. Others ringed the shadow-scorched edges of a burning pyre.

"They're burning them," I said slowly, tasting the foulness of my words and the air heavy with the smell of fire. It was the cremation of all things. Grass, root, pine, hair, flesh. It was all there, burning, mingling.

Wrong.

He tightened his grip on my wrist, pulling me in. "You can't go to them. They will not see you."

"But this is my home," I protested. "I need to find Mother." I twisted away from him, fury growing wild in my stomach. "Father." I ripped free. *"Elliot."* I stumbled into the clearing. Wave after wave of warm, fire-fed air pushed into me, drying my eyes and heating my lungs.

My home was an inferno of flame and smoke, cracking and groaning so violently, it was as though it were alive.

Dying, but *alive*.

The nearest legionnaire was tucked into the shadows of the Visstill, the golden metal of his breastplate charred and streaked with blood. He was gazing past me—eyes fixed on the pyre, the smoldering house, sparks exploding across the sky—and made to turn away, moving deeper into the trees.

"Stop!" I shouted, clawing my way through the smoke that drifted between us. "Please stop!" As I ran, darkness began to cloud the edges of my vision. "Stop!" I screamed again, crying out so forcefully that my voice cracked.

The legionnaire paused, turning toward the clearing—just as an explosion of red flame and dark, all-consuming smoke thundered behind us.

My home had collapsed into itself, releasing its innards to the earth.

I staggered sideways into the legionnaire, gasping, wild-eyed, and suffocating on both the smoke and my own panic. I should have fallen against the man's metal front, but instead I fell *through* him, crashing to the ground as he walked forward and through me.

This isn't happening.

I stumbled to my feet, lunged forward, and grasped for the legionnaire's shoulder, only to pass through him in a wave of shadow.

This can't be happening.

The Shadow Bringer emerged from the flame and smoke, shadows rolling from his shoulders in powerful waves. Soot marked his skin under his mask, ringing his eyes and wrapping around the hollows of his exposed jaw. I expected the legionnaire to notice, especially since the Shadow Bringer was wielding his sword, but he continued walking, completely oblivious to the Shadow Bringer's powerful, inhuman presence.

"Where are they?" he asked me.

"I don't know," I answered, miserable and aching. "I can't find them."

I looked toward the pile of burning bodies. If they were purging the Corrupt, then would Mother, Father, Elliot—?

He interrupted before I could finish that thought. "No, not your family. Who caused this? This is a warped dream, based on your current reality. There must be someone powerful at the root of it. Who deals with your Corrupt?"

"Lord Mithras," I said absently. "Our holy Light Bringer."

"Mithras?" he repeated, eyes flashing in revulsion. *"He is no lord."*

Another explosion shook the ground around us, filling the air with wood, stone, and debris.

And then fire rained down.

The Shadow Bringer threw up his arms, letting his blade fall to the earth, and from his hands he summoned a protective shadow that loomed as high as a mountain and crashed with the force of a storm-battered sea. It wrapped around us, forming a shield before the fire hit.

For a few silent moments, we were alone in the void, listening to the muffled crashing of my world—my burning, ravaged world—falling against our shield of shadow.

"I'm dead, aren't I?" I finally managed. "I died in the fire, just as my family did. That's why I'm stuck in your castle and can't wake up."

"No, not at all." He looked past me, eyes cold, as if he could see beyond his wall of darkness. "What you just saw was merely a half-truth, as most dreams are. It held parts of your reality, but not the whole. This isn't real."

I peered at the shadows, trying to see what he could see.

"You're lying," I said.

"I'm not," he said simply, shaking his head.

"This is exactly what I left behind before I fell asleep and dreamed of you." I cursed, a familiar rush of sorrow and fear ripping through me. "They're dead. I can *feel* it. I can feel myself dying, too."

Something snapped in me again, a familiar pulling of my ribs. Only this time, instead of connecting me to some power out of my reach, it connected directly to him. The Shadow Bringer turned to face me, eyes wild. Part of his neck was left exposed by his helm; his hair curled damply against it, melding with the soot that marred it. My attention drifted to his mouth. A smudge of ash was underneath his lower lip, all but enticing me to wipe it off. And his *eyes*. Shadows swirled in them, eddying between darker and lighter variations with every breath. They reminded me of stars—depthless constellations I wanted to get lost in. And, Maker, he was so *tall*. Powerfully built and capable of great, terrible things.

He's beautiful.

The thought surged up, unbidden, and nearly made me buckle.

"Again," he asked, alarmed. "How are you able to call on my power? What are you?"

"I'm not a monster," I snapped, finally releasing some of the pent-up emotion that I had been holding on to for days. "Don't take me to be anything like you, demon."

"Enough." He held me by my shoulders, pinning me to a tree with a grip of iron. His sphere of shadow released its hold, falling back and blanketing the scorched, ruined land around us.

He wasn't beautiful.

The Shadow Bringer would never be beautiful. There were his powers—the way he could control darkness and make it bend to his will. Then there were the demons that lived with him, haunting his castle with their screams. The tales had falsely professed his eyes to be red and his body fiendish, but he possessed many features that made him cold and cruel nonetheless.

"*Enough,*" he repeated, the color fading from his eyes, his lips. "Please."

He looked at me with wild desperation.

But I couldn't stop. The shadows roared.

"You're a demon, a devil, a *monster!*" I screamed.

His expression forfeited what his silence could not.

"You killed my sister! You killed my parents!"

Emptiness ripped at my stomach and cleaved my heart in two. It laid bare the space where I had a family who loved me and a home that protected me. Mother and Father, no longer Corrupt. Elliot, safe and without tears. A future and a hope for a better life. Without realizing it, I closed my eyes. I was screaming, sobbing, begging—for what, I didn't know. For this vision to be a lie. For the Shadow Bringer to end it all.

And the dark roared louder.

When the chaos settled, the shadows dropped, circling the ground in a low-lying fog and leaving the Shadow Bringer and me exposed. To my disgust, he was still holding my shoulders, and I was unintentionally leaning into him, face pressed into his armored chest. A quick shove sent him sprawling; he'd been drained of his shadows, which were now scattering to the wind and skimming the grass instead of returning to his body.

The sensation of us being watched snapped me to my senses.

Mithras, encircled by his Light Legion, was standing across from us, shoulders dusted with ash and boots marred by the Shadow Bringer's low-lying shadows. Peering through his mask, his eyes, golden and all-seeing, betrayed an expression of abject shock, and the legionnaires who had previously ignored us were now staring, mouths agape. We were still in this dream, but they could see us.

They can see us.

The Shadow Bringer, half-crumpled at my feet, cursed.

"You're the Havenfall daughter. Esmer," Mithras began, taking a step forward. Light threaded around his fingertips, dissipating some of the shadows that clung to him. "And what is that monster doing at your feet?"

The Shadow Bringer staggered upright. The fog began to move, darting around ankles and rising to meet his outstretched hands.

The Light Bringer's face paled. "You aren't meant to be free."

"Ah, Mithras," said the Shadow Bringer, his shadows beginning to hiss. "Your death will finally bring me peace."

"Monsters like you can never find peace," Mithras spat, the color beginning to return to his skin. "You will be banished to your castle immediately."

"No," the Shadow Bringer said menacingly. In an instant, his shadows became serpents, grabbing legionnaires and slamming them into the ground with violent *cracks*. He laughed and the darkness rose, swallowing any legionnaire who managed to escape the beasts' powerful bodies.

"After him!" Mithras yelled, but many of his followers were either incapacitated or drowning in the shadows.

I sidestepped a legionnaire who fell from the dark, blindly swiping a serpent off his throat only to catch a jab to the ribs from his comrade. I bent over, gasping for air. Fire stung my lungs as I tried to catch my breath.

It was here that Lord Mithras found me. He held his hands at his sides in a show of false civility, but his eyes were murderous. I stumbled backward, horrified by his anger and nearly tripping over one of the Shadow Bringer's serpents.

"Did you free the Shadow Bringer, Esmer? He was bound to that castle in order to protect the entire Dream Realm. We will be *eviscerated* with him roaming free."

"Of course not—never, my lord. I was his prisoner," I insisted, wincing at another sharp wave of pain from my ribs. "I saw you burning my home, my family. The villagers, too. Are they...?" The question burned off my tongue, tasting of ash. *Are they dead?*

Mithras made a sound of disappointment. "Don't sound so pitiful. As an Absolver daughter, you should know better than to question your Light Bringer. To burn is to purify. If their souls aren't purified, they'll be reborn in the Shadow Bringer's domain as his demons." Mithras held himself very still. "But perhaps you are right to be afraid. After all, you *have* been consorting with our kingdom's greatest enemy." He raised a hand, light simmering, and I flinched. The shadows nearest to me mimicked the movement, and Mithras cocked his head. "And manipulating the darkness yourself, no less."

"I-I'm not manipulating anything," I said, voice cracking. "My sister was killed by the Shadow Bringer. I want no part of this."

But the Light Bringer was not swayed. His hands glowed bright, drawing closer to me like flames on the pyre—and the shadows around me shot forward, slamming him to the ground.

Oh hell.

Mithras rose, eyes glinting. Golden, light-flecked blood dripped from his mouth, staining the top of his armor. "Well, well, well. I don't think you were held captive, Esmer. I think you sought him willingly."

"I didn't mean to hurt you, my lord. *That wasn't me.*" I said, equal parts shocked and distressed.

"I beg to differ," Mithras snapped, making a point to raise his burning hands. To my horror, the serpentlike shadows flared up, sensing my alarm. They hovered by my waist and looped around my arms, ready to strike. "The worst of humanity pulses through you, wicked girl. And to think I was prepared to bestow mercy upon you."

The light in his hands burned brighter and hotter just as his eyes began to glow, aflame with unspent fury. His mouth curled up, showing bloodstained teeth. A predator's tell before landing the fatal blow.

Mithras raised his fist and charged, sending a powerful blast of light at my head.

The shadows around me threw themselves into the light, but they were instantly destroyed, shattering as soon as their bodies met the Light Bringer's blinding flames. A serpent on my wrist tightened, yanking me down one second before the blast could touch me. I quickly rose to sprint toward what was left of the Visstill Forest, but the serpent pulled me back, almost as if it was tied to something—or someone—else.

The Shadow Bringer.

He looked as horrified as I felt, trying to pry from his wrist the serpent that tied us together like some unholy rope. It was clear he wanted to charge forward—to attack the Light Bringer—but I refused to let him. The Shadow Bringer and I grabbed the serpent rope at the same time: I yanked left; he yanked right. He was glaring daggers at me, clearly distracted, but managed to simultaneously blast darkness at Mithras, sending him flying.

Taking advantage of the momentary chaos, I hurled my weight toward the woods, desperate to break the bond that tied me to him. Unfortunately, the Shadow Bringer was dragged along, plummeting into my side. I kicked him, but the shadow bond only tightened, bringing us closer together.

"He's within my reach. For the first time in five hundred years, he's *within my reach*," the Shadow Bringer breathed, chest heaving. "Let me go, Esmer."

It was the first time he'd said my name, and it ignited something strange in my chest.

Disgusting.

"I can't." I tested the shadow again, but it didn't budge. It sat tight on my wrist, looping up and around my forearm in the same manner it clung to the Shadow Bringer's. "But maybe this binding will make you easier for the Light Bringer to kill."

"If I die," he said darkly, "your beloved Light Bringer won't forgive you. He'll simply chain you to the dark like a prisoner. Just as he did with me."

"He'd never make me inherit your darkness, Shadow Bringer. This is all just a terrible misunderstanding."

"You think so?" The silver in his eyes flashed. I had clearly struck a nerve. "Then know that your version of reality is built on lies and deceit." His riotous gaze fell to his gauntlet-covered arms. He flexed them, anxious to be rid of the serpent. Nevertheless, it clung on. "But I suppose that doesn't matter. Soon I'll be rid of you—for good. Mithras wouldn't have it any other way."

The darkness began to rush back to the Shadow Bringer, surging to his hands. What remained rose behind us in a threatening tempest, filling half the sky with a pit of starless night. The sudden influx of shadows left the clearing in front of us empty, void of anything but the Light Bringer, his legion, and—

Demons. Dozens of them.

Mithras pointed a deadly charge of light our way, screaming at the legionnaires to strike us and the demons—just as the Shadow Bringer brought the tempest down, swallowing us all.

11

My eyes creaked open, straining as the world wobbled alive.

Soft golden light worked through the air, and for a moment, I thought I was still dreaming. But the light fanned out, lapping against polished ivory, decorative gold metal, a small shelf of books, and paintings that wrapped around a domed ceiling. I felt plush velvet against my hands, even though they were bound by ropes. Heard horse hooves and the *clink* of rattling metal. Smelled honeyed wine, inked paper, and the subtle scent of something deliciously masculine. Expensive cologne, perhaps. What I didn't expect to see was the Light Bringer sitting across from me in the most extravagant carriage I'd ever seen.

"You're awake."

The Light Bringer, unmasked, lounged in the seat across from me. Although he held himself casually, his face contained a riot of emotion: unease, disgust, and confusion.

He leaned forward, looming over me. His bare face was striking: tan skin, molten gold eyes, and blond hair that fell to his shoulders, escaping the band that bound it. A beloved, golden king. He looked exceptionally younger than I had anticipated him to be, but his centuries of rule showed in his eyes.

"So, you've returned to us after all," the Light Bringer began, his full mouth slanting into a frown. I couldn't decipher his expression. Hatred? Condemnation? Every breath made it harder to tell. "Do you have anything to say for yourself?"

I inhaled sharply, wanting to answer, but my throat had closed again. A muffled *wheeze* croaked from somewhere within me. The Light Bringer unhooked a flask from beneath his mantle. He brought it to my lips, positioning it carefully so that it didn't spill, and I drank deep.

Water. Blessed, blessed water.

In any other context, I might have felt nervous being this close to him. *No one* was ever so close to the Light Bringer, never mind being hand-fed water out of his personal flask. But there was no time for those emotions. No time for formalities, either.

"Why am I bound? Where is my family, my lord?"

Mithras leaned back, and I noticed a faint scar splitting his brow.

"The Light Legion does not tolerate the Corrupt. Unmanaged, they will destroy a village. Unpunished, they will destroy a kingdom." As he talked, he removed his gloves and set them on the bench. A spray of blood marked them. "The Corrupt are known deceivers, worming their way into the light when they're still rotting from within. Fortunately, our Maker is a forgiving god."

"Where is my family?" I repeated, on the verge of hysterics.

"Where do you expect them to be?"

I halted. "What?"

He gave me a strange, inquisitive look, as though he was gauging something—or considering a new possibility. Whatever it was, the expression passed swiftly. "We began our purification ritual, starting with your parents, but the ceremony was breached by a demonic presence. It took a long time to reestablish the ritual and save what souls remained."

A deep, bruising ache dragged along my scalp and ended between my shoulders, forcing me to bow my head. Thoughts swirled around in bizarre fragments. Memories clouded in on themselves. Even reality itself—the reality of Mithras pinning me with eyes of burning embers—felt distant, somehow. I centered my breathing, focusing on the carriage's scent of wine, old books, and expensive cologne.

Mithras placed a hand atop my shoulder, grazing the edge of my neck.

"You paint a convincing portrait of innocence," he murmured. "Silas and Mila certainly believe you to be. But they have not known your kind as I do. They did not *see* you as I did." I tried to respond, but my throat was dust, my teeth carved from chalk. And even if I could speak, I didn't think the words would come. They were stuck to the walls of my mind, clinging to the shadows. "Even so, we agreed that you would be treated justly," he continued. "Your punishment will be suitable for your crime."

Again, Mithras offered his flask, and I drank.

"I have no reason to be punished," I managed, blinking away the haze that shrouded my eyes. "I want to see my family."

"You will," Mithras said simply. As if a curse had lifted, the pain instantly ebbed. "In heaven one day. That is, if your troubled heart is ever allowed entrance."

"Then my mother, my father—"

"Are with the Maker."

"And their bodies?"

"Were buried with the rest of the purified Corrupt."

My heart burned with grief. I wanted to sob, to hug someone, to *scream*. Mithras put his elbows on his knees, eyeing me warily. "We are currently en route to Istralla. Your brother is, too, since it is too dangerous for him to remain in Norhavellis unattended. If he is worthy, he can train at Citadel Firstlight and become a member of the Light Legion one day."

This made my heart ache, too. I had never considered the possibility, but Elliot would be a wonderful legionnaire. He was brave, empathetic, and kind. Everything the Light Legion should be. He deserved a future. He deserved the entire world.

"And what about me?" I rasped, tears pricking my eyes.

"*You* are being escorted to the capital for your formal hearing."

"What am I being tried for?"

"For consorting with the Shadow Bringer," he snapped, his hypnotic voice growing cold.

"I did not consort with him. My lord, he captured me."

His mouth twitched up in a tight, forced smile. "Then you're either delusional or a liar. Either way, it does not matter. I saw it with my own eyes. You were standing next to the Shadow Bringer and wielding his shadows as if his dark magic was your very own."

His words slid like fire down my spine.

Wielding the shadows *did* feel natural. Like they had always been a part of me.

"No—*no*. I wasn't with him," I insisted, the words falling from a tongue that felt too numb, too dry. "He captured me against my will. I was trying to escape." Tears slipped down my face. "I would never side with that monster."

The Shadow Bringer's deep, melodic voice rang in my ears: *What you just saw was merely a half-truth, as most dreams are. It held parts of your reality, but not the whole. This isn't real.*

Maybe there was a chance I was still dreaming.

I pinched the inside of my palm, wincing at the bite of my nails and the tight ropes still looped around my wrists. Pain could be felt in the Dream Realm, too, but this sensation was sharper and more complete. I wasn't dreaming. This was terribly, horribly real.

The carriage slowed to a stop.

Silas tapped lightly on the door before carefully opening it. The Light Bringer signaled him to speak.

"My lord, we must set up camp." Silas glanced at me uneasily. "The injured need to be freshly bandaged, and morale is low."

Mithras gave a curt nod. "Very well."

He made to stand, leaving me inside the carriage.

"This isn't just, my lord," I begged, feeling pathetic. "You haven't even heard my story."

"Oh, but your story has already been told," Mithras said angrily, snapping his mask back into place. He held me by my bindings, squeezing the ropes until they hurt. "You have earned your fate. Now be strong for your brother and face the justice you deserve."

I swallowed a scream.

I had thought that the Shadow Bringer's castle was a hellish nightmare, but that wasn't even close to the truth. *This* was hell. *This* was a nightmare.

And this was now my *life*.

Disembodied conversations drifted past the carriage, turning my stomach into knots. I begged the Maker to shield Elliot's ears, but if I could hear them, why couldn't he?

Oh, Elliot. He must think I'm a monster.

"She looks terrible. More corpse than girl," came a gruff voice.

"Have you seen how she stares at us?" a feminine voice added. "There's darkness in her eyes; she's Corrupt, clearly."

"It's disgusting," said a third. "Like the Shadow Bringer himself is in there just itching to crawl out of her skin."

Shocked laughter, a horrified gasp.

"Better watch your throats tonight," the gruff voice said. "She'll rip into them if left unattended."

"If the Shadow Bringer claimed her soul, it wouldn't really be her. It would be *him*. And if he got to us—"

"He'd devour us before anyone else in the kingdom was the wiser."

I nearly vomited at the thought. I'd never harm them. I wanted them to *live*. I wanted them to be free from Corruption just as much as I desired everyone in the kingdom to be free. But they didn't see that when they looked at me. They only saw a monster posing as a girl, a treacherous beast who would spread Corruption like a ravenous fire until the soul-stealing plague consumed Noctis whole.

We set up camp in a crescent-shaped glade. Legionnaires murmured furtively among themselves as they gathered firewood, righted their tents and bedrolls, and tended to both the horses and the Light Bringer's every whim.

Before long, armor had been carefully removed, and the group was largely nestled around a roaring fire, lounging in matching tunics and woolen pants. Dusk settled in, tickling our hair and necks with a cool, pine-scented breeze. Something shifted in the Visstill the later it became; nighttime sounds bloomed in the shadows as wind wended itself through the ancient trees, *whooshing* between bough and root as though the land was its hollow plaything. I prodded the ground with the toe of my boot, still bound and uncertain as to what I should be doing or where I would be sleeping. At the rate I had been ignored—or suspiciously glared at—it was likely there wouldn't even *be* a place for me to sleep.

Elliot, on the other hand, had a small golden tent all to himself. He was on the opposite side of camp, carefully isolated from me, and though we couldn't talk, it gave me comfort just to see him. He looked my way often; I couldn't tell if he was crying because he hated me, because he loved me, or because he mourned for Mother and Father the way he would soon mourn for me.

I wandered to the edge of camp and slumped into the curve of an unearthed tree root. Silas, likely ordered to watch me lest I make a run for it, stepped away from the fire to join me.

"All the way over here by yourself?" he asked, kneeling next to me. His face, a deep, beautiful brown, was freshly scrubbed, and his eyes, typically gentle, were sharp despite his casual tone. "You need to sleep at some point, you know."

Earlier, while the other legionnaires were occupied with setting up camp, Silas had tried to speak with me. He wanted to shed light and optimism on Elliot's future at Citadel Firstlight, but I was too uneasy to give him my full attention. But now, in the lonely, lengthening shadows of twilight, I wanted to talk.

"I wasn't about to escape, if that's what you're implying." I raised my hands, still bound by rope. "Wouldn't make it far, anyway."

Bound hands made basic things difficult: walking, sitting, avoiding obstacles—but especially moving through a forest such as the Visstill. I had learned that truth quickly when I went to relieve myself earlier, tripping over a branch but unable to catch my balance. I didn't have access to a mirror, but I was certain my face was scratched and my long hair messy.

Silas had been nearly smiling, but the expression slipped. "You're a perceived threat that we all witnessed. We must remain cautious." Silas took a swig from the flask at his feet, clearing his throat. "Many of us have had Corruption in our own families," he said, continuing. "We're familiar with it in ways I wouldn't wish upon our worst enemies. And we *definitely* have an enemy or two." His warm smile was back, but it felt empty. "Some legionnaires may hesitate to approach you, but it's only because they're afraid of what you might be."

At my silence, he faltered.

"There has never been a battle like the one last night." He added, taking a second drink from his flask, "Last night changed everything. The Shadow Bringer isn't supposed to be roaming dreams with someone like you by his side."

Silas offered me his flask, holding it steady so that I could easily partake. It was filled with a warm, bubbling cider, and it instantly eased some of my tension. "Then everyone truly *did* see me in the dream?"

"It—yes. Yes, we could. Do you remember the smoke that came from the scepter Lord Mithras held?"

I nodded. It smelled delicious, like sweet autumn leaves and ancient secrets.

"It is a kind of sleeping mist. It gives us the ability to walk between reality and the Dream Realm, but it also works as a sedative. Lord Mithras was purifying the most severe Corrupt in the Realm when you emerged from the shadows with that monster." He raised his face to the sky, closing his eyes. "Mithras will likely seek you tonight in your dreams. He wishes to see where your soul wanders. If you are telling the truth, then perhaps there is still hope for you."

I wasn't sure why he was confiding in me like this. Perhaps it was because I was going to die soon. The dead were quite efficient at holding secrets. Mila joined us, red hair full and immaculate, and leaned against another upturned root. It was a massive thing, nearly reaching her shoulders.

"Silas, Esmer is probably starving. Did you think to bring her any food?"

"I'm not hungry," I protested, but then, as if on cue, my stomach let out an unnatural growl.

When had I last eaten? Yesterday morning?

Mila rummaged through a pack at her side, fishing out a canteen, some bread, and a roasted duck leg wrapped in cloth. She handed them to me, giving me a sad half smile. "For our unexpected hostage."

"Thank you," I managed, taking a small bite of the duck leg. Fortunately, the rope was just loose enough that I could eat. "Please make sure my brother has food, too."

Mila nodded solemnly. "Of course. Already done."

She returned with more food and drink after making a stop by Elliot's tent, her arms overwhelmed with a jug of steaming cider, two jars of smoked pine nuts, and bits of roasted poultry. All from Norhavellis, I learned. Small tokens for their Light Bringer. We ate hungrily, licking the salt from our fingers, and settled into a somewhat regular rhythm as Mila and Silas traded stories of their travels. I eased into the conversation, thoughts of Corruption, death, and despair ebbing from my mind the longer we spent together, and I even managed a smile at one point.

A smile.

Guilt and grief churned in my stomach. I wasn't sure if I deserved to smile.

As the fire burned low, the legionnaires began the whispers of a song, their voices growing louder and more haunting as it looped, repeating for a second time.

Suff'ring in the silver'd pool
Alongside his shadow'd ghosts
But darkness fell, devour'd them all
Beware, the Shadow Bringer comes
So burn the light brightly and
Sing the song boldly
For we fear not shadow nor the night
For beware, beware, beware, beware
Beware, the Shadow Bringer comes
The shadows, they drown him
The light doth surround him
Bound to his darkness evermore
So beware, beware, beware, beware
Beware, the Shadow Bringer comes
Beware, the Shadow Bringer comes

They moved into a few other songs, some spirited, some somber, but I kept thinking of the first. It made me feel uneasy, exposed. I didn't like it at all.

As the legionnaires sang, distracted, Mila slipped me a vial of elixir. "I gave one to Elliot, too."

"Thank you."

I politely declined to share Mila's tent with her and nestled back against my tree root. We weren't friends, I reminded myself. And it felt more comfortable, somehow, being in the open air. The legionnaires were unbothered by my choice; several of them always stood guard along the camp perimeter, watching me and the woods for signs of anything unusual.

I arranged my rope-bound arms over my knees as best I could, trying to appear nonchalant and insignificant. Between my connection to the

Shadow Bringer and his demented world, my involvement in an entire village's damnation, and my likelihood of rotting in an early grave, it was too much to handle, too much to comprehend.

And then there were my parents. My poor, poor parents. I buried my face into my cloak, sobbing quietly. Eventually I dozed off, lulled by wind threading through the branches above me.

When I opened my eyes, I expected to be greeted by swaying tree-tops and the smell of breakfast at our camp. Instead, I woke in a sprawling room layered with ancient tapestries, dusty bookshelves, and the barest hint of candlelight. It smelled of night, rain, and old things. Of dust and objects left in obscurity for far too long.

And that's when I saw him.

The Shadow Bringer was sleeping in a canopied bed, cloaked in shadow, obsidian armor, and his typical draconic mask with its caged jaw. Silvery fabric curtained the frame around him, floating loosely in the cold, dusty air. He appeared frozen in sleep, silver-white hair pooling on the pillows below him.

I was in his room.

I was in the Shadow Bringer's *room*.

Creeping backward, I felt for a weapon while keeping my gaze locked on him. I was unsettled by his silence and lack of movement. Was he dead? I considered testing this theory, perhaps feeling for a pulse or a sign of breath, but quickly decided against it. Something told me that he was very much alive—just depleted from using whatever power it was that stemmed from him.

I found a steel fire poker leaning next to a cold fireplace, weighty and sharp despite the dust it left behind, then carefully slid within arm's reach of the Shadow Bringer's massive, lavish bed. Strange, that such extravagance could be found consorting with an equal amount of rot. The mix of luxury and decay was uncomfortable. Intolerable, even.

I drew up the fire poker, holding it over the Bringer's exposed throat. *Demon. Monster. Killer.*

Hate surged through my veins, nearly choking me. This man, the horrid origin of Corruption, damned my sister, cursed my parents, ruined Elliot's future, and wrecked any chances I had at normalcy. If I killed the Shadow Bringer now, perhaps Corruption would end, the demons would be destroyed, and all captured souls would finally rise to meet the Maker's holy light.

The poker hovered over the smooth stretch of skin just below his jawline. One swift thrust, and it would all be over.

Grrrrssschk. Rrrsssschk. Rrrssschk.

I froze, listening intently. The wind, perhaps.

"Let us out," a demon suddenly howled, snarling and groaning from just beyond his bedchamber door. "Set us free."

Something heavy slammed against the door, causing me to flinch and lose my balance. The fire poker slipped from my hands, sliding off the bed and crashing to the floor.

The Shadow Bringer's eyes opened, depthless and aching.

"*You,*" he rasped, caged lips close to my ear. He put his gauntleted hands over mine, cold and sharp, and my traitorous heart stuttered. "You don't need to panic—I can manage them. I always have."

He rose to his elbows as I felt myself slipping back into consciousness.

His hands were iron.

Then clay.

Then dust.

The demons repeated their chant as they threw themselves against his door. The screams layered together, rising and echoing in a hellish chorus.

"Let us out."

"Set us free."

"Let us out, let us out, let us out!"

The last scream yanked me back into the dream.

I was in the Shadow Bringer's bed, straddling his legs. I must have grabbed for him while I was falling out of the dream; his hands were firmly clutching mine. He let out a slow breath, fixing me with cold silver eyes that began to change from aching and depthless to something sharper and more aware. My breath hitched, and a horrific blush crept up my neck as I felt his armored hips shift under my thighs. We looked down at the same time, realizing just how close our bodies were.

Too close.

We scrambled backward as shadows roiled around us, tangling in their eagerness to obey each of our panicked wills. This was a mistake— a shadow looped around the Bringer's wrist, and my will must have called it forward, for it curled around my wrist, too, and pulled itself taut.

He cursed.

I cursed.

And the demons roared louder, bending the door to his bedchamber.

"The demons aren't usually this persistent." The Bringer shoved himself off the bed, cursing again when the movement yanked me sideways into his shoulder.

"I thought the mighty Shadow Bringer would have more control over his monsters," I said angrily, putting a step between us. We were near the door now—too near for my liking—and the Shadow Bringer was assessing its current condition. It seemed sturdy enough, but the demons were relentless, slamming their bodies into the wood. Two horns suddenly broke through, piercing the door. When the demon tried to retreat, the horns stuck, rattling the frame. "Or do they hate you so much that you *can't* control them?"

He glanced back at me, mouth slanting into a scowl. "I've never been their master—merely their keeper. So yes, they hate me. Perhaps you're familiar with the feeling."

Inexplicably, his baiting words made me blush.

The fire poker was too far away, but maybe I could manipulate the shadows to my advantage. I concentrated, willing them to slip under the Shadow Bringer's armor and grasp his throat like a constricting snake, but they merely wavered in place, useless and without form. It was wishful thinking, then.

Of course the shadows won't harm him.

"Tell me: When you woke in his presence, did your Light Bringer accept you without hate or fear? Were Mithras and his followers not condemning you to a monster's fate?" At my silence, he turned his attention back to the door, running a hand over one of the smooth alabaster horns that pierced it. The demon flinched at the Bringer's touch, splintering more of the wood. He added quietly, "If you hadn't interfered when I tried to fight Mithras, you would have avoided all of this. I don't know why the shadows listen to you."

"Maybe your hold on them is weakening," I guessed, trying to sound confident. As I said this, the shadows that followed him moved to trail behind me, lapping at my ankles. I tried not to shiver in disgust; if I could use them to my advantage without the Light Bringer seeing, I would. Anything to keep me alive. But I'd need to rid myself of them—and the Shadow Bringer—soon. "Perhaps they'd rather align with me than with a hateful villain like yourself."

"Would they, now?" the Shadow Bringer mused. "Interesting. If only you could wield them with any consistent effect."

"Then you're forgetting what happened in the water chamber," I remarked, another flush making me scowl in irritation. Maybe it was just my imagination, but the shadow tether between us seemed tighter. He was too close, too tall, too *attentive.* No one had ever looked at me like this before, and I didn't know what to make of it. "Maybe I'll try that again on the demons outside your door."

"You will not try that again."

"Of course you don't want me to hurt your precious demons. You're their *keeper,* after all."

"You are vexing," the Bringer bit out, touching the top of his throat. I wondered if he was remembering the swell of shadowed blood that had pooled there, leaking from his mouth. "The demons in the hall are much older and far more powerful than the fledglings in the water. What you accomplished in the previous dream won't work on them."

The horned demon began to twist, throwing itself into the door with a renewed fervor.

"You really should try to wake up. This won't be pleasant."

"It can't be any less pleasant than what I'd wake up to. I'm being marched to my death."

His pale eyes narrowed. "What do you mean—"

I cut him off, willing the shadows at my feet to rise. I didn't know what I was doing, not really; I'd intended for them to form a wall, sealing us off from the demons, but they rushed forward and cracked the door wide open. The shadows disintegrated at the contact, sinking back to the floor.

Demons—dozens of hideous demons—stood in the hall, gaping at us.

"Like I said," the Shadow Bringer sighed, yanking on our shadow tether so that I stood behind him, "you are very, *very* vexing."

The shadows rose at a twitch of his fingers, churning in front of us like a condensed thundercloud. A blink later and the cloud surged forward, pouring over the demons like a midnight tempest. The creatures tensed as the shadows washed over their broken bodies. They weren't being attacked, exactly, but it seemed they were being purged of something terrible. Shadows crawled from their noses and eyes, joining the dark around them, and their mouths remained frozen in silent screams. When the cloud finally settled, the demons were sated. Their rage and panic had cooled; the fight had left their hollow eyes. Eventually they slunk back down the hall, seeking solace elsewhere.

The Bringer's shoulders sagged. His shadows were now mere wisps, settling under furniture and sliding beneath rugs. Even the tether that had bound us had disintegrated, retreating inside a nearby vase.

"Wretched creatures," the Bringer muttered, crossing the room in a few quick strides. He made it to his bed—as if forgetting I was there, too—and quickly turned around, instead choosing a book-covered desk to lean against.

His room was opulent but uncared for. A tomb left untouched for centuries. I examined a vase overflowing with dead flowers. "How can you live like this?" I found myself asking. "You're the lord of nothing but dust and demons."

"It wasn't always this way. But it's difficult to be lord of anything when you're cursed to rot in a castle that no longer feels like yours, unable to leave and unable to purge this place of its shadows. Many would say it is a fate most fitting, but I vehemently disagree."

A dark laugh rose in the back of my throat. A monster wishing to absolve his own monstrosities was absurd. "Then perhaps you shouldn't have forced Corruption upon Noctis. You cursed an entire kingdom to live in fear and die in ruin. Your fate *is* fitting for such a crime."

His hands squeezed the edge of the desk, cracking some of the wood into dusty splinters. "My *fate* was torn from me the moment I was banished here. Time was stolen from me, my life was stolen from me, and—" Shadows flashed in his eyes, but he did not move. "I did no harm to you or your kingdom. Believe what you wish, but that is the truth."

My hands trembled with anger. He lamented his past and present, but what about Noctis's future? What about *my* future? There was nothing left for me. I should have had my entire life to look forward to— decades filled with purpose and joy. Perhaps even love. A family of my own, a house of my own, a *life* of my own. The Shadow Bringer may have been rotting in his castle, but I was rotting, too. And I didn't have a choice. I was inches from the Shadow Bringer now, glaring up into half-dead eyes spinning with whorls of silver and night. I hated him. He was the enemy of Noctis, the harbinger of Corruption, my family's killer, and my future's cruel thief. The tales made him out to be wicked, soulless, and cruel.

So why did he look so achingly sad?

I wanted to shove him. Wanted to grab him by his stiff shoulders and scream with the same agony and intensity as his demons. Instead, I said fiercely, "You have a responsibility to make things right. If you're truly as miserable as you say, then change your fate. If you can manage that, then maybe you'll be able to change mine, too."

"Perhaps Noctis can be salvaged, but I don't know where to begin." He crossed his arms, mouth tightening. "My power once called to the dark, and dark things were drawn to it—drawn to *me*. I once thought I could contain all the demons here while I waited for an absolution that never came."

The Shadow Bringer harbored demons within the walls of his castle prison to *protect* humanity? The tales never suggested as much. Still, the barest hints of truth were there, waiting for me to take notice.

"But you didn't fully contain all the demons."

"No," he agreed. "And perhaps they never were fully contained, if what you're telling me is the truth. The demons in my domain aren't Corrupting anyone; they're as trapped as I am."

"Which leaves those roaming the Dream Realm to their own devices."

Grrrrssschk. Rrrssschk. Rrrssschk.

We turned at the same time. A demon leered at us through the broken doorway, its shoulders so wide that it had to adjust itself to fit. It lunged for me, moving quicker than what should have been possible, its grin wide and hair-covered arms outstretched. Surprisingly, the Shadow Bringer threw himself in front of me, shadows up in defense, but he was either too distracted or too slow.

The force behind the blow was staggering, slamming the Shadow Bringer into the fireplace with a sickening crunch. He snapped to his feet, but the demon was faster. It grabbed the discarded fire poker, raising it to his exposed throat.

"Set...me...free," the demon rasped. "Five hundred...years."

For a moment, the Shadow Bringer's eyes widened, but he quickly shook his head, clearing whatever thought had just passed. He brought his hands to his throat, shielding it from the spike. "The curse has no end, demon. Put the spike down before I impale you with it."

"Five hundred...years," it repeated. "He...is...coming."

"You're delusional and broken, just like the others," the Shadow Bringer said sadly. "Pitiful."

And then he grabbed the fire poker, spun it around, and shoved it between the demon's eyes. It lurched back, poker protruding from its forehead, and lunged for me again. I spun to avoid it, diving for a half-open curtain at the far end of the Bringer's room.

A balcony.

Curse it all.

Lit by a dusting of stars, the balcony looked straight out of the pages of a storybook—perfect for romance or reminiscing, but not for outrunning demons. The ledge was too far away from the forest that sprawled beneath it.

"Let me *out*," the demon snarled. It tried to pull the fire poker from its skull, but it only managed to snap it. It wielded the broken piece like a dagger, poised and ready to strike me down. "You can free me."

My back slammed into the balustrade. The creature had cornered me into a place it knew I couldn't escape from. I willed the Shadow Bringer's shadows to race down my arms, covering them in thick, writhing darkness.

When the demon took its next step, poker raised to strike, I sent the shadows flying. They became swords, lances, pitchforks—and assailed the demon, sending it reeling into the Shadow Bringer, who had followed us to the balcony. They crashed into the other side of the railing, assaulted by shadows both knife sharp and corporeal. The demon took the worst of it, moaning from its injuries, but the Bringer was halfway off the ledge, cape pinned by spikes and blades. The part of his body off the ledge—his right arm, shoulder, and head—began to smoke, burned by an invisible force.

I had never heard the Shadow Bringer scream, but he did now, writing in torment. His gauntlet sunk into his right arm, melding with the skin underneath, and his moon-white hair began to smolder under his helm, just as his skin blistered and peeled. He tried to push the shadows away, but they wouldn't listen, wouldn't bend to his will. Whatever force was burning him was also keeping him from using his abilities.

And he was dying.

I didn't know what death meant in the Realm, but something told me the Shadow Bringer might not wake from this. And if he died—and the demons *didn't* die—what then? I'd have to face the demons alone. Perhaps they'd riot, overwhelm me, and escape, plaguing Noctis with a rush of Corruption.

He broke free from the shadows at the last moment; the force of it sent the demon plummeting off the ledge.

The Shadow Bringer crumpled. He sat perfectly still, eyes closed, leaning his half-melted body against the balustrade. His skin had already begun to heal, resetting back to its original state, but it wasn't quite restored.

"I'm tired, Esmer. I'm tired of living like this."

I froze where I stood. "I—"

"Do you see now? They accuse me of Corruption, but there are no captured souls here beyond my own. There are only demons, pulled here by my wretched power, and darkness. Nothing but rot and my ruined soul on display." His eyes fluttered open briefly before closing again.

"How can you expect me to believe you?" I asked in shock, tears springing to my eyes. He looked absolutely *wretched*. I'd never seen a person in such a state of decay. "What you're saying goes against everything I've been taught. It's a path I've walked my entire life."

"Then let me convince you otherwise," he rasped. "Help me find my freedom and purpose, and I will return the favor a hundredfold."

I raised my face to feel the wind. It swirled around us, fragrant with the scent of the sprawling wilderness below, and threaded through our hair, caressing it with smooth fingers. "The tales say nothing about how to free you. They scarcely mention your fate at all."

The Bringer let out a heavy sigh and opened his eyes. The shadows were back under his spell, but they felt empty and dull compared with how they'd been rioting earlier. "You said Mithras was marching you to your death. If he succeeds, you'll never leave. You'll share my fate, bound to this castle and unable to watch your loved ones grow older. You'll live here as Noctis sinks further into ruin, oblivious to the waking world and numb to the passage of time. Don't let them take you."

"It's already too late," I whispered shakily, heart sinking. "They're transporting me to Istralla for my sentencing."

"Then find my tomb," he said with sudden intensity.

"Your tomb?" I repeated, confused. "I'm not sure how your bones will help my situation."

"Not my bones," he growled. "If I still exist here in the Dream Realm, then my mortal body must live on in a fixed slumber. If you can wake me there, I can help you."

This was new, too. The Shadow Bringer was supposed to be a monstrous beast with fangs and claws, not a man with a living, breathing body somewhere in Noctis. My thoughts drifted, and I wondered what he looked like in his mortal flesh, if his sleeping body wore armor and a helm, too. Perhaps he'd have scales underneath all his layers of metal. Or, more likely, skin. Pale and flawless skin, like the stretch that could be seen around his lips and jaw—not the burning mess that was still trying to heal itself.

Stop thinking about his skin. Stop thinking about him at all.

I gritted my teeth, banishing the image from my mind. I didn't care what he looked like as a mortal. If his tomb could be found, and he was, in fact, asleep inside, I could convince the Light Bringer of my loyalty. I could help the Light Legion kill him, once and for all time. Still, I felt torn. Playing into his hand was a risk, and the Light Bringer might not even believe me.

"I can never accept your help. You're the keeper of demons, and—"

"Yes, just a monster ruling the Dream Realm from his cage like some twisted god," he snapped, voice dripping with sarcasm. "Walking into your dream was the first time I've left these walls in centuries. Unfortunately, as soon as you woke up, I was snapped back. I want out of this castle, Esmer. I *need* out." He stood, gripping the balustrade for support. One of his helm's horns, which had partially broken apart in his hair, dropped to his feet, rattling against the stone.

He gestured to a crescent-shaped glade in the distance; it was identical to the one the Light Legion was currently camped in. "There. In Noctis, my tomb is just beyond that glade. You're asleep there right now with the Light Legion, aren't you? Mithras has a sense of where I am, but he can't find me. Not the way you do."

"I really can't escape," I whispered, close to breaking. I had tried to shove away my feelings of grief, but they were now squeezing my chest in an iron vice. "You haunt me and won't let go."

"I know you want to kill me," he noted, bringing a clawed hand to my neck and dragging his thumb under my lip. He pressed softly, coaxing a shiver of shadow to rise between us. "Even though we share a similar madness, you'd rather die than accept my help. You'd let Mithras drag you to Istralla like a dog, even if that meant being slain by his blade. Even if you knew it wasn't true justice, you'd offer your neck to him."

Shadows began a slow twirl around us, lapping at our arms.

"I'll find your tomb, Shadow Bringer."

And after we kill you, the Light Bringer will surely trust me enough to set me free.

A slow, triumphant smile ghosted his lips. "If you can find my tomb and wake me, I will ensure that you're never scared or lost ever again. I will make them pay."

Strangely, I believed him. But I could never follow him.

He reached for me, and I found myself reaching back. But just as my fingertips met his, I was ripped away, his hands and castle spiraling into nothingness.

I stared past my steaming bowl of porridge, scarcely able to believe what I was seeing.

The legionnaires were awake. And *cheery*.

They moved about the camp in an efficient morning rhythm, none the wiser to what had happened in my dream. The demonic chorus, the wail of demented release—it took most of breakfast before my stomach stopped churning. Still, the dream lingered, even with Elliot sitting next to me.

Let us out.

Let us out.

Let us out.

The Shadow Bringer's breath against my ear, his eyes as they lit up, searching me.

Does he face those demons every night?

I took another mouthful of oats, awkwardly maneuvering the bowl in my bound hands.

Is he facing them now, alone?

All of what I knew about the Dream Realm stemmed from Weaver tales and Norhavellis's limited collective knowledge of both demons and Corruption. I had never been taught that the Shadow Bringer was trapped in his castle, unable to control the demons that stalked it. Or that his body slumbered somewhere in Noctis.

I shook my head, remembering when he had called my world *little*.

I had assumed he mistook my small world for a ruse. That in crafting a dream of my own, complete with my home, Norhavellis, and part of the Visstill Forest, I had been hiding some covert affiliation with whatever enemies he claimed I aligned with.

But my world really *was* little.

And when he called it little, he had sounded haunted by a yearning I didn't understand. There was distrust, sure, but there was something else, too. Something that betrayed the fact that he hadn't been apart from his shadows in many, many years. I nearly felt compassion.

But he needed to die. If I was to live, he *had* to die.

As soon as I was guided back into the Light Bringer's carriage, I told him everything I knew, spilling the Shadow Bringer's secrets like a spew of sour milk. At first, he seemed amicable. Earnest, even. But when I reached the part about the tomb, his expression turned violent.

My stomach twisted. This information was all I had left to trade, and if he didn't believe me—or worse, if he thought I was trying to manipulate him—he could see to it that I never made it to Istralla at all. Perhaps he'd proclaim me an active threat and behead me in this carriage, my blood staining the elegant fabric crimson.

"The Tomb of the Devourer," he murmured dreamily, surprising me. Then his eyes gleamed as a starving predator's would. "Where the Shadow Bringer's mortal body lies. And he told you this directly?"

I nodded, shoving aside my racing heart. "Yes. He showed me its location in a dream."

The Light Bringer leaned forward, knocking his knees against mine. Then he quickly wrapped me in an embrace, folding his gilded arms around my back. The gesture was so unexpected that I stiffened, unsure of proper protocol and overwhelmed at his sudden warmth. He smelled like honeyed wine and expensive cologne—a perfect, royal bouquet that I didn't want to sully or offend.

"How utterly *wonderful*, Esmer," he said into my hair, shuddering as he held me tighter. I couldn't move my arms; they were pinned to my sides. "You have done such a good deed in telling me this. My blade will sing when it pierces that monster's blackened heart."

I shoved aside the brutal mental image of a supine Shadow Bringer getting his chest cavity ripped apart by the Light Bringer's blade.

If I am to live, he has to die.

"That will be a good day, indeed, my lord. He is a plague upon our kingdom."

He dropped the embrace, regarding me seriously. "If you bring me to his body, your crimes will be absolved, and Elliot will be welcomed to Istralla under my direct protection. He will be given a limitless supply of elixir and will never know pain or fear again."

"My crimes will truly be forgiven then, my lord?"

"Yes. It is very noble to turn your affinity with the dark into something so worthy as this. It means you are still good, Esmer. Redeemable, even." He smiled at me broadly, teeth perfect and white. "I will make good use of you."

"I will serve however I can, my lord." My head spun, buzzing with this new possibility for my future. If I wanted it, I could have it. It was *so close*. With the Shadow Bringer dead, I could finally live in peace with Elliot. We could forge a new life and heal from our hurt together. We could forget that any of this had happened at all. "Thank you, my lord."

"Bring us to him. Bring us to the Shadow Bringer."

We rode into the late afternoon, wandering through the Visstill in what probably seemed like aimless, looping circles. As the sun arced above the treetops, shadows lengthened, blanketing the root-spattered ground in patches of thick darkness. Mithras stopped the carriage on occasion, conferring with me as he would a compass. The farther we traveled, the deeper the Shadow Bringer's pull.

I could *feel* him.

Eventually, we abandoned the carriage and horses altogether, continuing instead on foot while a small group of the legionnaires remained behind. It was now our third day of traveling in search of the tomb, of haunting fireside songs about Corruption and the Shadow Bringer, and of me strangely desperate to see him again. I hadn't dreamed of the Bringer since the night in his bedchamber, and it bothered me.

I chewed on the inside of my cheek, running through a mental inventory of everything I knew about him. Even with his half lies and vague insults, it was becoming more and more difficult for me to perceive him as wholly evil. I found myself wondering what his true name was. Or if he even had one.

He has to die, Esmer. His name is meaningless to you.

Mila sighed, earning a few semiannoyed glances from the legionnaires. "Where is this dreadful tomb?"

"Enough with the dramatics," Silas murmured.

"We've been traveling in circles for days, Silas. This tomb is a pest. Perhaps it doesn't even exist."

Silas looked uncomfortable. "Esmer wouldn't knowingly misguide us."

"There you have it," Mila said, shaking her head. She wore an array of small golden earrings, but they were barely noticeable in her hair. *"Knowingly."* She turned to me with a tentative smile, but doubt was clearly in her eyes. Over the past few days, she had become more and more suspicious of me. Why did I ever think we might be friends? "Are you purposefully misleading us? Or did you simply forget where we are supposed to be going?"

"I've never ventured out this far," I answered, bristling. "It does feel like we're circling something, though. I think we're close."

"I knew it," Mila said with a groan. Then she whispered to Silas, her voice conspiratorial, "The cross, the chip in the corner—it's the same rock we saw yesterday. What do you suppose she's getting at?"

"Save for finding the tomb, she's not getting at anything," Silas snapped, his mouth tight with exasperation. "And what makes you think *you* can spot the difference between one chipped stone and another, especially from a distance? They're rocks, Mila."

"Because I'm not spotting differences. It's where they're similar that matters," she retorted. They turned to each other, continuing to bicker.

Elliot tapped my elbow. It was hard to believe he was only ten; the past few days had simultaneously aged and depleted him. Though he was in clean clothes—the Light Legion had been considerate enough to pack a small trunk of belongings for the both of us—his brown eyes were dull and his mouth, usually quirked up in a grin, was in an emotionless line.

"I believe you, Esmer," he whispered. "I know you can do it."

Don't cry.

"Thanks, Elliot," I said, giving his hair a gentle tousle. Fortunately, the Light Bringer had decided to do away with my bindings shortly after I'd launched our hunt for the Shadow Bringer's tomb. "How are you feeling?"

"I miss Mother and Father."

I bit the inside of my cheek. *Don't cry.* "I miss them, too."

"I miss home. How it used to be. I thought I'd be happy to leave, but I'm not happy at all. And you know what?"

"What?"

"I wish we'd said goodbye. I wish we hadn't turned our backs on them and walked away."

A strangled, devastated sound tumbled out of me. I quickly clamped a hand over my mouth, hoping the legionnaires hadn't heard. "I know," I whispered, on the verge of tears. "But we can't change the past. Mother and Father are at peace with the Maker. We need to look ahead to the future."

He nodded, chin quivering. "It's hard."

"I know it is. But soon the Shadow Bringer won't be able to hurt us anymore. The Light Bringer is going to destroy him once and for all."

As if the Shadow Bringer heard me speak his name, I felt a long, insistent pull in the back of my mind. Suddenly, I could feel him every-where: sliding over the ground, whispering through the trees, rushing through our hair, and tangling in our clothes. His shadows—or were they *our* shadows now?—sat layered on top of nature's shadows, but they slowly crept out from their hiding spots, clearly beckoning me toward a deeper part of the Visstill.

Mithras caught my eye and raised his fist in a victorious gesture; he *knew*.

"Light Legion," Mithras began, projecting his voice over the travel-ing party as he drew me to his side. "We are nearly there. This tomb may contain the Shadow Bringer's monstrous body, but soon it will merely be a husk. We will slay the enemy. We will rise victorious and destroy Cor-ruption once and for all."

The shadows beckoned me toward a nearby hill, so we walked single file down it. My boots stuck into the hillside as we descended, squishing and pulling against mud from a recent rainstorm. Leaves were strewn everywhere, and the early-evening air began to chill, forcing the hair on my neck and arms to rise.

He's close.

As if on cue, a dark, towering structure emerged before us, shrouded by a copse of ancient, clawing trees. It was difficult to tell how large the Tomb of the Devourer was; its body, which sat behind an entrance so dark it seemed partially open, was dug into the innards of a hill, obscur-ing its size. And the light seemed dimmer here—the air heavier, colder. A slow-moving mist clung to the damp earth, threading out from the shadows and clinging to the tomb's vine-covered walls.

I fell into silence along with the legionnaires, squeezing Elliot's hand.

The Light Bringer, mask affixed and sword drawn, approached the entrance. At first, he said nothing. Then he murmured, so softly that it sounded like a shift in the wind, a crunch of someone's boot against the leaves, "May he rot."

"My lord? The tomb—" Silas began.

"May he *rot*," Mithras repeated, louder, stronger.

Rage and hunger burned in the Light Bringer's golden eyes, spilling over his taut, too-stiff body and trembling in his clenched fists. It trickled from the dust still floating from his hands. Without warning, he tore his mask from his face and hurled it into a nearby tree. It sank sharply into the bark, narrowly missing one of his legionnaires. The legionnaires flinched, some taking a step or two back into the forest.

"What do you use your eyes for?" Mithras asked this question to the nearest legionnaire, but it was clearly directed at all of them. "For what do we use our senses? Our senses of taste, touch? Of scent and sound?"

"I use m-my eyes to see, m-my lord," the man stuttered. His skin shone with sweat. "I use all m-my senses to serve the Light Legion. I use them for you, my lord."

"And what of the rest of you? Can you sense the darkness?"

The legionnaires nodded, expressions warring between duty and discomfort.

"Can you all sense it?" Mithras implored again, louder, more insistent.

"Yes, my lord!" the legion echoed.

"And can you spot it, even if it walks among you?" He arched his hands through the air, motioning at the depths of the forest. The shadows had lengthened, drawing attention to the encroaching darkness.

"Yes, my lord!" the Light Legion repeated, their voices rising as one.

"And would you drag it out of the shadows and bring it to the light? Bring it to me?"

They nodded grimly and bowed. "Yes, my lord."

"We must walk in the shadows," Mithras intoned.

"To walk in the light," they answered.

"Good. Set up camp," Mithras ordered. "We will soon reunite the Shadow Bringer with an eternity of damnation. He has no escape."

The legionnaires exchanged glances, clearly uneasy. Mithras's attention, meanwhile, lingered on me. And as the legionnaires scurried away to their various duties, fading into the night, I noticed that he was the only one without terror in his eyes.

14

My dreams were playing tricks on me.

The moon had shifted, revealing a hauntingly beautiful man with moon-white hair, bloodless skin, and eyes made alive by churning shadows. I couldn't move, couldn't so much as turn my head, but I could see him as clearly as I could see the embers of the legion's dying fire.

The Shadow Bringer.

His movements were stiff and strange, as though he was uncomfortable in his own skin. And maybe he was. Where his skin was porcelain smooth in the Realm, it was now marred by bruises and hollowing dips under his eyes. He looked awful—and more human than ever. I tried to see his facial features more clearly, but it was painstakingly difficult to focus. He wore a helm, much like the one he wore in the Dream Realm, but it was in terrible condition. He flexed his pale fingers. Dried red blood still clung to his skin, and his ripped clothing was markedly darker in several places, smeared with dirt, dust, and even more blood.

His? Someone else's?

My eyes drifted shut. I was imagining him. He was not real.

He isn't real.

Slowly, I began to feel the ground beneath my back, the wind pressing against my face, and the grip of my hands clutched over my dress. I took a furtive glance around the camp, expecting the legionnaires to be awake and aware, but they remained silent and still, sprawled out atop their various bedrolls. Ashes floated in the wind, leftover from both our hurried evening meal and charred torches half-burning on the ground.

Too still.

Silas reclined near the half-dead campfire. His eyes were closed, face unlined and unconcerned. I touched his neck, feeling for a pulse, and nearly buckled with relief when I felt the weak *thump* of his heartbeat. Not dead, but nearly. And where was Elliot? Frantically I scanned the clearing, unable to find him. But then I saw the Shadow Bringer's tomb and I *knew*.

My blood chilled.

The Tomb of the Devourer, watching over the sleeping camp like a yawning beast, stood open, a wound of black marking its entrance. Someone had moved the stone slab, leaving the entrance unguarded and bare.

Elliot. If he hurt Elliot...

Consumed with fear and rage, I sprinted into the tomb. A weight washed over me as I entered, a silent scream begging me to leave. It was dark, damp, and emanating with despair. But I couldn't leave—not until Elliot was safe and the Shadow Bringer was dead.

The prince of darkness was easy to find. He knelt at the bottom of a staircase by two skeletons, tears gleaming silver in the half-light of the tomb.

Grief was familiar to me. It lived in the heart of Norhavellis. It had lived in my mother and father after Eden's death. It lived in Elliot, who had watched as his goat, a soft, gentle creature that he'd bottle-fed from birth, was dragged into the Visstill by creatures with white fangs and hateful eyes. It lived in me. *Suffocated* me.

Apparently it lived in the Shadow Bringer, too.

I hesitated at the top of the staircase. He had put the Light Legion to sleep—had put them to sleep and climbed back into the Tomb of the Devourer as if he wanted me to find him.

Who *was* the Shadow Bringer, really?

A commander of demons? An immortal devourer of dreams?

The murderer of Eden, Mother, and Father?

In his current state, he looked no different than a weak, half-dead man who'd recently bathed in blood, sweat, and dirt. A man engulfed in sorrow and delusion. Moonlight filtered in from outside, casting the blackened walls in a strange, undulating light. It felt as though I was walking in a dream—not stepping into a grave in the middle of the Visstill—and I moved forward carefully, slowly descending each step as the Shadow Bringer knelt over the bones at his feet. I was halfway down the stairs when footsteps sounded from behind me. They were meandering and slow. Heavy in weight, as if their owner wanted to be heard. Hope leapt in my chest. *The Light Bringer.*

He strolled into the tomb, unmasked and partially armored, his golden hair made dull and dark by all the shadows. Still, his eyes glowed as if lit by some internal flame. The Shadow Bringer stood slowly and laid a hand on the tomb's lower door. He took a deep breath, as if to prepare himself for something—as if to speak first. But his lips did not move.

"Esmer," the Light Bringer announced in greeting, his low voice sinister. It sent shivers down my back. "Taking an evening stroll?"

I shifted uneasily. What *was* I doing here? Everyone else had been put to sleep by the Bringer, and yet I had followed him into his tomb. Mithras may have had doubts about my allegiances before, but he'd entertain no excuses now.

"I thought I saw the Shadow Bringer take Elliot, my lord. I came here to rescue my brother."

"Such bravery," the Light Bringer said approvingly. "And would you be capable of saving your brother? Would you destroy the wicked Shadow Bringer with your bare hands?" He gestured toward my hands, which clearly held no weapons. "Quite impressive for a mere village girl. Your mother and father must have taught you well."

Father had trained me in some things: tending animals, fixing fences. Basic archery and swordplay. Mother had, too. The proper way to heal cuts and bruises. How to read and start a fire. What oils to use in the finest—or most putrid, depending on what was available— perfumes. Which plants to use to season the barest of dishes. How to care for others. How to find the good in people, even when there appeared to be none.

How to hope for a better future despite the darkness surrounding us. But neither my father nor mother had taught me how to deal with a situation like this.

"Oh, and the Shadow Bringer. A pleasure to see you in the flesh after so long." Mithras directed his attention away from me, crossing his arms and widening his stance. "Did your guilt wake you from your sleep? Or was it the screams of every poor soul you've ever killed?"

The Shadow Bringer faced Mithras head-on, rage and exhaustion shadowing his eyes in equal measure.

"Perhaps it was my will to finally be free," he answered at last, his tone matching Mithras's.

"Then you are delusional. Do your delusions speak to you? Do they appear to you as ghosts? Perhaps they take the form of those two skeletons at your feet." The Light Bringer descended the stairs quickly despite the dark. I backpedaled, twisting to avoid him so he could reach the Shadow Bringer more easily.

But instead of heading past me, Mithras went straight for *me*, grabbing me by my wrists and slamming me against the stairwell. "Eager to meet your fate, are you?" he snarled. "Then *embrace* it."

I thrashed against him. Wherever his hands touched, it *burned*. His skin was fire made physical, a flame with a body and a voice. My bones were melting, heating to a warm, pulpy liquid under his touch.

"You will regret hurting her," the Shadow Bringer warned, tone like ice.

"I am a reasonable man," Mithras said to me, ignoring the Shadow Bringer and clenching my wrists tighter. Heat was spreading, spiraling into my forearms. For a moment, his eyes flashed a rich, bloody red. "I considered giving you mercy—a chance to redeem yourself after the wicked display from your mother and father. But I have again found you consorting with the devil himself. A devil who calls ghouls his friends." He let go of me then, causing me to tumble the rest of the way down.

The Shadow Bringer rushed to meet me, ready to tend to my wrists, but the fire had no lasting effects; my bones were pain free and whole.

"And to think you were so eager for me to kill him." Mithras made a sound of utter disdain. "How disappointing."

"I *do* want him killed," I insisted, eliciting a look of cold rage from the Shadow Bringer.

"No, you don't," the Shadow Bringer urged. "Remember what you've seen. Who you *are*. Your presence alone urged me to wake up. I could feel your call. You're like me—"

"I am nothing like you," I snapped, taking a pointed step away from him and toward the Light Bringer. "My lord, I—"

"*He is no lord.* I would tear that word from your lips if I could," said the Shadow Bringer.

Mithras laughed. "You are a wretched stain on this earth, Shadow Bringer. The world will be better off without you in it." He drew a golden sword from his side, its blade long and cruel. "Truly, some would say it's miraculous that our paths crossed. You came close to freedom, Shadow Bringer. But our light will always damn you back to the hell you crawled from."

Darkness crackled at the edge of my peripheral vision.

"I welcome you to try," the Shadow Bringer answered. His voice was frighteningly calm as he pulled me, despite my protests, behind him.

Then the Shadow Bringer moved, springing on Mithras in a blur of metal and swirling shadow. His own blade of obsidian—drawn from his palm as it had been in the Realm—behaved strangely, interacting with the shadows as it cut through the ancient, stone-damp air. The darkness was drawn to it, sparking across its surface in wild, random arcs. Mithras did not flinch. Instead, he leaned forward into the Shadow Bringer as he charged.

Their blades met in a hard, violent *clang* as gold hit obsidian.

"You're weak," Mithras spat, shoving the Shadow Bringer sideways with a forceful thrust of his blade. "Your shadows are empty. *You* are nothing."

"And you are no lord," the Shadow Bringer growled. He parried, sending Mithras reeling toward the staircase.

"Let me remind you." Mithras drew his sword upward. Bright, raging light spiraled down into the tomb, curling against its dark recesses and resting upon the skeletons, bathing their bones in a blinding haze. "I am the Light Bringer. The chosen," he continued. Light settled brightly against Mithras's blade, igniting it in a white glow. "As I will live in glory, you will rot in the shadows."

One side step, a duck, a counter. A sweeping, violent sideswipe. A lightning-fast parry.

Mithras and the Shadow Bringer fought with maneuvers so automatic and instinctive that each movement seemed part of a larger dance. And despite the strangeness, the impossibility of it all, Mithras didn't cower from the Shadow Bringer's shadows, even as they shifted to seal their commander in a second skin. Their duel felt like a familiar fight— one waged before, somehow. It was mesmerizing.

A battle between warriors of power and practice.

There was the Shadow Bringer, with his tattered black armor, silver-gray eyes the shade of a churning sea, and face hidden by his draconic helm. White hair tumbled down his pale neck, resting in loose, mangled curls.

Then there was the Light Bringer with his immaculate armor, strong features, and golden eyes that could condemn with a violent fire.

Just as it seemed Mithras and the Shadow Bringer would fight for hours, too evenly matched for a clear victor to emerge, the Shadow Bringer's darkness began to falter. He glanced at me as his shadows began to fade, an eerie expression on his face. He looked as though he were already dead. Hollow, gaping eyes. Ghostly skin marked with welts and gashes from the Light Bringer's blade. Cold, pale lips glossed with blood leaking from his cheek. A walking corpse, a man half-alive.

I'm not sure how I knew, but I *knew*. He needed me.

He wants me to call on his power—like I did in the Dream Realm.

Though we weren't dreaming, being inside the Tomb of the Devourer bent the laws of reality itself. Here, shadow and light danced together, alive and singing. I could feel the shadows. They gathered around me, twining in a heavy cloak across my shoulders. They were there, roiling, powerful, and ready for my command. I needed to reject them unequivocally.

But I also needed a weapon.

Something to fend off the Shadow Bringer. Something that would allow Mithras to triumph once and for all.

Mithras. If I chose the Light Bringer, there would be no going back. The Shadow Bringer would die. I squeezed my eyes shut. Why did my stomach hurt? Why did I feel *guilty*? Maybe it was the image of the Shadow Bringer wretched and shaken as he'd knelt by the entombed skeletons at his feet. Or the Shadow Bringer with his protective shield of shadow when fire had rained upon us. Or maybe it was that look he had given me just now. A simple, veiled plea for help.

The Light Bringer deflected another of the Shadow Bringer's sweeping blows, ducking as he countered, and moved clockwise, forcing the Shadow Bringer to stand with his back exposed to me.

I had to make a choice. *Now.*

Delving into the power at my shoulders, I stepped back, balancing its weight as it grew in size. My channeled shadows flickered in and out of more physical forms, shifting from a thousand daggers to a kaleidoscope of broken glass to a billowing fog. I gritted my teeth against the pain. It was all so heavy.

A sword. Morph into a sword, a scythe.

The shadows twitched, twisting into a vague, sharp shape before fading back into mist. I groaned, shaking from the effort. The shadows weren't listening. Why weren't they listening?

Bind the Shadow Bringer—lift and pin him against the wall.

Again the shadows twitched, gathering together as Mithras and the Shadow Bringer continued their battle. They pooled toward the floor, crept out toward the ceiling, but they disintegrated before reaching their human target. I cursed quietly under my breath, attempting to weaponize them once more. The Shadow Bringer looked at me again. Only this time, his eyes were not dead. They were not hollow or weak.

They rioted in the colors of a raging storm.

The Shadow Bringer sprinted my way, ducking as the Light Bringer misjudged the weight and timing of his swing. I froze, thinking he was about to attack me, but he merely grabbed my hand. His skin, typically covered in the Dream Realm, felt cold and stiff, like it hadn't experienced human touch in many, many years.

"What are you—" I cried out.

He drew my hand to his chest, resting it against the shredded cloth of his armored tunic. I felt it then, what he was doing; my shadows teetered over my shoulders, rising to merge with his own. Night, shadow, darkness—they became one above us, tousling our hair and clothing in their swirling, churning wind. The merging force lifted the curls from my neck, grazing skin that was damp with sweat. It mingled my sleeve with the ragged edge of the Shadow Bringer's.

I nearly sobbed at the sensation; it felt glorious.

Mithras's eyes widened at the sight of us. He remained near the staircase, firm in his stance, but he did not approach us. "Look at you!" he began, shouting over the storm above. "A perfect, poisonous match." He let loose a short, barking laugh. "And like the shadows you are, the *nothing* you are, you will both be burned down by the light." Mithras beckoned around him. His blade glowed in the same ethereal light that shone from his eyes. "I'll never let you free. This place of rot and ruin was made for you!"

Giving a snarl of frustration, the Shadow Bringer squeezed my hand tighter, drawing more shadows into the air. They loomed over us, beautiful and terrifying. He roared, charging the mass of dark magic into Mithras—

Just as I commanded it back.

The shadows heaved against the Shadow Bringer's limbs, flinging him to the ground with a sickening *crunch* as his helm slammed into stone. The Shadow Bringer struggled to stand—he struggled desperately, fighting against a sea of darkness that sought to consume him whole.

Blood pounded in my ears. *What have I done?*

I looked up at the Light Bringer, expecting him to be smiling as he witnessed my allegiance.

Instead, he looked utterly horrified.

15

Mithras blinked, as if waking from a dream. "No," he said, distantly, wretchedly.

The legionnaires, awake at last, entered the tomb, rushing to their lord's side.

It was all too much—suddenly, agonizingly, it was all too much.

Something hit my back, heavy and hard, sending me sprawling into the dirt. A legionnaire was on top of me, blade poised over my throat. Several more were over the Shadow Bringer, ready to slice his head clean off. Stories whirled through my head, one after the other. Stories that would explain my innocence, that would prove the Shadow Bringer deceived me, used me. But as these stories eddied in my mind like the shadows pulling at my clothes, I couldn't shake the feeling that I was lying to myself. The Shadow Bringer's hollowed, marred face sprang into my heart, unbidden and unwelcome, reminding me of the connection we had and the brief feeling of rightness that had come over me when I'd had possession of his power. Of *our* power.

The shadows made me feel as though I had, despite everything, a purpose.

From above the stairs of the tomb came a wild, unhinged laugh, snapping through the haze.

Mithras.

The Light Bringer dragged a hand across his swollen mouth, smearing the blood that occasionally pooled from it. A few strands of hair, wet with blood and dirt, stuck to his jaw. His eyes were cold despite their golden color, daggerlike and violent, and the flesh of his face had sunken, much like the Shadow Bringer's had. It accentuated the scar that split his brow. A legionnaire offered him a bit of cloth, but he pushed it away.

"Like calls to like," he murmured.

Like calls to like.

A lord of demons, connected to *me.*

"Our Maker is with us, even in the dark," Mithras intoned. "We must walk in the shadows."

"To walk in the light," the Light Legion answered, voices wavering.

When Mithras spoke again, it was to the Light Legion.

"You have done well, faithful legionnaires," he said sadly, blood trickling from his lips. He wiped at it, dragging it back into his mouth. Several legionnaires looked down, away—averting their eyes from their lord's sunken skin, bruised body, and bloodied teeth. "Forgive me."

And then he exploded.

Light shot from his body as a cloud of daggers, slicing into his legionnaires. They screamed in shock, leaping off the Shadow Bringer and me as they tried to defend themselves. Those who ran met Mithras's blade on the stairs; those who didn't run died as his volcanic light poured into their mouths and out of their eyes. It left them in strange skeletal husks inside their armor, as though their very essence had been dragged out from under their skin. In the chaos, what remained of the Shadow Bringer's shadows carried him deeper into the tomb.

When the dust settled, all the legionnaires were dead.

All of them save Silas, who was at the tomb's entryway with Elliot unconscious in his arms.

"Elliot!" I screamed. But he did not stir. *"Elliot!"*

"Listen quickly and carefully," Mithras ordered, eyes wild as he grabbed me by the hand and yanked me up. I screamed, thrashing as hard as I could, but he was much stronger. "I will protect your brother and give him a privileged life in Istralla. In return, you will guard Noctis from the monsters the Shadow Bringer harbors. With him you will shield our world from the darkest shadows of the Realm."

Bile rose sick and violent in the back of my throat.

"No," I choked in fear, skin clammy and cold. Fear of the tomb—fear of the *Light Bringer*. The tomb would kill me. There existed no food, water, or light. There existed no way out, save for the colossal door of iron and stone at its front. I struggled against Mithras, trying to run for the stairs. "Let me go! I can't believe you *killed* them!" I screamed. "Silas—help me!"

But Silas didn't move. He didn't even *acknowledge* me.

"This tomb is a font of darkness," Mithras explained, forcing my attention back to him. "You will inhabit it physically and tether yourself spiritually. Asleep, you will draw the Dream Realm's demons to you, binding them to the Shadow Bringer's domain. In theory, your combined power should bind more demons, saving more human lives."

A few threads of shadow rose in response to my terror, but I couldn't focus—couldn't control them. With a quick wave of his hand, Mithras extinguished them.

"I sensed it when I first met you," Mithras insisted, turning to face me. "Power in the Realm is distributed to dreamers of similar capabilities. You are every bit as capable as he is—you just need time to practice, is all." He added, voice lowering, "And besides, even if you *didn't* have power of your own, you're still able to bolster his. You give him a strength I hadn't imagined possible."

The Shadow Bringer's voice came to mind. He had already warned me of this.

If he succeeds, you'll never leave. You'll share my fate, bound to this castle and unable to watch your loved ones grow older. You'll live here as Noctis sinks further into ruin, oblivious to the waking world and numb to the passage of time. Don't let them take you.

"You're sentencing me to die in this tomb," I sobbed. "I just want to be with Elliot. Let us go. *Please.*"

"What other fate would you prefer?" Mithras drew close, eyes wide and desperate. I took an uneasy step back, heart thundering. "To simply rot into the earth, leaving behind no legacy, no meaning, no purpose? The tomb will be the safest place for you; Istralla will be the safest for Elliot. The safest and the most necessary."

"Corruption is overrunning our kingdom," Silas added, his voice colder than I had ever heard it. "If there is a chance this helps us bind more demons, then hope will spread, illuminating our kingdom in the light of the Maker."

Silas turned, half-hidden by the tomb's entryway. One more step and I'd never see Elliot again. I surged forward, screaming, but Mithras hauled me back, binding me to the wall with two shimmering bands of light.

"Remember, the Shadow Bringer is a necessary darkness, even though you've been taught otherwise. I do *not* desire his death or his release." Mithras considered me fiercely, as if he wanted me to understand something that I was not fully comprehending. "So above all else, do not harm the Shadow Bringer, and do not release him from his tomb or his castle. We need him there. *I* need him there. Swear to me, Esmer. Do *not* release him. If you do, the deaths of these people will have been for naught."

"If you wanted to spread the Maker's light, then why did they need to die?"

Beyond the tomb's entrance, wind groaned softly through the trees, rustling leaves and speckling dawn's early sunlight across the expanse of the clearing. I stretched myself upright, standing as tall and as straight-backed as I could. I needed to find strength somewhere, so I drew it from my family. I drew it from Father, who had patrolled our home without fear. Every night he had battled demons. Demons of the unknown, demons of the twilight. Demons of dread, demons that made sounds as they shifted in the woods, snapping twigs and howling at the stars. Demons created out of fear. Demons built out of Corruption. I drew it from Mother, too, who had shielded Elliot and me from Corruptive fates. I drew it from Eden, who had shown me kindness even though I persuaded her to dream. I drew it from Elliot, who faced life with joy even in the darkness.

All wasn't lost. It couldn't be. I needed to steel myself for what was about to come—for what my fate had conspired to be.

I need to survive. Whatever it takes.

Mithras regarded me with cool detachment as he responded: "Because *no one* can know where this tomb is, not even my legionnaires. This place must fall into desolation like it always has. Like it was *meant* to." Without warning, he dissolved my bindings and shoved me backward. "And *you* will keep it that way."

Then he slammed the tomb door shut.

The Tomb of the Devourer was silent, heavy, and endless.

Half-delirious with exhaustion, grief, and fear, I stumbled forward, feeling my way through damp tunnels and crumbling stairs as I tried to avoid the Light Legion's corpses. Without torchlight or a moonlit sky, the tomb gnawed at me, flooding me with its ancient scent and eternal dark. The walls were strange, thrumming with a soft vibration that made the space feel alive, somehow. As though it had been waiting for me all along.

As though it wasn't just the Tomb of the Devourer but *my* tomb, *my* grave.

This is what it must feel like to be buried alive.

I swallowed back tears, coughing as I breathed the dusty air. Where was the Shadow Bringer? He was nowhere in the silence, the dust, the rotting stone. My hand was searching the walls for a clue, a sign—when I tripped into something dry and rattling.

Bones.

As the sound echoed off the walls, I waited, silent, fully expecting that the Shadow Bringer would reveal himself. When he didn't, after minutes—perhaps hours—had passed, my only companions, darkness and two skeletons, mocked me.

Maker, help me.

I paced around the chamber, dragging my hand along the walls for support as I went. The movement reminded me of when I'd first entered the Shadow Bringer's castle, encased in darkness; it wasn't until my eyes had adjusted that the space had revealed itself. But there were no lights here. No gilded chandeliers or candelabras, no mirrors by which candle-light could reflect. Still, there had to be a door or a passageway. His shadows had carried him somewhere—but where?

"You can appear anytime now, Shadow Bringer," I said, my voice higher in pitch than I had intended. Perhaps the Shadow Bringer was dead. Maybe I was doomed to rot alone in this pit of darkness. "Haunt me like you usually do."

I clung to the stone, slowing my breathing and counting to ten.

No.

The Shadow Bringer was here, somewhere. This prison was his, and he was within—in the dark, in the cold, in the shadows. I could feel him. I pulled my arms in tight, fighting the chill seeping into my dress. The vibration, that steady *thrum* of power, was back, this time closer than before. It hummed steadily under my fingertips, calling me to the center of the tomb's innermost wall. Here the stone felt different, as though it was made from another material altogether. Curious, I traced a finger over the wall, flinching as my hand passed through. The stone parted like dust or smoke, swirling apart like a curtain. I inched my hand forward, shivering as the substance lapped against my wrist, fore-arm, elbow.

Then, as though the substance was alive, it grabbed my arm and *pulled.*

I shrieked, mortified, as the wall passed over me in a quick, freezing blast. It was like jumping into a pond on a summer night and slipping under a crust of warmth left over from the sun's scorching heat, to then reach the darker, colder depths below. I pushed up against the hidden chamber's floor, scrambling to get my bearings. The space was surprisingly vast; my own home could have fit within it five times over, and I still couldn't see past the shadows that obscured its edges. Stones arched overhead, curling into a central orb that gave off a slow, meandering light. A slab of obsidian sat underneath the orb, as if patiently awaiting a sacrifice, and thousands of blue quivering flecks illuminated the cavernous ceiling beyond, mimicking stars.

It didn't take me long to find him after that.

He sat against one of the twisting, arching stones, leaning back with his neck exposed. From his wounds spun thick tendrils of shadow, crystallizing as they drifted up toward the orb. One of the deepest cuts—an ugly, unforgiving gash across his chest—gave off the blackest substance, trailing over his skin and tangling in his hair. His helm's caged mouth, along with one of its draconic horns, had broken off, leaving more of his hair and mouth exposed.

A beautiful and haunted man, indeed.

"End it," he said to me, his voice echoing strangely in the cavernous space. "That's why he brought you to me, isn't it? Then *end* it. Finish what you started. It's what you've always wanted."

A sound of disbelief escaped my lips. "I'm not here to kill you, Shadow Bringer."

"Why not? Do you no longer see me as the monster you've been taught to fear? All it took was seeing your lord slaughter his loyal followers," he bit out.

"You are a necessary evil," I said simply. It was a cold truth and perhaps not the entire truth, but the Shadow Bringer did not so much as flinch. "You harbor demons that would otherwise overrun Noctis. So no, I can't kill you. But until I know the full truth behind Corruption and how to stop it, I can't trust you."

"So, I am not a monster but a *tool*." He let loose a sigh. It was the only proof he was even breathing. "Leave, Esmer. You don't belong here."

"I can't. The Light Bringer sealed the entrance."

"You should have escaped while you could." He stood to his full height, and that strange dark smoke rippled around the lines of his body. Within a blink he was looming over me. "Do you know what it's like to spend life in a cage?"

"I know enough," I said, meeting his eyes as evenly as I could. Maybe I was clouded by exhaustion, but I did not feel fear when I looked upon him. "A lifelong sentence of Absolver duty to Norhavellis and never being able to leave the village. Corruption destroying families and leaking from the eyes of those too young to even know why. Not having a choice—or the ability—to say no to those with more power than me." I stopped, frustrated at the emotion rising up my throat.

"My mother once told me that living a caged life is like being a wolf confined to some desolate enclosure," he began, threading his fingers through some of the shadows that rose from his injuries. "You snarl and howl, desperate to sink your teeth into something tangible, but you have no way to explore the vast wilderness just outside your reach." He made a fist, squeezing a thread of shadow until it broke apart. "You can almost feel the earth beneath your feet or the wind on your skin, but you're trapped. You ache for the unknown, where the rest of your life— every possibility, every hope for the future—waits, but you can't move."

So, he truly had been mortal at one point. He had a *mother*. The tales never told of such an origin, never humanized him at all.

"I've felt that way before," I whispered. "I desperately wanted to escape my life for something better, but I never could. And now I have nothing." I brushed my hand across a shadow as it moved to touch my shoulder. "It's a horribly accurate comparison."

"It is, isn't it? Ironically, my mother used to make that comparison to encourage me to dream. Whenever I was facing some challenge in reality, she'd tell me to escape to the Realm and let the Weavers guide me." He looked away, swallowing hard. "If only she knew I'd spend most of my life imprisoned in the Realm, never having a choice."

"Did your mother pass before you were locked away, then?"

"My mother and father both died when I was a child. They never knew what I would become. And now you're here facing the same fate."

His eyes slid to mine, gazing at me intently. "I know your pain, Esmer. I know what it feels like to grieve so deeply that it changes the essence of who you are."

He was suddenly too close, too overwhelming. Had the Shadow Bringer been a normal man, perhaps I would have felt the heat diffusing from his skin. Instead, his nearness felt like a cool, tantalizing brush of midnight air. He searched my eyes, breath hitching at whatever he found in them, and then spun on his heel to walk to the obsidian slab, pieces of his ragged clothing sliding across the floor.

"What is that?" I asked, following.

"A means to an eternal slumber," he answered. The slab, its edges curling upward, was surprisingly pliant to the touch, its surface reflecting the light from above. "If you fall asleep here, the tomb will anchor you to the Dream Realm. But being physically joined to the Realm has its consequences. Your mind will slowly distort, and your memories will fade—all while you lie comatose."

I nodded. "The tales say that Weavers took precautions against such a fate. They'd periodically wake so as not to lose themselves to the Realm."

According to the tales, Weavers once rose from their sleep to attend the most extravagant and pivotal moments in Noctis's history. They were present for the crownings of kings and victories in war. They were honored guests at citywide celebrations, deity-like in the fanfare they caused. Though waking from the Realm was a risk—it made the Weavers susceptible to death and aging—they were protected and beloved by the people.

"Weavers be damned," the Shadow Bringer snarled. "For five centuries I lay upon this stone, waiting for a release that never came. Death would have been preferable."

A shiver coursed across my skin. He had been locked inside this tomb in an eternal sleep for *centuries*. I couldn't imagine what he had lost during those years, what he had forgotten. I shuddered to think what I, too, would lose or forget if the Light Bringer chose to never release me.

"Do you honestly believe you were wrongly imprisoned?" I asked, lowering my voice. It felt as though I was broaching something forbidden. "Only your wickedness is recorded in the tales. There's no trace of goodness in the stories we are told."

"I don't know." The Shadow Bringer placed his forehead into the palm of his hand, clenching his jaw as though his thoughts physically pained him. "Threads of memory, broken moments in time—that's all I have. And they don't always tell me what I've lost or what life was like before."

"That doesn't seem like much, then."

"No. But I do feel a deep hatred toward the Weavers and Mithras. That I know to be true." He looked at me again, long and hard, as though he was considering a decision. "I slept here for centuries as my soul withered. Perhaps I was good once, and perhaps I can change Noctis's fate, but I don't know that there's anything good or worthy left in me. You need to understand that."

Something didn't feel right. It was in his eyes; in the way they shifted, lowering.

"You look as if you could use some rest," he murmured, his voice a soft caress. His words felt like silk or velvet—a deep, rumbling purr. "Come, lie on this stone. Let me ease your burdens." His words had an irresistible pull, and I found myself surrendering to the exhaustion that was weighing me down. As I lay on the slab, the stone seemed to soften and embrace me, soothing my weariness.

I nodded in agreement, thanking him.

Didn't I?

I sighed, my eyes heavy and warm. Or maybe I didn't thank him. I couldn't remember.

"You're all that I have left," I admitted quietly. "Do you know that?"

The Shadow Bringer leaned over me, exposed lips a breath from my own. "That isn't true."

"But it is," I breathed. Tears ran down my face, bubbling up from where I had suppressed them earlier. "And it is heartbreaking."

"I heard you scream for 'Elliot.'"

"He's my little brother," I whispered. "The Light Bringer took him."

I felt a hand—*is it a hand or his shadows?*—slide around the nape of my neck, threading my hair with long, cool fingers. I shivered, leaning into him as he held me, and marveled at the new shade of darkness spinning around us. I reached out to touch it, to see what it felt like—and realized it was rippling from my own skin.

What is this? I thought I asked. *What is this coming from my body?*

But my eyes were heavy again, and the stone so soft and welcoming.

Something brushed my temple, my cheek.

And then I felt no more.

PART TWO

To Wake Where Shadows Gather

Dreamer, dreamer—wake up."

I sighed, burrowing into the silky depths of my bed. "Go away."

"How long do you intend to keep us waiting?"

"Us? Is Mother there, too?" I nestled deeper into the bedding, tugging a particularly fine blanket up to my nose. It smelled of juniper, night, and the brush of rain on fallen leaves. "I'm not ready yet."

"We have not the time as you do," the voice said irritably, as if I were a petulant child.

"We wait. *He* waits," said a second voice, its tone more gravelly than the first.

"But I've waited longer," the first voice snapped.

A groan crept out before I could stop it. Why were Elliot and Mother so insistent? Didn't they know how exhausted I was? My bones were stone, my skin a sheath of molasses. I couldn't possibly do what they asked.

"Wake up," the first voice urged.

"Wake up," the second echoed.

"*Wake up*," they commanded together.

"Fine—I will," I mumbled, rubbing my eyes and giving the room a bleary once-over. Everything was so dark, so formless; had they not thought to light a lamp? "Where are you?"

"We're here," the voices said as one.

Ice gripped my spine, spiraling up toward my neck. The Shadow Bringer's room hit me with all its force—its every shadow, its colors and smell. I threw back the covers, mortified that part of me still yearned to curl up in his blankets, to breathe deep the scent of night and rain on his pillows, and sleep.

Where did those voices come from?

A quick scan of the Shadow Bringer's chamber told me I was alone, but there were too many places to hide, too many corners that could cloak or conceal. And what was that dragging noise coming from the hall? I squeezed my elbows, wishing that I were wearing the Shadow Bringer's menacing armor instead of the full-length dress that manifested on my body whenever I dreamed. I'd have felt much safer under a sheath of metal.

Maybe that was why he wore all those layers.

"Come to me, shadows," I said, attempting to sound strong and confident. I waited, expectant, trying to quiet my breathing. My heart was panicking, clawing at my throat, which made it difficult to hear the demons in the hall. Were they watching, waiting? Did they know I was here, alone? "Shadows, come forward," I hissed again, feeling ridiculous.

Why aren't they listening?

"Let us out!" a demon suddenly shrieked, slamming its weight into the door. The walls trembled at the force of it, letting loose a few books and a lot of dust.

Strength and confidence be damned.

"Please," I begged, glancing around wildly. Where were the shadows? It had felt easier to summon them before; what was I doing wrong? I focused on my hands, acutely aware of the emptiness there. Nothing prickled at my palms or flooded my chest. There was no rush of energy, no thrum of the Shadow Bringer's lingering power.

I was truly alone, without anything or anyone protecting me from the demons.

"I'll mount my defense the old-fashioned way, then," I said through gritted teeth. And I went to work.

By the time I was finished, the back of my dress was damp with sweat, clinging to my skin as I knelt to inspect my work. A tower of interlocked furniture—the Bringer's sumptuous chairs, bookshelves, and bed—was now shoved haphazardly against the door. It was fine enough, I supposed. At least a demon would be met with some resistance before getting the chance to eat me. For good measure, I climbed through the maze of furniture and shoved a piece of iron—the scepter of some sculpture—through the door handle.

Better.

I sank into an armchair I had left behind. As with my other Realm adventures, I felt no hunger, no thirst, no urge for bodily functions; but cold, warmth, and the dusting of pain could easily seep in. And seep they did.

Night air swept in from the balcony, chilling my sweat-slicked skin and rustling the curtain it passed through. It mingled with the many candelabras, tossing their flames close to death, and roved back to me, forcing shivers down my arms. It nearly made me forget why I was there in the first place. The Shadow Bringer had locked me here somehow, trading places so that he could be free from this cage of demons and darkness.

I muffled a scream into my hands.

The Shadow Bringer must have known he could bind me. That was why he had led me to his tomb. He'd intended to lead me there, bind me, and then what? I considered the possibilities. Would he seize Istralla and unleash his demons on all of humankind? Spread Corruption further and more pervasively? Destroy all the elixir stores?

Why did I get so close to him? And why didn't I stop him when I had the chance?

I walked to the curtain of billowing fabric, determined to somehow stop the wind, when a strange noise whistled in the distance.

"Dreamer," it keened, and I recognized it as the voice from earlier. The voice I had thought to be Elliot's.

Under the unusually bright and silver-tinged stars, the Bringer's balcony was a sight to behold. Dark roots entwined with ironwork, forming sculptural motifs across the castle walls, and the floor was a glistening, star-flecked obsidian that felt like silk underfoot.

"Have you finally the wits to see us? Here, here," the voice whistled again, echoing out from somewhere below the balustrade.

I peered down at the forest, uncertain as to what I'd find.

"Ah, dreamer," the familiar gray-haired demon called. "Quite some time it has been."

The demon seemed more human than before, its eyes no longer seeping and its cheeks less like the curves of a skull. Even its posture seemed more composed—tall and graceful, not hunched and dragging as though the weight of hell rested upon its shoulders. Or maybe it was just the starlight playing tricks on me. Stars and the shimmering blue orbs that floated through the forest's many trees.

"Where is he, dreamer?" a second demon asked, slinking from the forest. This one wore a short cape, unlike the long, meandering cloth of the first, and glared up at me with eyes of coal. "What have you done? Where is he?"

Surely they meant the Shadow Bringer. If they knew he was gone, what would they do? Would they try to take advantage of his absence and overrun me?

"He's inside," I answered, turning my shoulders as if to leave. "In fact, he's calling for me. I had better return before he notices I'm speaking to monsters in the woods."

The first demon grinned and tilted its head. "You're cold. Has he not attired you with one of his cloaks? They are rather extravagant, but practical enough. Quite suitable for times such as these."

"He already offered," I bluffed, hoping they weren't catching on. "I declined."

The second demon scoffed. "You would spite him in such a manner? How loathsome."

The grin of the first demon widened. "Quite loathsome, indeed. But I do forget—our poor demon-riddled minds are so fragile, you know—our lord has only a single cloak, typically affixed to his shoulders. He does not lend it willingly."

"I spoke too quickly. I only meant that he offered me a *blanket.*"

"Hmm. A blanket, you say? Strange—my memory has returned. Our lord always adorns his personal guests in cloaks. Yes, most definitely cloaks. A welcome gift, if you will."

Color rose to my cheeks, clearly revealing my frustration, so I stepped back into the shadows. I wasn't sure how well the demons could see, or how powerful they were, but I didn't feel like finding out.

"Retreating so soon?" the first demon questioned. "Are you certain you wish to do that?"

"I won't tolerate your tricks, demon. Leave me be and go back to where you belong."

"And where is that, dear mortal? Where is it that we should go?"

I didn't answer. Instead, I turned on my heel and marched back inside, clenching my jaw against their varied and clever taunts. The conversation had felt almost preferable to the uncertainty and loneliness that dwelled within the Bringer's chamber. *Almost.*

I spent the next few hours searching through the Bringer's things, hoping that his real or imagined cloaks would emerge. His room was cavernous, stretched tall by ribs of obsidian and adorned with inconceivable opulence, so it took some time to look through it all—even with half its furniture piled against the door. I found books both strange and familiar; some pages were empty, some burst with poetry, art, and music. Then there were some Weaver tales, though they no longer felt like tales at all. They seemed living and true, depicting both Mithras and the seven Weavers in ordinary settings and conversations. And then there were the citadels Firstlight and Evernight.

In these books, Citadel Firstlight was a haven in Istralla for the Weavers and their acolytes; it provided resources, training grounds, and a means for the Weavers to delegate among earthly rulers. On the other hand, Citadel Evernight was a place where nobles and their families could dream in profound ways; it was there that collective Dream Realm feasts and balls, lavish affairs beyond the imagination, could occur without restriction.

There were also two unnamed dreamers of great talent.

The young men were anomalies, failing to possess a specific affinity to any Weaver, but their acclimation to the Realm allowed them to join the Weavers' ranks regardless. Pages spoke of their raw, unprecedented ability, describing the ferocious battles they led with the Weavers against demons and their false gods.

I read until my eyes hurt—until the pages blurred and the words swam.

Moving to the floor, I cradled my head in the crooks of my arms. Above me, dramatic seascape and mountain paintings, easily the height of three or four men, crawled up the walls to coil around a great chandelier. The paint broke apart in some places, slipping out of the canvas to float alongside the shadows.

It was a beauty both strange and breathtaking.

The floor held me for some time, ghosting its phantom shadows over my skin and toward the balcony, where they disappeared. Despite its opulence, the Shadow Bringer's room felt empty. Void of warmth, hope, and joy.

It ached for something, but I wasn't sure what.

I woke in a pile of silken pillows and feather-soft blankets, bathed in the strange scent of a thunderstorm mixed with dusty furniture. I pressed my face to the nearest pillow and breathed in, relishing it. It reminded me of a fog-covered field, but with a subtle undertone of woodsmoke and old books.

"Let us out, let us out, let us out!" shrieked a demon far too close for comfort.

I sprang to my feet, disoriented from the low candlelight. My heart plummeted as the chamber sharpened into focus.

"Oh, Maker," I gasped in dismay. *"No."*

The barricade of furniture I'd piled high against the door was gone. Every chair, every desk, every book was now precisely placed, resting exactly where it had originally been.

"Let us out!"

I made to slam a chair against the bowing door but quickly changed my mind. A chair would be nothing against the strength of a demon; I might as well use a scrap of lace to stop the force of a river.

Maybe there's a way out through the balcony. A hidden ladder of some sort.

Two familiar demons sat against a pair of trees below the balcony, their distorted faces mocking and cruel. One was sharpening a piece of metal, carving its edge into something gleaming. The other simply looked bored.

"Dreamer," greeted the gray-haired demon. It took the second demon's improvised weapon and tested it on a section of its long cape, nodding appreciatively when it sliced straight through. "Still without that cloak, I see. Here to delight in this good morning?"

"This is no morning." The sky was the color of sapphires and turbid, ancient wine. Without the balcony's candlelight and the forest's silvery-blue orbs, the demons would have been altogether obscured. "How is this morning"—I motioned wildly at the sky—"and what about any of this is *good?*"

"Ah, that. Should we tell her?" The long-caped demon glanced at the second, its expression thoughtful, but the gesture was ignored. The second demon merely continued sharpening its makeshift blade. "Very well, I will tell her." The first demon looked back at me and grinned. "We aren't in the mortal world, darling. Our eternal night is, well, eternal."

"But we are all dreaming. Can't the structure of day and night just be altered?"

I thought back to when the Shadow Bringer's dungeon had shifted, transporting me to my home in Norhavellis. Or when wings had burst from the Bringer's back, carrying him high over the Visstill.

"No. This domain was permanently set to protect our lord. Or to punish him—we aren't certain. Have we decided our opinion on that?" The first demon glanced at its companion again, and again it was ignored. "As I said, we aren't certain. So eternal night it is."

I cursed under my breath. The forest below was a long way down, dropping farther and farther away the more I looked. Without wings or the Shadow Bringer's magic, I'd have to physically descend the wall. Or jump. And neither option seemed very realistic.

"Are you in distress?" the long-caped demon inquired. "You seem a bit distressed."

"No."

"If you ask our lord nicely, I'm sure he would quell your troubles," the demon said, its cracked lips widening into what could almost pass as a smile.

"I'm sure he would."

The demon inside the castle—still clawing at the Shadow Bringer's door—roared, its howl rattling the chamber and echoing out into the night.

"He's in a mood today, hmm?" the talkative demon from the forest commented, leaning back into its tree. The second demon from the forest, silent and sullen, still hadn't joined the conversation, clearly preoccupied with its weapon. "Trouble sleeping?"

"Enough with your games," I seethed. The demons clearly knew more than they were choosing to say, likely withholding information that would enable my escape. "You know that scream wasn't his."

"Could have fooled me," the demon said with a careless shrug, crossing its feet.

"I need to wake up from this dream," I said tersely. "Tell me how."

The demon thumbed its gray chin, considering. "Quite a dangerous venture, that."

"I don't care what I have to do. I don't belong here, and I need to go home," I said.

"You truly wish to wake?"

"Yes," I answered fiercely.

The long-caped demon's grin widened even farther. "Then you must first go to sleep."

The second demon slammed its blade into the grass. "Your attempt at wit is making me lose my own," it hissed through bared teeth, nearly spitting from the force of its words.

A roar suddenly erupted from inside the castle, along with the shuddering *crack* of a door splitting open.

A new demon lurched toward the balcony from inside the Shadow Bringer's bedchamber, spindly arms trailing like liquid across the stone.

Its spine was long and crooked, needled with twigs and fur, and its face—if it could be called a face—was the skull of an elk. I reeled backward as it approached, frozen with terror. My hands were empty, bereft of either steel or shadow, and I could do nothing but watch, horrified, as the demon slunk forward. If I jumped from the edge of the balcony, would I wake in the Tomb of the Devourer? I shook my head. *No*—my body was physically tied to the Realm. If I died here, I might not come back on the other side.

I might not come back at all.

"Out," the elk demon rasped as three others joined it from inside. The balcony trembled from the weight of their collective steps, shivering as I did when I looked upon their bodies. Atop each neck sat a skull; there was the elk of the first, a horse on the second, a bull for the third, and something fanged and serrated atop the fourth.

They lifted their skulls toward the midnight sky, raising their faces to meet the wind.

The elk demon growled, towering over the balustrade. "Where is he?" Its voice rumbled and cracked around each syllable, as if it hadn't spoken a coherent sentence in centuries.

The long-caped demon from the forest stood from its sitting position, stretching its gangly limbs and stifling a yawn. "Whatever do you mean? You should have passed our unruly lord on your way out of his bedroom."

As an answer, the quartet of demons on the balcony made furious, animalistic noises.

The sullen demon from the forest, previously silent as it sharpened its makeshift blade, pointed its weapon at me. "If he isn't in there, then ask *that* one where the Shadow Bringer is."

The elk demon turned to face me, halting its jagged movements. For a moment, it simply stared, its empty sockets suggesting vision that saw movement and shape beyond the physical. Things deep within the soul. Then it stepped forward again, slowly dragging itself to me. I pressed myself flat against the balustrade, attempting to still my shuddering limbs.

I had almost succeeded until it bowed low enough to scent the air by my neck.

"Something of his resides within her," the elk demon growled.

The fanged demon stalked closer to the elk demon, followed by the horse and the bull. It looked ready to jump, its clawed hands gripping at the stone. "She has been here before," the fanged demon realized. "Perhaps she is his replacement—or perhaps he has abandoned us."

The horse demon joined in, circling me. "Where is he? Where is the lord who would not release us?"

I held my chin high against the demons' menacing faces. I had neither steel nor shadow to fight with—only words. "If you so much as touch me, the Shadow Bringer will exact his revenge upon you all."

"Do not trick us," bellowed the bull demon. "He cares not for you nor anyone."

The fanged demon hissed. "Your death would be of little consequence, dreamer."

Beneath me, the balcony cracked.

No, no, no.

I staggered against the crumbling stone, swaying, reaching, grasping for *anything*—but the demons, in the chaos, thrashed their limbs into the banister. They shattered the stone, flinging it wide and far. A large piece of the broken castle crashed into my chest, pinning me against the balcony and slamming my skull into the floor with a sickening *crack.* I didn't know where the screams were coming from—if they were from my lungs, my mind, or some nauseating union of both. All I could see were the demons. A horde of skulled, broken beasts crawling, climbing, and lurching their bodies from the Shadow Bringer's castle over the edge and into the forest. Shrieking with glee. Roaring with pleasure. Crushing others as they clambered for their freedom.

Hundreds of demons pouring into the night.

I woke in darkness upon the Shadow Bringer's floor.

The dark had become a living, breathing thing, forcing its way into my eyes and nose. It hurt to breathe. Cold air swept over the blankets still strewn about the floor, flipped the pages of books left unread, and whistled through unlit chandeliers and candelabras.

For the first time, the castle had not restored itself.

Drawing a velvet blanket around my shoulders, I stumbled to the balcony, cursing my fate and contemplating whether or not to yell into the night. If this was to be my eternity, my mind would surely disintegrate before I saw the light of day again.

I shivered from a new kind of fear. Just how long would it take for me to wake up from this?

When I was little, the idea of dreaming had felt precious and wondrous. Sacred, even. Before the Shadow Bringer existed, to dream was to receive a gift from the Maker; in a dream, one could relish in hope and wander in possibility. Eden and I used to whisper about dreams, worried that Mother or Father would hear and think we were being disrespectful. But we enjoyed imagining what the Realm might look like. How the Weavers dressed, talked, moved. We would curl under a tent of blankets with our Weaver tales, spinning stories of adventure. We discussed how a dream might feel—conjectured the sights and sounds that we might experience. We wondered what it would take to become a dream warrior of legend, or to have a Weaver choose us as a follower. But most of all, we wondered what we might have to do to escape our twisted life in Norhavellis.

I laughed, the sound of it weak and small against the void around me.

What I wouldn't give to have that life back.

Fear was a battle I couldn't win here. It suffocated me—crawled over my skin, squeezed my heart, chilled my bones. There was always the crumbling *crack* of a stone that sounded like footsteps, a whisper of wind that sounded too near to a breath. I knelt behind a statue, drawing the blanket close. If I concentrated, I could pretend I was a child in Norhavellis, spinning tales of wonder with Eden.

Dreams weren't meant for *this*. Fear, sorrow, hatred—dreams were meant to quell these things. Not ignite or reaffirm them.

From my burrow of velvet and stone, I watched in horror as a figure leapt to the castle's highest spire. It was tall and spindly, bone-white skin glowing as though it were the moon and stars. Sweeping tendrils of hair flowed out from its skull, webbing the castle in black.

A demon?

For a moment, it stood, motionless, its face tilted downward.

I couldn't tell where it was looking; its face was shrouded in shadow, its limbs half-cloaked by its hair. I sucked in a slow, steady breath and held it, flattening myself against the statue on the balcony.

Don't see me. Don't see me. Don't see me.

As though it could hear my thoughts, the creature cocked its head.

Then it descended.

It floated through the air, landing elegantly in a pile of its robes and hair. The creature—the man—looked my way, his face a serpentine array of angles. His mouth was a thin, cunning frown, his nose a sweeping line between listless eyes of coal.

And atop his brow sat an ivory crown.

"You needn't cower so," the serpentine man said, acknowledging me but maintaining his distance. His voice was slow and melodic, a dusting of silk upon stone. "Had you answered the door, I would have entered properly."

I lifted myself from my burrow. "It isn't my door to open."

"Darkness beckons to the isolated. If you do not open the door, you will still be found," he murmured, his eyes clouded in thought. Then, as if a weight was lifted from his skeletal shoulders, he sighed. "But I digress. Will I be invited indoors, or shall we continue this charade on the balcony?"

"Who are you? Are you of the demons?" I asked.

"At one time or another, we are all nearly demons."

I clenched my jaw. "That isn't an answer. I asked who you were."

"And I owe you nothing, dreamer." He fixed me with his eyes of coal. "But I will give you my name, because you already know it."

For a moment, I studied him, the angles of his dark, intelligent eyes, the ghostly undertones of his voice. He spoke as though he knew sorrow, despair, and death—knew them so intimately that he no longer feared them.

He looked nearly the same as his image in the book of Weaver tales.

Somnus, Weaver of the Past, introduced himself and bowed. "A pleasure."

W hat a wretched condition this castle is in," Somnus observed, inspecting the Shadow Bringer's chamber with a scornful eye. He lifted the edge of a ruined painting, its canvas ripped into long, oily shreds. Silver light ebbed from his fingertips and illuminated the paint. "A shame, considering the hope and wonder that were imbued in its mortar."

He trailed around the broken pieces of the room, pausing every few steps to examine a shredded book or gouges clawed deep into the walls. His every movement was smooth, careful, effortless; refined over the course of centuries, his body carried itself with perfect precision.

Somnus was a ghost formed into life, a living specter of a man.

It was said Weavers created everything in the Dream Realm, blending landscapes and simulated realities like they, too, were the Maker of their worlds. Some dreamers could alter pieces of their dreams, adding context or adjustments as their minds saw fit, but most dreams were the direct creations of the Weavers behind them.

"You speak as though you built this place," I said. At Somnus's inquisitive expression, I worked to retract my statement. "I mean—"

"No. It is not of my creation; my domain rests elsewhere." Somnus dropped the jeweled tapestry he was examining. It gleamed as it fell, curling over his pointed boot. "But you think it is beautiful, do you not? I forget how grandiose the Realm appears to a dreamer, even in its ruin. And this castle is merely one thread of the Realm's entirety."

I didn't respond, holding my arms close.

"Dreams have become fickle, shadowed things. To truly dream—" He paused, his depthless gaze narrowing. It was clear he wasn't satisfied with my silence. "Surely the experience is exquisite in your eyes."

"It is beautiful," I admitted, reluctant to specifically acknowledge the beauty of the Bringer's castle. The Shadow Bringer was a mortal enemy of the Weavers; any affiliation with him here—beyond my chance appearance in his castle—was an enormous risk. I pretended to examine a flameless candelabra. "Though I'd prefer a bit of light."

"Beauty can be found in darkness, dreamer. You needn't be afraid of acknowledging your affiliation with the Shadow Bringer, even though he did cause quite the turmoil some five hundred years ago."

Oh hell.

I whirled on Somnus. "You know what I'm thinking," I observed accusingly.

He shrugged. "I merely witness impressions. Small shivers of emotion and belief." He stared at me, all knowing. Dangerous. "But I am experienced enough to know what they mean."

Realization crashed against me, heavy as the sea; Somnus wasn't here to make small talk, to comment on the beauty of the Realm or the state of the Bringer's castle. No—his eyes spoke of something deeper, deadlier. His posture reeked of bloodlust even amid its grace.

"You're here to kill him, aren't you?"

Somnus considered me for a moment, assessing the way I stood, the clench of my jaw, the shaking in my hands. "Not yet, dreamer. I merely bore witness to the darkness escaping his castle, shattering what was left of his domain's boundary. I thought I'd find him here, but all I see is you."

"That's because I was tricked into taking his place. He isn't here."

"Is that the sole purpose for your presence here, then?" Somnus motioned around us—at the Bringer's crumbling chamber, at the night leaking in through the uncurtained wall. "Because you took his place in the mortal world?"

"What else would I—"

"That is not the only reason you are here, dreamer." Somnus pulled a weapon from the fold of his robes. It was a blade forged from the night sky, its handle carved from onyx and ivory. Tiny stars danced along its edge. "Your purpose is beyond that. *His* purpose is beyond that. But a thousand demonic souls, freed? A transgression of incredible concern, considering they were contained here for nearly five hundred years prior."

I swallowed back the fear rising in my throat.

Where had they gone? What had I *done*?

"I couldn't stop them," I whispered miserably.

Somnus approached, gliding silently across the stone. I thought he was positioning his body to attack, but he instead offered me his sword. It was a twin to the Shadow Bringer's, pure black and deadly sharp.

"A token from the Maker Himself." I tensed, watching as the weapon rippled with power. Weaver or not, I had no idea what his intentions were. "Use it to channel the gifts you were given."

When I made no move to take it, Somnus gently placed his hand over my own.

"Why do you hesitate?" he asked.

"Because I don't understand why you're offering it to me."

"And *I* don't discern why the Maker does what He does. I only act upon His command, trusting that He sees further than I do." A corner of his mouth lifted. "Also, you are weak and fearful. You need a weapon if you wish to be of any consequence here."

Well, then.

Color rose to my face as I accepted the blade, lifting it gingerly. Cool to the touch and thrumming with power, it felt no heavier than a small broomstick.

Somnus dipped his head in a small bow. "May it protect and guide you."

"How is it meant to be used?"

"As any other weapon is used. Be merely its bearer, and it will destroy you. Meld with it, and you will conquer." He parted his hair, and a curved sword emerged, its blade much like the fang of some enormous beast. "It can also be hidden on your person when not in use. Do you have a preference as to where?"

I thought for a moment, remembering how the Shadow Bringer had pulled his blade from his left palm. An easy spot to access and as useful a spot as any.

"The palm of my hand," I declared.

Somnus nodded, approval in his serpentine eyes. "Place the blade here"—he positioned the sword above the center of my left palm, its point nearly piercing the flesh—"and use your will to command it under your skin."

I did as he specified, taking hold of the hilt and balancing it above my palm. I lowered the sword slowly, carefully, imagining that it wasn't a sword at all but a delicate breeze or a wisp of smoke. But I hesitated. So instead of passing through me like smoke, it passed through very much as a physical sword would.

"Maker's light," I hissed, stanching the shadow-tinged blood with my sleeve. If Somnus noticed the abnormality in my blood, he didn't say. "How is it even possible to bleed here? None of this is—"

"Real?" Somnus asked, sheathing his blade back into his hair. "There are different parts of the Realm. Some are more physical in nature than others. Try again."

"I—" *I don't know if I want to try again*, I almost said. But Somnus gave me a withering look so filled with expectation and mild disappointment that I changed my mind. "Fine."

I took a full breath, centering my focus back on the sword. It seemed to mock me, gleaming as it was, wondering why *I* of all people was to be its master. Closing my eyes, I again imagined that the blade was nothing but a shadow. I envisioned a creeping, sword-eating darkness coiling up its length, rendering it entirely into mist. Slowly, I let the weight of the mist pull itself down, focusing on what it felt like to have the substance pool in my hands. Then, my right fist fell empty against the palm of my left, and I opened my eyes.

The sword was gone.

I flexed my hand open and shut, marveling at the sensation of the sword within. My palm ached, thrumming with cold and heat and the sensation that something within it wanted *out*.

"You need to test it," Somnus advised.

"Yes," I agreed, surprised at the new sense of purpose that pooled within me. The sword was a vein of power, a weapon both familiar and new. "But against what?"

Somnus beckoned me to follow him. "Something that will prepare you to face all the darkened souls that fled from here."

We walked through the castle, silent save for the sweeping of Somnus's hair upon the stone. He moved as if he knew the castle intimately, never hesitating about which staircase to descend or hallway to follow. Candelabras ignited beside him, glowing from orbs that spun out from under his hands, and the castle slowly melted into life as we ventured through. The light slid over paintings taller than trees in the Visstill, over waterfalls crawling like honey from statues of lions and serpents.

But the farther we walked, the more we saw decay, rot, and ruin.

Dry, snakelike branches, rattling as they burst from the ground, clawed against paintings, ripping them. Arched ceilings adorned with whorls of silver and draped in star-specked gossamer crumbled as we passed underneath, showering the air with dust and revealing the sky above. Then there was damage the demons had left behind. Each room held impossibly high claw marks and teeth left scattered in piles of rubble and cloth.

The main vestibule, the lavish entryway where I'd first met the Shadow Bringer, was a mess of broken furniture and dust; it looked— and smelled—as though it hadn't seen light, fresh air, or humanity in years. What I remembered as vibrant shades of emerald, plum, and wine were now pale and lifeless, and the array of golden mirrors and candelabras were reduced to shards upon the floor.

"Decay can settle so quickly," Somnus remarked. "This castle is merely a husk without its ruler. It is simply mesmerizing."

Mesmerizing?

With all the rubble and lingering shadows, it felt as though a demon would appear at any moment. There wasn't anything mesmerizing about that. Somnus beckoned to a passageway below the vestibule; it coiled down in a steep descent, veiled in a haze of shadow. From it, a familiar smell emanated. Something damp and cave-like.

"Come, dreamer. We are nearly there," said Somnus.

I struggled to keep up as we descended, worrying that my feet would tangle in Somnus's hair. It was a sleek, beautiful curtain, trailing behind him like a cape, but it was far too long for someone to safely follow. The more I studied his hair, the more I wondered if it possessed a mind of its own. And maybe it did. Whenever my footsteps trailed too close, it would shift away just in time.

I thought I heard Somnus chuckle once or twice. Likely mocking my skittishness. But I couldn't be sure.

We ended up in the Bringer's water cavern, its wet stone and twilight greenery a mangled smear of what it used to be. The candelabras were extinguished and tangled over by vines, causing the space to be cast over by a strange, pervasive darkness. Even the central pool, its waters previously lit by starlight, seemed empty and dead.

"Ah, and another place lost to time," Somnus said, his voice echoing.

He spread his hands wide, orbs springing from his fingertips and diving deep into the pool. As his hands followed, the water erupted into a burst of starlight, mingling with orbs that danced slow, meandering arcs beneath its surface. Depthless as the pool was, there were no signs of monsters lurking within. It felt clean, inviting, even. I found myself standing over its waters, watching as Somnus traced symbols and figures over the silver light.

"You are ready, I assume," Somnus murmured, continuing to thread shapes into the surface. "Use what you were given, and conquer all that you face."

I stared at the surface, expecting something to jump out at us. The water rippled, steady and bright, iridescent with stars. Clear and demonless, it held no clues about what he wanted me to see. I turned to Somnus, several questions upon my lips.

But he was gone.

Before I could react, a force cracked against my shoulder. My balance was already unsteady from the half-light of the cavern and the power vibrating under my skin. I tripped, flailing.

The water caught me quickly—but it was no longer water at all.

I was in a pit, a forest of snow-covered bone and rot spanning beyond it. And in the center was Elliot, his eyes bruised and hollow.

E lliot!" I screamed, lunging toward him. But my legs wouldn't move—they were stuck underneath me, caught by something dark like mud but thick with bone, rot, and other disgusting things. It clung to my feet and forced me into stillness.

Elliot hunched over his knees, thin arms gripping his sides. His hair was dirty and matted, his clothes nothing but long, dwindling rags. They reminded me of the gray demon's attire—nothing suitable for a human boy.

"I'm sorry," he moaned, sobs racking deep and heavy from his chest. "I'm sorry, Mother. I'm sorry, Father. I'm sorry, Esmer."

I took another look at my brother. He was thinner, smaller, his voice wavering and more childish than I had heard in some time.

"I'm sorry!" he howled again, raising his face toward the endless pit of bone, snow, and filth.

The pit changed as he howled, slowly unfurling one of its edges. A winged demon peeked over this unfurling edge, its skull ringed in horns that crowned red smoking eyes. Where its face should have been was a mask of swirling darkness, devoid of features save for those eyes, and its body was colossal, clothed in armor that formed to every crevice of its unnatural shape.

Every inch of my body screamed at me to run.

Run.

My mouth felt dry, my bones liquid and soft under my skin. This demon reeked of ancient, all-seeing power that felt familiar, somehow. I couldn't place it, but the sensation that I had seen this demon before somewhere—or that this demon had once seen *me*—tugged at the back of my mind, desperately begging me to take note.

Elliot howled louder once he saw the demon, crying to a snowing, horrible sky.

"Elliot, look at me!" I fought against the ice-slicked wind that was now whirling around the pit. It stuck to his back, froze against the strips of his rags. "You need to wake up right now! Fight it—fight this! You can't let it get you. *Please!*"

Somnus had thrown me into one of Elliot's nightmares from back when he was dying of fever after Eden's Corruption. I had been thirteen at the time; it was a year that had no end or beginning. There was only hunger, darkness, and the lingering stench of death. Mother and Father had managed to provide us with elixir—the Norhavellian supply, I knew now—but only after Elliot had told us of his wicked dreams.

They had been horrific, those dreams. Filled with things most vile and terrifying, they were far worse than any of the stories we had known. But he had kept them from us for a time, convinced that his silence would mean our safety. He thought his dreams were his fault. That he had done something to deserve them.

But he had never mentioned a demon.

The demon descended slowly, crawling over the lip of the pit and staring hungrily at my brother. Elliot sniffed, his slight shoulders trembling, and tilted his face toward the sound of my voice.

"I'm your sister—it's *me*. It's Esmer."

Recognition dawned in his dull eyes. "Esmer? You look different...."

Boom.

Continuing to descend, the demon grew closer and closer, its eyes glinting with hellfire. Its armor shifted with each step, the sound of it echoing, booming—a deep rumbling that shook the core of the earth.

Boom.

And as it walked, my body sank deeper into the mire. First my ankles. Then my shins. It reached for my thighs, bit deep into my hips. A breath later, and it was seeping up over my stomach, cold and foul.

Boom.

The muck was heavy now, squeezing my ribs like a vise.

From within my palm the sword began to thrum, reminding me of something vital.

Use what you were given, and conquer all that you face.

I looked in newfound horror upon the demon. I sincerely doubted Somnus meant conquering *that*. It didn't seem conquerable in the slightest, but it was the only danger here—and I was the only one with any power to stop it.

"Maker help us," I muttered, pulling the blade from my palm.

As soon as the blade met the air, three things happened: The demon positioned itself to jump, its cloudlike maw parting to reveal black teeth; Elliot started running; and the ground below me solidified, spitting me out. Instinct told me to raise the weapon high, focusing every ounce of my willpower into making it do whatever it was supposed to do. The metal, reflecting a glorious night sky within its body, began to glow, and snow circled in a pattern around it, swirling rapidly like a blizzard might.

"Help!" Elliot screamed, stumbling to kneel behind me. I spared a hand to hold him to my side. "I-it's *cold*, Esmer. I w-want to go home."

"I do, too, Elliot. But first I need to defeat this demon."

Ice coated Elliot's eyelashes and clung to my hair in clumps. I blinked back tears, focusing, trying my hardest to see beyond the swirling wall of snow. The demon was out there somewhere, lumbering its way toward us, but the snow obscured it.

Boom.

"It hates the light," Elliot warbled.

My breath hitched. "How do you know that? You've seen this demon before?"

Elliot nodded, hiccuping.

Without warning, the demon attacked.

It barreled at us from the vortex of wind and snow, its body so massive that parts were still obscured in gray, milky mist. I swung the sword up, willing it to make contact, begging it to burst with a light so bright, it would force the creature back—and the blade began to glow, gleaming with the force of a million stars. It parted the snow and ice, lifted parts of the fog. The demon hesitated, leaning back into the mist. It was working; the light truly was warding it off. I grinned in utter disbelief.

It's working.

But suddenly, just as quickly as it had ignited, the sword went dark. It faded into a regular blade, something that one might find forged at a village blacksmith's. Elliot and I looked at each other, horrified. The demon lurched forward, lowering its depthless face to meet my own. It didn't speak, exactly, but I could feel its raw hunger, its boiling rage. A primal, all-consuming *want* to devour me whole. This creature was unlike anything I had encountered before. It dwarfed every demon in the Bringer's castle. It made them seem insignificant and small.

And it was about to consume Elliot and me alive.

I shrieked as it reached for us, unable to keep a sound of horror from escaping my lips. It pinned us to the ground with a press of its claw, nearly forcing the sword from my hands. Elliot howled miserably, squirming against the thing's charred flesh, but the effort was useless; its claw was the size of a carriage, easily crushing our bodies.

"You are mine, dreamer," the demon thundered, its words more akin to a storm than true syllables. It loomed over me, commanding my attention with its smoking red eyes. I couldn't make myself look away. "Eons I have waited for this moment. It shall not be taken from me."

Tears leaked from my eyes, stinging my frozen cheeks with their warmth. Somnus had sent me to this dream for a purpose, but I had failed him—failed my brother, too.

"You are but a shadow; I shall be the sun," the demon roared.

I ground my teeth in frustration, throwing my weight up into the demon's claws. If Elliot had battled Corruption when he was at his sickest, he would have died. Quickly. Fever had already wasted away his body for months; the physical deterioration in deadly combination with the psychological deterioration that came from Corruption would have been unthinkable. An unwanted image of the Shadow Bringer danced in my peripheral vision, taunting me. He was strong where I wasn't. He had power and command over his surroundings in ways I only borrowed. Enemy or otherwise, had he been here, he would have been able to do something.

This is his fault. All of it—

"You claim to know a man's guilt without first knowing his soul?" Somnus's voice rang, piercing sharp and clear through my mind. *"This reality is beyond that of your Shadow Bringer's. Use what you were given; see the light within the darkness and let it sing."*

At Somnus's direction, I began to see something within the demon: a small vein of light, trickling out from a crack in its armor. The light was no larger than a wisp of hair or the stem of a flower; still, it was there. Waiting. Watching. Yearning to escape the confines of the demon's thick armor and rotting heart. It reacted to my sword immediately, glowing brighter and brighter as the blade absorbed the shadows around it.

The demon made a miserable, furious sound, its teeth flashing once before disappearing into its clouded face. It drew its claws up as it roared, shaking its crown of horns. Elliot and I scrambled away, tripping over ourselves as I fought to hold the sword upright. Shadows were pouring into the sword now, gushing from the demon in a river of darkness.

"It's shrinking!" Elliot exclaimed, looking on in wonder as the demon folded into itself. And as the demon shrank, Elliot's skin cleared;

his eyes became bright and luminous, his hair gleaming with shiny curls. No longer was he clothed in rags, either. He wore garb suitable for a young prince. Even the snow had stopped, replaced by a shower of light.

Within seconds, the demon was reduced to the height and stature of a goat.

Its horns were brambles, its stormy face a mere puff of smoke. I stood over it, slamming my sword into the exposed flesh of its stomach. It made a squealing, whistling sound, falling to the ground in a fit as it tried to back away, but I held on, cutting straight through flesh, blood, and bone. Only the back of the demon's chest plate, still cupping its skin despite its reduced size, stopped me from piercing all the way through.

A rhythmic sound echoed over the pit.

The edges of the pit began to flatten, shivering down until the landscape was smooth and uniform. The mist cleared, as did the shadows that had flowed from the demon's body. An army was revealed, led by a man surrounded by floating swords, a ghostly woman draped in silver and white, and a man armored in crimson and gold.

Xander, Weaver of the Present; Theia, Weaver of the Future; and *Mithras*.

"Stay close," I said, motioning for Elliot to step away from the demon. It gasped out irregular, shallow breaths, releasing a final *wheeze* of air as the sword slid out from its stomach and back into my palm.

"Your report was lacking," Xander, Weaver of the Present, intoned to a soldier at his left. Hundreds of soldiers, faces obscured by masks, stood behind their respective leaders, each marked by the color of their leader. Xander's were in iron, Theia's in diamond, and Mithras's in gold. "This 'threat' is merely a pup," Xander noted.

The ironclad soldier bowed his head. "I'm sorry, my lord. Perhaps the demon moved dreams."

"Enough. It is done," Xander responded, commanding and clear.

Chestnut hair swept back from his temples to rest under an iron crown, framing a strong, shrewd face and bright eyes.

The Light Bringer kicked the demon's lifeless body, knocking loose one of its twiglike horns. "'A face wild as a storm, body protected by the Maker's stolen armor.' A false report, indeed. Pathetic creature," Mithras said, making a face.

"I wouldn't let it sully my boot," Xander said, mouth twisting in displeasure. The ground was stained heavily by the demon's blood, and he stepped to avoid it. "Come, let us return to the citadel."

"Ahem," Theia said, gesturing delicately at Elliot and me. Her pale eyes were wide, her silver hair glossy and full of light, but her form felt false in its perfection; she seemed a sculpture, an animated painting—not living, not breathing. "The dreamers are here. They appear to be lucid."

Their attention snapped to Elliot and me, instantly wary. But the more they examined us, the more they grew uninterested. It was clear we were of no importance. Still, Mithras strode over to us, his golden eyes showing boredom and vague curiosity—but not recognition.

"Is it true? Are you aware, dreamers?" the Light Bringer asked, looming over us. "How rare."

"I can't believe it's you!" Elliot exclaimed, completely ignoring his question. "Fighting demons and stuff—*wow!*"

I gripped Elliot's shoulder, pulling him back a step.

Theia's pale lips drew into a smile. "Just as I said. Lucid."

Mithras's gaze grew distant. Then he placed a single gloved finger against Elliot's brow.

"What are you doing?" Elliot asked innocently, a version of his younger self once more looking from Mithras to the Weavers, then to me. "Your finger's cold."

And just like that, Elliot disappeared.

"*No!*" I lunged forward, unthinking, and swung my fist straight into Mithras's jaw.

Stunned, he fell backward, slamming into the pool of demon blood.

For a second, he was silent, disbelief and rage boiling in his eyes. Then he roared, scrambling upright.

"I merely *woke* him. I should take your—"

"Have grace," Xander admonished. "A hunt, no matter its length or success, does not warrant such base behavior."

Theia nodded, crossing her arms. A row of bracelets trailed up her forearms, linking sporadically to her gossamer sleeves. "He speaks the truth. We must save our energy for what matters." She turned toward her legionnaires, headpiece gleaming. "Ensure that one's memory is adjusted."

Mithras's eyes bore into me, cold and shallow despite their honeyed color. I watched as he readjusted his expression, masking his hate with something resembling indifference.

"My apologies, dreamer," the Light Bringer murmured, giving a short bow. "It has been an arduous day."

I nodded and gave him an understanding smile, willing myself to hide the emotion warring in my veins. "Forgive me for striking you," I offered weakly. "I was merely overwhelmed by your presence."

"You are forgiven," Mithras said, lifting my chin. "It is rare for us to come across a dreamer who is lucid." He smiled sadly, as though he felt pity for me. "Your memory of this dream will fade, but you needn't be afraid. The demon you faced today will no longer haunt you."

No wonder Elliot never told us about seeing a demon. The memory was taken from him before he ever had the chance.

"Why are the Weavers hiding themselves from Noctis?" The question stumbled out of me, uncertain but decisive. "We've been waiting— *begging*—for the Weavers' return. For all we knew, the Shadow Bringer killed them all."

"You know nothing, dreamer," the Light Bringer snapped, looking at me as though I were an insect. "Why don't you take your elixir next time?" he added angrily, leaning over me. "Your brother, too. Continue sleeping in blissful unawareness of the demons that lurk just beyond your subconscious. It is better that way."

Anger and disbelief burned bright behind my temples. "Is it?"

"Tell me, what do you think it is? What do you think you *know*?" Mithras grabbed my wrist, forcing me forward. His hand was upon my forehead before I could duck out of the way. "You are of no significance, dreamer. Go back to the life from which you came."

And then, like glass, the dream shattered.

A gentle wind lapped against my cheek, bringing with it the deep, lingering scent of a forest at midnight. It swept along the curves of the pillows under my head, stirring up notes of juniper and rain. I sighed in contentment, happily stuck in the in-between of wakefulness and sleep. It wasn't often that Elliot allowed an open window while we slept—something about his fear of birds—but he must have decided that the fresh air was worth the risk.

Mother must be burning a fresh candle. Or mixing some new curative, perhaps.

I breathed deeper, trying to decide what the scent reminded me of. The Visstill? No, it was too complex, too dusty. It smoldered with something like incense, something similar to old wood, and twisted itself around a mist-covered field brimming with wild, beautiful things. It was divine.

Elliot curled up next to me, his breathing even and slow. I smiled to myself as I listened to him breathe, reminiscing about the days when he'd pile all his blankets and stuffed animals onto my bed so that he'd be protected from all sorts of things: winter winds that leaked into the creaking walls of our attic room, loneliness, or even the watchful eyes of a monster in the shadows. He was braver than he realized, my brother. Though he never quite understood why.

I reached out to tousle his hair, finding instead the stiff, cold skin of his neck.

"You're freezing," I said, tossing him one of the blankets that towered over me. I adjusted my reach, curling a hand in his hair. It felt softer than usual—not tangled and coarse. "Mother finally got you to brush your hair, huh?"

Elliot didn't answer, so I cracked open an eye.

And nearly jumped out of my skin.

Sleeping next to me, nestled deep in an extravagant pile of pillows, was the Shadow Bringer. Black armor clung to his half-blanketed body, darker than ink and lustrous with newness and quality. Not a single piece was out of place; gone was any trace of the tattered, injury-soaked material of his earthly attire. And he was back to his true form: mouth irritatingly tempting, skin clean and bloodless, and moon-white hair pooling over the velvet beneath him. The only flaws were in his helm; one horn was still missing, and the lower half of his face was no longer caged in metal. His lips, now freed from their iron bars, were unsettlingly close to mine.

I was still studying them when his silver eyes flicked open.

"This is simply the way I am," he murmured, voice thick with sleep. "Cold." He gestured to where my hand still clung to his hair, and I choked on my response, scrambling to the farthest edge of the bed.

A strange half smile ghosted his lips as he settled back into the pillows.

"It's good to see you, Esmer."

"You *tricked* me," I ground out, embarrassment shifting into something coherent and sharp. My new weapon prickled under my skin, dancing with anticipation. "You put me on that stone so that I would replace you here."

For a moment, he looked ready to deny it. Then he said, fixing me with a bright, unbreakable stare, "I did."

I was not expecting a confession.

Nor for him to look like he did, lips caught in an earnest expression.

"What have you been doing all this time? Spreading Corruption, growing your army of demons?" I asked.

At his silence I barreled on, grabbing his shoulder without thinking. Even over his armor, his body was so cold. It felt as if I were touching a corpse, not a man with blood running through his veins. "Who have you killed? What evil acts have you—"

"I have done *unspeakable* evil," he interrupted, mouth slanting into an expression that showed part of his teeth. "In one year, I razed Noctis to the ground and forced all of humanity into chaos and war." Shadows rippled from his eyes, spinning like smoke. "All but those I deemed worthy are Corrupt."

"You're mocking me," I seethed, moving to swipe at the rising shadows. He caught me before I could. While he felt cold, his body was solid, a weapon meant for battle and bloodshed. "I've only been here a few days. A year is impossible," I said.

"One year," he confirmed, his smile growing wider. "Haven't you figured out that the Dream Realm works differently than the mortal world?"

As he moved to still my thrashing, blankets shifting down from his body, I suddenly realized that the scent of juniper, night, and rain was *him*. Against my better judgment, a warm flush raced across my skin. The effect he had on me was becoming difficult to ignore.

"A year has passed, and my demon army is infinite, nourished by Corrupt souls. We are thousands strong, and I've returned to the Realm as their king," he explained.

"*Liar.* How can you command your demons if they're gone?"

His eyes flashed, revealing the smallest shred of disbelief. Had he finally noticed the silence beyond his chambers?

I continued, imagining the rage that was surely churning within him. "They escaped off your balcony—they're *free*. If you hadn't left, they'd still be contained."

Shadows rioted around his arm and swept over the skin where my sword hid. I dug my fingernails into my palms, readying myself for the fight that was surely about to begin. I could still smell the blood of Elliot's demon on my weapon; I had reduced it from a colossus into nothing at all.

Use what you were given, and conquer all that you face.

The Shadow Bringer had tricked me. *Baited* me into taking his place. I had felt sympathy for him before. Fascination, even. But maybe that had all been for a reason—to get me here where I was at this moment, his exposed throat a mere breath from my hidden blade.

He sat up straight, smile vanishing. "Esmer, I never left the tomb. I tried for days, but the stone wouldn't move."

The blade in my palm felt distant. It slid away, no longer interested in a fight. "It's becoming difficult to tell when you're lying or when you're telling the truth," I said.

"I haven't been lying. I assumed you knew I was teasing you."

"No one in my position would have assumed you were teasing," I snapped, incredulous. My pulse was racing; I didn't know why. "In case you've forgotten, it's only acceptable to tease someone if you *like* them— and if they like you back. You betrayed me and left me here to rot, so you can't possibly like me, and I feel nothing but hatred toward you."

"I don't blame you for hating me," he breathed, turning his back to me and putting his feet on the floor. "But if I remember correctly, we held no alliance. I wouldn't call it betrayal if we were never truly on the same side."

He had a point.

"Still, I—"

"And you tried to kill me. Several times, I should add," he said, turning to look at me. "You likely *still* wish to kill me."

He had another point.

"You can't blame me for feeling that way," I said.

He shook his head. "I don't. As you shouldn't blame me for taking measures to ensure my freedom, even if it meant that others might suffer. Others who tried to *kill* me. Betrayal is an act reserved for family, comrades, or lovers. We are none of those three things."

"And yet you came back," I snapped.

Above us, I could hear his chandeliers swaying softly. It was a sound I had never heard before, likely because there had never been true silence in his castle. There were always screaming demons or unsettling sounds from the hall. The lack of sound was strange. Strange and unexpectedly peaceful.

"They really are gone, then? The demons have escaped?" he asked, feeling their absence as much as I did.

"I couldn't contain them. I had no chance," I confessed.

"Then I need to find a way to call them back, or else Corruption will spread ruthlessly throughout the Dream Realm. It will be worse than ever before."

A resounding *crack* thrummed from the ceiling, sending a web of hair and a massive chandelier crashing to the ground. Dark stones ricocheted across the floor, cracking against the bed, and an obsidian statuette the size of my forearm slammed into the Bringer's back as Somnus unfurled from the rubble.

"Your escalating personal drama, *enthralling* as it may be, is distracting." Somnus plucked one of the chandelier's arms from where it tangled in his hair, eyes narrowing in distaste. "Your castle is a wreck, Shadow Bringer. Have you not had enough time to get your affairs in order?"

"Somnus," the Bringer snarled, shadows writhing about his shoulders and down the length of his hands. The room darkened, shadows deepening and drawing near.

"Shall we talk, or do you insist on violence?" the Weaver said, baiting the Bringer.

"I have no words." The Bringer let loose a primal, gut-wrenching roar as he leapt into Somnus.

Shadows tore over them like a crashing wave, and they both fell through the front of the bedchamber, tumbling down to the floor below. I staggered from the canopied bed, glancing at the hole where the chandelier once hung. A wisp of a blanket, one of the Bringer's silk-lined ones, hung by a corner in the rafters, the only evidence of where Somnus had made his perch.

Had Somnus *slept* there?

"I have spent centuries imagining how I'd kill your kind!" the Shadow Bringer bellowed, snarling again as a massive *crash* echoed up through the chamber. Somnus's laugh rang out, clear and full of mirth. "You are not allowed to come *here*"—*Crash! Bang! Crack!*—"and tell *me* what to do."

Somnus released another mirthful laugh, forcing another roar from the Bringer.

I ventured to the stairs leading from the Bringer's room, tucking back into what was left of the wall, and watched as the shadows poured below, seeping from cracks and corners and under the edges of furniture. They billowed out from holes in the walls and floor, swept out from the underside of my hair. All rushing, desperately, to the Shadow Bringer's aid as he raged.

And rage he did.

The Shadow Bringer was wrath embodied, his shadows a vengeful sea of bite and fury. With a slash of his hands, they rose as one, and with a dip of his shoulders, they eddied under and around him. They moved as he moved; he was a living, breathing shadow himself.

It was difficult not to stare—not to gape in admiration as he fought.

But Somnus moved like a shadow, too. The Weaver of the Past was true to his name, flitting in and out of sight as though he were no more than an afterthought, a slip of some long-forgotten memory. The Bringer's shadows couldn't reach—couldn't quite wrap their tendrils around his ghostly form. Somnus swirled around the room in wide, sweeping flashes, dodging the castle's deteriorating structure with the ease of a centuries-old legend.

Then it stopped.

The shadows slowed to a drip, inching forward like a crawling, sluggish thing, quivering around the Bringer's body as he halted in midair, his face twisted in pure, unadulterated wrath. Somnus stood before him, lacing threads of silver through the air. They coiled outward, holding back the Bringer in an enormous web.

Somnus walked to a mostly upright armchair and sank into it with a sigh. "And greetings to you, too, Shadow Bringer. Obstinate as ever, I see. A pity, as that will make things a bit more vexing for me." He thrummed the edge of the chair, vacantly draping a leg over a piece of rubble as though it were a footrest. "I thought the years would have aged you. Though I cannot recall your hair being quite so pale, and you are a degree angrier than you ever were."

The Bringer, frozen in time, fought to speak, jaw clenching and eyes wild.

"What is that? I seem to hear something, but it eludes me," Somnus murmured, feigning a troubled stare around the room. When his gaze sharpened back to the Bringer, his lips angled up in a serpentine grin. "Aha: You appear to be stuck in my web. Allow me to free you." The web gleamed, visibly loosening around the Bringer's upper half.

The Shadow Bringer took a deep, ragged breath. "Let me down."

"Apologies," Somnus said, his voice dropping into a conspiratorial whisper, "but my web will not loosen. You understand."

The Bringer's only answer was a strangled curse.

"Esmer, do come join us." Somnus beckoned, motioning a bone-white hand in my direction. I took a seat atop an overturned chest, careful that its broken edges didn't cut the backs of my legs. "We have much to discuss."

The Bringer cursed again. "Do we, now?"

"Oh, we do, Shadow Bringer. Verily, we do. If you'll be *good*, that is." Somnus threaded his fingers through the web; at his touch, the silvery threads tightened, earning a grunt of discomfort from the Shadow Bringer. "The ward protecting this place has been broken, rendering you as vulnerable as a bird with clipped wings. You could flee...." A thread of his web quickly trimmed pieces of the Shadow Bringer's and my hair, and another thread launched them toward a hole in the ceiling. As soon as the locks touched the air beyond the ceiling, they burned, shriveling into puffs of ash. I flinched, horrified. "But something is preventing you both from leaving this place."

My stomach dropped.

I hadn't imagined that I'd be trapped like the Shadow Bringer. Locked here, yes, but not trapped to the point where if I tried to leave I'd burn. Suddenly I felt too overwhelmed, too powerless, too *small*. I was trapped. Truly and utterly trapped. I needed to figure out how to escape. How to leave this place forever and wake up—even if it meant that the Shadow Bringer might wake up in the Tomb of the Devourer, too.

The Light Bringer's voice rang clear through my memories, a frantic warning.

So above all else, do not harm the Shadow Bringer, and do not release him from his tomb or his castle. We need him there. I need him there. Swear to me, Esmer. Do not release him.

I shoved Mithras's command aside, trying to stay focused. Perhaps he'd have a different opinion now that the Shadow Bringer's demons had been released.

"You cannot die without first fulfilling your Maker-given purpose." Somnus crossed his arms, looking to the hole in the ceiling. "Corruption is festering past the point of no return. It needs to be wiped out for good, and I have a few theories about how your abilities can help us. If your domain does not implode on itself first, that is. Or if you're not too twisted to manage."

"I will never help the Weavers," the Bringer snarled.

"Not just *your* help, Shadow Bringer. We need both of you. You both have certain talents that may prove necessary if we wish to be rid of the demons once and for all," the Weaver said. "Regrettably, your talents are wasted while you remain trapped in this cesspit of a castle."

Certain talents?

As if hearing my call, a few shadows slipped around my ankles, waiting for a command. I nudged them away with my boot, not wanting them to draw Somnus's attention. With my luck, they'd charge him like a feral cat.

"Then summon the rest of the Weavers here, nullify the curse, and be done with it," the Bringer said.

Somnus's thin mouth tightened. "It is not that simple. The Seven are not fully convinced of your innocence, and many are still in hiding, weakened by the demons that plague us. What locks you here binds you regardless of their influence. Only you can solve your freedom now. And the two of you must work together to solve it quickly, or else you shall both perish."

"We'll never escape, if that's the case," I grated out. The Shadow Bringer's castle was massive, but its ornate walls were starting to close in. "The Shadow Bringer and I aren't allied in the slightest."

"Perhaps not," Somnus said, giving an elegant shrug. "I would not know. However, there is something dark in both of your pasts that is haunting you. Something that appears to be haunting you still. My intuition tells me therein lies the key to your survival. Or your demise." He shrugged again. "That is for you to decide."

My stomach instantly knotted.

Something dark in both of your pasts. My past was filled with haunts and hurts. Darkness clung to it like tar, seeping into wounds both fresh and buried. Grief washed over me, ever suffocating. Eden, dead. Mother, dead. Father, dead.

Elliot, gone.

The Shadow Bringer made a sound of utter disgust and said: "The only thing haunting me is *you*, you—"

Somnus sighed, and the Bringer went still, mouth locked in a snarl. His eyes blinked, furious; it was the only movement he was capable of. "It seems you have lost all sense of civility in your imprisonment. You are filled with rage and bitterness and not much else," Somnus said, his eyes softening a touch at this observation. Then he said, turning to face me, "Esmer, perhaps you have an idea of what haunts you. I sent you to visit a dream where the darkness was strongest. What did you see there?"

A winged demon peeked over this unfurling edge, its skull ringed in horns that crowned red smoking eyes. Where its face should have been was a mask of swirling darkness.

Merely remembering the demon sent shivers of disgust down my arms. The fact that it felt familiar, somehow, unnerved me even more. Had I dreamed of it once? Why did it *know* me?

"There was a demon unlike anything I'd ever seen."

"And what did it look like?" Somnus asked.

"It had red eyes that burned like fire, and its face resembled a—"

"Storm." The Shadow Bringer finished my sentence, no longer frozen. "And it has armor. And horns." We locked eyes, an uncertain understanding forming between us. "I dreamed of such a demon as a child."

I nodded grimly. "My brother did, too."

"Interesting," Somnus murmured. "The Weavers believe this same demon is orchestrating part of the Dream Realm's Corruption. Unfortunately, it continues to elude us. We receive reports of its whereabouts, but whenever we are on the cusp of finding it, it either disappears or proves indomitable. It may be stronger than any of us are capable of handling." He placed his hand upon my shoulder, looking unexpectedly sympathetic. "Esmer, this demon has been hunting your family. First, your sister. Eden." A chill raced over my skin, settling hard in my stomach. "Not long after, it found Elliot. That was the dream you just experienced." I squeezed my hands together, horrified at the truth beginning to unravel. "Most recently, it claimed your parents. Naturally, Elliot would be next. Then you, of course. If you survive long enough for it to find you, that is."

I chewed on my thumbnail, trying to come to terms with this terrifying revelation. If I dwelled too long on the fact that Elliot might still be hunted by that demon with smoking eyes, I'd lose what little shred of control I had left.

The Shadow Bringer's shadows raced up Somnus's web, ripping it to shreds.

"Unless you are proposing something that results in both my freedom and your head atop a pike, *get out of my castle and never return*," the Bringer threatened.

Somnus's eyes flashed in irritation. "I came here to request your aid in destroying this demon, and to offer my assistance in helping you flee. If you will not heed my request, then go ahead and rot inside these walls as the world crumbles around you. Despair as the demons you unleashed prey upon Noctis." He added coldly, looking at me, "Your brother included, Esmer. Your time is running out; if you do not find a way to escape this wretched place, your soul will fester here forever."

And with that, he vanished in a swirl of black.

Later that night, if time could even be measured in the Dream Realm, the Shadow Bringer and I stood on his balcony and watched in horror as stars began to fall out of the sky. Every few breaths, a handful would drop. And when the stars dropped, so did part of the castle. Sometimes, the crash of stone would be far away—a distant rumble as a piece of it broke into dust. Other times, it was extraordinarily close and made us flinch. Part of the balustrade broke away with a *crack*, nearly catching my boot. I reeled backward—straight into the Shadow Bringer's armored chest.

I spun around, glaring at him accusingly, and he scowled as though he wanted to throw me off the balcony just to see what would happen. Another *crack* rang out as a stained glass window broke from a lower floor.

"So, your castle really is crumbling. And everything else around it," I said to break the silence.

"It appears that way, yes."

He sounded almost pleased. It was maddening.

"And you chased away our only hope of ever escaping." Somnus hadn't come back; I didn't think he ever would.

"I did."

"And if this world, this—"

"Domain," he completed.

"—crumbles, then we'll be trapped in the Dream Realm forever."

"Correct. We will never again wake in reality and will be confined to the Beyond, which is—"

"The Dream Realm equivalent to hell," I finished.

He crossed his arms as a smirk dusted his lips. "Very good. You're catching on."

"You seem awfully calm." I was livid.

He shrugged. "I have nothing to lose. I've lived in damnation for five centuries; perhaps an eternal stay in the Beyond would pale in comparison."

More stars were released from the sky, glittering as they fell. If the dark purple sky was a tapestry, then the stars were the stitches holding it in place. As it became undone, patches of pure, soul-eating black stared back at us, a steady reminder of what was about to become our world.

"See, that's where we will never be the same. Because I do have something to lose." I glared up at him, trying to ignore how magnificently tall he was and how that height affected me. His lithe body was built for destruction, but it was also unfairly proportioned. Unfairly *perfect*. "I have Elliot. My brother needs me alive and breathing in reality, not stuck in a dream. Surely you have something that you desire enough, too."

"I didn't say I *never* had anything to lose." His silver eyes swirled with shadow; he was clearly contemplating something. "At Somnus's suggestion, there is one tactic we might attempt. But it is a gamble since we're on borrowed time."

"And? What is it?"

"We can walk through past dreams to get a better sense of how to free ourselves. But we will only have a few tries to get it right."

"How many dreams? How many tries?"

He stared at his domain, watching as it slowly tore itself apart. "Perhaps only three. One dream per day."

"Then we have to choose them carefully." I thumbed my lower lip, considering. "Surely there's some clue in your past that will lead to our freedom." And there it was. *Our* freedom. I wondered if he heard it. "Somnus said that the horned demon might be the key. Can you think of three dreams where it was significant in some way?"

The Shadow Bringer ran a gauntlet through his hair, appearing quite vexed. "One."

"Then we'll begin with that one. We need to start somewhere." Another shattered window, another *crack* as part of his castle fell. I wondered how the dream would manifest. If it was anything like the one I'd created, it would consume our immediate surroundings. "Let's go now."

"Visiting my past dreams requires more concentration. They are a part of my subconscious," he said, placing his hands over his armored hips. Maker, he *was* vexed. "I haven't dream walked in some time. My body has been too tense to focus."

"Too *tense?*"

"Too many demons to be on guard against."

"So you're a bit out of practice? What is considered 'some time' to you?"

"I haven't dream walked since before I was locked in here. It could go wrong."

My eyes widened. "Surely not wrong enough that it would be worse than our current fate."

"No, but I might send us somewhere useless." He glanced away, cursing as more stars fell. "My memory is distorted. You've been here a few days; can't you already feel your mind breaking apart? Imagine five hundred years of this."

I shivered. I knew *exactly* what he was talking about.

"We don't have a choice, Shadow Bringer. We need to go—we need to go *now.*"

"Ah," he muttered, rolling his shoulders.

He was stalling. Why was he *stalling*?

"As I said before, past dreams are inextricably connected to the sub-conscious. I can't summon a dream on a whim and walk through it as you did."

"How, then?"

"It's only possible if we're both in a relaxed state of sleep."

I made my way to one of his armchairs as he went to his bed. I curled into the leather, ignoring the chill in the air and how uncomfortable my dress was becoming. "Sleep it is, then. I can handle that."

"We need to be in closer proximity," the Shadow Bringer said, clearly irritated. As though I wasn't understanding him at all. "Stop fidgeting in that chair and join me in my bed."

I blinked open an eye, instantly wary.

"You say that so easily. Like we're *friends*. As if I should listen to you without reason and trust that you won't devour my soul or strangle me in my sleep."

He scoffed in exasperation. "I've watched you sleep before and have never harmed you, have I? In fact, when I watched you sleep in my tomb, I felt no malice, even though you had very nearly killed me. I felt only guilt at leaving you there alone." He made a small sound of disbelief, as if he could hardly understand it himself. "Is that enough to convince you I'm sincere?"

Three things slammed into me at this admission.

The first was that the Shadow Bringer could, perhaps, feel emotions other than anger and misery. The second was that he watched me sleep and it quite possibly *vexed* him to do so. The third was that I was physically affected by him, more and more, in ways I wasn't willing to admit.

My days spent in the Dream Realm must have indeed warped my mind.

"Fine." I climbed into his canopied bed, trying not to think about how much I wanted to bury my nose in his pillows and breathe in his scent. Instead, I lay atop his blankets and faced away from him. "So, I just need to relax, then? You'll do the rest?"

"I must," he murmured.

He shifted so that he faced away from me, but the movement was barely perceptible. His bed was simply too massive; I could have very well been alone and not noticed a difference. Shutting my eyes, I tried to focus on my breathing and not the panic rising in my chest.

"Are you cold?" he asked. "We need to reach a deep state of rest within our subconscious minds. That won't be possible if you're shivering."

He drew a blanket over me—one he likely conjured out of thin air—and promptly removed his arm. But it was no use. Every *crash* sounded like a demon breaking through the door. I hadn't been shivering; I had been *flinching*.

I hated myself for what I was about to ask. "Can you...um."

"What is it?"

"I used to share a room with my sister," I murmured. "After she died, it was my brother. Whenever one of us was anxious or fearful, we'd sometimes sleep with our backs to each other. To feel like we were less alone."

The Shadow Bringer went unnaturally silent; I thought he didn't hear me.

"The sounds of your castle breaking apart are too similar to..."

"The demons?" he supplied.

"Yes," I admitted, my voice a low whisper.

The bed shifted as he drew near me, gingerly placing his back against mine.

I hated craving this shred of simple comfort after everything I'd been through. Hated that it had to be *him*. But if escaping this castle required me to successfully dream walk, I'd do whatever it took. Even if that meant pretending this monster's back was Elliot's or Eden's. But the more I tried to get used to the feel of him, the more uncomfortable I became. He was too cold, and his armor was far too sharp and rigid. One of his overlapping metal feathers bit into my shoulder blade, making me readjust to accommodate it.

"Why are you always in armor?"

He laughed dryly. "I've slept in my armor for as long as I can remember. There's no use for comfortable things in a pit of darkness."

No use for comfort? His bedroom was filled with hundreds of books, elaborate paintings, and plush armchairs. He had a balcony that overlooked a sea of stars. A canopied bed with luxurious pillows, heavy blankets, and silk sheets.

"Your bedchamber is filled with comfortable things. All this velvet and silk."

"Then I suppose over time the armor has become a part of me." He shifted again, and I could feel the metal feathers sink until they were smooth against his back. He fit more easily against me now, his shoulders cold but no longer sharp. "I have no reason to wear anything else."

"Well, now you do. You're not very comfortable to lie against."

He sighed through his nose and went silent again. For a moment, I thought he had fallen asleep.

"You're still shivering."

"I'm not shivering," I insisted, flinching as another part of his castle dropped away with a *crack*.

A curtain of shadow suddenly rose from the floor, cocooning the bed in a sphere of darkness. It made a low *whooshing* sound as it swirled around us, perfectly replacing the erratic *cracks* and *bangs* from the rest of the castle. The comfort it brought was immense; my breathing evened out almost immediately.

"Thank you," I said, burying my nose into his pillows and hoping he didn't notice.

His breathing hitched. Perhaps I'd struck a nerve.

But then I felt him relaxing, too, stretching his long, armored legs so that they brushed against mine.

"I need to thank you, too," he murmured. "This is the first time in five hundred years that I haven't fallen asleep to demons screaming."

I swallowed hard, uncertain as to what I should say.

"May it be the first of many," I finally whispered. "I never want to hear their screams again."

A few soft, slow moments passed, marked by the even *whoosh* of the cocoon.

"Esmer," the Shadow Bringer suddenly said, his tone deadly serious. "I will do what I remember, but if this goes awry, we could find ourselves trapped in a deep layer of the Dream Realm. Or some false, incorporeal pocket. It could take us years to escape if a Weaver doesn't intervene."

"We don't have time to consider hypotheticals, Bringer."

"It wouldn't be fair if I *didn't* consider this very possible hypothetical with you. Because if I don't go deep enough, the dream might be useless, wasting a day and bringing us closer to our ruin. Do you accept that kind of risk?"

I didn't hesitate to answer. "I do."

"I could go alone," he urged. "Even if I became trapped in a deeper level of the Realm, time would function as usual on this layer. You'd wake up after a restful sleep, and I'd wake up, too; only I'd be a few centuries older."

"Then don't trap us. Guide us true."

He made a sound of approval, shifting again so that his spine better aligned with mine.

"Sync your breathing with mine," he prompted. I could faintly feel the deep rise and fall of his breaths.

In, out.

In, out.

In, out.

My mind lifted, guided by the Shadow Bringer's inexplicable prodding. He urged me to follow.

And so I did.

For the first time in years, I woke to the sound of laughter.

It rang out from the belly of a child and boomed deep and hearty from the throat of an older man. Perhaps the child's father or grandfather. Laughter in its purest, sweetest form. The kind of laughter that could drive out fear and replace it with something warm and beautiful.

The Shadow Bringer loomed above me, scowling. "Can you stand, or have you lost the use of your legs?"

"Aren't you demanding?" I remarked, matching his tone.

We were in an empty parlor. Lavish and pristine, its walls and floors were bedecked in patterned rugs, bookshelves carved into trees and horses, embroidered chairs, and several paintings of a happy, beautiful family—a father, a mother, and their dark-haired child. I sat up, watching as mist filtered through windows that dotted the room's length. Its only exit, a towering archway, swirled with more mist, obscuring whatever rested beyond.

"Follow me," he said with a sigh, stalking toward the arch. "It's as I feared; my memory is too distorted. This dream isn't where I meant for us to go."

Instead of following, I ruffled through a vase of wildflowers and peonies, dipping low to breathe in their scent. A feeling of dread rose up, unbidden. A feeling of sinking, of dirt being shoved in my throat, and walls closing in.

Focus, Esmer.

From beyond the mist, laughter rang out again, snapping me from my spiraling thoughts.

I set the vase down, ready to clear my mind and move forward. "So, where are we? Do you recognize this place?"

He took a cursory glance around the room. "It feels familiar. I may have lived here once."

"It looks similar to your castle," I said, pointing to a landscape I'd seen in the Shadow Bringer's antechamber. "Though yours is obviously more somber. And in ruins, given its demonic residents."

"*Former* residents," said the Shadow Bringer, his voice lifting in false wonder. "A horde of demons unleashed upon the world. What would Mithras say?"

"The demons wouldn't have escaped if you hadn't forced me to be your sacrifice," I snapped.

"Sacrifice? I tried to make you my *heir*. But how fortunate for you that—"

"*Fortunate* for me? If it weren't for you, my sister and parents would be alive and I'd be home and at peace with my family. Not here with you in an eternal nightmare."

"I already told you. I didn't harm your family."

"How can you be so sure? You don't even remember how Corruption started, Shadow Bringer. You have scarcely any memories at all, even though the tales blame you with absolute certainty." I crossed my arms, daring him to speak. When he didn't, I barreled on. "If I help you through this, you owe me something in return."

"Your promised freedom should be motivation enough."

"Not when my freedom means a pitch-black tomb with no food or water. Or the Light Bringer deciding I've broken our agreement and punishing Elliot. I want to learn more about this demon—and hopefully this gets us closer to escaping your castle—but it still forces me to place a lot of faith in you." I sank into a sofa, picking at the fraying edge of an embroidered lion. "Faith that I don't quite have at the moment."

The Bringer shot me an exasperated look. "You're overestimating how much choice you have. Hurry up. We need to keep moving before the dream collapses."

Try me, Shadow Bringer.

Sweeping an arm out, I gestured toward the parlor's several book-cases. Thick, leather-bound tomes sat within each one, some organized by color, others by topic or even length.

"Perhaps my *choice* could be to first read every single book in this place, since you want me to 'hurry up' so badly." I picked one at random, flipping through its gilt-edged pages, then another, a red monstrosity with an embossed shield in its middle. Each held words—clear, coherent words. Strange that a dream could be so detailed and visceral that it mimicked reality itself. I'll admit I was being childish, but a few things needed to be made clear if we were going to work together as a team. "Every single one. Even the storybooks with all the illustrations."

Like a warrior drawn to battle, the Bringer approached, armor gleaming wickedly. "Then I will destroy them before you can," he threatened, shadows darkening the edges of the room and crawling toward his out-reached hands. "Or I could pick you up and drag you with me. Your *choice*."

There was that flicker again, just below my wrist.

Now wasn't the time to battle the Shadow Bringer—not when I was pitifully untrained and he looked perfectly capable of strangling me with a single curl of his index finger. But my sword was insistent. It itched underneath my skin, forcing my attention as though it were suffocating on blood and bone.

He caught the uncomfortable expression on my face. "Fitting. You're afraid of me," he noted. "Perhaps I won't need force after all. You'd follow me regardless, fearful for your life."

"I am absolutely not afraid of you," I shot back, wincing again as the sword prodded my palm.

"See? You flinch from me." The Bringer snarled, crossing his arms in a mirror to me. "So, what would I owe you for your cooperation?"

"What I want is your knowledge," I began, taking a small bit of satisfaction at the surprise on his face. "Teach me how to use the shadows, or other ways of power in the Realm. And then, when we're free from your castle, you will do everything you can to stop Corruption. Even if that means partnering with the Weavers and treating Somnus with civility."

"What you're asking is no simple task. Stopping Corruption isn't like bandaging a small cut. It's a centuries-old wound as wide and weeping as a tempest."

"Your memory is broken. Perhaps you're just forgetting how," I said through gritted teeth.

The Shadow Bringer pinched the skin between his brow, considering. Then he said quickly, meeting my eyes, "Fine. But I cannot agree to partnering with the Weavers. Or Mithras. Not when I'd rather see them dead."

Begging to be unleashed at the most ill-timed moment, the sword launched from my palm, warming with life when its hilt met my hands. It thrummed softly, as if it held a soul within. And maybe it did. The soul of a demon so powerful that it could warp mountains and blot out the sky. A demon so mighty that Xander, Theia, and Lord Mithras sought to crush it with the power of their three legions.

The Bringer recoiled, staring at me as though I'd grown a second head.

He dropped his gaze to the sword, mouth thinning. "Did Somnus give you that?"

I gripped the handle tight. "I know how to use it."

"Good," he said simply, unsheathing his own blade. It was a brutal thing, a twin to my own. Pure, light-eating black. "Show me you're not afraid of the shadows that bind us."

With a snarl, he pounced, blade raised high and shadows storming in his wake.

And something in me snapped.

My sword unlocked some raw, instinctual knowledge about battle. How to parry and block. How to handle the weight of a blade and prepare for the onslaught of another. How to study an opponent's body and react accordingly. So when I met the Shadow Bringer's powerful swing with a counter of my own, his eyes widened—then gleamed bright with some feverish, unhinged thrill. Shadows ebbed to their corners as the Bringer launched forward again, slinking down into the floor as though he wanted this fight to be between us, and us alone.

But that wasn't what I—what the *sword*—wanted.

We wanted the dark, wanted the rise of shadow and night under our control. The shadows rushed toward me, clinging to my feet and dancing along the lines of my arms.

"They truly *do* answer to you," the Shadow Bringer pondered, cutting right and aiming a strike at my shoulder. I deflected easily, intuiting where to position the blade. "But can you control them?"

"That's where I need"—I ducked under another of his swings, using the rug underfoot to steady my balance—"your *help*." Shadows clung to the both of us now, rising from our bodies like second skins. Around the Bringer they roiled, reflecting his fury and challenge, but around me they shuddered, quivering between varying levels of opacity. "And you need mine."

A strong wind began to circle the room, overturning chairs, shattering glass, and scattering books across the floor. It centered on the Shadow Bringer, coiling through the shadows that now wrapped his limbs and towered high atop his back. In a few moments, he had transformed completely, black wings unfurling from his shoulders and new armor covering most of his skin in dark, sharp edges.

"Do I?" he asked, slamming his blade into the ground. Shadows exploded over the room, sucking away all light and color. "I've thought of a different proposal. One that involves ripping this dream apart from the inside and then doing the same to my domain. After that, we can crawl out of the Beyond and end Corruption on our own terms."

"That is a terrible idea," I hissed.

The walls bent in and out, flexing like some giant, breathing creature. They shook under his destruction, rattling as he peeled away their layers. But even as the walls fell, they resisted—reversed back into place as though their creator, somewhere beyond this scene, fought to repair each broken piece.

Then something changed.

The Shadow Bringer's face twisted from triumph to alarm; his eyes widened, and his jaw clenched against whatever internal demon he was battling. Underneath us, the floor gave way, collapsing in on itself as mirrors shattered and furniture fell into cracks, disappearing into the void below.

I screamed, staggering aside as a bookcase nearly crushed me, and tripped on a globe as it rolled into my shin. I fell toward one of the widening cracks, scrambling to grip something, *anything*, as the void, gaping open like the maw of some ungodly monster, pulled me down. It was just a dream—*everything was just a dream*—but fear, dark and terrible, jolted through my skin, physical as fear could be.

As if roused from a stupor, the Shadow Bringer snapped his eyes to mine. He dove in a whorl of shadow and feathers, pulling me against him just as the ground dropped away with a final *crack*.

For a few wingbeats, we were silent, suspended in the air and staring into the emptiness below.

The Bringer's breathing was more ragged than I expected, his chest rising and falling in deep, labored pulls. Even his eyes looked pained. Haunted. Guilty. It didn't make sense. He had tried to rip the dream apart—wasn't this what he wanted? What was the point in regret *now*?

My fingers clung to his shoulders, desperate for a better grip. One slip—or one change of the Shadow Bringer's mind—and I'd plummet.

"I'm not going to drop you," he snapped, annoyed. Still, he made a point to reposition his arms. "As I said, we must walk these dreams together. That can't happen if you fall into an abyss."

"We won't be walking in *any* dreams if this is how you'll be acting,"

I cut back. "You said we had only three dreams. *Three dreams* until your domain shatters with us in it. I would much prefer to not end up in the Beyond."

Almost imperceptibly, his claw-tipped fingers tightened. "I might be able to warp this dream into another. If we don't wake up from this, we won't waste another day."

"You're mad," I criticized.

"I'm not in my right mind, no." *And I haven't been in some time*, he seemed to imply.

Debris continued to fall as the room disintegrated around us, swallowing any hope of its restoration. Stone collapsed into vapor, books ripped themselves apart as they burned, and the painting of the family tore itself into shreds. I half expected the seven Weavers to appear in front of us, shaking their heads in dismay at our complete and utter failure.

The Shadow Bringer cried out in pain, arching his back as though he were struck by lightning.

Screams lurched from his throat, even as he ground his teeth against them. His limbs shuddered under the weight of whatever was attacking him, and in the chaos, his grip slackened. I buried my hands in his armor, but the material was slippery, liquid.

I gasped, barely holding on as his body continued to thrash in pain.

And then the wings upon his back melted into dust, sending us plummeting into darkness.

I can't remember when I stopped screaming.

Something wet pressed against my cheek, reeking of dead fish and rotting wood. I sprang up, horrified—only to find mud dripping from me. Cold, slimy, foul-smelling mud. It coated the side of my face, crawled down my neck, and burrowed itself all over the folds of my clothing.

Great.

I wiped it from my eyes, trying to focus on the dimly lit landscape that surrounded me. From what I could see, I sat before a dark pond, its edges webbed in cattails, haze, and scum. A shadow of something splashed atop the water before disappearing again, impossible to see below the surface. At the sound of someone spitting, I whirled around. Dull gray eyes met mine through the mist.

The Shadow Bringer coughed, flicking mud from his gauntlets in disgust.

"My power is beginning to fail," he muttered. As if to demonstrate, he opened a fist, scowling as a small shadow appeared. It quivered pathetically before vanishing in a puff of smoke. "I will soon have nothing."

"How is that even possible?"

"I don't know." He made a frustrated, violent sound. "It was a mistake to take us here. I should have taken us back to the castle and started anew."

Erratic splashing of a large, unknown creature sounded again over the water.

I shuddered. "I'm really not looking forward to that demon finding us."

"You want *it* to find *us*?" The Shadow Bringer gave a small, dreadful smile, catching me off guard. "We can find it ourselves."

"And how do you propose we do that, Shadow Bringer?"

"We find my past self. If we can find him, the demon will surely follow." His smile slipped, discarded like an ill-fitting mask. "Something about this place feels familiar. I think there is a village beyond the mist."

"A village, out here? Are you sure?"

He tilted his head, considering. "Mostly."

I sighed, eyeing the forest and the strange, clouded pond. A cottage, filthy and falling apart, stood at its edge, but there were no other signs of human life. No lights, no voices. Only the sound of water lapping against mud and the occasional splash of some creature in the pond. I shivered again.

"Lead the way, then."

And he took my hand, guiding me forward.

There was not a village beyond the mist. There was an entire *city* beyond the mist.

Built from luminescent stone, a large city sprawled from the forest, fading into the distance as it trailed along the edge of a sea. A lively wind, rising from the water and swirling through the streets, dusted the air in salt, citrus, and something nostalgic and sad. I lingered for a moment, trying to place the particular scent, but as quickly as it appeared, it vanished into the night. I glanced at the Shadow Bringer, who was analyzing the city, his expression unreadable. The shadows that had lived within his eyes were broken, stripped away with the rest of his power.

"Do you know where we are now?" I asked.

His mouth opened slightly, as if he were tasting the seam of some long-forgotten memory. "Istralla." Then, more confidently, "This is Istralla."

"The capital of Noctis," I murmured, looking around with a new sense of purpose.

While this wasn't how I'd envisioned seeing Istralla for the first time, it felt wonderful nonetheless, watching as the city sparkled with promise and light. But the longer I looked, the quicker its fine edges began to unravel. Some structures made sense—sprawling cottages, an open-air marketplace, dress shops—while others twisted into bizarre shapes and sizes. All around us, buildings shifted into trees, trembling between forms at the edge of our vision, as others faded in and out, disappearing and reappearing in time with our breathing.

The twisted beauty of a dream, I supposed: half reality, half but a shadow of truth.

I started to comment on this observation, but the Shadow Bringer was no longer at my side. Whirling around, I scanned the forest and the city's edge. Had he been forced out of this dream, somehow?

Then, there he was, waltzing into what appeared to be an inn.

"Are you *kidding* me?" I seethed, hurrying to follow.

The inn seemed rather nondescript in comparison with Istralla's more extravagant buildings, filled with regular-looking people gathered around regular-looking tables and the warm glow of a hearth at its center. The Shadow Bringer was easy to spot, a smear of darkness amid colorfully dressed patrons.

"I take it you have some kind of lead?" I asked under my breath.

He ignored me and stalked toward a noisy group of men, glaring daggers into the deepest parts of their souls as they laughed around ale and a half-eaten roast.

"Begone," he snarled, seizing a dinner knife and holding it under the nearest man's chin. "You have no place here. Leave, and I will spare your throats."

I sucked in a breath. He was hopeless. An utter *fool*. Without his powers, how could he antagonize an entire crowd of people—some of whom were armed—and survive? Dream or not, a battle was still a battle.

Taking a step back, I ducked behind the largest man I could find, his belly spilling over the table at which he sat. If I hid, maybe I could avoid being associated with the Shadow Bringer altogether.

"My companion and I have need of your table," he added, gesturing to where I hid. I recoiled, waiting for people to start staring. Or attacking. But the men didn't so much as glance up from their food and drink. Irate, the Bringer continued, lowering his voice into a deadly command. "I will not ask a second time."

Still, the men refused to move. They continued joking and carousing, drinking heartily and laughing deeply. I watched, mildly amused as the Bringer's expression slipped from disbelief to utter fury.

"I warned you," he said simply, slamming the knife's hilt into the man's skull.

Except it didn't *slam*, exactly.

The hilt bounced harmlessly off the man's head, no more a threat than a push from an infant.

The man reached up to pat the spot where the Bringer hit him. "Aye, boys, I'm thinkin' there's a bug flyin' round here. Just bit me on the head!" The Shadow Bringer tried again, throwing his full weight into the swing. "Aye, ouch! It just 'appened again!"

His companions gave a pointed look about the room, laughing wildly.

"Mate, there ain't any bugs flyin' round here."

"No, I swear it! The spot's itchy an' everythin'," the man protested, much to the hilarity of the others. Huffing, he pointed dramatically at a fly buzzing around the ceiling. "See? *See?* There it is!"

Another man chimed in, jabbing him playfully in the side. "More like yeh've drank too many ales for that thick skull of yours to 'andle."

"Aye, shut it," he responded, shoving himself away from the

table—nearly colliding with a visibly disturbed Bringer—and stormed out of the inn. His companions followed shortly after, quickly downing the rest of their ale on the way out.

After a short pause of his own, the Bringer sat down, selecting the most shadowed part of the table to sulk.

"No effect, huh?" I asked, sitting across from him. On my way over, no one acknowledged my existence. Not one person looked up, even if I nudged their back or waved my hands in front of their face. "It's like we're ghosts."

The Bringer grunted in agreement, steepling his hands under his nose. "Some dreams are like that. It means that these patrons aren't real; they're merely figments from the dreamer's imagination."

"*Your* imagination, then?"

He ignored me, instead sweeping his hands across the table to grab an empty cup and plate.

"I think we have more important things to figure out than feasting on imaginary dream food."

He shot me a withering look. "Do we, now?" At my confused silence, he touched the edge of the cup, concentrating as it filled itself with a ruby-red liquid. Wine, likely. *Or the blood of his innocent prey*, I thought darkly. At another touch, the plate—and then several more—bloomed with fresh fruit, seared meats, and a slice of mysterious dessert. "Go ahead, figure out your important things. Then you can watch me eat, if that's what you would prefer."

I crossed my arms. "I don't want any of your food."

"Good. Because I did not offer you any."

Insolent bastard.

"How is this allowed, anyway?" I asked, gesturing at his admittedly delicious-looking treats. "I thought you couldn't use your powers."

Selecting a cut of lamb, he took his first bite, frowning slightly as he chewed. "If an act of creation does not disrupt the dream's purpose, then it is allowed."

As I watched the Shadow Bringer eat, slightly amused that he was now able to eat through his half-broken helm, I wondered at the point of it all. Was it for the sake of normalcy, to eat and even sleep in a dream? It made sense, I supposed. If I had been locked in a castle for centuries, maybe I'd want to keep human habits, too. He brought the cup to his mouth, drinking deep. But when he brought the glass away, sensuous lips flushed with dark liquid, he still wore a frown.

"For someone eating food fit for a king, you sure scowl a lot."

"Envious, are we?" he asked, taking another sip. Still, the scowl stuck.

"No. I'm not hungry," I protested, crossing my arms. Just as my stomach unleashed an absolutely pathetic growl. An instinctual reaction at seeing food, probably.

The Bringer's mouth ticked up, taking pleasure in the fact that he'd caught me in a lie.

"Suit yourself," he drawled, leaning back to glare at the ceiling and finish his wine, which refilled itself whenever the liquid dropped too low. "I will continue relishing my 'food fit for a king.'"

I eyed an especially beautiful strawberry, unable to ignore the hunger prying at my insides. Maybe I'd spoken too soon. Why *wouldn't* I want to partake in a feast fit for a king? Plopping the berry into my mouth before I could think otherwise, I closed my eyes, awaiting a delicious, tart burst of juice.

Instead, rancid slime filled my mouth, causing me to gag.

"A hatred for strawberries. Interesting."

"What? No. It was rotten—" I choked as its taste clung to my tongue. Grabbing the nearest cup, I motioned for the Bringer to fill it. "Fill this—please—*ugh*." I took a drink before the liquid had even pooled halfway up the glass, desperate to rid the foulness from my mouth.

Except I almost spit *that* out, too.

I hadn't taken more than a few sips of wine in my entire life, but the taste of it never bothered me. No, normal wine was fine. It was the fact that the Bringer's concoction tasted watery, mud-like, and vaguely sour.

"Is there a problem?" he asked.

I gaped at him. "Do you not taste it—or smell it? It's all wrong."

At first, the food and drink appeared perfect, pristine. But now the truth of each smell was unmistakable: The fruit was rotten, the meat was burnt leather, and the dessert looked to be powdered with ash, not sugar.

"Ah." His eyes widened behind his helm, a rare glimpse of mortification dawning there. "My ability to conjure food was stunted in the castle. I may have forgotten the taste of things."

His sense of taste was forgotten? More like absolutely *destroyed*.

"How long has it been since you ate something from outside of the Dream Realm?"

The Bringer stopped to consider, still drinking from his glass. "Five hundred years, give or take."

My mouth dropped open. "Five hundred *years*? Maker, stop drinking that—you'll poison yourself."

"It is fine enough for my tastes." He avoided my attempts at stealing his drink, waving the glass just out of my reach. Still, when he took another sip, his mouth twitched in displeasure. "But if it does not suit yours, craft your own."

I inspected an empty cup, willing it to fill to the brim with a rich, fragrant wine. When nothing happened, I sat back in frustration. "It's not working."

"In my castle, you walked into an entire dream from memory. A cup of wine or a slice of bread should be simple."

"Coming from someone who can't even make a strawberry taste edible," I muttered, earning a stiffening of the Bringer's posture. "What?"

He moved closer, the wine stain on his mouth looking more and more like blood. "You insult me casually for someone who desires my knowledge."

"Show me how, then. It can be the first thing you teach me. As per our bargain."

"That's what you want your first lesson to be? A tutorial on the art of food?"

"I'm just interested in the act of creating, is all," I said, bristling.

And it was true. I wanted to be free from the Dream Realm, but part of me also wanted to learn more about it. What it meant, how it worked—how to move within it and become powerful enough to withstand a demon's attack. Dreaming had proved itself to be a double-edged sword of beauty and pain, reality and illusion, and I couldn't deny that parts of it were fascinating. If that meant cooperating with the Shadow Bringer, then so be it.

"Are you, now?" With a slight furrow to his brow, the Bringer grabbed my empty cup. "Perhaps I'll attempt to explain. But I expect you to produce something edible."

I couldn't help it. I almost smiled.

He must really miss food—even though he's trying to hide it.

"Then I'll make you the finest wine in all the world," I said.

He tilted his head, nearly smiling himself. "We will see."

The Shadow Bringer explained the process with a surprising amount of care, detailing the importance of past experiences and memories as key ingredients when crafting something in a dream. Even if the creation was a new object or special ability—something like wings, or erupting fire from one's fingertips—it needed to be drawn from memory to be fully functional. Effective wings, for example, required the memory of birds in flight, the feel of feathers, and the sensation of jumping and falling. But when honed correctly, imagination could be even stronger. A dreamer with a strong imagination could craft extraordinary, lifelike creations, drawing from thoughts as powerful as memory itself. Untamed, however, imagination held risk. An imagined sword might erupt into a serpent. Or a candle. An inferno, even.

As I concentrated on the glass in front of me, I leaned into both techniques, remembering a summer drink of plum juice and crushed rose petals but also imagining what it might feel like to taste liquid silk. The glass filled slowly as I decided upon the right color, finally settling on a shimmering purpled ruby.

I drew the glass to my lips, expecting something dreadful.

At the first sip, it tasted wild. Fragrant rose, oak, and plum. It wasn't wine, exactly, but it wasn't juice, either. And the texture was exactly as I had imagined: Softer than silk upon the tongue, it slid down my throat like a caress, tingling as it moved. The Shadow Bringer must have noticed the delight in my expression—or the rapidly dwindling liquid in my cup—because he snatched it from my fingertips, looking quite smug as he brought it to his lips.

"Hey, I wasn't finished!"

The Bringer gave a throaty, contented sigh as he polished off the drink, likely not intending for the sound to be heard. His eyes flicked up, a command plainly written there. For a moment, I wondered what it would be like to not taste food or drink for five hundred years. Was it really possible to forget something as fundamental as *taste*?

Based on the Bringer's euphoric expression, it seemed so.

"Fine, fine. I'll fill it again. Just—stop staring at me like you want to eat *me*," I said, face warming under the heat of his stare. "I have to concentrate."

This went on for some time. I would imagine some new drink or food, and we'd partake in it together, the Bringer in a constant state of muted awe as he remembered what was lost. And he loved it all— bitterness, richness, sweetness—and demanded more, tempting me to try new and outrageous creations from my own imagination. Milk in the form of snowflakes. A crispy peach. A sugared flower, its petals dusted in a honeyed perfume.

We were in the middle of trying an edible moon, its glowing surface made of lemon and airy, cake-like dough, when the whole inn erupted in a cheer. I nearly fell out of my chair at the sound, so used to the quiet hum of the inn's banal chatter.

"Too much wine?" he asked, leaning forward to steady me.

"Of course not," I snapped, unwilling to admit that I did, in fact, feel a bit lightheaded. An imagined feeling, but one I couldn't quite shake.

"Here." He swept a finger underneath my lip, brushing off a stray droplet. "As I said before, imagination reigns supreme in the Realm." He examined his thumb, now slightly damp, then licked it. "Experiences feel immersive here. Sometimes more so than they do in reality."

"Well, I feel more like a ghost, considering we don't exist to anyone here." Alarmingly, I could sense another flush rising on my skin; I hoped it wasn't visible. "What about our creations?" I eyed the half-eaten moon, wondering what would happen if I threw it across the room. "The people here can't see us, but can they see what we've made?"

"If they can, they're too hollow to care. The original dreamer, however, may notice."

"You mean *you*? We are in one of your past dreams, aren't we?"

"Indeed we are."

"Where could you be?" I mused, scrutinizing the faces around us.

None seemed aware that we—or our piles of plates heaped with interesting combinations of food and drink—existed. And if the dreamer was a past version of the Shadow Bringer, no one looked even remotely like him. Not that anyone could, exactly. Even with his face still partially covered by his helm, he was deadly in his beauty. And was *his* skin a little flushed from the wine, or was I imagining that, too?

Definitely my imagination.

I stood up, ignoring my dizziness, and attempted to see what the crowd was staring at. How much time had we mindlessly wasted? Had we missed something important—some clue that would help us escape his castle?

Among the crowded bodies, I spotted a raven-haired boy, his eyes warm under the inn's light. He waved a ribbon overhead, its length glistening like scales, and began to recite some kind of wild, theatrical tale as the crowd looked on, mesmerized by his every word. I leaned in closer, trying to make out what he was saying.

"Come back here," the Shadow Bringer protested, vaporizing a few plates to make room for more. A thread of shadow—just a shiver of his power—snaked out and grabbed the back of my dress. "Next I will try a vegetable. A carrot, perhaps."

"We just ate a moon, and you want a *carrot?*" I asked, laughing. The Shadow Bringer returned my mirth, a crooked half smile on his lips. I dragged a hand through his thread of shadow, snapping it. "I'm trying to listen to that boy. Maybe he's important to the dream."

"I do not care about some pointless child."

Maker, he *sounded* like a child.

"Well, maybe you should, considering we have no other leads to go on."

The boy raised his voice, almost as if he knew the Shadow Bringer was ignoring him, and continued on with his story, flinging up his ribbons in a dramatic sweep. At the same moment, the Bringer sent another thread at me, this time aiming for my feet, and I was too distracted by his half smile to notice. I twisted, trying to catch myself, only to land squarely in his lap—just as the boy's ribbons turned into a trio of serpents, writhing their gilded bodies as they soared overhead.

This caught the Shadow Bringer's attention.

He slid a hand over my waist, pulling me away just as one of the ribbon serpents would have careened into my head. Unfortunately, the timing was a bit too hasty. His chair toppled out from underneath him, catching our legs and sending us sprawling. For a single suspended moment, we were tangled in each other.

A droplet of wine trailed from his mouth, and it took everything in me not to trace it with my hands. Or my lips. The roar of the inn dulled to a muffled growl.

What was *wrong* with me?

I shoved the feeling down, mortified. I had never been in a romantic entanglement, never experienced what it was like to touch and be touched, never felt what it was like to be loved and cherished in a way that only a lover could. Logically, my reaction could be blamed on that. He was a beautiful man, and he was staring at me as though I was beautiful, too.

His proximity was *really* making it difficult to see him as a villain.

But then, as moments do, it shattered.

"And I battled them all!" the boy shouted, wielding an imaginary sword as he pretended to fight the serpents. "They threatened our lives. They wanted to drag Istralla into the sea!" He ducked as one of the serpents dipped lower. The crowd backed away, muttering in astonishment.

"That boy. Is he someone important?" I asked shakily.

The Bringer muttered something noncommittal, slowly easing us both to our feet.

"But do not fear. I vanquished the demons! So, you are safe now, and you owe that safety to me," the boy declared, grinning with all the pride in the world. And he bowed low, the hem of his oversized cloak touching the floorboards. "Now," he continued, straightening himself, "my winnings, please."

The crowd didn't move; they were too preoccupied with eyeing the flying serpents.

"Oh. Um, sorry," the boy said sheepishly, turning the serpents back into ribbons with a wave of his hand. "I had them under my control, you know. You were never in any harm. I promise."

The Shadow Bringer returned to drinking his wine, no longer interested. "Greedy child. Desperate to rid the poor of their coin, even while dreaming."

It wasn't coin that the boy was after, though. As he moved about the inn, he collected donations of food and drink, using his cloak as a makeshift pack to carry it all. He arranged his growing collection as he went, ensuring that nothing spilled. Loaves of bread, a small sack of potatoes, three bottles of milk—he took it all, thanking each patron with a beaming smile. When he made it to the back of the room, nearing where the Bringer and I sat in our shadowed corner, his eyes lit up.

"Now what is *this*?" the boy wondered aloud, bounding over to our outlandish plates and scooping up the half-eaten moon. He was a striking boy: fine, noble features and black hair curling to his shoulders. "A ball of cake? Huh."

"Ridiculous child," the Shadow Bringer scoffed, making the moon disappear with a quick wave. "These creations are not for you."

"Was that really necessary?" I whisper-shouted. Even though it was clear the boy couldn't hear or see us, I still felt as though he could.

The boy stared at his empty hands.

"It's already happening," the boy muttered, brimming with great sorrow. "I must hurry. No time to waste."

He snatched two of our plates, tucking them into his cloak and hurrying away before the Bringer could react. Halfway through the crowd, the boy turned around, rushing back to our table to snatch a cinnamon cake from under the Bringer's nose.

"Why you—" the Bringer started, grabbing the boy by the wrist. It was useless, though. The boy couldn't be held. As if he had grasped smoke or water, the Bringer's hand merely slipped away. But not before the boy glanced up and showed us his eyes.

Expressive and framed in dark lashes, with the beginnings of small silvery shadows dancing within their depths. I didn't have to guess; I knew immediately who this boy was.

And, based on his stunned expression, so did the Shadow Bringer.

We sprinted through Istralla under a film of salty mist, trailing the boy as he ducked into the surrounding forest. Even with his pack of food and drink, he ran as though he carried no extra weight, darting under boughs and avoiding roots with expert precision. The mist didn't burden him, either; it was denser now, clinging to every surface and suffocating the air.

"So that boy—he's really you," I panted, struggling to match the Bringer's pace.

"Evidently." The Shadow Bringer lanced me with a brief, annoyed look over his shoulder. "Remember what I said about imagination. Keep up."

Keep up? My legs felt like rocks and my head swam from all the wine, but I was dreaming—and I was running as if I weren't. I should have been nimble, not trailing behind the Bringer and tripping every few steps.

Working through my imagination, I shielded my feet from rocks and twigs, lightened my limbs, and lengthened my stride. My dress was next. It was useless and flimsy in this terrain, so I altered it into dark, close-cut pants and a belted tunic. A biting wind cut through the trees, impossible to ignore, so I added a silken cloak lined with thick, comfortable velvet, taking inspiration from the Bringer's attire and giving it properties of smoke and shadow. Running became easy, instinctive. The more I focused on what was in front of me, the simpler it felt. So I fixed my eyes on the Shadow Bringer, mimicking the way he moved.

And the Shadow Bringer moved as he always did: like a creature of living darkness.

Even without his shadows to strengthen his steps, he ran through the forest as though he were a spirit that dwelled within it.

"Do you know where we're going?" I asked, releasing a stream of pent-up air. I didn't feel like a creature of living darkness, but at least I was keeping up. "It's your dream. You really should know."

"I have an idea." The Bringer spared a glance over his shoulder, evidently surprised that I was still there. Or maybe he was surprised that my clothes now looked a little like his. "Your heart doesn't beat in the Realm," he added, picking up his pace. "Eliminate its influence, and you'll stop gasping for breath every five steps. We breathe here merely out of habit."

"I'm not gasping. And my heart is fine."

"You are. And it is not."

Unconvinced, I brought a palm to my chest. And my wrist. And my neck. But my body was quiet. Nothing but a hollow, silent shell. "Where is my heart?"

"Ask the Maker."

"I'm asking *you*, Shadow Bringer."

He sighed. "The Maker designed it, fearful that humankind would forget themselves within the Realm. It's one technique of many used to determine whether one is awake or simply dreaming. Out of habit, however, dreamers still tend to breathe. Or to feel the ghost of their heartbeat."

"Strange," I murmured.

In the Realm, blood spilled. Pain bloomed. Emotions burned with rage and chilled with fear and loneliness. The Dream Realm could look and feel real even during its most unbelievable moments. But no heartbeat? The Realm was a strange place, and this was perhaps its most unnatural quality of all.

The Bringer stopped, and I collided into his back. "What are you—"

"Get down," he commanded, yanking me to the grass.

We had arrived at the pond. The cottage, its walls decaying and covered in filth, was no longer dark or silent; its windows glowed with light, and conversation drifted from between its cracks. Inside, the boy could be seen talking with two adults—his parents, perhaps, since they shared his dark, finely crafted features—as he offered bundles of food with a hopeful smile.

"I thought we couldn't be seen," I observed, shifting so I wasn't eating the leaves of the undergrowth the Bringer had thrown us into.

"It depends on the dream," he said simply, peering intently at the cottage and everything else beyond it. Mist passed around us like a shroud, lingering atop our backs and turning the Bringer's hair into a veil of its likeness.

"Then why are we hiding, exactly?"

The Shadow Bringer looked at me as though I were a fool. "The demon."

I ripped my attention away from the cottage, eyeing every shadowed corner within the clearing. And there were *many* shadowed corners. Most of which were also draped in mist.

"You're the *Shadow Bringer,*" I remarked, sounding more nervous than I wanted. Where was the demon hiding? What could he see that I couldn't? "Subdue it with your wicked might or something."

"My wicked might?" He reached out as if to grab me by the chin, but stopped, instead fixing me with an exasperated stare. "If I were its lord, then why would I be hiding in a bush? You're a foolish creature."

"I'm no more foolish than you," I shot back. He made a logical point, but his tone irritated me. I wasn't a foolish creature. I wasn't something to be ignored or thrown aside. And I had a name. "I'm eighteen. Not a foolish creature—an adult."

He arched an eyebrow. "Age does not beget maturity."

"That's interesting, considering you've been alive for centuries and are still a—"

"Time doesn't exist when you're a ghost," he said angrily. "It stopped for me the day I was sentenced to rot in my castle."

"I see," I said, biting my tongue against another cruel retort.

"If you wish to prove your worth, Esmer, then call out your sword and give it to me. I have a demon to kill."

"Use your own sword," I snapped, bristling. If I gave away my sword, my *only* weapon in the demon-infested Realm, I wasn't sure I'd get it back. And I really didn't want to take that risk. "It's mine."

"My power is weakening. Not yours, it appears." He moved closer, his body nearly touching mine. If I leaned forward, we'd be embracing. "Give it to me."

"I don't think so."

His scowl twisted up a bit, revealing the edges of his teeth. From my angle, they looked more akin to fangs. "Am I to strangle the demon with my bare hands?"

"I'd love to see it," I challenged. "I'm sure you'd fare just fine."

My palm tingled, thrumming with power and urging me to let out the sword underneath. Gritting my teeth against the discomfort of burning skin, I willed the sword to return to the depths of its original resting place.

But the sword fought back. It sprang to life in my hands, gleaming wickedly, and the Bringer pounced, making to pry it from my fingers.

Except the sword resisted, slamming him hard on the ground with a blast of shadow.

He gaped at me from where he was thrown. "You willed it to *attack* me," the Bringer spat, flicking some dirt from his helm.

"I warned you first. It listens to me, not you." Except I wasn't sure *why* the sword had exploded like that, throwing the Bringer back with monstrous force, but he didn't need to know that.

"Do you want to fight the demon all by yourself, then? Because that reality is imminent."

Definitely not. "No, but—"

The door to the cottage swung open, revealing the raven-haired boy. His face was red and splotchy, tears shining silver upon his skin, and the half-formed sounds of a violent argument followed him.

"You wretched beast!" screamed the boy's father. From the window he had appeared handsome; now his face was skull-like and quickly turning gray. "You are a curse to all who know you. Filthy, *filthy* boy!"

The boy tried to speak. "I just wanted to help—"

"You are not our son," the woman joined in, flinging her own words of condemnation into the night. She, too, had been beautiful, with black, flowing hair and fine, feminine features. Now her skin festered, sagging into deep, dripping wrinkles that opened into sores as they melted off her face. "A son would not make his parents choose between their lives and the life of their child."

"A son would not dream when he should be working to provide."

"A son would not let his parents die!"

Together they screamed at the boy for stealing their food and leaving them to starve. They blamed him—damned him—for *everything*. Their hunger, their poverty, their pain, and even their deaths. It was all the boy's fault. It would always be his fault.

The Shadow Bringer looked away, cursing low and deep.

This dream was terrible and cruel. It was the kind of dream I was warned about as a child—a dream of unimaginable pain, brought on by a demon who sought nothing but to devour souls.

But this dream of a young Shadow Bringer from over five hundred years ago was all wrong. Dreams like this weren't supposed to have existed back then. They *couldn't*. Not before Corruption and the rise of the Shadow Bringer.

"Why are they treating you like this?" I asked, horrified. "They're your parents, aren't they?"

"They are."

"So the dream is distorting them? It's taking your memories of them and twisting it into something worse."

He didn't answer.

"*Their food always disappears!*" the boy howled into his empty hands. Except they weren't empty—not exactly. Two ugly red welts bloomed across his skin, wrapping down his palms and up his forearms. "Why? Why does this always happen to me?"

The boy's parents loomed over him, forcing him to kneel.

"I just want to help you," the boy sobbed. "I just want you to love me."

"We will never love you," his father snarled, spitting at the boy's hands even as he grasped for their feet. "You're a pitiful excuse for a son."

"I miss you both so much," the boy cried. "Why do I only ever see you in my nightmares?"

"Because only good boys have good dreams. You're a worm who belongs in the dirt and the dark."

His mother reached down, and for a moment, it looked as if she might embrace him. The boy looked up, hopeful even through his tears. But just as her nails grazed his cheek, she slapped him. Hard.

Instinctively, I lurched forward, but the Shadow Bringer grabbed my arm, pulling me away.

"You don't need to see this."

I dug my heels in. "He needs our help, Bringer."

"There's no time," he said, shaking his head. "And even if there was, it would not change anything."

"But—"

"It's coming. The demon is coming."

From the pond a creature began to emerge, a behemoth of dark, purpled skin. Its skull was distorted, its mouth a mass of long, curling fangs that bent all the way back into its spine. It lacked arms or legs, so it dragged itself to the shoreline in heavy, sliding pulls, and red smoking eyes peered around, searching for something. It looked different from how it had appeared in Elliot's dream, but I knew in my soul they were one and the same.

Demon.

"The good parts of the dream never last," the boy lamented, throwing his fists into the ground. He didn't seem to notice the demon. The cottage started shaking, its dirt-covered walls leaking something dark and foul. *"Why does nothing ever last?"*

The boy didn't *seem* like a threat to humanity. He was vulnerable, ordinary. Not the Shadow Bringer, not the Devourer, not an enemy of humankind. But perhaps he had more power than he let on.

The Shadow Bringer stiffened. "I think I remember what happens. I subdued the demon myself."

"Really?" I asked. The boy hadn't even noticed the demon yet. The monster continued to drag itself to shore, working its fangs as it tasted the mist. Everything in me screamed in resistance, battling our silence. Our stillness. I wanted to say something, *do* something. The boy, alone and visibly helpless, didn't stand a chance. "You don't even see it yet."

The demon was at the shoreline now, pulling its body from the water.

"I..." The Bringer paused, visibly working through something. "Any moment now."

The young Bringer looked up then, finally aware of the monster in front of him.

"And what are you doing here?" the boy asked, gray eyes unflinching. "Are you here to mock me? I've seen you before. I am not afraid."

"You should be afraid, human," the demon growled, rising up to show its full height. "Do you think me some feeble part of your imagination?"

"Everything here is from my imagination," the boy said simply. His face scrunched in concentration, almost as if he were willing the demon away. "It is time for you to leave."

"How prideful," responded the demon.

The boy laughed. "Just wait. You will be gone before your next breath." But as he stared, focusing on the beast's every distorted feature, nothing happened. The demon was still there. When the boy spoke again, his voice cracked. "You're still here. Why are you still here?"

"From the lake I have watched you, observing your failures. You will never save your mother. You will never save your father."

"Shut up."

"They will starve, they will wither."

"I said, *shut up!*" the boy screamed.

"They will die."

"You don't know that!" The boy ground his teeth, glancing at his mother and father. They pressed against the grime-stained windows. Tears fell from their eyes, curving down their cheeks only to fall into their screaming mouths. "You know *nothing* of me or my family."

A pit formed, heavy and horrible in my stomach. This dream was not intended for my eyes—this was private, fragile, raw. Dreams always held pieces of reality; a dream's composite parts might be fantastic or bizarre in nature, but the core of it, the very deep and innermost core, was tied to the dreamer's reality.

If this dream was an indicator of the Shadow Bringer's past, it revealed a life riddled with fear, poverty, and hatred. And a hopeful, imaginative boy trying to make everything better.

"They will hate you, even in your dreams. You will never be loved again," the demon said.

"You can't know that," the boy protested. But his words were weaker now, aching. Doubting. "How can you know that?"

"You have no purpose. What do you live for?"

"What kind of question is that?" The boy swiped a tear from his eye, the skin underneath blooming red with frustration. "And you never answered my question." Behind him, the voices of his parents rose in anger and bite. "Why are you still here? Why can't I erase you?"

"Because I am not of your kind, human."

"Then what are you?"

"I am no one," the demon divulged, "but I can become you. I will ease your hardships. I will right your injuries." The demon slid forward. The growl in its voice softened, contrasting with the violence pouring from the cottage. "Let me free you from your miserable life, child. Come forth and I will gift you eternal rest."

Beside me, the Shadow Bringer cursed.

I whirled to face him. "You said you *killed* the demon. That's a little different than letting it devour your soul."

"I did kill it," he insisted. "But I don't remember when it happened. Or how."

As the Shadow Bringer and I deliberated what was happening—and if we should do anything about it—the boy appeared to be considering the demon's offer. His shoulders drew in, heavy with some unseen weight, and his eyes closed in concentration.

"Come to me," the demon purred, lowering its head so that it was level with the boy's, "and never again will you feel pain or sorrow. Your loneliness will ebb into darkness. And the darkness is where you belong."

"Where I belong?" the boy echoed, lifting his eyes. Gone were their lively sparks of shadow; his eyes had flattened into something hopeless and sad. "The dark has followed me since before I can remember. I am tired of the dark."

"That is only because you have resisted it," the demon answered easily. "You are a part of the dark. And the dark is a part of you." It twisted its maw into what resembled a smile. "It is your purpose."

"I have never known a purpose," said the boy. "What would I do with it?"

The demon began to move. Wherever it slid, a piece of the boy's dream fell into decay, and when it gave a deep, guttural inhale by the cottage, the voices inside were silenced. I twisted my hands in the grass, unable to watch any longer.

"Bringer," I said insistently, hoping that he would agree with what I was about to say. "Before you came back to the castle, Somnus showed me my brother's dream. I saw this demon there, too, but I was able to reduce it into nothing with my sword."

"What are you implying?"

"Well, if I can do that again, maybe I can save you."

"This is a dream. A *memory*." Still, something new dawned in the Bringer's eyes, mingling with his doubt. "We shouldn't have the ability to alter it."

"But what if we could? This is the past, but we're from the present. The *future*. Maybe *we* were the ones who attacked this demon. You don't remember how it happened. It's possible."

"Impossible," the Shadow Bringer breathed, slowly shaking his head. In front of us, the boy froze, staring up at the demon as it coiled around him. Its mouth widened, revealing the abyss-like length of its throat. The Bringer snarled in disbelief. "Why am I not doing anything? Why am I letting it get so close?"

And then, with a delighted scream, the demon swallowed the boy whole.

The demon slid over the cottage, sweeping a lazy tongue across its teeth.

"Damn you," the Bringer growled, surging from the ground. Had he his full powers, a whorl of mist and shadows would have been rising with him. Instead, he had only me. "Release him," he commanded, his voice deadly in its severity.

"You are not of this dream," the demon rasped, inhaling slowly through its nostril slits as if it were tasting us. I shuddered, feeling positively violated. "Or of this time. But you both have darkness within you. What is it that you seek?"

"I said to *release him*," the Shadow Bringer repeated with a snarl. "He is not yours to keep."

"But he *is*." The demon dropped its head so that it was beholding its own midsection. The skin there was smooth, motionless. No sign of life from within. "The dark is where he belongs. I am defending his birthright. His fate."

"No one's birthright is to belong in a demon's stomach," I said, standing my ground beside the Shadow Bringer.

It grinned, flicking its tongue as it slid toward us. "I disagree, human. Especially when the bond is so symbiotic."

"Demons steal birthrights and ruin fates," I insisted, summoning every ounce of my remaining courage. "There is no bond to be had."

Angry tears burned at my eyes, reminding me of every twisted, Corrupt body I'd seen. Corrupt children, their lives broken forever. Men and women who would never experience a true, restful sleep. Lives ripped apart before they could be fully experienced.

"Oh, how little you see," the demon purred. "This is the beginning of something glorious." It was close now, the arch of its skull touching the trees above us. "I've always wondered what it would be like to breathe your mortal air."

"On my call, distract it," the Shadow Bringer murmured, scarcely moving his lips.

My stomach dropped. "What do you mean?"

The demon rumbled on. "I want to wear your skin. Bleed your blood."

"According to your own account, you were 'able to reduce it into nothing,' Esmer." The Shadow Bringer looked very much as though he wanted to roll his eyes. For the sake of my dignity—or perhaps his own—he didn't. "I'm going to bind the demon so you can safely try that technique again, but I need you to distract it first. Just hold its attention. Speak to it."

I nodded grimly, biting the inside of my cheek. "Fine."

"Soon I will know how it feels," the demon said, eyes glistening in ecstasy.

I felt the Shadow Bringer's hands on my shoulders, a brief graze of cool metal. Then he shoved me forward—right in front of the demon—with what I *swore* was a chuckle. I spun back to yell something unkind, but he was gone.

The demon fixed its red eyes on me, saliva dripping from its teeth.

"Your skin is soft. Your blood is fragrant. I think I prefer *you* to the willful child inside my stomach."

Shuddering in disgust, I lifted my sword. It glistened with life, even in the murky half-light. "You won't take either of us, demon."

"Come here, girl. A truth, for one of your pretty teeth."

The demon moved to attack, handling its body with startling speed and flexibility. As it slid, bones began to grow out from its back, forming into the shape of six arms. Arms edged in long, brutal claws. I lurched sideways, trying to dodge, but I was too slow. A claw caught my side, tearing into my tunic and the skin above my ribs. I crashed into a tree at the force of it, gasping as I fought to catch my breath. The injury throbbed as wet, bloody shadows dripped down my ribs.

The demon moved again, fast, too fast, striking me down a second time.

The demon tilted its head, considering me. "You fascinate me, dreamer. Fragrant, indeed, is your blood. How might I spill more of it? Let us see."

A flash of something dark and quick caught my eye: the Shadow Bringer, under one of the demon's arms. He had become a ghost, a memory, silently threading something around the demon's arms, spine, and head. Something thin, hairlike. Threads of shadow, spiraling out from the Bringer's hands as he wove them tight.

I gritted my teeth against the pain blooming in my side, determined to do what the Bringer had demanded. *Distract it.* I struggled to my feet, meeting the demon's gaze. "You're stronger," I ground out, holding my bleeding side. "How did you manage to grow all those arms?"

"I am fed by the one who sustains me. I am made strong by his blood, his bones, and his darkness."

My stomach churned in response. How many children perished in the bellies of demons? How many rotted into Corruption there, believing every lie that their cursed dreams fed to them? Gently, meagerly, light began to unfurl from my sword. I focused on growing the blade's light, letting my anger and desperation fuel its strength, and imagined that the light could move, quick as a whip and as fluid as the wind.

The demon chuckled. "Bind me, you bind the boy. Kill me, you kill the boy."

At the demon's threat, I hesitated. What if the demon was right and I *did* hurt—or even kill—the boy? Would the Shadow Bringer die, too? Demons were masters of lies and half-truths, so it could be lying. But maybe not. Corruption bound a demon, physically and mentally, to its chosen human. Maybe that truly was the dark reality of it all: To kill a demon, its human must be killed, too. There was no salvation without death, similar to the Light Bringer's creed.

"You may join him in my entrails, if you would prefer," the demon rumbled. "I can arrange it."

I glanced toward where I thought the Shadow Bringer stood, but he was nowhere to be seen. I wanted to be brave, wanted to play the hero, but fear was threatening to crumble it all. The demon was a monster—a *monster*.

"Let him go," I said, my voice fiercer than I expected it to be. "What do you want in return?"

"Your soul," the demon said simply, licking its teeth. "If you wish to save him, you must offer yourself." The demon made to taste a blood-tipped claw, its face bright with triumph, but its arm jerked to a stop before it could. Bound by the Shadow Bringer's threads, the demon couldn't move. It roared, struggling mightily against the shadow bindings even as they cut deep into its skin. "Cursed dreamers—what is this?"

The Shadow Bringer burst from below, using his patchwork of threads to climb the demon's back. As he climbed, he sent a quick breath of shadow into the demon's red smoking eyes, blinding it. The demon roared again, and quickly, wildly, the pond began to rise. Its scum lapped against my feet, ankles, shins—just as the Bringer finished his climb, making to wrench one of the demon's horns from its head.

The horn broke free with a brutal *snap*.

The demon hissed, thrashing in its blindness. It caught the Shadow

Bringer off guard, and he fell, crashing through his threads and snapping them. He cursed, making to grab a thread, a bone, a horn—but everything slipped from his hands, just as the demon broke free an arm.

It happened fast.

The demon threw its arm into the Bringer, crushing him against the pond-soaked earth. I expected him to rise immediately—to shrug off the demon's arm that pinned him underwater—but the demon persisted, leaning its weight into his chest as he drowned. I lunged for the demon, sword raised, just as the demon grabbed for its broken horn. Hissing, growling, *grinning*, it drove the horn down, stabbing clean through the Bringer's armor. Clean through his chest.

"*No!*" I screamed.

It was as if the horn were in *my* chest. I couldn't see the Shadow Bringer, couldn't see if he was moving. Dark, bloody water pooled from where he was pinned.

The demon turned. Its vision had been restored; hatred burned in its eyes.

"Now it is your turn," it said simply, just as its bindings dissolved.

It rocked forward, widening its mouth into a colossal, endless hole. I couldn't move. Mud clung to my legs, rising with the water. Frantically, I lifted my sword, desperately calling to its light.

Too late.

The demon brought its jaws over my body.

In the belly of the demon, I found the young Shadow Bringer.

He knelt in a shroud of mist, framed by a void of black. There wasn't much to him, really. Just a tangle of skinny limbs and too-large clothes, eyes wide and sad under curls of raven hair. A far cry from his future self—what he would one day become. His hands grasped at the mist, as if he wanted to squeeze it into submission. Or maybe it was simply to ground himself to something. Anything.

I approached him, surprised when his gray eyes lifted.

"I thought I was alone," the boy whispered. He sounded distraught that I was there with him. "Did the demon devour you, too?"

"I think so," I croaked. My throat was surprisingly raw and painful. Had I been screaming?

I took a moment to study the demon's pit. It sloped up on all sides, globe-like, and a dark fog crawled over the ground. Time, light, and color didn't exist.

There was only the young Shadow Bringer and me.

It was disturbing that I hadn't woken up—that I was truly *here*, rotting inside a demon's stomach. I let out a tense, frustrated breath. This was the Bringer's childhood dream, but it also felt real. Present. *Alive* somehow, and not just a memory.

Turning back to the boy, I asked, "Are you hurt?"

"I don't know," he admitted, frowning as he examined his arms and legs. "I don't feel anything." He didn't appear to have any physical injuries, but his expression told of a different kind of pain. His real wounds were hidden, sharp, suffocating. He met my eyes again, as if he wanted to say something but wasn't quite sure how. "The demon said I would never feel pain or be lonely again. So why do I—" Suddenly, his face crumbled. He turned away. "I don't know why...."

Without thinking, I put a hand to his back. It was how I comforted Elliot when he was sick or scared; a touch to remind him that he wasn't alone. The boy flinched at first, hesitating, but a breath later, he relaxed, slumping forward to rest his chin atop his knees.

In an instant, the young Shadow Bringer had become what he truly was: a boy. And I realized I didn't even know his name.

"I'm Esmer," I offered quietly after a few moments had passed. "You don't know me, but I want to help you get through this. *We* will get through this."

The boy lifted his head. "Esmer," he echoed, testing the word. "I have a unique name, too. I am Erebus."

Erebus. It was a lovely name.

"Did the demon promise *you* anything?" Erebus asked intently. "It told me I would find where I belong. My purpose."

I think I prefer you to the willful child inside my stomach. A truth, for one of your pretty teeth.

I could almost feel the demon's dry, rotting breath on my face.

"The beast seemed more interested in how I would taste," I said, shaking my head in disgust. "We didn't get to the part where it promised me riches or good fortune."

"The demon said it knew me, but it never even said my name. Isn't that strange?" he asked.

"Demons are liars," I answered. They were parasites, too, desperate to become what they consumed. And I had unleashed hundreds of them upon my kingdom. "Maybe the demon had a few of your memories or guessed what you were feeling. But it didn't know you. They never truly do."

I placed a hand on the pit's wall. It resisted my touch; something on the other side was pushing back. "I think this pit is one of their tricks. An illusion, maybe. We just need to figure out how to break it."

Erebus watched me with a mixture of curiosity and dismay. "It's rare to speak of demons so boldly." He drew closer. "Are you from Citadel Evernight?" He must have seen the genuine confusion in my reaction, because he continued, adding quickly, "Never mind. Someone from Evernight wouldn't be here. Weavers don't care whether we live or die."

A distrust in the Weavers, even five hundred years in the past? I couldn't help pressing the boy: "Why won't the Weavers come? Aren't they supposed to be protecting dreamers?"

Supposedly, the seven Weavers prospered before the Shadow Bringer rose to power, gifting humanity with handcrafted, Maker-blessed dreams. It would be years until the first outbreak of Corruption. So why *was* Erebus left to face a demon by himself? Weavers protected the world from demons, hunting any that slipped through their veil. Would they not go after this one?

"You really think that?" Erebus spat, clenching his fists. "They never protected me. Not from this nightmare. Not from the demon. Not from anything. They *abandoned* me." I began to hear the similarities between his voice and the Shadow Bringer's. The hatred and the deep, burning sorrow. "Everyone else dreams like we're meant to. Everyone else can fly and do magic and *see* things. My dreams turn into nightmares, and they end with my parents dying. And it's always my fault."

Erebus placed his hands next to mine. Instead of pushing into the demon's strange, globe-like stomach, he pulled. The substance melted into shadow as it stretched, clinging to his hands. Several handfuls of shadow later, the globe still held firm. Huffing from the effort, he turned to me.

"My mother and father thought I was special. Funny, isn't it? They said the Weavers would take me to Evernight, and we'd never go hungry again." Shadows danced in his irises. His face, elegant despite his youth, was caught between calculated fury and something more desperate. Colder. "But then they died, and no Weaver ever came. The demon told me the dark was my purpose. You said it doesn't know me, but I think you're wrong."

As if in response to Erebus's proclamation, the dark deepened around us, encroaching on the mist. It moved over the boy who would grow up to be the Shadow Bringer with shadows dancing on his fingers and sorrow swimming in his eyes.

An image of the Shadow Bringer flashed before me. Was he still in the dream, crushed under the weight of the demon's horn? Again, as if in response, the demon's stomach began to change.

Water pooled at our feet, falling from its sky and seeping thick down its walls. The more I thought of the Bringer, bleeding and broken at the bottom of the pond, the faster the water rose. I shoved the memory of him away, fighting for control of the globe's form, and the water slowed to a stop.

But as the water stilled, the dark drew nearer, tugging at my hair and crawling spiderlike down my throat. And with the dark came unspeakable thoughts. Visions of sobbing mothers with terrified children clinging to their arms. A village armed with smoking torches and bloody mouths. Noblemen dreaming peacefully in beds carved from the bones of the less fortunate.

Erebus stood silent and wide-eyed beside me, experiencing visions of his own.

"Erebus, look at me."

Erebus worked his mouth open and shut, but no words came.

"No one is made for the dark. You might *control* the dark, but it isn't your purpose. Nor your essence," I said.

Shadows burst in from all directions, swirling up in a thick, bubbling fog. They began to obscure Erebus from me, as though they were set on eating him alive.

"What do you know?" Erebus finally shouted, whirling to face me. "The dark listens, and I listen back. It knows me better than anyone." He showed me his hand. Even as the shadows obscured him, they danced around his fingertips. They were beautiful, in their own way, shimmering faintly with small flecks of light. "My power scares people," he said, lowering his voice. "It scared my mother and father. It scares you, too. You're afraid of me."

Erebus stood tall, daring me to say otherwise.

My heart broke for him and his distorted view of himself. How could the dark be someone's purpose? Why did it linger around Erebus—around a boy who should have been safe in a Weaver-crafted dream and not rotting in a demon's stomach?

I held myself as he did, bold and unwavering. "I'm not afraid," I said, meeting his defiant glare. "I've seen the dark, too. I've lived in it."

As a child, I spent days adventuring in the Visstill. I enjoyed reading by the barn and delighting in the reckless joy of a season without Corruption. There were beautiful days in my childhood. But after Eden's death, the shadows stretched higher as the sun dipped beneath the trees it once smiled upon. I remembered the circle of torchlight, wavering in the long nights when the elixir supply was down to its final dregs. I remembered the desperation forming in my father's eyes. The rage in

223

my mother's. The fear in my brother's. Perhaps I ran from the shadows for too long, repulsed by how they whispered to me, linking me to the Shadow Bringer.

But that was a mistake.

The Shadow Bringer's life was wrought with darkness, but that didn't take away his admirable qualities. He was clever. Imaginative. Unflinching even in the face of despair. Powerful despite centuries spent in a looping nightmare. Maybe the Bringer's shadows were beautiful; maybe mine could be, too. Perhaps I didn't need to flinch from my past or my darkness as though they were shameful cloaks to be stuffed away.

I could bravely wrap them around my shoulders and be free.

"Knowing the dark doesn't make you a monster," I continued, assured in what I was saying. What I was trying to make him *see*. "It's what you do in the darkness—and how you rise to overcome it—that matters."

"You're lying," Erebus accused, taking a step back. "*No one* knows what it's like to live in the dark. Not the way I do." His eyes brightened in the fog. "You're not really here, are you? I imagined you to protect myself."

I reached for his hand, just as he began to melt into the dark.

"Erebus, *no*," I insisted, begging him to stay.

"If my purpose is evil, then what good am I?" he said. At this point, he was nearly gone. His limbs were caught in the shadows, half-eaten. "Where do I belong if I'm a monster? Nobody loves or protects me. Perhaps my mother and father did, once, but they're dead now."

Lunging, I managed to grab his arm. The shadows retreated at the contact. As his shadows overlapped, folding in and out, their light—just a handful of tiny shimmers a moment before—grew strong. "Just because there's darkness, it doesn't mean all the light is gone. Look—see? And you do have somebody, Erebus. You have me."

And I have you, too.

"I…" Erebus began to whisper something but stopped, watching the light dance within the shadows. Together the twin energies radiated from his hands, blanketing the pit. The heavy fog disappeared, replaced by a sea of stars.

Together, we looked in awe at the transformation.

Soft, twinkling light came to rest upon Erebus's face, illuminating his hesitant wonder. Slowly, his desperation faded. Slowly, his breathing quieted.

"I never knew," he whispered, lifting his arms. At his call, some shadows dropped, coiling elegantly around his shoulders and forming a cloak on his back. Others tangled in his hair, shaping into a loose crown. Power radiated from him, wild and true. "I thought the dark was a terrible thing. But this feels different. I can control it." More firmly, he repeated, "I can control it."

The sides of the demon's pit began to splinter and crack.

"These walls aren't going to last much longer," I observed, sidestepping a piece of the globe as it fell. "I don't know what will become of us if that happens, or if we can still escape. But we need to try."

Erebus turned to me. His eyes were burning. "I'm going to rip us straight from the demon's stomach. I swear it."

From the ferocity in his expression, I believed him. "Good. Then the beast won't be able to hurt anyone ever again." *Nor will it continue to hunt me, my family, and the Shadow Bringer.*

Erebus nodded. A swath of darkness pulled itself from the sky, moving to rest atop my shoulders, too. It felt warm. Comforting, even. I leaned into my new mantle, savoring its touch.

"I'm sorry for saying I imagined you." He smiled then. His expression held sorrow, but amazement, too. "You just seemed too good to be true, is all."

Erebus held out his hand. I took it.

And the globe cracked in two, bursting with the light of a million stars.

27

Am I dead?

For a time, there was nothing but stark, blinding light. It surrounded me with its fullness, swallowing my screams. I searched for a shape, a shadow, a movement, *anything*. But the light persisted, overwhelming despite its emptiness. My hair floated to the sides of my face, fluttering along the edge of my cloak. Slowly, I began to feel weightless. Free, even.

But everything was wrong. It was suffocating, this light. This *silence*.

I glanced at my hands. They were empty, missing the boy's brave, reassuring grip. He had wanted us to escape the pit together. A terrible thought slammed into me: Maybe I hadn't made it. Maybe I was dead or lost, stuck in some eternal Dream Realm afterlife when all I wanted was to be alive on earth and safe with Elliot.

The thought sickened me.

Vaguely, I felt something brush my fingertips. I reached through the ripple of light, grasping for what I had felt. If it was Erebus, I wanted him to know that he wasn't alone. But as I stretched, the light expanded outward, drowning my face and crawling into my nose. I squeezed my eyes shut.

My throat was full, bubbling over.

I'm dying.

The light stilled, dampening into gray. Just as something—*someone*—finally reached for me. Their hands were armored and as cold as ice, but they held on. My eyes flew open.

And for a moment, the world stood still.

The Shadow Bringer, more statue than man, was suspended in a pool of silvery water. His eyes were closed, lashes resting atop frozen cheeks, and his hair pooled about him in a ghostly crown. Gone was the lifeblood from his skin; he was pallid as a corpse, lips drawn together in a colorless line. It struck me again how beautiful he was. Even with a helm drawn over most of his face, his beauty rivaled the moon's. But the Shadow Bringer had once been just a child. A mortal—a *boy*—with fear, hope, and dreams in his bones. And he had a name.

Erebus.

My eyes drifted to his chest. The demon's horn had been thrust through his ribs, pinning him to the bottom of the pond. I shuddered, imagining how it would feel to be impaled like that. To be left to die, speared to the mud like an insect. I pulled on the horn, hoping that I could dislodge it from his chest. Death and life in the Realm were mysterious, fickle things. The Bringer looked dead, but he also never had a heartbeat. And neither did I. My chest was empty, motionless as his.

It was then I realized I hadn't been breathing. And I didn't need to.

When I felt I was drowning in the Shadow Bringer's cavern, perhaps it was only because I *believed* I was drowning. Maybe there really was hope after all.

Gritting my teeth, I held the horn and pulled hard. I groaned at the weight of it; bubbles poured from my mouth. But my effort was useless. The horn was too heavy—too slippery under my hands. I couldn't lift it, even as I tried to imagine it as light, weightless, and brittle.

A large, misshapen body moved through the water. A thing that looked very much like the red-eyed demon.

I wrapped my arms under the Shadow Bringer's shoulders, moving closer to him than I had ever dared. His hair, silky and ticklish, brushed against my face. If I couldn't lift the horn, maybe I could lift the Shadow Bringer off it. I just had to angle him correctly, pull him up before the—

I froze, panicking.

The demon was close—too close. It kicked up sediment from the bottom of the pond, clouding the water and obscuring my view of its body. Just a few seconds more and it would be upon us.

Holding the Bringer tight and trying to ignore how cold and empty his body felt, I swam up with all my strength.

The demon lunged toward us, stretching its mouth wide.

Too late—it's too late.

Its body circled us, breaking through the sediment. I looked on, horrified. We were weak. Powerless.

We'd *failed*. And the cost was devastating.

Because of this demon, I would be imprisoned in the Dream Realm forever, never able to return home. Never again would I see a real sunrise, enjoy real food, or watch real people living real lives. Because of this demon, I'd never get to hug Elliot or watch him grow up. I'd never even see him again. I buried my face in the Shadow Bringer's chest, shutting my eyes as the demon's teeth closed around us. The Shadow Bringer wasn't a monster. He wasn't some creature in the dark worthy of being hated and feared. Not like this demon was.

But just as the demon's jaws began to squeeze shut, surely sealing our fates, it disintegrated.

And just like that, everything changed.

The pond's waters shifted into something pure and crystalline. I could nearly smell it. *Taste* it. Floral and crisp: mint, wildflowers, and fresh air. The pond floor, slick with mud and decay, transformed into a slab of dark sapphire. Any debris—anything other than pure, sparkling water—dissolved. Golden light, filtering down from above, washed over it all, hinting of a radiant sunrise just beyond the surface.

Though I wasn't breathing, I wanted to. I wanted to drink it in; I wanted to fill my lungs with this scene.

Even the Shadow Bringer was changing. His skin warmed, lips shifting from deathly gray to a pale pink. The demon's horn disappeared, too. Though the Bringer's armor had a hole in it, his chest was smooth and intact.

With the horn no longer pinning him down, we began to rise. As soon as we broke the surface, the change in the dream was evident. The cottage was gone, as were the scum-lined cattails and perpetual haze. Instead, a field of wildflowers swept as far as the eye could see, each glowing as if it held a candle within its petals. Trees curled over the field, immensely tall and impossibly magnificent; their bark was iridescent and their leaves glittered like precious jewels. A sunrise shimmered above, glowing plum and gold.

And in the middle of it all, shadow and starlight spinning from his hands, was young Erebus.

He was smiling—*beaming*—as he worked, forming rolling hills and emerald rivers, clouds of silver dust, and a million stars to rest within his golden sky. From the ashes of his family's cottage grew an obsidian tree, its many branches filled with the same glowing flowers in the field. I had never seen a boy so happy, so *free*. Even Elliot, ever the sweet, brave optimist, never truly looked the way Erebus did now.

Without demons or Corruption, was this what dreams had the power to be?

It left me longing for something I didn't quite understand. Like I had missed something important my entire life, something critically significant to my happiness and purpose. Carefree joy. Endless possibility.

Still damp from the pond water, I scarcely noticed as tears slid down my face.

I pulled the Shadow Bringer to the bank, setting him in the flowers. They fluttered against his body, an array of glowing colors swaying gently in the breeze, and their light, mingling with the sunrise, softened his edges and hollows. He looked as though he was one breath away from opening his eyes.

And surely he was breathing. *Right?*

The Bringer had said that breathing was a habit—that dreamers did it regardless, despite not having true heartbeats. I knelt over his chest, waiting for a breath's telltale rise and fall. I gave it a moment, then another, counting my own breaths in the meantime.

Thirty seconds passed. Sixty. One hundred.

His chest remained motionless.

Strangely, I felt irritated. He was the almighty *Shadow Bringer*, for Maker's sake. Yet here he was, drowned, freezing, and powerless, defeated by the very monster we needed to overcome.

"You're not dead, and the demon is gone," I said, wanting to grab him by the shoulders and shake him. "You're going to miss the rest of the dream, Bringer. Wake up."

Beyond us, Erebus continued to weave beautiful new creations. A great bird, its wings a blanket of midnight. A cloak of stardust, onyx, and velvet, which he threw over his shoulders to trail along the ground. Sometimes he flew; sometimes he jumped; sometimes he simply stood within his flowers and smiled.

For a moment, I thought he looked my way.

"Erebus!" I waved my arms, straining so that he could see me. The flowered meadow was wide, and its iridescent trees partially obscured the Bringer and me. Erebus started to move toward us, but another moment passed, and he turned, walking away. "Erebus, I made it out! You did it—we—"

A hand grabbed me by the sleeve, pulling me down to land half-draped across an armored chest.

"Don't say that name," the Shadow Bringer thundered. And then he coughed, struggling to find his voice again as his hand dropped from my sleeve to my thigh. He didn't seem aware of the touch; his shadowed eyes weren't fully focused. "I am no longer that man. His name shouldn't be spoken."

Before I could think, I threw my arms around his shoulders.

A laugh slipped out, then it turned into a sob before I could stop it. I didn't know why I was crying, but it felt good. It felt *freeing*. Surprisingly, the Bringer leaned into my touch. He wrapped his arms around my back, holding my hips with one forearm and my shoulders with the other. Though his arms were armored, they weren't uncomfortable. In fact, I was surprised by *how* comfortable they felt.

"You're crying." He slowly brought his hands to my jaw, pressing against the line of tears that still slipped down my skin. "Why are you crying?"

"I don't know," I admitted, leaning back so that I could see him. Shadows slowly spun in his eyes; they were more beautiful than I'd ever seen them. "I thought you died."

"And that makes you sad?"

"Of course. We're allies, aren't we?" I whispered. "It wouldn't be fair for you to abandon me so soon."

"Mm," he murmured in agreement. "I remember the rest of the dream now," he said suddenly, drawing me back into his chest. A soft, astonished noise slipped out of me. "You pulled my younger self from that demon's pit. It's rare for the Maker to allow a lasting divergence from the past, but it was *you*. My anchor." He cursed, almost as if in disbelief. "And to think I once thought you my enemy and my ruin."

"And what do you think of me now?" The words tumbled free before I could stop them.

"I think you are my equal," he declared, breath ghosting my cheek as his hands drifted to my shoulders. "My salvation." Warmth burned from where his hands ghosted my skin; I'd never felt such a sensation before. I wanted more of it. I wanted *him*. "You carry so much guilt on these shoulders. So much fear and heartbreak," he observed.

He held me on a precipice, held my glass heart in his metal hands. One squeeze and it would break, shattering into a million jagged pieces. "You see that in me?"

"I see all of you, Esmer." My breath stilled, and he continued: "But it's as you told me—'knowing the dark doesn't make you a monster.' You're more than your fear. More than your heartbreak." His hands slid down my arms, tangling in the shadows that were lazily curling around us. "More than the limits you've placed on yourself. You're the only person alive who—" He swallowed hard, cutting himself off. "I only mean to say thank you. That's what you need to hear. Not anything else my imagination conjures up." He looked past me, gaze settling on the flowers and trees instead of the flush racing across my face. "Where are we?"

"We're still in your dream," I answered.

He instantly tensed, scanning the sky. *He thinks the demon is still alive.*

"The demon is gone," I added, waiting for him to relax. But the tension did not ease from his bones.

Instead, he looked even more agitated. He peered down, noticing the gaping cloth at the center of his chest. "Ah. Now I remember." His voice dripped with venom. "I was staked to the bottom of the pond and left to rot." The shadows in his eyes sharpened around his irises. "If that demon is still hunting us, we need to find it again. And soon."

The intensity in his gaze made my neck burn. "You should try speaking to your younger self. We might be able to learn more about why the demon was hunting you."

The Bringer closed his eyes, slowly shaking his head. "The past self isn't allowed to communicate with their present or future self. But perhaps you can speak with him."

I waved at Erebus, hopeful that he could see me. He was so close to us—looking our way, even. Surely he'd be able to talk, just as we had done in the demon's pit. But the more I waved, the more it was apparent that he couldn't see us. We were veiled from him, just as at the start of the dream.

"Forget it. He can't see you," the Bringer said.

Ignoring his dismal tone, I asked, unable to hide my wonder, "Can all dreamers do what you're doing?"

"Do what, exactly?" He was looking at Erebus, too. "Spin in circles? Grow a flower? That's nothing."

"How is that *nothing*? You're creating a world of your own from nothing. It's amazing." The dream was gaining life and depth; different sights, sounds, and scents continued to bloom around us. "And you look so happy. Like you finally found your purpose."

"Is that what you see in the boy?" The Bringer shifted so that he was mostly sitting up, hands slipping from my back. He watched Erebus for a few silent moments, pain spinning from the shadows in his eyes. "You're wrong. I never knew my purpose."

"Maybe you forgot it," I challenged. "But that doesn't mean you never had one. Or that you still don't."

Erebus had a future. A fire for life. A *heart*. What happened to him that he lost it all?

"And if I asked you to name your purpose, what would you say? Would you tie it to happiness? Family?" His jaw clenched as his tone turned spiteful. "Or perhaps to self-righteousness. To *justice*. To ridding the world of evil—and of monsters who belong better in the dark." *Of people like me*, his eyes seemed to add.

"That's a ridiculous thing to say. The dark isn't the end. What you manage to create out of darkness," I said, motioning around us, "*that* is what matters."

"So you have sympathy for my fate and hope for my future?" His upper lip curled, defiant. "Careful. You're almost making me believe it."

I was mad. Fuming. He was *impossible*. "I might have hope for you, but I certainly don't have sympathy or pity," I snapped, lifting myself from the ground. The sudden movement made me dizzy, but by standing I could see more of what Erebus had created. "Unless you want to talk about how pitiful your castle is. . . ."

The Shadow Bringer laughed, not entirely disagreeing with me.

Mist descended over the sunrise. A lone figure walked from it, hair dragging through the flowers and dusting over robes made of black feathers and dark, plated silver. An ivory crown, rising into sharp, blade-like points, adorned his brow. His face was skeletal, black eyes listless and wise. *Somnus.*

Erebus didn't move. In fact, he stood taller, facing Somnus without fear.

"Erebus," Somnus said in greeting. If Erebus was surprised Somnus knew his name, he didn't show it. "Your creations have echoed throughout the Dream Realm. It is no small wonder for a dreamer to create without a Weaver's guidance."

"A Weaver's permission, you mean," Erebus remarked. Despite the bite in his words, his tone was flat.

"That is because the Realm is dangerous, dreamer. Particularly when it is stretched by your own hand." Somnus selected a flower at random, holding it up to the rising sun. "One slip of your mind, and something innocent grows fangs."

The flower burst into flames. Somnus closed a fist over it, sending smoking tendrils into the air. When he next opened his fist, he offered the hand to Erebus.

Erebus stared at the hand, neither taking nor refusing it. "What do you mean by this?"

"We have been watching you, Erebus. Join us at Citadel Evernight." Softly, he added, "You are worthy."

The Shadow Bringer launched himself forward. He half ran, half staggered to where Somnus and Erebus stood, a weak shroud of shadows trailing him. They couldn't see him—they didn't so much as blink in his direction as he approached—but that didn't deter him.

Though weakened, the Bringer, mantled with the ghost of his power, moved with violence in his blood.

"They can't see you!" I shouted, running after him. "What are you even—"

"You say you have hope for my future," he began, charging for Somnus just as Erebus stepped forward, "but this is the moment when my past begins to rot. If there's a chance I can stop it, I need to try."

Erebus was going to accept Somnus's hand. There were embers of power and pride in his eyes; his was the expression of a boy who had finally been *seen*—but not without hardships. A boy who knew the value of what was being offered, despite his distrust of the Weavers.

"Don't take his hand!" The Bringer crashed into Somnus, but it was like hitting a wall.

A wall that could also *explode*.

He flew backward upon impact, skidding wildly through a patch of Erebus's brightest flowers. A tree halted the Bringer's momentum; he crashed to a stop against it, head slamming sideways into its jeweled bark. If he cried out in pain, I didn't hear it.

Erebus placed his hand in Somnus's. And just like that, the dream collapsed.

he Shadow Bringer's domain was rapidly deteriorating.

The iridescent forest had dropped away, only remaining as a thin ring around the castle itself, and in its place was something difficult to comprehend. I squinted at the horizon from his balcony, desperate to decipher the scene. At first, I could only hear water lapping against a shore. Then the deep thrumming of bells and a low, melodic humming. There was also the scent of something ancient and nostalgic. The starry sky had broken apart, replaced by whorls of silver, purple, and midnight blue. A sky clothed in eternal twilight.

And when the scene finally pieced together, revealing itself in its entire glory, my breath held.

In Norhavellis, water pooled in shallow rivers and cattail-lined ponds. It poured from the sky, collected in puddles, and forced pastures into muddy pits. It sat heavy in gray clouds, fell like fingers against my bedroom window, and soaked into my shoes as Eden, Elliot, and I raced home from the village. Anything grander—seas, lagoons, lakes so wide a fleet of ships could sail through them—was a tale to be read about. A story tucked away in a book. This was something else.

The sea circling the Shadow Bringer's castle was *alive*.

Part of its body rolled and surged like a willful horse, swelling into the sky. Other parts dipped low, cowering like a wounded fawn, or stretched taut and still. The water's crystalline skin, reflecting the twilight sky, stretched over each wave and melted into the horizon. It was untamed, glorious, and absolutely terrifying. But despite its force, the sea was contained; glossy stone, shaped in a perfect arc, formed its limits, and a magnificent tower anchored its center.

"You weren't meant to see that entire dream," said the Shadow Bringer, joining me on his balcony. Bits of shadow clung to his edges, trailing down his newly armored arms and back. They had grown in number since I'd last seen him. "It is a wretched part of my past."

"Are you okay?"

"I'm fine," he snapped.

Stubborn, stubborn man. "You don't have to hide your hurt from me, Bringer. I'm not going anywhere."

"That's only because you can't run. If you had the choice, you would."

I shook my head, exasperated. "No, I wouldn't. Where would I even go?"

"Anywhere. Everywhere." He turned, briefly fixing me with a haunted stare before facing the sea again. "This is the Nocturne, as I'm sure you're aware," he announced suddenly, gesturing at the swelling waves. *Changing the subject.*

"I'm not aware. The Weaver tales never mentioned anything like it."

"There's more to the world than a single book of Weaver tales. You've never even seen a sunset outside your village."

"I've been to places beyond Norhavellis," I said, bristling.

"A distorted, half-formed dream in Istralla hardly counts."

"I don't see why not." I raked through my memory, searching for another example. "And there's also your castle."

His eyes, ringed by his shadows, narrowed. "Paying visits to my castle counts even less. You need to see more of the world, Esmer. I wish that for you, even if I can't be with you when it happens." He stormed off to a different part of the balcony, shadows hesitating a moment before trailing him.

"I don't know what things were like five hundred years ago, but people's fates are a bit more limited now. We don't have dreams"—I matched the Shadow Bringer's pace, walking shoulder to shoulder with him—"or adventures." Pointedly, he avoided my gaze. "So forgive me for not being as knowledgeable as you."

He spun to face me, catching me by the wrist. The movement was impossibly fast, marked by shadows with a faint glint of starlight within them. I snatched my wrist away, darkness trailing behind.

"I see your powers are back. You should be happier now, at least," I observed.

For a moment, he looked confused. Then he glanced down, noting the shadows as they rolled off his body. "I've lived with these shadows for centuries. They're a part of me, but they aren't a source of my happiness."

"You *have* a source of happiness, then? What is it?"

He scowled, turning to face what he had called the Nocturne, and my face began to heat with a surprising amount of regret. We had just relived a deep, vicious trauma from his childhood, and here I was interrogating his happiness. Of course he wasn't happy. How could he be?

"I'm sorry, Bringer. I didn't mean—"

"Enough," he muttered. "I've heard enough for the moment."

Glimpses of color and light began to shimmer within the Nocturne. If I focused on a particular area, the color and light sharpened, briefly taking shape. In one section, I saw a moonlit house with a family embracing on the porch. In another, a girl walking through dry sands, white pillars, and winged statues. Then a woman smiling by a field of shining crops. A man riding a horse down a narrow road with a cave at its end.

"What are those things in the water?"

"Dreams. The Nocturne contains them all. Weaver-crafted dreams and the ordinary kind." He pulled his gaze from the waves and settled it on me. "What do you know of the Dream Realm? Its configuration and how it functions."

"Well, there are—or *were*—seven Dream Weavers." I counted them on my fingers. "Somnus, Xander, Theia. They control dreams of the past, present, and future. Then there are the elemental Weavers: Fenrir, Nephthys, Ceres, Lelantos. Fire, water, earth, and air."

"And where do they reside in the Realm?"

"They each have a territory. They're like miniature worlds or kingdoms in the Dream Realm."

He nodded. "They call their lands—which include any permanent acolytes—domains. And all domains border the Nocturne. The nearness is important since that's how the Weavers access their intended dreamers. It's an anomaly that my domain is so close to the Nocturne; at this rate, it will soon be consumed by the sea." He pointed at the Nocturne's tumultuous waters. "Over there. Notice the mountains? The barest hint of clouds? Lelantos's domain." Sure enough, there was a faint mountain range in the distance. He pointed in another direction, toward a darker sky and shimmering line of emerald. "Ceres's forest. Nephthys's domain is next—you can tell by how it glitters. She thoroughly enjoys her jewels."

"Are the Weavers there, right now? In their domains?" I had to ask.

He considered the question, thinking. Remembering. "In a sense. Their souls manifest within the dreams of the Nocturne, perpetually monitoring humanity's dreams. But the Weavers themselves could be anywhere. Feasting and drinking with kings and queens on earth, creating pretty things within their domains in the Dream Realm, or persuading dreamers to following them as acolytes."

"Five hundred years ago, perhaps. None of that exists in the present," I noted.

For a moment, genuine concern flickered in his eyes. Then it faded, quick as smoke. "So you have claimed." He made a dismissive gesture. "I don't know what happened to the Weavers after I was banished. It is difficult to watch the world when you're confined to the company of demons and darkness."

I shivered. I couldn't help it. It was madness—*madness*—to even imagine his existence.

Let us out, let us out, let us out!

How many times had he borne witness to those hellish screams? That he was even capable of a smile, or a coherent sentence, was a testament to his strength.

The Bringer ran a gauntleted hand through his hair, unaware of where my thoughts had turned. He continued: "Next to Nephthys, you cannot tell from here, but there's the most foolish-looking palace. Fenrir's. He—" The Bringer finally noticed me watching him instead of looking wherever he was pointing. "What?"

"Nothing." I managed a smile, much to the Bringer's irritation. For all his supposed hatred of the Weavers, there was no mistaking the genuine interest in his explanation. And if he knew each of these details, his memory must have returned, too. Or at least in part. "Carry on, please. I'm learning quite a lot."

"Are you, now? I don't see how you're learning anything at all by watching *me*."

I suppressed a laugh, instead motioning toward the massive tower at the Nocturne's center. It was a colossal, beautiful thing, glowing through its various spires and archways, and as the waves dipped, several bridges were revealed, spanning out like the spokes of a wheel. "Whose domain is that?"

The Bringer's eyes darkened a shade. "That is Citadel Evernight."

Evernight. I knew that name. "In the demon's stomach, your younger self asked if I was from there." I'd read about it in his books, too, but I wasn't about to let him know I'd been searching through his things. "And Somnus"—I searched for the right word. *Invited? Called? Coerced?* I settled on the first—"invited you to it."

"Invited?" Apparently, I'd chosen the wrong word. "I was not *invited* to

Evernight," the Bringer continued. "I was *forced* to Evernight. After years of neglect, Somnus cornered me at my weakest. If it weren't for him, perhaps my fate would have differed." For a moment, a smile ghosted his lips. "You know, it was once considered an honor to be chosen as a permanent dreamer of the Realm. To be summoned by a Weaver to hone your dreaming talents at Evernight as a student. A *scholar*. You'd even have your family generously compensated in return." He spun to me, suddenly asking, "Do you want to know how my parents died? Or how they were in life?"

The voices of his mother and father, shrieking at a young Erebus through the walls of their decaying home, came rushing back.

A son would not make his parents choose between their lives and the life of their child.

A son would not dream when he should be working to provide.

A son would not let his parents die!

I shook my head. "That dream depicted them cruelly."

He smiled again, but it felt cold. "My dreams were always that way. They would begin one way and twist into something else by their end." His hands clenched at his sides, shadows twining between his fingers. "That is how I first learned to manipulate them."

"And by being able to manipulate your dreams, you thought a Weaver would notice you. You thought you'd be chosen," I said.

"Only the most exceptional dreamers could generate a dream of their own will. And I was one of them." His voice chilled as he continued, slipping into something lifeless and bitter. "But months passed, and no Weaver ever took notice."

"Because your power stemmed from shadows and not something simpler, like fire or water?"

He nodded. "And when my parents learned the truth of my powers—that they were grounded in shadow, and not an element or a time construct—they began to despise me. They said I was evil. A cursed child, sent to ruin them. And in a way, I did." He fixed his shadowed gaze on me. "In my time, families with wealth and power hired dream interpreters. Sometimes dreams were simple in meaning.

Sometimes not. An interpreter ensured that the Maker's message was clearly heard and followed."

"Interpreting sounds like an incredible amount of responsibility," I said.

A cold half smile. "Indeed. And if the dream's interpretation was incorrect or ill received..." He drifted off, and my imagination began to wander to dark places. Places where the dream interpreter was shunned or even killed.

Eventually, he continued: "My mother and father interpreted dreams for a wealthy family in Istralla. They were well-known for their interpretations, always clever, precise, and true. They eventually caught the eye of the king."

"So they began interpreting the king's dreams?"

"For a time. And for a time, we lived in luxury, with our own wing in each of his palaces. But it's a funny thing, wealth. Power. They destroy as easily as they create." He laughed, the sound cold and miserable. "Our new status destroyed my mother and father. As I grew older, they consulted me for answers. They told me the Maker had dulled their vision, but I think they just grew complacent. Lazy. So they came to me. Even in their hatred, they relied on me. A child of darkness, secretly interpreting the dreams of royalty."

A ripple of cold crawled over my skin. I didn't like where this was going.

"One day, I was asked for my opinion of the king's dream. In his dream, he saw a great, blazing sun and a shadowed moon. At first, the dream was peaceful—everything in perfect balance. But as the dream went on, the moon crept closer to the sun, ate it, and became something else. Something *other*. A thing made evil and cruel."

"That's horrible." Shuddering, I pressed my hands to my side, willing them to warm.

The Shadow Bringer walked closer to the edge of the balcony. For the briefest of moments, it appeared as though he wanted to fly into the Nocturne's depths.

Then he sighed, shaking his head as if to clear it. "The king's dream wasn't a simple nightmare. Nightmares are personal; they uproot the dreamer's deepest fears. His was a vision of the future. A warning. After the moon ate the sun, it bathed the land in darkness, swallowing all light. The king saw this happen. He also saw something emerging from the dark: two swords. One white, one black."

A staging of the dream appeared from the Bringer's hands, formed by shadows of every size, color, and texture. I watched as the storied king rose from between his fingers, desperately swinging the twin swords against an unconquerable evil. It was a violent, hopeless fight. One I never wished to see again.

The king's swords shattered before a single blow was ever landed.

The Shadow Bringer went on. "The sun represented the king, and the moon represented a great demon. The dream's warning was complicated and deadly. It warned that the king would be Corrupted by evil, and someone would seek to defeat the king using two powers: justice or logic, the white sword; and war or deceit, the black sword. But neither would suffice."

In the shadowy reenactment, the king's mouth widened in a silent scream.

"The future would come to pass regardless," he said.

With a clench of the Shadow Bringer's fist, the king was put out of his misery.

"That dream was intended to warn the king of his demise. It was *his* responsibility to recognize the impending evil and to prepare for it in different ways. When I gave my opinion of the dream, it wasn't well received. My parents chose to tell the king a different interpretation— one that veiled the dream's warning into something more palatable. But someone close to the king had overheard my original interpretation." Absently, the metaled ends of his fingers flexed open and shut. "The king was furious. He condemned my parents for their deception. Banished and starved them. They died of disease within a year."

"What happened to you, then?" I whispered, horrified. An image of him sprang up—of a young Erebus, desperately trying to feed his parents with food that never satisfied. A nightmare meant to trap and destroy. "You were just a child. You interpreted as you knew how."

The Bringer saw the look on my face. Saw the other questions lingering there.

Were you punished—like your mother and father? Were you left to a rotting shack in the forest, left to starve?

"I wasn't punished for their crimes."

"Why?"

"There were other uses for me. I was kept in the palace as the king's chosen interpreter, for one. It was there that I met Mithras. The king's only child." The Bringer's mouth tightened. "He shouldn't still be alive, Esmer. I don't know what sustains him, but it isn't natural. Only Weavers are intended to be immortal."

"Perhaps he's cursed as you are."

"Perhaps." A strained, irritated breath passed through his nose. "In those early years, we grew to be something like brothers. Though I was rarely allowed to leave the palace, Mithras did everything in his power to ensure I was treated as an equal, even if that meant sharing clothes and eating from the same table. When we were in the Dream Realm as Evernight scholars, we'd spend our spare moments practicing swordplay or reading stories as you and your siblings once did."

"That's difficult to imagine."

He shifted his gaze from the Nocturne to me. Something burned there, simmering deep within the shadows. "I know. But loneliness can command a strong and desperate pull."

We stood in silence for a few moments, looking out across the Nocturne. What a terrible fate for a child—a wretched foundation on which to build a life. It explained more than one of the shadows that darkened the Bringer's eyes.

"The Weavers oversaw two citadels," he began, switching subjects. "One in Istralla, Firstlight, and one in the Dream Realm, Evernight. Firstlight allowed for Weavers to maintain relations with earthly rulers.

Sponsorships from various kingdoms and such. Evernight is beyond explanation. A rigorous academy, a decadent fantasy, a symbol of Maker-given prosperity."

I looked to Evernight, at its glowing spires and impossible proportions, beckoning to us. Without understanding why, I took a step forward. Then another. Before I realized it, I was leaning over the Shadow Bringer's balcony and staring deep into the Nocturne, wondering what it would feel like to swim beneath its waves. Could I swim through it—all the way to Evernight? What would it feel like? Would it warm my skin or chill it further?

I studied a particularly tall swell, considering.

The Bringer yanked me back. "Be careful. It's known to call dreamers to its depths."

I gritted my teeth, eager for the Nocturne's call to fade yet reluctant to be released from the Shadow Bringer's arms. "What would happen if I fell into the water?"

"Well, considering we're both cursed, you'd probably burn. Generally, however, most dreamers walk in. Willingly." He frowned. "If properly trained as a scholar of Evernight, you'd enter the Nocturne in order to influence the dream of another. On behalf of your bonded Weaver and at their direction."

"And untrained?" I asked.

"Untrained, you would drown yourself in the Nocturne, jumping from dream to dream until you lost all sense of who you were or why you entered the Dream Realm in the first place." A wicked gleam formed in his eyes. "Dreams are feeble things, meant to live and die by the will of the Weaver who built them." He drew near. "You'd wake as a hollow shell of your former self, unable to recall the most basic elements of your identity."

"That's terrible. Why would the Maker—" Then I noticed a faint smirk on his lips. "You're joking," I said incredulously. "You're actually *joking.*"

"I am not," he insisted. But the smirk grew, widening his mouth as it bloomed. "There are many things I do well. There are fewer things that I do willingly. Joking is not something I do well *or* willingly."

Without warning, a deafening sound echoed across the Nocturne.

Dmm. Dmm. Dmm.

It sounded like a death knell. No—louder.

Dmm. Dmm. Dmm. Dmm.

After the seventh bell, the air stilled. I expected the worst. A monster, rising from the Nocturne, water dripping down its scales. Or an evil darkness, devouring Evernight like the moon in the king's dream. Instead, the Nocturne's waves fell at once, smoothing into glass, and seven great bridges were fully revealed, spanning across the sea from Evernight into the Weavers' separate territories.

"Evernight's call," the Shadow Bringer explained. "The bells ring to summon the Weavers."

"For danger or for amusement?"

"Sometimes danger, demons and the like." He walked back inside his bedchamber, arranging himself atop the bed in a stiff, uncomfortable-looking line. "Sometimes amusement. Either way, it doesn't concern us."

I followed his lead and climbed into his bed, pulling a slip of quilted velvet up to my nose. Maker, the smell was divine. "What do you define as *amusing*, Shadow Bringer? Paint me a picture."

He propped his head up on an elbow, peering at me from under his draconic helm. It was beginning to look quite lopsided; its caged mouth and one of its two horns had broken off, and I desperately wanted to yank off the rest of it.

"My amusement used to be dreaming. Flying over the Nocturne with outstretched wings. Imagining and creating entire worlds." His voice grew soft, a velvet purr. It was positively distracting, though I doubted he was even aware he was doing it. "Now the only thing I can qualify as amusing or enjoyable in the slightest has been the time I've spent with you."

I promptly turned around, shocked. I did *not* want him to see the flush rising to my face.

"Your standards for entertainment are a bit low. I don't know that I'd qualify this as either amusing or enjoyable." That was a lie. Parts of these dreams *had* been exhilarating. But if I focused on the darker moments—the hurt, the grief, the terror—they threatened to devour me whole. "Particularly since our eternal damnation is imminent."

"Yes. There is that." I felt the bed shift as he moved closer, once again enveloping us in a *whooshing* cocoon of shadow. Only this time, instead of his back, I was clearly pressed against his chest. "We still have two dreams left. We just need to find something in one of them that helps us break free."

He lifted my hair with a brush of his hand, fingers briefly grazing the nape of my neck. His clawed gauntlets were perpetually cold, and his unexpected touch felt electric.

Get ahold of yourself. He was moving my hair because it was in his way. Not because he wanted to touch *me*.

"What do *you* define as amusing, Esmer Havenfall?"

"I'm not sure. Reading? Daydreaming? What most girls my age would qualify as *amusing* hasn't happened yet."

A pause. "What's that?" He dared me to go on.

"I've never had a lover." I hated how exposed I felt around him, how *right* it felt for his hand to be threaded in my hair. "And if our souls really do become lost at the end of this, that means I'll die before having experienced all that life has to offer. Just as you'll die without having experienced freedom outside the Dream Realm in centuries. It's terrible. And wretchedly inconvenient for someone who has never even been kissed."

"You would desire such a thing?"

"Well, of course," I said with a laugh, turning to face him. "Doesn't everyone?"

His gaze dropped to my lips, a silent and shocking question. I hadn't expected for our conversation to turn *this* way. Hadn't imagined that he'd even consider doing what his expression now suggested. But his lips were slightly parted, and his helm had broken away just enough around his mouth and jaw to make it possible.

I nodded yes before the moment could be ripped away.

He brought his lips to mine. The kiss was soft, slow, and achingly tender. Just a graze of his sensuous mouth. But where his lips were soft, the rest of him was firm, rigid, and unyielding—a man encased in obsidian armor from his feet to his brow. The top of his helm felt cool against my forehead, his nose a mere suggestion in the shape of the metal. Still, while his mouth was pressed against mine, I scarcely noticed. Warmth surged through my limbs, pooling pleasantly in my stomach.

He leaned away too soon.

"There," he murmured, voice a shade darker than I'd ever heard it. "A first for both of us. Perhaps now our spirits will be less discontent after we perish."

"Perhaps so," I agreed.

I ached to kiss him again. To kiss him back *fully*.

I wanted to lift his helm from his face and thread my fingers through his moon-white hair. To arch into his chest as his arms pulled me closer. To explore more of him, chasing that warm, tingling feeling as he explored more of me, too. I wondered what more skin might feel like. Maybe it would feel safe. A comforting nearness that would push away everything terrible and cruel about the world.

But it could feel like betrayal, too. Like blinding, teeth-gnashing guilt.

I turned back around, my nonexistent heart racing at a steady, frantic pace in my chest.

The second dream began with a starlit sky. Floating, untethered, *free*.

And then we plummeted like stones, crashing into a floor of black marble. I gingerly untangled myself from the Shadow Bringer's long limbs, trying not to think about our kiss. We had fallen asleep in close proximity, his mouth near my ear, his gauntleted hand atop my waist, and his armored legs a close shadow around mine. But he never touched me in a way that wasn't strictly necessary. Never crossed that unspoken line.

"Where are we now?" I asked, reeling from the splendor surrounding us.

Vast and domed, the dimly lit chamber was adorned with painted murals depicting strange dreamscapes, celestial beings, and dreamers in various states of sleep. A long line of people, clad in nightclothes, stood in front of the murals as they waited to reach a circular dais draped in blue velvet. At the center was a willow tree, its long, slender branches slipping into a pool of starry water that encircled the dais and poured backward out of the chamber. There were two figures in front of the tree. One sat in a throne-like chair; the other stood at his side.

"Welcome to the Evernight Dream Temple," the Shadow Bringer

announced, helping me up. Hazy stars, almost as if they were pulled from the sky beyond, drifted into the chamber from the missing wall, casting ever-changing patterns on the floor. Several began spinning in slow circles around us, and he gently parted them with his hands. "Here the dreamers visit the kingdom's esteemed dream interpreters. All from the convenience of dreamers' mortal beds."

"It's beautiful," I breathed. "I would have done anything to visit a place like this if I knew I could."

"It used to be common. Dreamers would visit if they were struggling to make sense of their dreams, which happened often, or if a Weaver felt a dreamer was following a self-destructive path and needed clarity. For the dreamers who sought the temple willingly, most simply wished to know whether their dreams were Maker-sent, Weaver-sent, or figments of their own twisted minds."

"Are we here to get our dreams interpreted, then?"

He nodded grimly. "Yes. And hopefully we can speak with the interpreter before the demon appears. I can feel it lurking."

I shuddered. I didn't see the red-eyed demon anywhere, but that didn't mean it wasn't hiding in the shadows.

"Keep in mind that the first dream was, for the most part, a singular dream. A distorted nightmare of sorts. *This* is a memory of a collective dream. We can only participate here as much as the Maker wills."

An older man wearing a long robe and feathered slippers pushed into me.

"Go on," the man demanded, his half-hooded eyes glassy with sleep. "Go forward to the dais."

The Shadow Bringer shot him a look of icy, utter disdain, but the dreamer either couldn't see him or wasn't paying attention.

The dream, ever so slightly, flickered.

"You need to calm down," I ordered, grabbing the Bringer's hand before he could attempt anything drastic. "This dream relies on the strength and tranquility of your subconscious, correct? Because I think I'm starting to understand something."

"I am anything but tranquil, Esmer."

I fought not to roll my eyes. "If you let your emotions get the better of you—your rage, your disgust, your *hate*—then this dream will shatter before we can even meet the interpreter, yet alone confront the demon."

"So what do you wish for me to do? Be civil?"

"Yes. Be civil."

His eyes widened a touch, as if this was the most ridiculous concept he'd ever heard of. But then he sighed, a terse breath through his lips, and slowly squeezed my hand.

"I don't wish to be civil," he said darkly, giving me a deadly half smile. It was positively *violent*. "But for you, perhaps I will put my rage aside. Reserve it for those who truly deserve it."

Dozens of dreamers had formed a queue behind us, slowly materializing into the temple chamber each time a new dream was interpreted. From what I could see, interpretations held a specific pattern: The dreamer would approach the dais, images would appear in the water, the tree would glow one of several colors, and finally the interpreter would relay a brief message. Then the dreamer would vanish, presumably sent back to their earthbound dwelling. It appeared that the central figure was the main interpreter, whereas the figure next to him was perhaps his guard. Sometimes, the guard leaned sideways, sharing a laugh with the interpreter. Other times, he stood still and serious, glaring daggers at any dreamer who dared get too close or too comfortable.

"If the tree glows a color, the dream was sent by an elemental Weaver," the Shadow Bringer explained. "Red, blue, green, or brown for Fenrir, Nephtys, Ceres, or Lelantos. If the dream is from Somnus, Xander, or Theia, it will harden into either bone, iron, or diamond. If it turns black and charred, that means the dream is a nightmare. Some worthless figment either conjured by the dreamer themselves or under the influence of a demon."

Soon, we were near the front of the line.

With each step, the air grew thick with anticipation, as if the very atmosphere hummed with the secrets of the universe. The air that surrounded the dais was blurry, as if time itself was beginning to distort. The interpreter motioned us forward, his hands covered in black leather.

"Approach the water," the interpreter commanded, his voice a dark, haunting melody. "Look into its depths and show me what you seek, dreamer."

"Listen to him," the Shadow Bringer urged. "Look into the water and focus on your desire for freedom. Think about breaking away from my castle, and ask the Maker to help you. The Nocturne and your subconscious will do the rest."

I looked up, meeting the interpreter's silver-flecked eyes. Eyes I'd know anywhere now. *Erebus.*

My breath stilled; my chest *burned.* He was even more beautiful than I'd imagined he'd be.

His hair, raven black, swept away from a pale, perfect face that balanced masculinity with something so refined and so elegant that he was difficult to look at. With his helm on, the Shadow Bringer was a striking collage of sharp and captivating pieces: eyes, lips, jaw, metal. Unmasked, with all his features revealed, he was a masterpiece.

"Why is—"

"Don't acknowledge me," the Shadow Bringer murmured just as a shadow ghosted across my lips, silencing me. "It will draw the suspicions of Weavers or dreamers, which could jeopardize the dream's viability. Just...be careful. And be especially mindful of *that* one."

That one? Reluctantly, I tore my eyes from Erebus to his guard.

Not guard—the Light Bringer. Mithras.

Mithras, his honeyed eyes sparkling with humor, stood next to Erebus, arm casually draped atop the back of his chair. Erebus's cape billowed behind him like the wings of some nocturnal creature, complementing the finely tailored clothes he wore; Mithras, on the other hand, wore a white shirt that was open at the collar, black slim-fitting pants, and golden adornments that gleamed even in the dimly lit room. Both wore similar signet rings; both had the trappings of two beautiful young princes in their primes.

The water was still and depthless like an all-seeing eye.

Odd.

When I looked, I could feel the water looking back. Waiting. Assessing. Probing for ways to help me *see*. Something tugged faintly on my mind, coaxing out a memory. I followed the Shadow Bringer's instructions, focusing on my desire for freedom. Vaguely, I could sense my mind drifting to Elliot, but I pulled it back, focusing instead on my dream of the Shadow Bringer's castle and the invisible bindings that trapped us there. The Nocturne wanted more—it felt unsatisfied—so I gave it more context. Corruption and my frustration because there was no cure. Eden, Mother, and Father. Aching for a normal life outside of Norhavellis. The terror I felt whenever I thought about Elliot. My connection with the Shadow Bringer.

My deeply *unsettling* connection with the Shadow Bringer.

Erebus could see some of what I was showing the Nocturne—pieces of the Shadow Bringer's castle, the demons, my family—but other parts were swept away, hidden as if only for the water itself. The willow's branches sank idly into the liquid, softly swaying.

Show me how to be free, I thought.

Show me how to save us.

Show me how to save all of us.

Suddenly, the temple began to glow with a radiant, overwhelming light. The tree was turning gold, lit from within as if by the sun itself. I felt warmth spread through my limbs, a pure aching *rightness*. Tears slipped down my face because, for a moment—for once in perhaps my entire life—I finally felt nothing but peace, hope, and the reassurance that everything would be fine. The dreamers behind us were similarly amazed. Some wept; others simply beamed in outright joy.

The Shadow Bringer stood at my side, utterly speechless. He cast a beautiful shadow with the sun dancing in his eyes.

The dream flickered again. We were running out of time. *Hurry.*

"Your dream is Maker-given, dreamer. A light in the darkness," Erebus said, standing to get a better look. Beside him, Mithras was staring in similar wonder. "Nightmares are false; they exist to misdirect, twist, and misalign dreamers with their true purpose. Weaver-sent dreams are messages meant to inspire, teach, warn, or guide—all depending on the Weaver. But Maker-sent dreams serve a greater purpose. They can alter the fabric of the Realm itself."

"What does my dream mean?" I urged. "Can you tell me what I should know?"

Erebus closed his eyes, considering. Then they opened quickly, snapping back to mine.

"I cannot. Maker-sent dreams are not for me to interpret. I can only tell you that you are on the right path and that your dream serves an important role in the fabric of our world."

"That tells us *nothing*," the Shadow Bringer spat.

"Is there truly nothing you can tell me?" I implored, echoing the Shadow Bringer's frustration.

Erebus peered into the water. "When I try to interpret your dream, shadows cloud my vision. The only thing I can glean is that you are meant to walk through this darkness in order to find what you are looking for. Keep moving forward, and trust that you will reach your purpose. I'm sorry I can't tell you more. I wish I could."

Suddenly the dream quivered, fraying at its edges.

In the open space behind the dais, the Nocturne could be seen in all its great expanse. But something was terribly wrong. A murky presence had formed on the horizon, and it was sliding through the water, turning the sea black in its wake. With every step, the dream temple shook.

"I see you, dreamers," the shape rumbled, its voice shaking the foundations of Evernight. The dreamers around us, including Erebus and Mithras, began to fade, unaware of what was happening. "You will not run."

In a blink, the intruder was upon us. Its colossal face peered through the temple's open wall, skull ringed in horns that framed red smoking eyes. Its face was still a mask of swirling darkness—a terrifying storm cloud that sought to devour more than just bones and blood. It hungered for the very fabric of a person's being, the threads that held souls together.

"You fight against your fate; you are meant to succumb to the dark. It is in your blood," the demon spoke to me.

The Shadow Bringer grabbed me by the waist, urging me to run. He sent a wave of rolling darkness into the demon's head, but it was useless. The demon merely laughed, a strange, hideous sound that felt too similar to the crash of thunder, and began to smash the temple wall so that its body could properly fit.

"We need to wake up, Bringer. We have no chance."

"No, we don't," he agreed, holding me tighter. "This isn't natural; this demon is so powerful that it's destroying the threads of time itself."

The demon grabbed the willow tree with a massive claw. Instantly, the bark charred, turned black, and erupted into flames.

"Hold on," the Shadow Bringer urged. Our shadows swept us forward, desperate to save us.

"If you continue squirming, dreamers, I will find other ways to pry you apart," the demon warned.

"Ignore it. Keep running—"

"I know!"

"I will start with your brother, Esmer Havenfall. If you do not succumb, I will tear him apart limb from limb. I will dismember him and make you watch."

Fear, sharp and deep, twisted my stomach, sending my mind reeling. Demons were liars—deceivers and weavers of ugly half-truths. But this demon already knew Elliot. Had tried to devour him once. Had *hunted* for my entire family, if what Somnus said was true.

The demon pulled the tree out by its roots, throwing it at us in a fiery, smoking spiral.

And then the world went black.

30

We woke in the Shadow Bringer's bed, haunted and shaking. We had no time.

"We need to go further into my subconscious," the Bringer said breathlessly, fingers shaking slightly as he formed the shadows around the bed, cocooning us from the sounds of destruction. "This is our final opportunity. I need to be able to sustain the third dream long enough for us to explore it fully."

I helped him construct the veil of shadows this time, strengthening it with threads of my own magic. Almost instantly, a small weight appeared to lift off his shoulders. Still, he seemed distracted. Unfocused. I felt similarly untethered. My mind was a raging pit of despair, filled with a deep, nauseating terror at the prospect of Elliot being hunted by that demon.

He brought his gauntleted hands to my face, gently easing them through my hair.

"Before we enter the final dream, I need you to know something," he said.

"Hopefully you're not about to tell me that you're actually a figment of my imagination."

"What? *No.*" The shadows in his eyes danced, an unexpected display of mirth. "I am real, Esmer. All of this, all of *me*, is human. From the moment I met you, you've never ceased to remind me of that fact." His shadows stilled, and for a moment, I thought he was going to kiss me. But something in him resisted. "I was only going to say that first, you must know that I will do whatever it takes to free us from this castle. Even if it means that you're freed and I'm not."

"That isn't the plan, Bringer."

"The second is that I will destroy the demon before it can hurt you or your brother," he continued, ignoring my protests. "I will tear the Dream Realm asunder before I let that monster harm you. Now," he continued, voice shifting into a deep, melodic purr, "I'm going to ease us into this final dream. Listen to me. Imagine with me. Have you ever been to a ball?"

The question was so unexpected that I laughed. "They're not exactly commonplace in Norhavellis."

But Eden and I always dreamed of what it would be like to attend one.

His smirk was back—almost a smile this time. "Then let us disrupt one."

I'm not sure what I expected to come next, but it wasn't a *boat*. We arrived upon a sleek, elegant vessel adorned with two throne-like chairs. As soon as the Shadow Bringer and I sat, the boat tilted forward, cutting soundlessly across the Nocturne as it headed toward Citadel Evernight.

I fidgeted in my chair of tufted silk, wishing I had something to brace myself against. I had some experience riding horses, and I had been inside the Light Bringer's carriage. A boat was another thing entirely.

I bit my tongue against a sentence that would have betrayed my unease, instead forcing myself to stop glancing down at the Nocturne—with its eerie stillness and faint, slithering shadows—and to instead look up at the towering structure that was Evernight. Closer now, its walls seemed carved from a mountain. It rose in jagged swaths of stone, forming the base of seven massive arches, and within each arch flowed a waterfall, pouring into the ancient sea below. The tops of the arches seemed to be circling something—exactly what, I couldn't tell. It was too far up in the sky to see.

For an academy, it was breathtaking.

But it was more than a school for dreamers. It was a training ground for talented scholars, but it was also a temple for slumbering mortals to have their dreams interpreted, a host for decadent revelries, and an important meeting place for the seven Weavers and their followers.

The boat rocked to the left, almost sending me careening into the Bringer's shoulder. I tried to counteract the next motion—surely a dip to the right—but I guessed wrong. My hip slid awkwardly against the silk, sending me off the seat and onto the floor. Reflexively, I grabbed on to something to steady myself.

Unfortunately, that something was the Shadow Bringer's thigh.

He stiffened at my touch, thoroughly disrupted from whatever musings he had been lost in.

"Easy," he muttered. But instead of ridiculing me, the Bringer simply offered me his hand. I took it gratefully, settling back into my seat with no small amount of embarrassment. "The Weavers enjoy making the Realm as lifelike as possible. Some of their creations—such as this boat—translate better than others, as you have just discovered."

Other boats could be seen in the distance, carrying their appointed dreamers in vessels similar to ours. And sure enough, they rocked and swayed just as much as we did.

"Interesting," I managed, gripping the edge of my seat. "I can't say I understand the logic. They could have made it glide, or fly."

The boat suddenly righted itself, cutting through the water like a hot knife through butter. As it picked up speed, a soft wind, touched by twilight and the scent of the Nocturne, gently lifted my hair. The only indicator of the Bringer's influence was a haze of darkness at the ship's underbelly.

And the Bringer hadn't even twitched a finger.

"Let's see what we can make it, then," he said playfully.

The boat tripled in size, stretching itself tall and wide as it grew to fill the waterway. A carved figurehead emerged from the front, shaped into the visage of a one-winged angel, and black sails, glistening like a blanket of stars, unfurled from its new mast. Saturated in ink, the boat—now a magnificent ship—became a thing of darkness.

The Shadow Bringer gave me a pointed look, clearly amused with his abilities.

I found myself leaning into the wind. It was a strange feeling, being whisked away to a ball with the Shadow Bringer at my side, and I tried not to think about the previous dream or my nauseating fear about Elliot's safety. I considered instead what we were about to face. Because even while the Shadow Bringer seemed at ease in his vessel of darkness, there was trepidation in his eyes. As though he knew what was coming. Or, if he didn't, his instincts knew.

I didn't have time to ask.

A crowd filled with dreamers was gathering in front of Evernight as they stepped off their various ships. I couldn't tell who was a Weaver, who was a regular dreamer, or who was a scholar of Evernight. To me, they all looked the same: clothed in outrageous colors and textures and outfitted to look like kings and queens. But even in their finery, it was *us* they stared at. Hundreds of eyes, bright with envy—no, *hunger*—at our ship's power and beauty.

They were staring at us, too.

"They're staring," I hissed. "Why are they staring?"

Unbothered, the Bringer leaned back into his seat. "Because I gave them something to stare at."

"Right. Well, they look like they want to eat us." I mimicked his posture and leaned into the silk. If he wasn't concerned, then maybe I didn't need to be, either. "If they attack, I hope you're as confident mounting a defense as you are in your shipbuilding. It'll be you versus a few hundred."

"Just me? You have a maddening habit of wielding the shadows, too," he murmured, clinking the tips of his armored fingers together. "You should be perfectly capable of defending yourself. Me versus half of them, by my count."

"Fine," I agreed with a grin, shivering with delight when the shadows rose to my call, pooling around our feet and dancing across our limbs. Then there was my sword, thrumming reassuringly under my palm. "Me versus half."

Once our ship slid to a stop in front of Evernight, I fully expected the crowd to storm us. But as we stepped off the ship, their eyes drifted elsewhere. As if the ship had never existed at all.

As if *we* had never existed at all.

"My ship wasn't a part of the original dream, so it can't be remembered for long," the Bringer explained, making his way to Evernight's main entrance. There were three passages cut into the citadel's mountainside: The left went down, the right went up, and the middle went straight. So far, none of the dreamers had approached the middle; masked gatekeepers, clothed in black with silver insignias on their chests, directed the dreamers left and right. "And even if they acknowledge us, our impression will be fleeting. We'll neither be truly seen nor fully remembered for long, no matter how memorable one might be." He said the last part coyly, clearly meaning *me*.

Face burning, I noted the crowd's excitement. They were radiant, beaming and chattering as if they were about to experience the most glorious event in all their lives. Still, I questioned whether they truly couldn't see us. Some looked as though they were purposefully *avoiding* eye contact with us.

"Think of this night as a frozen memory," the Bringer continued, failing to notice the dreamers who had quietly begun to watch him. They whispered as we passed, glancing at him from the corners of their eyes. Some looked on in admiration, others in outright fear. "We can do whatever we wish within it."

"His hair and his helm, what do you suppose...," one anonymous voice said audibly.

"Perhaps it is the theme," said another.

"But that look in his eyes. Don't you think...," the first went on.

Others looked at me, too. Not so much in awe or fear, but jealousy. Anger, even.

"No one has ever seen her here before," a third voice hissed.

"A new scholar, perhaps," another wondered.

"He would never...," a fourth voice gasped.

"Evernight is permanently housed within the Realm, so there is never a primary dreamer," the Bringer continued, oblivious. As we passed through the crowd, some of the bolder ones reached out to feel the edge of his cloak. "No singular Weaver in control, either."

I swatted at a man's too-eager hand. "Um, Bringer..."

"Lord Erebus," announced a gatekeeper, stepping in front of us and sweeping into a bow. He adjusted his collar as he rose, fixing me with a curious once-over. A silver mask covered most of his face, framing the top of his mustache. "You may pass, of course, but the Seven have decreed specific attire for the dreamers."

The Shadow Bringer stared at the gatekeeper as if he had grown a second head. As if growing a second head would be more likely than him actually *seeing* us and, consequently, *talking* to us as though we were regular dreamers and not the Shadow Bringer and his companion from five hundred years in the future.

"I must also take the name of your...partner," the gatekeeper stammered, flustered by the Bringer's silence. "She is not listed on the register—we did not know you would be bringing a guest—but I will, of course, make all suitable arrangements. How nice it is that you brought..."

"She is—" the Shadow Bringer began.

"My name is Esmer," I interrupted. I tried to look as pleasant as possible, even as my name echoed in the crowd. *Esmer. Esmer. Esmer.* By the fourth *Esmer,* my name was written on a scroll that appeared from thin air. "What attire is appropriate?"

The gatekeeper straightened. "It is the Revel of Rebirth, my lady.

Weaver Lelantos has prepared the appropriate specifications to honor the occasion." He pointed at the left passageway. "Evernight scholars will attire you within."

"Thank you," I said, feigning nonchalance. As if I knew exactly what he was talking about.

I gave the Bringer a pointed look. *Frozen memory* this definitely was *not*. It all felt strange, wrong. As though we were intruding on a life already lived. Was it possible that the Bringer did something to skew the dream? He ran a finger along the armor at his neck, fidgeting with one of its points. I had never seen him *fidget* before.

The Bringer noticed me looking at him. Shadows spun slowly within his irises as he unhooked his hand from his neck.

"Have a glorious Revel, my lord," said the gatekeeper, bowing again to the Shadow Bringer. He gave a third bow, this time to me. "As may you, Esmer."

At once, a silver-masked girl with golden brown skin and hair braided like a crown emerged from the left passage, wearing black robes lined in silver. An Evernight scholar, I assumed, based on her intelligent, appraising eyes and the quiet, confident way she carried herself. She appeared to be my age, if not younger, and I found myself wondering which Weaver she had pledged herself to. Ceres? Theia? I bit the inside of my cheek, undecided. I had no way of knowing what her gifts were, so guessing would be useless.

"Welcome to Evernight, dreamer. My name is Aris," she said, regarding me with polite curiosity. It was different from the curiosity of the gatekeeper, or the judgmental crowd. "Please, follow me. I can escort you personally." She nodded to the Shadow Bringer, as if her escorting me was a personal favor. "Have a glorious Revel, Lord Erebus. Ceveon and Sorren are inside."

The Bringer's face twisted into cold indifference. "Of course they would be."

Maybe he would have said more, but Aris gently touched my arm straightaway, cuing me forward. Evernight gleamed overhead, beckoning me to experience something that was only available through the pages of a storybook. Yet still I hesitated.

I should be excited, I told myself. Elliot would be excited. Eden would have been, too.

I looked at the Shadow Bringer one final time, perhaps seeking his approval or reassurance, but he didn't notice me. He was too busy glaring at Evernight as though it was a foe to be conquered, killed, or strangled with his bare hands.

I turned back to the passage, frustrated.

Maybe I was right to be worried after all.

The moment I stepped over the threshold and into Evernight, a warm breeze licked my boots, curled around my legs, and skimmed my back. Then it cupped my face, examining me, before whisking through my hair and away to something else.

"What was that?"

Aris squeezed my elbow. "It's Evernight. It does that to dreamers—skims their bodies and reads their minds. Like a thorough guard. Or nosy grandmother."

"Bizarre," I breathed, wondering what Evernight saw when it examined me. Did it know that I was from a different time? Did it even care? I glanced around, half expecting to see eyes on the walls.

"When it first happened to me, it felt similar to the attentions of a curious dog," she said, chuckling softly. "But don't be alarmed—it happens to all of us. To some, every time. For others, just once and never again."

"What does it do if it doesn't like what it finds?" I asked.

Aris shrugged. "That depends. Evernight could deny you entry or throw you out. Or it might steal your secrets and deliver them straight to one of the Seven."

I did not like the sound of that.

"So did I pass its test, then?"

"Possibly. But sometimes Evernight chooses to do nothing, even if it questions your origins or intent."

Before I could ask more questions, the passage opened into an excessively opulent chamber. My eyes burned from the brightness of it, just as my nose burned from the smell. Jasmine, lemon, rose, pear, vanilla. Other things that I couldn't name. Things I had never smelled before but wanted to. Vanity mirrors lined the walls, each with its own golden chair, and botanical arrangements in glass vases sat between each mirror, growing so long and unruly that they trailed to the floor, eventually crossing stems and growing into intricate shapes, whorls, and paths.

Aris stood by me as I stepped to the side, watching as women in an array of colorful dresses, each more gaudy and more intricate than the next, filed in. They chatted excitedly among themselves, taking their seats in front of the mirrors. Once they were seated, male and female scholars, dressed in black with the silver insignia of Evernight on their robes, at once began assessing and altering the women's appearances. It was a kind of magic that only a dream could produce—instant changes of hair color, makeup, adornments, clothing—and I couldn't help staring. It was fascinating, and most scholars needed only a minute to work their magic.

One minute of concentration and anything was possible.

Hair of all colors, textures, and lengths was shaped into elegant styles without a single pin. Dresses were shortened, fabric loosened, colors lightened into ivory, rose, and peach. Masks were added last. And while the dresses, makeup, and hair varied from woman to woman, every mask had the same ornate design: carved ivory, inlaid feathers, and rows of delicate beadwork lining the edges. Despite the masks, the women looked lighter as they left the chamber. Unburdened.

Well, *most* of them.

"Hideous. This color doesn't suit me at all," a woman at the mirror complained. She pinched her skin as she examined her eyes, lips, and cheeks. Her scowl deepened the longer she looked. "Sorren always used a shade darker—less plum, more berry." The attending scholar brushed a hand over the woman's face, delicate as a breeze, and the makeup changed. I had thought it looked fine before. But the woman smiled, finally pleased. "There. I look beautiful now, don't I?"

The scholar nodded, bowed quickly, then promptly moved on to the next dreamer.

"He probably thinks he's too good for this work now," another woman remarked. A scholar was in the middle of fixing her hair into a loose braid atop her head. "You saw how he looked at us the last time. Pride is such a sin."

The first woman rolled her eyes, adjusting her flowing skirts as she rose. "And an unhoused dreamer is still unhoused, no matter what friends they keep. One would think Sorren would understand that by now."

"One would think," the second woman echoed. Her attendant finished her hair, and she beamed at herself in the mirror. "Lovely." To the first woman, she said sweetly, "Have a glorious Revel."

The woman returned her saccharine smile. "And a glorious Revel to you, too."

Aris gestured at a chair to my left.

"May I?" she asked, waiting for a nod before setting her hands on my head. Her fingers meandered through the strands, gently lifting them from my scalp. "Your hair is a fine color—and quite full. It needs little else." She let the strands fall; at once they became untangled, glossy, and loosely curled. "Unless you'd prefer something more eye-catching?" Aris gave a subtle nod toward the woman at my right.

The woman was in the middle of admiring her hair, which didn't look that different from a large bird's nest. Even for a Realm style, I imagined it must feel heavy and awkward, but the woman seemed pleased with herself, ignoring her attending scholar's suggestions.

I winced. "Definitely not."

"Good. And besides, you don't need the distraction," Aris agreed, turning her attention to my face. She brushed a hand over my cheeks, my nose, my eyebrows. Lightly pinched my chin. Took the edge of her pinkie nail and traced the shape of a half-moon on my forehead. "Let's accentuate your eyes, add some shimmer to catch the light, and use a darker rose for your lips. What do you think?"

I looked at myself in the mirror. Tried—and failed—to envision what she was planning. My eyes, lashes, and brows were already dark. My natural lip color was muted. Unremarkable.

"I don't usually fix my face with powders and paints," I admitted, trying not to fidget under Aris's scrutiny. "So I'm not sure."

"Oh, this is far better than those simple embellishments. Promise. Now, let me see."

And before I released my next breath, my face changed.

It was as she had promised. My features darkened, becoming more defined and commanding, and the color on my lips made them appear fuller. Tempting, even. And at my temples, brushed artfully into my hair, was a shimmering silver dust. I had worried she would make me unrecognizable, but I still looked like myself. Polished and beautiful, but myself.

Aris gave an approving nod. "You look lovely, Esmer. Lord Erebus will surely think so, too."

I blushed. Actually *blushed*. Over a simple compliment.

Aris must think I am incredibly vain. Someone easily swayed by pretty words—just like all the other women here.

"It is not wrong to acknowledge or appreciate your own beauty," Aris remarked, as if hearing exactly what I was thinking. "In fact, I think it is rather honorable to recognize beauty in yourself. No matter which form it may take."

She was sincere. But I had already averted my eyes from the mirror.

"Thank you," I managed. "Truly."

"Of course. Now, for your attire." Aris took a step back, assessing. "You will want to match Lord Erebus, I presume. He does favor his black, but this Revel requires a lighter touch."

I bristled. "I don't have to match him."

She gave me a peculiar look. "You are his guest, are you not? It is tradition to honor your Realm host."

"And I would honor him by matching him?" I pictured the Bringer and me entering the ball together. Envisioned the hundreds of eyes as they swiveled to stare, fixating on our matching dramatic capes, devilish armor, and pointed boots. What a pair we'd make. A very obvious, not-blending-in-at-all pair.

"Yes," she said with a smile. "But your attire would not be identical to his, if that is what you are imagining."

"It wasn't." *It was.*

Soft fabric cocooned my old clothes, squeezing, shaping, and stretching them into something new. As the cocoon unfurled, it revealed floating layers of dove gray silk, sheer sleeves that fell from my shoulders to my wrists, and a wide, somewhat-revealing neckline. Delicate slippers cushioned my feet, molded to me as if I had worn them my entire life. Last, a mask nestled itself to my face, curving elegantly over my nose and eyes. It was gray, not ivory like the others, and a simple, flattering shape that matched the silhouette of my dress.

My breath caught as I studied myself.

I had imagined, when I was younger, what I might look like in a princess's gown. Eden and I had shared many of these daydreams as girls, describing what we'd procure when we could finally visit a proper dress shop. What we'd wear to balls or garden strolls with wealthy lords and handsome princes. What we'd wear to our own weddings, even. In truth, we had little understanding of what people wore outside of Norhavellis. What colors were favored or what quality satin or velvet felt like. All we had were storybooks and the imaginations of children. And even with all my lavish daydreams, never in my life had I imagined donning something so magnificent.

"Go on, take a twirl," Aris said, grinning. "This may be my best work yet. Come, now."

She guided me into a spin, making a sound of approval as my dress gently floated behind me.

"How long have you been a scholar here in Evernight? You're very talented."

We completed a second spin. "I was recruited at thirteen with my twin brother. It was Theia, Weaver of the Future, who found us in a dream and assured us of our potential."

"So you study under Theia's guidance, then?" I asked, curious about what it was like to study in a place such as Evernight.

But instead of answering, she dropped my hands. "I should escort you to the Revel. I've taken enough of your time."

Wait—no. "If I said something wrong, I'm sorry," I said quickly, stiffening at the sudden change in her tone. What unspoken line had I crossed? If I had already blundered so severely, I wouldn't last five minutes at the Revel. "Erebus has told me some things about Evernight, but he tends to be a little cryptic. My question wasn't intended to hurt you, but I apologize if it did."

She held my stare, challenging me. Finally, she let loose a sigh. Her defensiveness weakened. Snuffed itself out like a dying flame. "No, I overreacted. To answer your question, I have no assigned domain. I've yet to be formally selected by a Weaver, even though Theia sought me out in a dream all those years ago. A Weaver can sense potential in scholars and even their likely specialty, but dreamers don't always develop their abilities enough to join a Weaver's domain as one of their acolytes after completing their studies at Evernight."

"So why haven't you been chosen? You're very talented."

"You flatter me," Aris said softly. "Modifying appearances is a common ability in the Dream Realm. I have not shown significant potential in what *matters*, which is showing talent in one of the seven Weavers' areas." She added, voice lowering, "If I'm not selected by eighteen, I'll be deemed unhoused. Then I will either work to maintain Evernight until the end of my mortal days or be banished from the Realm forever. I'll never be able to join a Weaver in their domain or do anything of true purpose or importance." She squeezed her hands together. "My brother and I turn eighteen at the end of this year."

I shook my head, contemplating the reality of that fate. "And your brother? Does he face the same future as you?"

She nodded, eyes downcast. "If he isn't chosen, he will be devastated. We've both trained years for this, but he's the one it will hurt most." Aris coughed, straightening her black skirts with a flourish. "I'm sorry for rambling. I should get you to the Revel before Lord Erebus hunts you down himself."

Before we left, I caught my reflection a final time. I almost stumbled, noting something different in my eyes.

There were shadows in my irises, swirling and vibrant.

Just like the Shadow Bringer's.

I smelled the next room before I could see it.

Salt and flowers. The wormy odor of fresh earth. The brush of a storm-soaked wind. Tree roots, pine needles, and sun-warmed fur. Damp rocks and cracked acorns and sweet dandelions. Tart berries. Gentle touches of lavender, sage, mint. And roses. The soft, powdery scent of roses. Peonies. Tulips.

And about one hundred other things that I couldn't name.

"It smells..." I wasn't sure which word could possibly do it justice.

"Most say 'heavenly.' But I've heard one or two dreamers who thought it too rustic. As if the smell of earth is a thing reserved for animals." Aris took a deep, cleansing breath. "Or those of common blood."

"That's ridiculous. It smells incredible. Like joy and wonder."

She led me to a glass bridge that split the center of a cavernous antechamber. Except there was no ground under the bridge—no visible ceiling, either. Only pillared walls connected the room's various parts. Under the bridge was a vista of a great forest, and above the bridge, where the chamber's ceiling cracked apart, was a cyclical sky. Dawn, day, dusk, night. The sky rotated quickly, mesmerizing in its pure depiction of the sun, moon, stars, and clouds. It illuminated the bridge and the forest with new colors every few steps.

It was life itself, captured in a room.

No, it was more than life—it was idealized beyond what would be possible outside the Realm. The trees were too even, the sky too wondrous, the flowers too full, the rocks too precisely placed. Still, I couldn't help recognizing the chamber's majesty. It was, after all, the essence of earth made into its fullest potential. And as we walked across the bridge, my footing unsure in my new slippers, I breathed deep and examined all that I could.

A strange emotion welled up in my chest, hollow and uncomfortable. I wanted to share this experience with someone. Wanted deeply, achingly, to share what I was seeing, hearing, and smelling. Eden and Elliot would have loved Evernight. It was the culmination of everything we'd ever imagined: bright, beautiful wonders in a place safe enough to fully enjoy it. No demons, no darkness, no hunger, no fear. It was why, I think, Eden had finally relented when I'd begged her not to drink the elixir. Because dreaming *just once* would be worth it. And for hundreds of dreamers centuries ago, it *was* worth it. I swallowed hard, focusing on my footsteps instead of the pain in my heart.

And the Shadow Bringer—I'd very much like to watch his eyes as he beheld this room.

"Every year, a different Weaver is charged with furnishing Evernight," Aris explained, softly interrupting my wandering thoughts. "It is Weaver Ceres's year, though she is not in charge of this season's Revel."

Furnishing Evernight. As if the scene were no more elaborate than a rug or a houseplant.

She pointed at the sky, growing heavy with the colors of dawn. "This room is enchanted to change at precise points on the bridge. But only to the beholder." She gestured at a family ahead of us. They laughed as several plumed birds flew overhead, circling once before diving underneath the bridge. "By the time we reach that point, it will be day. But they will be farther along, so they will see the onset of dusk. Three cycles pass before we reach the end."

"It's beautiful."

"It is. And tedious," Aris sighed. "And a few hundred paces too long."

"What's the purpose of it, then? To be beautiful and tedious?"

She shrugged. "Evernight serves a different purpose for each of its inhabitants. And it's best to be aware that some purposes are more sinister than others."

At its end, the bridge forked into three paths. The dreamers, dressed in their finery, continued forward. Their accompanying scholars did not. With a quick curtsy or bow, each scholar left them to continue on. Alone.

"Go to the middle bridge," Aris directed. "Revels are for the Weavers, their acolytes, and dreamers. We scholars have other matters to attend to."

"Like making dreamers look acceptable?" I asked, fluffing the folds of my dress.

"You look more than acceptable," she said approvingly. "You should be thankful I found you. Others would have put you in yellow. Or worse, pink."

"If that's the case, I'm very thankful. I doubt Erebus would recognize me if I were wearing pink," I said with a grin. Aris returned my smile, but her expression felt a little sad. And expectant, somehow. "I hope you're chosen by a Weaver," I added. And I meant it. "I hope your brother is, too."

Aris bowed, and when she stood again, she straightened her back and held her chin high. "Enjoy the Revel. Perhaps I will see you again, one day."

And she left me to continue alone.

I hesitated at the end of the path, taking a grounding breath. In the flurry of being whittled into a finer, more elegant version of myself, I had nearly forgotten where I was. And, perhaps even more importantly, where the Shadow Bringer was.

And where *was* the Shadow Bringer?

More dreamers passed by, continuing to the Revel. Women in floating gowns and glistening facial adornments. Men, some with their eyes and lips defined by paint and powder, in equally brilliant clothes. Supple fabric, open necklines, dramatic hemlines, intricate layers and beadwork. There were a few children, too; some of the younger ones beamed with excitement, but others seemed listless, as if they'd already been to Evernight a thousand times, and this was just another boring familial requirement. Adults and children. Beautiful, chattering dreamers of all ages.

But no Shadow Bringer.

Maybe he'd decided to pursue whatever it was he wanted to do now that we could be seen and felt. Maybe he'd figured I'd only get in his way. I gritted my teeth, considering. Okay, so maybe I *would* get in his way. But that would only be because I was brave enough to try.

I decided to follow the next family, a man and woman with their son and daughter, slowing my pace so as to not draw attention to myself. The mother and father walked with fluid movements and raised chins, maintaining their grace and poise even in the casual audience of their immediate family. The guise of Realm attire couldn't hide what—or who—they probably were: royalty. Or near enough to it.

My mother and father had tried to mimic that kind of elegance once. Tried to fold it into their steps and smear it over their hard edges and dirt-covered lines. A tired king and his dutiful queen.

I folded my arms over my chest, frowning at the turn my thoughts had taken.

Who was I to judge my parents? I was just as broken as they were. *If not worse.*

The middle passageway brightened significantly as we neared the exit, widening and arching up in time with our progress. At the top, the bridge paused in its ascent, caught by a swirling veil of mist that obscured our steps.

The daughter visibly balked, shivering as soon as the mist touched her skin. "This had better be good," she said with a sigh. "The last time they did the mist, it was so dull. And the mock *battles*. Who even cares about war demonstrations? There are only so many ways someone can die."

The brother glared at her, more than ready to participate in a battle of his own with his sister. "You think everything is boring. I should throw you over the bridge. Then you wouldn't have to suffer the intolerable dullness any longer."

"Is that how you punish your servants, too? Throw them over your drawbridge? How utterly simplistic," she hissed, flicking her hair over her shoulder and quickening her steps. "I may tire of boring things, but at least I have more creative pursuits than throwing my heart at every man or woman who looks my way. Unlike you, who spent the last Revel with that pathetic lord's ugly son."

"Ugly?" he snapped back. "*Ugly?* What's ugly is your gross stain of a dress. Why would you ever wear orange?"

"How does this look orange to you? It's *peach*," she insisted, nearly shouting. But she picked at her dress, anyway, examining the fabric. "Just—just stop talking to me. I don't need the validation of a fool."

Their mother spun around, her mouth frozen in a serene smile. Which made it all the more frightening as she said, "What is truly *dull* and *ugly* is finding yourself sitting in your bedchamber, miserable and alone, while everyone else in society is enjoying the Revel. Your father and I can see to it that you never attend one again."

The siblings immediately straightened their backs and squared their shoulders, as if to remind their mother how prim and perfect her children truly were.

I couldn't help it. I laughed.

The mother had already turned around, no longer bothered by her children's bickering, but the brother and sister spun at once, eyes wide behind their masks.

"The audacity," the sister gasped, mortified.

The brother frowned at me before dragging his eyes from my feet to the top of my curled hair. Then he smirked, as if discovering a strange, disturbing secret. "You're some fledgling acolyte's new pet, aren't you?

You must be so overwhelmed." He made a point to look around us. "Oh dear, I'm sorry. Have you been forgotten already? You poor thing. The acolytes can be so fickle."

"I'm no one's pet," I snapped. "And my *friend* is waiting for me inside."

"It really is a pity to Revel alone. And in such a depressing dress, too," the sister added.

The brother cocked his head and thumbed his chin. "Actually, it's quite a nice dress."

"It absolutely is not," the sister insisted.

"Who made it? And your face. The glamour that they did with your eyes is striking."

"What do you care about that wretch?"

They turned their backs to me, more engrossed in their own bickering than my dress or the shadows swirling in my eyes. The mist snapped at their heels, partially obscuring them despite their nearness.

And just as quickly as they lost interest in me, the mist lifted.

The coliseum that appeared before us was straight out of the pages of Elliot's favorite Weaver book. Rows upon rows of gilded seats circled the coliseum floor, flush with dreamers partaking in the finest food, drink, and entertainment. Winged beasts, their intelligent eyes sparkling with amusement, flew between the columns, making the children laugh. Evernight scholars, masked and smiling as though they, too, were enjoying themselves, performed various feats atop floating platforms— everything from adorning dreamers' attire with feathers to commanding the air itself to carry guests to and from different parts of the coliseum. Chalices automatically refilled themselves with sparkling liquid, and platters were always brimming with colorful, strange, and fragrant dishes. Dreamers crowded the seats in their ethereal dresses, silky shirts, and perfectly crafted masks, smiling, laughing, flirting—vying mightily for the attention of others.

Everything felt vibrant, fresh, *alive.*

Some dreamers swiveled to regard me with curious or scrutinizing eyes, but mostly I was left to wander without interruption. If they remembered who I was from the Shadow Bringer's dramatic entrance, they didn't show it. The sweet-smelling food, the heady wine, the rows of beautiful people—it was all more seductive than a lone girl who may or may not have been associated with their lord Erebus.

I took a seat and picked up a stray goblet, curious to taste the flavor of an Evernight drink. I knew I needed to find the Shadow Bringer, but couldn't I enjoy myself in the meantime?

Stop thinking about the Bringer; he clearly isn't thinking of you. Or looking, for that matter.

Clarity burst through me as I drank from the goblet, cooling my skin and tingling across my tongue. The liquid tasted of fresh rain, of morning mist, and a little like the gasp of air you take while running— the breath you force into your lungs when you're at the peak of exhaustion, giving you a glorious burst of raw, powerful energy. It tasted of freedom and redemption and hope.

A bit like the sky, I thought.

So I took another sip. And another. I tried all kinds of drinks and food, each tasting more brilliant and more invigorating than the last. The more I consumed, the more I craved.

I wanted more, more, *more*.

For what felt like forever—and not nearly long enough—I laughed, smiled, drank, and ate with the masked dreamers around me. Watched as great winged beasts flew overhead. Smiled at the compliments from men and women. On my dress. On my skin. On my beauty. Everything was lost to me. Time, purpose, and logic. Anything that wasn't here, now—none of that mattered.

And as more time passed, the more I felt as though I belonged among these mysterious, beautiful people. Maybe I didn't want to go back home after all. If I forgot my purpose, maybe I could stay in this place forever. Here I could be what I was meant to be: beautiful, glorious, free.

Free!

As the night—or day, because who could tell?—spiraled on and the winged creatures stopped their flights, the conversation slowed to a deep, vibrating *thrum*. At the height of the silence, the dreamers' attention snapped to a mist-veiled archway on the opposite side of the coliseum.

"Has that always been there?" I asked, taking another gulp of my drink and settling back into my chair. The young man beside me, a cousin of a king from some faraway kingdom, wrapped his hands around my waist. "I hadn't even noticed."

"It has," he whispered into my hair, toying with my curls as he added a small braid. He took his time, deliberately forming the braid as slowly as possible, but I was strangely unbothered. I was more transfixed with his eyes of molten green. "The Weavers are about to make their procession. How thrilling."

Glee built in my chest, heavy and overwhelming. The anticipation of something new, something *better*.

Fenrir, the Fire Weaver, appeared first, stalking out of the mist like a lion after a long and glorious hunt. His body, loosely draped in robes the color of wet blood, displayed a wealth of black tattoos. They clawed up his chest, stopping at his jaw, and his rich brown skin shimmered faintly, a striking backdrop to the ruby crown atop his braided hair. But his eyes were something else; they burned with a fire so bright and so piercing that it hurt to look at him, even from across the length of the coliseum.

His acolytes fell in line behind him, all clothed in the color of wet blood, too. They bore their lord's sigil proudly, rubies gleaming from their throats and hands, and walked down the coliseum steps with power, glory, and purpose.

Nephthys, the Water Weaver, came next, more stunning in person than in any storybook illustration. Dark blue hair curled over bronze shoulders, trailing down her jewel-dusted back, and ocean eyes sparkled above a mouth pursed in mischief.

And pride, I thought.

A sapphire crown arched across her brow, matching the blue pearls beading her bodice and skirts. Her dress moved as water would, pooling from one step to the next. Like Fenrir's, her acolytes emerged behind her, wearing extravagant blue silks, matching sapphires, and beaded slippers.

Then there was Ceres, the Earth Weaver, garbed in wildflowers, undergrowth, and leaves. A horned headpiece curled from her scalp, embedded with emeralds and dripping with what looked like spiderwebs, roses, and small skeletons. She was a walking contradiction, portraying the bonding tension between life and death, growth and decay. And her followers held themselves as she did. Steady feet and steadier hands, rooted in the earth. Only they didn't wear spiderwebs or dying things. Layered in green robes and dark leathers, they looked practical—grounded. As they walked, their emerald amulets glittered.

The three time Weavers emerged next: Somnus, Theia, and Xander.

Somnus slipped from the dark like a snake unbound, clothed in black and a crown of bone. Xander stepped to his left, the immortal warrior with a king's all-knowing gaze, crowned in iron and flanked by floating swords. Theia completed the trio, draped in translucent fabric and a brilliant diamond crown. Their acolytes emerged together, all in armor. They looked ready for a war, not a party, and they held themselves as such.

Trained. Expectant. *Aware.*

The man beside me put his mouth to my ear.

"The two strays are next," he whispered. His breath was hot on my skin and as sweet as rotten plums. A shiver of revulsion crawled down my neck at his nearness. "How delightful."

I angled my shoulders away from him, twisting free from his arms. "Who?"

He drank from his chalice, not bothering to wipe away the liquid that dripped down his chin. "The special little lords of light and dark. You really haven't been to Evernight before, have you?"

Two figures, both in black leathers, appeared under the arch. The left wore a circlet of gold; the right, a circlet of obsidian. At the top of the coliseum stairs, they shared a genial smile.

Mithras and Erebus.

Two men flanked Erebus as he made his way to the coliseum floor. The first walked with confidence and easy grace, nodding at the patrons nearest to him. He was tall—as tall as Erebus—with caramel-brown hair, light brown skin, and an easy smile. The second kept a quieter, more calculated presence. Pale and mean eyed, with sleek black hair falling to his jaw, he glared at the stands as if making a judgment about every patron in attendance.

"Lowly bastards," the man beside me grumbled. "An unhoused should never be made into something they are not. It's like giving a pig a crown and calling it a king."

"They appear quite powerful to me," I said, ignoring the man's crude dig.

"Unhoused, scum, pigs. They're all the same. Mithras and Erebus were both scholars at Evernight, but they never possessed a specific affinity." The man shook his head and took another sloppy drink from his chalice. "Fortunately for them, they demonstrated power in other ways and became the Realm's most illustrious demon hunters."

"It sounds like they're of great value to the Realm, then."

"The Weavers may think so, but that doesn't mean all Revel guests agree," he responded, low and guttural. For a moment, his green eyes darkened, becoming something evil and wrong. But it was only for a moment.

He took a final swig. The darkness was gone, replaced by mild boredom.

My skin prickled, buzzing with anticipation and fear that carved away my clouded edges. It didn't seem possible that Mithras and Erebus would be friends—even five hundred years in the past—but there they were, chins raised high and smiling across the coliseum as if they were celebrating something magnificent. They frequently turned to each other, sharing some secret joke or another.

They looked happy. As if the world no longer weighed on them.

And just like that, the host of the Revel finally appeared.

Lelantos, the Air Weaver, jumped from the sky in a burst of blue, sparkling lightning. As he dropped, he splayed his arms wide and the sky changed, shifting from twilight into clouds heavy with storm. He pulled the clouds closer, closer, and closer still, forcing them to spiral around the coliseum. The clouds moved quickly, spinning faster and faster, sparking with light and booming low with thunder. And as the clouds spun, the coliseum began to spin, too; it slowly rocked on its axis, tilting slightly to the left. Then the right.

Finally, it *cracked*. In a rush of wind and lightning, the coliseum lifted into the air. I gripped the edge of my seat, trying to anchor myself to something—anything.

The green-eyed man laughed at me, reaching for my hips. "Easy. It's not as though they'd make us fall into the Nocturne."

I stood up. Shoved myself out of his hands.

His eyes burned with rot, twisting into malice. "Where are you going? You don't know anyone here. Pitiful little dreamer, all alone."

He rose to face me, squeezing my shoulders as the coliseum shook. No one noticed or cared. They were too busy laughing about the Revel's newest entertainment. His lips bent into a sneer all the way up to the edge of his mask.

"You don't belong here. Why don't you just *wake up*—"

He didn't get to finish his sentence.

Wings, unfurling in a *snap* of feathers, burst from our backs.

And just as the coliseum rose, it fell.

I t was something out of a story. A fiction.

A dream.

Now clothed in the Revel's biggest surprise—*wings*—dreamers and the Weavers with their acolytes floated in the clouds above the Nocturne. The coliseum had dropped back down, settling far below us into Citadel Evernight, and the green-eyed man had turned his back to me, no longer interested in my attention. Gone were our intoxicating refreshments and tepid conversation; now came freedom, possibility, *flight*.

Having wings wasn't so bad, I decided. They worked without any conscious input, moving behind me in long, graceful beats, and if I positioned my body in just the right way, they responded instantly, moving with me. If I angled my shoulders to the left, they angled, too, twisting me sideways. If I leaned to the front, they lifted up slightly, carrying me forward. It took no time at all to become accustomed to my wings—to flying. It was as natural as breathing, as smooth as walking.

Dream logic.

Lelantos, the Air Weaver, flew overhead, darting between the clouds, mist, and lingering sparks of lightning, fine-tuning his finishing touches. He summoned a flat panel of clouds to rest below our feet, marking the boundaries of his sky-bound creation, and twisted other clouds into spires that mimicked the shapes of marble pillars. He left us open to the world, as he formed no ceiling or walls around the pillars, but there wasn't much to see. The panoramic view of the Nocturne was marred by his storm.

When he was satisfied with his ballroom in the sky, Lelantos floated above us all, his great tawny wings forcing a wind to thread through our whimsical clothes and carefully placed masks. His own mask of bone curved over one side of his face, framing one-half of his hawkish gaze. He wore robes of fur and leather, his broad chest open to the air, and his full lips were curled in enjoyment.

"Dreamers!" Lelantos shouted, silencing the crescendoing music and lingering chatter. "Welcome to the Revel of Rebirth. You were brought here for a purpose, as you always will be. Rebirth comes when a nightmare is disturbed by the dawn of freedom. Rebirth means hope, glory, *wings*."

He paused, letting the impact of his words sink in. The air became heavy in his silence, weighted by possibility. Even Erebus and Mithras, now in matching white wings, looked to Lelantos in anticipation. For *what*, I didn't know.

And how convenient that the Shadow Bringer was still missing.

Uneasy, I glanced around, trying again to find him among the dreamers. He should have been obvious enough, but everyone's wings made it difficult to see. The wings obscured, masked, hid. Just as I swore I saw his moon-white hair or armor of liquid night, a wing obstructed my view, hiding whatever I thought I saw.

"To you, I am the Air Weaver: king of the sky, ruler of the winds, and harbinger of change," Lelantos continued. "But tonight, I am the master of this Revel. And a glorious Revel it shall be. Now the storms will cease, the rain shall recede, and the dawn of freedom will be upon us."

Lelantos spread his hands wide, and for a moment, I could have sworn that his pale eyes met mine. But just as the moment came, it passed, and with a final flourish of his wings, the skies listened. The storm quieted to a purr. The clouds dissolved. The rain, mist, and lightning ceased. And millions of stars, as gloriously bright as the heavens, slid into place around us.

The dreamers had been silent out of respect for Lelantos; now they were silent for a different reason altogether.

It was as the Air Weaver said. This was hope. Possibility. Freedom. *Rebirth.*

Wind, fresh with the scent of the Nocturne, swept in among the dreamers. Hints of salt, moss, and violets. As the wind swept in, so did the music, commanded by some unseen source. And just like marionettes on invisible threads, we began to dance. The steps were intricate and grand, but I didn't need to know them. As long as I relaxed my body, it moved without my input, falling into the natural ebb and flow of the movements. My wings spun me in place or guided me to a new partner; my hips twisted and my arms dipped of their own accord.

Some partners were talkative and genuine, complimenting my dress or sharing in the latest Realm gossip. Others were like the green-eyed man. At the outset, they were enchanting and interested in learning more about who I was—my past, my status, my hopes and dreams. But a few steps later, their sinisterness would begin to leak through. Their eyes would gleam red, their grips would tighten, and their mouths would wet.

My current dance partner was like this. He was an older man with a graying beard and a warm, booming voice. I had thought him kind at first. Charming. But he had since lost that innocence. Now as he looked at me, all I saw was a terrible, gnawing violence. It smoldered in his pale blue eyes, puffed out from his nostrils like smoke. I wanted out, out, *out*—

Suddenly, my wings faltered, as if forgetting the next step in the waltz. The man and I stumbled, falling into the path of other dancers. I glanced around, desperate to catch the eye of another partner.

"Get *away* from me," I demanded, fear sharpening my tone.

In return, he smiled, as if my struggle entertained him. "This isn't how you treat a nobleman."

Then the man—*monster*—caught my wrist, trying to pull my body back into his sweat-slicked hands. I resisted, slamming an elbow into his chest, but his grip was like iron. I couldn't break free. Why wasn't anyone watching? Why didn't anyone *care*?

But then someone did.

Erebus.

His partner, a beautiful woman donning a rose-colored dress, was gazing up at him in adoration. But Erebus's smile was stiff, his eyes distracted. Searching for something, just as mine were.

When he saw me, he dropped her hand.

A jolt snapped like fire through my bones. The feeling wasn't dissimilar to the effects of the drink I'd tried earlier: a flash of breathless power. I became all too aware of myself. The neckline of my dress, the color on my lips, and the soft shade of gray fabric that complemented his own attire. I hadn't realized it earlier, but now it was glaringly obvious. I assumed I'd be matching the Shadow Bringer.

Not *Erebus.*

Alter it. Alter it as you did in the last dream. Shift it before he can see—

But nothing happened. Even my blade, which had jumped through my skin before, felt tired and dull. Sluggish, as if in a deep sleep.

"Your turn is over," Erebus told the bearded man, smiling thinly. His voice was just as rich and commanding as the Shadow Bringer's, but he spoke with more poise than the Bringer ever did. "Find a new partner."

After only a moment's hesitation, the man released me.

"It was a memorable dance, dearest lady," he said, dropping into a bow and pressing a prickly kiss to the back of my hand before I could snatch it away. "Enjoy the rest of the Revel."

Erebus's silver eyes meandered along the lines of my body the way a man might look at his lover, but there was no warmth in his gaze. His unmasked eyes were sharp and guarded as they beheld the folds of my gray dress. The way my curls fell over my shoulders. The jewelry at my throat.

"You're wearing my favored color," he murmured, taking my hand and pulling me to his chest. His gloved thumb brushed over the spot where the man had kissed me, as the dreamers around us stared. "Most Revelers prefer bright colors, but I would rather be surrounded by the depths. Isn't that strange?"

"Not at all. There's a certain comfort in the dark," I answered honestly. "Especially in a place like this, so filled with chaos."

"You understand, then." He smiled, squeezing my hand as if in reassurance, but his eyes were still cold. "Are you a lord's daughter? A cousin of the king? It's rare to see a new face; I'm curious."

"I'm of no importance." I pulled back a step, conscious of the way his eyes betrayed the forced warmth in his smile. Speaking to Erebus felt strange; it was almost as if he knew I didn't belong there. "Just a dreamer at their first Revel."

"In one way or another, everyone here is important."

"Especially you, it seems. The dreamers can't stop looking at you," I said.

He pulled me back to him. Grazed the tips of his wings over my own. "Are you so sure? Look around—it is only *you* they see."

He was right.

The dreamers' stares were brimming with jealousy and anger, and in their collective rage, no one so much as blinked at Erebus. A different girl might have felt fear or even triumph at that jealousy—at all the attention that came with being the person who transfixed their beloved.

"Why did you request to dance with me?" I had to ask.

He hesitated. As if even *he* didn't know why he'd sought me out.

"You were due for a new partner," he said finally, guiding me into a slow, graceful spin. My wings complied, following his lead.

"But I wasn't. The dance was only halfway through."

"Was it?" he asked, feigning indifference. "I thought it was nearly over."

Maker, this man is every bit as stubborn as his future self.

I skimmed my hand along his shoulder, moving it absently toward the black hair that rested there. What had turned it white? Had the Bringer's castle leeched all color, all *soul*, from his body, rendering him bitter and bloodless? Erebus shared many similarities with the Shadow Bringer, but he radiated life in ways the Shadow Bringer did not. Erebus's eyes were sharper, his skin darker, and his lips more precisely defined. And there was a sense of self-assuredness in the way that Erebus carried himself. He was less haunted and burdened. More certain of his path and his purpose.

Our eyes met again. This time, whatever he saw in my gaze gave him pause.

He dipped his head, bringing his mouth to graze the edge of my ear. "Listen carefully and respond as truthfully as you are able. What is happening outside the Dream Realm? You're new here; you will be able to answer more clearly than the others. Has the sickness spread?"

"Sickness," I echoed, a chill spreading over my skin. *Corruption.* Did he not have a word for it yet? "Do you mean Corruption?"

Erebus's mouth tightened. "That is an accurate way to describe it. What have you seen?"

"It's dreadful," I whispered. The dreamers around us were switching partners, but we did not stray from each other's arms. "It killed my parents and my sister. Eden," I clarified, as if her name mattered to him. "She was young." My voice caught, tangled by emotions that twisted my heart into knots. "She had her entire life to look forward to."

But then I *killed* her.

I encouraged her to dream, and a demon found her. I wrought the shadows underneath her eyes. I caused the blood on her skin and the splinters on her coffin. I ruined a life that was not my own. Then her death rattled an honorable mother and father into committing unspeakable acts, ripping apart the lives of countless others.

I wanted to say this and more, but the shadows in Erebus's eyes made me pause. They swirled, pooled, darkened. I first guessed the emotion to be anger or horror, but it felt different. More depthless and aching.

Sorrow, I realized.

Was he trapped here, in Evernight? Why couldn't he just wake up and investigate himself?

I spoke my questions aloud: "Why can't you go see for yourself?"

He blinked, a flash of sadness breaking through his careful guard. "It is not as simple as that." He dipped me in perfect timing with the other dreamers, causing my feathers to brush the clouds underfoot. Once upright again, he spun me back to his chest. "I intend to fix this world," he murmured into my hair. "There will be no more sickness or death. The dark must be destroyed."

I realized something then.

Erebus was, indeed, more certain of his purpose, but that purpose wouldn't lead him to glory or happiness. He was bound for five hundred years of torment at the hands of a thousand monsters, and a detestable new moniker: Shadow Bringer.

"Whatever you're about to do...it doesn't end how you wish it to." The words stumbled out before I could stop them.

Five hundred years of darkness. Five hundred years of rotting away in the dark. Alone.

"Who are you?" he asked, silver eyes searching mine. "Have we met before?" His grip tightened. I wasn't sure if he was aware of it. "You look..." He drifted off, analyzing my face. For a moment, it seemed as if he might rip off my mask.

Far below us, perhaps within the halls of Citadel Evernight, a bell clanged, and the skies darkened.

Erebus stopped, suspending us in the air.

"I'm afraid that's all the time I have left," he said, smiling sadly and releasing my hand. "I hope to see you again one day. I intend to revisit this conversation."

"Wait, Erebus, you don't—"

But he had already turned his back to me and dived between the pillars.

Gone.

My wings beat behind me, silently churning the air. What was I supposed to do now? What was my purpose here?

And just as I was about to dive after Erebus, I finally felt *him*.

The Shadow Bringer.

I spun around. Unsurprisingly, he was still in his black armor, sharp boots, and taloned gauntlets. The metal gleamed wickedly under the starlight, so at odds with the soft hues of the other dreamers, and his matching mask, no longer a draconic helm, was lined in obsidian points. But no one cared. Most of the dreamers who'd once looked upon me as prey had now moved toward a fresh offering of food and drink.

Which left the Shadow Bringer and me alone in the deep, endless night.

His wings were black and glossy, grander and more resplendent than I'd ever seen them. They stretched behind him, shimmering like a midnight river set aglow by the stars, making him appear taller and more intimidating than he already was. How silly that I'd ever thought wings looked impressive on the other dreamers. The way they looked on dreamers was *nothing* compared with how they looked on the Shadow Bringer.

His were menacing and tempting. And I wanted to touch them more than ever.

Strange.

The Bringer took in my dress. I could have sworn his masked gaze lingered there—in the shape of it. In the folds, the fabric. On my wings, soft and gray. And last, he focused on my eyes. His mouth slackened. I wasn't sure he even noticed.

"You appear to be in your element," I managed, heat rising to my temples. I had meant to tell him about Erebus, but the thought had promptly drifted away. "Your wings suit you."

"As do yours." It seemed as though he wanted to say more, but he shut his mouth before he could. His skin betrayed him, though; a flush was definitely at his temples, too.

The music soared, light and free. A crescendo of stringed instruments so perfectly harmonious that it made my heart lift. We were the only two partygoers not dancing.

"Where did you go?" I finally asked without revealing my yearning. *I was looking for you. I missed having you by my side.*

"I didn't intend to leave you for so long." He swallowed hard, as if deliberating whether to tell me a truth or a lie. "I was visiting with old friends." His voice broke a little, cracked and splintered at that single admission. "Or watching them, really. What can a man say to his ghosts?"

A truth. A haunted, heartbreaking truth.

"Mithras was my friend, once," the Bringer continued, looking out at the sky. "But he betrayed me—and it happens tonight, at this Revel." He ran a gauntleted hand through his hair. "My memories come in pieces. There will be some cue. I should recognize it and know."

"So we have more time, then?" I asked. I then tried for something more playful, wanting to ease the sorrow in his eyes that so clearly mirrored Erebus's. "We could dance."

"I am not dancing." He added quickly, "I don't dance."

"Your past self would disagree. I was just dancing with him, actually."

The Shadow Bringer tilted his head, considering. "Were you, now? You should know I only learned to dance so I could appease the Weavers who held these cursed parties."

"What I'm hearing is that you are, indeed, *very* capable of dancing."

He grabbed my hands and pulled me to him.

"Only this once," he warned. "Just to stop your pestering."

Despite his initial hesitation, he guided me through the music, keeping up even as the pace frenzied. Our wings beat in unison. We twirled across the clouds, lost in the soaring violins, the complicated spins, and the beauty and wonder of it all. Before the first song ended, he was already flushed and smirking.

And so was I.

"How can you do that without flinching?" he asked, guiding us to a more secluded part of the clouds. Toward the pillars and the stars.

"Do what?"

"Touch me," he answered, bringing his gauntleted hand to the back of my neck. "Like this."

Like—*oh*. My left hand was perched on his shoulder, absently threading through his hair.

"I must be hypnotized by your impressive dancing skills," I said to save face.

"Hmm," he murmured, bringing his hand back to my waist.

"It's nothing, really," I insisted. "Your hair looked soft, is all."

The fingers around my waist tightened, metal talons digging into the silk.

Oh? So this isn't anything, either, then? his hungry grip seemed to suggest. But he pushed too hard, talons pinching my side, and I flinched.

He began to pull away from me, removing his hand from my waist.

"I have nothing against your hands," I said, making a point to squeeze the hand that held my right. "But they are encased in knives."

He cast a fleeting glance downward, apparently startled by the realization that his hands were, indeed, encased in metal.

"I've worn these for so long," he noted quietly, flexing his fingers. "Dreamers wear gauntlets or gloves to remind themselves they aren't in reality. A kind of protection, really—dulling the senses so we never forget what the Realm truly is. If we forget, then we might never choose to wake. We might forget where we are, who we are, and *why* we are." He added, eyes darkening, "The sensation of touch is a powerful thing to get lost in. I've rarely allowed myself to enjoy it."

He looked at his hands again, weighing, considering. Finally, with a slight shift in his eyes, the gloves drew back, melting into the spires that lined his forearms. His right hand, now unbound, stretched against my back; his left hand roved the curves of my fingers. The shadows in his eyes were on the brink of shattering. He clenched the fabric at my back, as if that would anchor him.

I couldn't help wondering again how long it had been since he'd felt the touch of another. There was solace in the warmth of skin on skin. To have that feeling dulled or removed entirely was unthinkable. The Bringer's expression changed; the cold mask of indifference was coming back. Without thinking, I pulled his hand to my face.

"Bringer. Look at me."

For a breath, his hand stilled on my skin. His expression was guarded, unreadable. But then his thumb brushed my jawline. Long fingers stretched across the curve of my neck, winding into my hair. The braid the dreamer had given me gave him pause, so he unbound it—whether by his magic or his hands, I couldn't tell—then snagged my lower lip with his thumb. The shadows in his eyes darkened, beckoning, then eddied away.

"You're beautiful," he murmured, skimming his thumb across my mouth. "I've always thought so. Did you know that?"

Maker, my skin was warm. *Of course I didn't know that.*

His touch lingered, then drifted, and before doubt could take hold, I leaned in, pressing a soft, tentative kiss along the line of his jaw, just below his ear. With his helm cast aside in favor of a mask, the air between us shivered with intoxicating tension. I lingered there, close enough to feel his breath, frozen between the urge to kiss him again and the desire to savor this moment a little longer.

"As are you, Shadow Bringer. You're the most beautiful man I've ever known."

His breath hitched as he pulled me close, tilting his face so that his mouth hovered over mine. In that suspended moment, uncertainty flickered in his eyes, as if questioning whether I truly wanted this. Desperate to erase his doubts, I cradled his face in my hands, fingertips tracing the features left exposed by his mask. I could feel the tremor in his touch, but I also felt his longing—the yearning to lose himself, if even for a moment. To kiss me. *Hard.* But instead of my mouth, his lips unexpectedly found my neck.

I gasped, arching into him and giving more access to that skin. Skin that was now absolutely and unequivocally burning.

He made a soft growl against my neck, dragging his teeth down the column of my throat. My eyes fluttered shut when I felt him there—brief brushes of his lips and tongue punctuated by the graze of his teeth. Teeth that I had once imagined would tear through my bones and devour my soul.

A slow, deliberate kiss near my ear had me writhing, pulling him closer.

Time stopped. The stars were slowly twinkling out—and something was terribly wrong.

"Esmer," the Shadow Bringer said, his voice suddenly cracking in horror. "I remember now."

Something snapped in his eyes. Something wild, fierce, unbound. He stumbled back, wings shuttering. Hesitating. He flew to the pillars, just as Erebus had. It was all so similar—his expression. The urgency.

The look of death in his eyes.

Only this time, when he jumped, I followed.

I thought I could fly.

I was wrong.

Outside the bounds of the Revel, my wings were worthless and limp. Wind ripped into my face, swept through my hair, and tangled my dress's delicate layers. A slipper—then another—fell off my feet. My mask slipped past my chin, catching at my neck, and I clawed at the silk ribbon and beadwork until it, too, fell away. I cursed loudly. The roar of the wind carried that off, too.

But I was dreaming. *Dreaming.* I should have been able to fly.

Why can't I fly?

I tried to summon my imagination, but my thoughts were jumbled. I couldn't think beyond the roaring wind. Couldn't see beyond the hair that whipped into my eyes. My wings twitched, slowly slumbering into life, but it was too late.

Without anything to steady me, I plummeted like a rock. And slammed face-first into the Shadow Bringer.

He spun around with a snarl, wings flaring, and twisted a hand in the front of my dress, pulling me close. With his other hand, he unsheathed his blade and thrust it under my jaw. It was all so instinctual—a cloak of violence worn a thousand times.

"You *fool!*" he shouted, stopping our plummet with a single push of his wings. "I nearly cut off your head. I thought you were a demon. Or a—"

"Do I *look* like a demon?" I snapped, clinging to his chest even as I pushed his blade away. "And since when do demons wear dresses, or silk slippers?"

His eyes were unusually sharp as he stared at me. "You can't control your wings."

"Clearly not."

"Then why did you jump?" he asked, repositioning me in his arms. "It was pure foolishness to follow me."

I thought I could fly. And I wanted to help you.

"Take me back to the Revel so I can keep dancing, then," I said, but the words snagged. Felt dry and wrong.

"It's too late for that," he said, eyes hardening. "We have a future to mend—if we're not already too late." His chest heaved against mine, betraying every emotion that hid behind his wall of shadow. I had never heard him sound like this. So broken and frantic.

"Five hundred years. *Five hundred years* of rotting away in the dark. There has to be a way out," he said.

The Nocturne stretched below us, still as glass, reflecting the sky's remaining stars. Near the horizon, the barest hint of dawn trickled in. For a moment, it was just us, the clash of sky against sea, and our mingling breath.

"Your village and its Corrupt have confined you. Stifled you. Forced you to live a life you didn't want for yourself." His voice broke then. "Now consider what that miserable reality would do to you over more than five lifetimes. Five lifetimes alone."

Visions—*memories*—flashed before me, demanding my attention and pulling me under. They made me into the Shadow Bringer. Made me see and feel the world as he did.

Erebus waded into the Nocturne, cloak dragging underneath its starlit waters.

Here was what he had waited for. His power; his purpose.

It was all for this.

But when he placed his bare hands upon the waters, ready to destroy the demons once and for all, the Nocturne changed. To his horror, the water darkened, twisted, and boiled. Cracked apart like hollow bones. Demons roared under its waves and broke free from its depths. They screamed violently into the night, desperate for blood and dreamers' souls. The Nocturne's shadows—its darkness—could not be cleansed. Erebus could not do it. He had failed.

He stumbled back.

Mithras was wrong. Their plan for Erebus to cleanse the Nocturne while Mithras gathered the hidden demons infesting the Revel—all to be crushed by the combined power of the seven Weavers, ending the demonic plague on the Dream Realm—was wrong. Erebus was no hero. His powers held no noble purpose. He was a blight, a curse, a disease. And for that, humanity would be destroyed.

Erebus looked to the sky, desperate to find his golden-eyed friend.

Mithras was flying above the Nocturne, ringed by all seven Weavers. Erebus almost shouted for him, but the words died in his throat. Mithras's eyes were hateful as they beheld Erebus, and the Seven's power rumbled around their immortal shoulders. Mithras and the Weavers weren't here to help him; they were here to fight him.

Mithras's betrayal clawed down Erebus's chest, callously ripping him apart.

Somehow Mithras had known this would happen. Erebus wouldn't purge the Nocturne's darkness like a hero. No, he'd be caught summoning demons from the Nocturne like an infernal villain. With a roar of rage and despair, Erebus tried to escape the Revel by forcing himself awake.

But he couldn't. He was trapped.

And so he fled.

Erebus escaped to his castle, his haven, his palace of shadow that had been his personal training ground. The only place he knew where he might be able to defend himself.

The Weavers charged him at his castle. Mercilessly attacked him in a swell of grief and fury.

"*Shadow Bringer,*" *they cried, damning him.* "*Demon lord. Devourer.*"

Rock crushed his outstretched arms; his left dropped, useless. But even mangled and broken, trembling and bloody, Erebus's right hand held, commanding the dark as it threaded together the final stitches of his domain.

"*You will not take my soul!*" *he roared.*

And the Realm roared back.

Years later, the shadows in his castle curled toward him, rolling around his shoulders in a hideous cloud. Perhaps a minute passed. Perhaps a century. How could he tell? His senses were cut off, his hands heavy and numb. But it did not matter.

Nothing mattered anymore.

He was no longer Erebus; he was the Shadow Bringer.

At first, the Shadow Bringer had counted the days. Scraped them into his bedchamber walls. Etched them in the pages of a book. But the living shadows—the monsters, the creatures, the demons—began to infest his castle. He wasn't sure how they appeared, only that they were trapped here as he was. Some could haunt the surrounding forest, but most, like him, were bound to the castle's walls. They curled around his soul as if they owned it.

And perhaps they did.

Their unholy power was clearly his, too; they were sated by his shadows and desperate for their release. The Shadow Bringer shuddered as a demon outside his door screamed.

His eyes were heavy, and his heart was full of hatred.

Centuries later, the Shadow Bringer felt the knock before he heard it.

Felt her walk up the castle steps as if she crawled over his skin.

He snarled, charging through his castle's broken innards. After all this time, they had finally sent someone to kill him. He scarcely remembered who "they" were, but he knew she did not belong in his domain. Did not deserve to see him like this.

Enemy. Enemy. Enemy.

The Shadow Bringer stood at his mirror and wiped blood from his throat, his chin, and his lips. It soaked into the cloth, staining it black. She had used his power—too much of it—to sate the demons in the water, and somehow caused him to bleed.

He had forgotten he even could. And it was all because of her.

How dare she enter his castle, his fortress, and try to manipulate his power? He had sensed it when they had first met. The shadows had bent to her will, loosening around her chest when he had meant to keep them taut. A vision of her drifted to the front of his consciousness. Her, standing in the middle of that cold pool, starlight pouring through the cracks and gleaming in the water, in the stone of the cavern walls, in her eyes. Her dark eyes, filled with—what was it?

He wasn't certain, couldn't recall what those emotions were named.

How dare she disturb his peaceful agony?

And he didn't even know her name.

The Shadow Bringer blinked hard, clearing mire from his thoughts. He did not feel the cold from the Tomb of the Devourer as it seeped into his bones, did not feel the hollows under his eyes growing tighter and deeper. For days he had tried to escape the tomb, but it was useless. The door wouldn't open. He shook his hands through his hair, kicked the ground with the heel of his boot. Darkness, everywhere.

He avoided the bones at his feet as he descended farther into the dark. And he tried not to think about Esmer as the walls drew nearer around him. But it was impossible.

He couldn't stop thinking about her.

The Shadow Bringer staggered to where he had left her. The chamber was undisturbed, a shadowed cathedral with a living sacrifice at its altar. Esmer's hair, so dark it was nearly black, curled over the stone.

She was beautiful.

He had resisted thinking—or feeling—as much, but he couldn't deny it. Hadn't been able to since he'd first met her. In a different time, perhaps he would have told her.

Except—

Was that her brow tensing, her mouth twisting into a grimace? He blinked again, *struggling in vain to rip the image from his sight. When Esmer had first closed her eyes, sinking into the oblivion he had so carefully prepared for her, he imagined he would feel hope. Relief. Triumph. He had theorized that she'd be able to replace him in his castle, that the curse keeping him imprisoned would allow her to remain there in his place while he hunted Mithras down and shoved a blade through the traitor's heart. Esmer had his magic, after all.*

But the tomb door wouldn't open, and a deep, roiling pit of regret and self-hatred was beginning to eat him alive. If he didn't join her in the Dream Realm, it would consume him, body and soul.

He lowered himself next to her, folding his hands over his waist. Perhaps he'd regret this. He was returning to his prison, after all. But his will to see her again and the rage he felt for Mithras were stronger than his will to succumb to his circumstances.

And so he closed his eyes.

The Shadow Bringer stole the glass from her lips, placing it against his own.

Around them, the inn was a cacophony of laughter and conversation, but he scarcely noticed. He was more focused on Esmer and her ability to create such delicious food and drink out of nothing. She had done well—surprisingly, wonderfully well—for someone without any formal instruction. What she had accomplished took most dreamers several years at Citadel Evernight to fully master.

It was strange to feel this way. To smile and for it to be true.

He took a long drink, longer than he should have, letting the warm, unfamiliar feeling settle back into his stomach with the rest of the wine.

Esmer had saved him.

She fought for his life and his redemption, even in the face of the demon, and had emerged victorious. He clung to her, still damp from where she had pulled him from the water. His vision was smeared, thoughts torn beyond recognition. Vaguely, he felt his hand drop into her lap.

He did not move it.

Esmer's eyes reflected the stars.

Dark and rimmed in artful gray, they shone brightly, brilliantly—at him. Even masked, they held power.

She was stronger than she realized. The shadows listened to her, heeded her will and her spirit. Even now, the darkness inside him sang to the darkness inside her.

The Shadow Bringer danced with her as he instinctively knew how, the precise memory of lessons having long faded from his mind. He worried that he would forget the steps, the rhythm, the sequence. That he would forget what it was like to lose himself to music. But their movements were natural. Easy. He could lose himself in this dance, this music, this night.

He could lose himself in her.

But as he looked back into her eyes, to that power lingering there, his wonder became clouded by doubt. She could not—would not—be his. Not in this broken world. He first had to change the future.

He had to change it for her.

The memories snapped away.

I was back in the Shadow Bringer's arms, held high over the Nocturne.

"What was that?" I whispered. The words trembled. The emotions of his memories had overpowered me, grabbing ahold of my own with taloned claws. "I saw you—I *was* you."

"That was the power of the Nocturne. Or Somnus. I don't know why those memories were shared. I…" His mouth worked open and shut, words failing to come just as a gentle wave of vulnerability swept in, breaking in the depths of his eyes. "I saw you, too. Your home in Norhavellis. What happened five years ago with your sister, Eden." He cupped my face, gently stroking my cheek. I nearly shattered at the touch—and the compassion in his tone. He didn't blame me; he never would. "The elixir shortage. The Corruption of your parents and what you had to do to survive."

We had wanted to share, I realized. *Wanted* to share these memories—these raw, broken fragments—with each other. Remnants of his emotions spilled over, running down my face. Loneliness, anger, desperation. But also trust. Courage. Longing. They bubbled up in my heart, sank deep into my skin.

"Then you'll know I intend to continue surviving. And I want you to survive, too," I said seriously, and I knew he understood. "We need to see this dream through until the end."

"In a few moments, I will step into the Nocturne. Just as the dawn breaks, I will sink my hands into its waters," he said, regarding me fiercely. "I will try to purify it, just as Mithras and I planned. I will try to tear away the dark, just as I did in the demon's stomach. But I will fail."

"And the demons will come."

He shook his head. "The demons are already here. There were demons at the Revel."

The green-eyed man, I realized, horrified. *The Revelers with wickedness in their words and their hearts.*

"Why didn't anyone say anything—do anything? How were they roaming so freely?"

"It was all a part of my and Mithras's plan. We tricked powerful demons into attending the Revel in disguise, promising them a chance at humanity. A chance to mingle with the wealthy and select their pre-ferred hosts. In return, the demons would abandon their war on the Weavers. No longer would they plague the Nocturne's dreams." His hands tightened around me. "It was all a lie, of course. Lies, everywhere. From both parties." He looked away. Gritted his teeth as he glared up at the Revel. "That's all the demons ever want—freedom. They want to walk upon the earth and breathe its air, just as we do. But that would be chaos. It cannot be allowed to happen."

"But it did happen. It still *is* happening."

"It wasn't intended to happen, though. There is no meaning or value to Corruption. No reason for the loss of dreams."

"How did Mithras betray you?" I asked, wondering aloud what I'd wanted to ask ever since I'd seen Erebus and Mithras together in the coliseum. It was clear that they respected each other both as comrades and friends.

The Bringer's eyes hardened. "While I was mining the dark from the Nocturne's waves, Mithras was supposed to gather the Revelers—the demons—and lure them down to the sea. The plan was to ambush them and destroy the Nocturne's shadows in one fell swoop, all with the Weavers supporting us."

"But something went wrong. I saw it break apart in the memory you showed me."

He nodded. "At my touch, the Nocturne cracked open, releasing every shred of darkness it held into the Realm, unbound. And when I turned back to Evernight, horrified at what I'd done, Mithras and the Weavers were already there, watching me. Mithras hadn't lured the demons down; he'd brought only the Weavers. All so that they could witness me summoning demons like a monster." He looked away, noting the faint shape of Erebus on the rocks below. "They didn't even give me the chance to explain myself. The Weavers attacked as one, with Mithras leading the charge."

My wings stretched behind me, slowly coming to life. I could feel the Bringer's power working through me, bidding my wings to move. When they steadied at last, the Bringer let go. "Thank you."

"That wasn't me," he said softly. "This power is yours now, too. It has been yours from the moment we met."

Dawn taunted at the horizon. We flew to the Nocturne, wind sweeping over our bodies and lingering between the feathers of our wings. It felt glorious, this flight. I wanted to savor it. I wanted to stretch my wings as far as they'd go. I wanted to rise high above the Realm and see it all. Every domain. Every secret. Every hidden, quiet place.

But there was no time.

Erebus was a blot on Evernight's shore. He crouched low upon the rocks, wings draped behind him like a magnificent, snowy cloak. He didn't hear us coming, didn't see us as we landed behind him. But the skittering of rocks sent him running, sprinting to the Nocturne's waters as if a horde of demons were at his heels. And maybe he thought that they were.

Erebus's wings dissolved into smoke, propelling him forward. What had made us quick in the skies made us cumbersome on land, and Erebus knew this. *Recognized* this. The Shadow Bringer willed his wings away, too, just as I did, but he was too late. Erebus crashed into the Nocturne, arms outstretched.

And he sank them deep within the water.

"*No!*" the Shadow Bringer roared.

It was a nightmare replaying itself. A terrible memory unlocked, only to be relived with no salvation. The water began to bubble, boiling underneath, just as it had done in the Bringer's memory. Then it cracked, snapping apart like an overfull vessel.

Erebus stumbled as demons swirled into life around him.

He had seemed so composed at the Revel—both commanding and strong. In control of his emotions and his path. When I looked at him now, I saw the boy back in the woods, fearing for his life. A boy doubting his purpose and his worth.

The Shadow Bringer, furious at his own failure, lurched forward.

He followed Erebus into the churning waves, thrashing against the demons as they fought to overpower him. The water was no longer clear. Instead, it appeared as ink would, opaque and endless. It rose to meet their calves, thighs, hips, chests.

Then it washed over their heads, swallowing them whole.

I halted at the edge of the rocks, stunned. If I jumped in, what could I do? Would I lose myself in the Nocturne, just as the Bringer had warned? Demons swarmed around the sea, crawling from the inky water. Others flew overhead, mocking. One dipped down—too close—and clipped my hair with its claws. When it flew away again, it was howling. Screeching into the night with a desperation so animalistic, it made my skin crawl.

I unsheathed my blade, gripping it with no small dose of uncertainty. Fear had made it easier to summon. But fear had loosened my hands, too. Made them weak. Made them tremble. Made them cold all the way down to my fingernails. The sword had worked before on *one* demon, but what could it do against the might of one *hundred*?

Another demon dropped toward me, feet skimming the Nocturne. Its wings were stunted and frail. Too feeble to hold the weight of its body. It crashed into the rocks with a pathetic cry, shivering as it tried to stand.

Do what you're capable of. Kill it.

The thing finally managed to stand. It peered at me, eyes wide and glassy. Water dripped down its wrinkled face, dampening its fur.

Now—before it attacks.

I could feel my blade's power. It thrummed underneath my hands, waiting to be used. *Pleading* to be used. I knew what it was capable of, but I couldn't bring myself to do it. Because the demon looked so *sad*. Fearful and uncertain, just as I was. It continued to shiver, glancing between the sword in my hands and my stricken face.

When it sensed I was no longer a threat, the thing sank to its belly, crawling into a nearby hole, and gave a small warbling cry before falling silent. My sword hung limply from my fingers, scraping against the rocks.

What was I *doing*?

Tears sprang to my eyes, unbidden and unwanted. I stumbled back to the Nocturne. I could feel the Shadow Bringer's darkness—the shadows that lingered, even now. Shadows that trailed behind him as he sank deeper, deeper, *deeper* into the water until I couldn't see him anymore. And through that swell of darkness, I could feel his pain. The deep, aching sorrow at seeing his tragic past lived out again. The indignation—the *anger*—at fighting himself. The pain of drowning. The fear of being lost to the Nocturne's dreams.

And there was something else, too. A longing for someone.

A longing for *me*.

I fell to my knees, numb to the demons dropping from the sky and crawling from the water. The Shadow Bringer was lost to the Nocturne. And if he was ever to come back, *I* had to save him. *I* had to fight for him—*now*—before he fell deeper. This felt real. This *was* real.

I sank my hands into the water, reaching for his threads of shadow. For the trail of darkness that lingered behind him like unraveling strings. I wrapped them around my arms. Willed them toward me with everything I had. And then I pulled. Mentally and physically. I pulled *hard*. Even as the demons screamed. Even as they rushed toward Evernight. I ignored them all, shut out what I couldn't understand, and focused on the Shadow Bringer.

Erebus was there, too. I could feel him as I called to the Shadow Bringer. Erebus was falling fast, lost between the Nocturne's dreams and the demons breaking free from it. Again I saw that boy back in the woods, fearing for his life. Despite his rank, despite his power, he was just a boy. A boy doubting his purpose and his worth as they crumbled between his fingers.

So I called for them both. Summoned the shadows that spun from each of them.

And when I saw a body emerging from the deep, I lunged for it.

"Hang on!" I screamed, grabbing for his arms, his shoulders, *anything*. Miraculously, I found his hands. And he held on.

But just as I pulled him up, I slipped on the rocks, falling sideways. Something grabbed for my foot, dragging me down. Pain lanced up my leg, red-hot and searing. Whatever tore at my foot was moving up my skin, climbing its claw up my leg as I fought to swim back to the surface. But the thing on my leg was stronger. It viciously pulled me down, down, *down*.

Faintly, I began to hear a song. A whisper of a memory, calling me deeper.

Elliot's arms, wrapping me in a hug.

Mother's hands, tying a ribbon through my hair.

Father's eyes, bright with approval—with joy. At *me*.

Eden's voice, begging me to play.

Esmer! Esmer, come here. Come see.

Eden, begging me to stay.

Esmer, please. I miss you.

I wanted to follow the Nocturne's call. Ached to follow those voices—those memories—down, down, down. But before I could, the Bringer heaved me out of the sea and into his arms. A curtain of shadow followed behind, twisting around us like a blanket.

"They were just dreams," he spoke into my hair, easing me to the ground and into his lap. "Just dreams."

The Shadow Bringer was cold and wet, but I didn't care. I clung to him with all the strength I had left, almost shattering at the contact. I wanted more than anything to bury my face in his chest and cry. But when I tilted my head up, expecting to see the man I had grown to cherish, my mouth fell open.

He was the Shadow Bringer—but he was also Erebus.

His eyes were the same, a brilliant silver with shadows melting from their edges. But his moon-white hair was black as night. His skin was darker, too. It spoke of a life lived away from dreams. A life lived in the sun. Most shocking of all, though, was that his face was bare. His mask was gone, lost to the Nocturne. He was so beautiful, so utterly *alive*, that it made me ache at every pulse point.

"What have I become?" he asked, noticing the shift in my expression and the black, tousled strands that fell to his shoulders. "Who am I, Esmer?"

I cupped his face, marveling at every perfect feature. Who was he? I considered the question seriously.

"You're a prince of darkness," I began, tracing his cheek with my right hand as he leaned into my left. "A fearless warrior, a talented dreamer, a brilliant mind," I continued, moving from his temple to his hair. He listened wordlessly, completely enraptured by my voice and my touch. "A beautiful soul whose shadows mingle with my own. A man who is, despite everything he's endured, *good*. A man my soul had been yearning for."

I pressed a quick, impulsive kiss to his lips, and he shuddered.

"Just as I've been yearning for you," he said roughly, his large hands circling my waist as he kissed me back. It was passionate and all-consuming, an explosion of desire that had been suppressed for far too long. I gasped as he held me tighter, enjoying the pleasant flutter in my stomach that his eagerness coaxed out. But the kiss was over as quickly as it began. When he pulled back, his eyes were shining. "A light in the bitter dark. A clever, bewitching girl who rose above the darkness that sought to consume her whole."

The shadows around us tightened, cocooning us, shielding us from the Nocturne's incessant pull. It made me remember the shadows that had called to me during all those bleak, lonely nights in Norhavellis. The shadows I'd tried desperately to ignore.

"I was just a shadow of myself before—" He stopped abruptly, understanding flashing across his face. "I was a shadow of myself; a shadow missing its whole. *You* merged us. Now I have everything. My memories, my power, my *life*—I have it all."

"And that...upsets you?" I asked, not grasping why he suddenly looked so pained.

"No," he answered, holding my chin as he searched my eyes. "But what you just did defies simple dream logic." He turned away, warring with something within himself. "Something isn't right, Esmer. It shouldn't be *possible*—"

A warbling, desperate cry made us both jump up; the demon I had spared earlier was crawling toward us on the rocks. Before we could understand what was happening, it shuddered violently as its wings fell off, its fur melted into skin, its wrinkled scalp grew hair, and its limbs arranged themselves into shorter, more precise variations. Variations that were indisputably human.

"You saved me," the woman sobbed, grasping at the stone as she tried to stand. "I was trapped in that monster's body, but together you pulled my soul free."

Together you pulled my soul free.

Together.

That admission rocked something deep inside my heart, a part of myself that had been aching to find its purpose for far too long.

The woman looked down at her hands, which were smooth and no longer clawed, then closed her eyes, smiling widely as her body began to disappear. "I'm being called home," she cried. "I'm home."

And then, in a burst of star-flecked shadow, she was gone.

"Her soul was *trapped* in a demon's body?" I said, my mind racing to make sense of the preternatural transformation.

"She looked just like the demons in my castle," the Shadow Bringer sputtered. "Maker, even her cries sounded like them."

That's it.

It was the answer to a question that had disturbed me since I had first set foot in the Shadow Bringer's castle. His demons wanted out— but perhaps what they wanted was more than just freedom from the castle? They didn't listen to the Shadow Bringer as though he was their lord; rather, they were bound to him as though his darkness called to some hopeful, desperate part of themselves. Except the Shadow Bringer hadn't realized this—hadn't known how to use it in a way that could free them.

But somehow, together, we could.

Together we just did.

"What if that's where souls go after they're fully Corrupt?" I began, starting to formulate a theory that left me nauseated. "A demon can fully take over a dreamer's physical body, but where does the human's soul go in the meantime? The tales say *you* devour the dreamer's soul if the Light Bringer doesn't reach them in time."

The Shadow Bringer shook his head. "And we both know that isn't true."

I thumbed my chin. "Corruption can be a slow process. A progressive descent into a full demonic takeover." I shivered in disgust, remembering Eden as she lost her battle to Corruption. Sometimes she was lucid. Herself. But in a matter of days, she was more demon than girl. "When Eden was herself during her Corruption, she'd tell me about her visions. They were scary and very...dark. I always thought her Corruptive demon was tormenting her during these dreams, but maybe she was actually *inhabiting* her demon."

"And when Corruption fully occurs, the process is permanent," the Bringer supplied.

I stumbled on, growing more and more certain that I was right. "It would make sense for the dreamer's soul to anchor itself to the closest thing resembling a body. And that that body would be the demon's. A soul for a soul, a body for a body."

The Bringer looked utterly horrified. "If this is true, it will change everything."

"Those demons in your castle—what if those were *people*? The souls of those lost to Corruption and left uncleansed by the Light Bringer."

He shook his head. "Impossible. They have never displayed any semblance of humanity."

"But neither did that woman," I insisted. "While trapped, the souls might forget they were ever human in the first place. And our shadows are the key. Our shadows can *free them*, Bringer."

Overhead, in the clouds, Mithras jumped down from the Revel.

He was coming to betray Erebus—coming to show the Weavers that his friend had summoned demons from the Nocturne. And once the Weavers knew, it would be chaos. We would be hunted, just as Erebus was all those years ago.

For a moment, I thought Mithras's eyes flashed red.

But before I could tell, the Shadow Bringer sent us away in a flash of roiling darkness.

35

The Shadow Bringer and I stumbled back to Evernight.

"Hurry," he murmured, grabbing my hand and leading us through a hall lit by floating candlesticks. "We need to reach my chambers before the Weavers interfere."

Outside the corridor, the sounds of battle pressed in. Demons screamed as Weavers and their legions rose to meet them, the ringing of metal as it met claw and bone punctuated by a great, roaring wind and the crash of booming thunder.

It didn't take long before I was thoroughly lost. Evernight was a maze teeming with hidden hallways and opulent rooms. It was magic in its purest form, beauty summoned by the wildest and most eccentric of imaginations—yet somehow also convoluted and strange. We turned a corner and began to ascend a glass staircase, narrowly avoiding dreamers and scholars as they raced around us.

We pressed on, looping around a window-lined hall and up a smaller, cruder staircase cut from stone. Unlike the rest of Evernight, this section felt private and secluded. There were no people, no sounds other than our own. Even the ruckus of battle had dampened to a dull rumble.

And then we were alone.

It was a dark, elegant room, furnished in blue silk, marble tile, and several sprawling rugs. There was a bed on one end, tucked into a corner by three large windows; a balcony; a plush seating area; and several candelabras emitting soft, blue-hued light. On the other side of the room were several bookshelves lined with ancient-looking texts. A fireplace was centered inside the longest bookshelf; it was cavernous and carved with figureheads of a dragon, a wolf, and a stag.

"Is this your room?"

A fine mist of shadow spread from his fingertips, sinking into the walls and settling underneath every stone, tile, and rug. *A ward*, I thought. Something to protect us—and to keep others out.

"It was." He stood just inside the entryway, as if unsure of where to go next. "Though I was rarely here to enjoy it."

I tried not to think about what, exactly, he did—or didn't do—to enjoy the room.

"It's still strange to see beds in the Dream Realm."

"It is strange, isn't it?" the Bringer mused. "Like the food and drink we consume, sleeping in the Realm is a functional comfort. At Evernight, sleeping slows the mind and allows the dreamer to easily transition back into reality. In Noctis. More talented dreamers can force themselves awake without sleeping, but that takes practice. Many scholars can't do it with regularity."

I recalled my early dreams in the Shadow Bringer's castle. Despite my best efforts, I couldn't wake up on command. The demons in the woods had cornered me, so close that I could see the saliva dripping from their cracked lips, and *still* I couldn't wake.

He looked to the windows, almost as if he expected a demon to be peering in. "Sleep is a formality as much as it is a comfort. A reminder of what is...and what was."

What is and what was.

And also a way to return to the Shadow Bringer's castle. A way to discover our fates.

For a long while, the Bringer and I fought it. The raw, instinctual desire to sleep. To fall into a soft mattress, curl up in a blanket, and burrow deep into a pillow. To forget the day and begin anew. But slowly, our conversation faded. In the low candlelight, the Shadow Bringer's eyes became dark, pooling shadows. He dragged his palms to his brow. Sat there for another moment, shoulders tight. Waiting. Then he slammed his fists into his knees and stood.

"We can't keep this up, Bringer. If sleeping will help us travel back to the present, then we need to—"

The Bringer spun around, wild-eyed. "This is the third and final dream. What if we wake and this was all for nothing?" He took a deep breath, trying to steady himself, but his chest continued to heave. "If we wake up in my castle, unable to walk free after everything—" He cut himself off. As though he had admitted something he didn't want.

The pain in his eyes was too much.

"Perhaps it would help if you took off your armor," I suggested. "You need to relax."

The Bringer sighed, releasing some of his tension. The shadows in his eyes swam deep and thick. *Like syrup*, I thought. And then he conceded. His armor melted off his skin, replaced by a dark blue robe. My eye snagged on his chest. Followed it until his skin disappeared under a swath of silk. I wasn't sure if he wore anything else underneath.

"If I'm to wear this, you must wear something more suitable, too, then."

He tilted his head. Slowly, my Revel dress, still wet from the Nocturne and half-torn from our flight, shifted into a soft, flowing robe that mirrored his. His eyes melted as they beheld me. Turned raw and depthless—a testament to some unnamed emotion roiling underneath. Something primal, instinctive.

Something that spoke loudest in the shadows of the night.

I touched his hands, desperate to finally study them. His fingers, strong yet slender, curled around mine, tracing my wrists and brushing across my palms. His touch felt so unbelievably real.

"Why do you insist on doing that?" he asked, staring at my explorative fingers.

I dropped my hands, embarrassed, only to find him pulling them back.

"I simply asked *why*. I never asked you to stop," he said, voice lowering to a rasp.

Because I want to lower your shields. Ease the pain from your eyes. My face flushed as I looked at our intertwined hands. At his stern, hungry expression. The way his body seemed to curve around mine, craving closeness. How his lips parted slightly as he searched my face. All my logic—every critical, careful instinct I had—became buried underneath something else. Something I wasn't familiar with.

"I haven't held someone like this before," he murmured, restraint still apparent in his shadowed gaze. "I don't know how."

"I don't know, either," I breathed. "But I want to."

"Why?" There was that question again.

Why, indeed.

I grazed his neck with my fingertips, raven hair sweeping over my skin. "You don't deserve to be alone any longer."

"So it is because you pity me?" he asked, voice scarcely above a whisper.

I shook my head, irritated that he wasn't understanding. How could I simply *pity* him after all we'd been through? "No, not at all." I paused, my lip caught between my teeth. "It is because I want you—and I want to keep being with you, even after we wake up. I am yours, if you'll have me. Wherever our dreams take us."

We stared at each other for a few breathless, quiet moments. All that could be heard was the deep, hypnotic *thrum* of the Nocturne in the distance. And he still looked so damnably uncertain, as if he wasn't sure he even deserved my touch. He was so broken, so deprived of sincerity. I wanted to tear those thoughts from his mind.

"Then that makes you a fool," he said finally, shaking his head. "A complete and utter *fool*. You do not want this. This is nothing you should want—"

I grabbed his face and pulled it to mine, kissing him directly on his mocking, irritatingly beautiful mouth.

He pushed away, eyes wide. Shadows still, for once.

Weighing. Measuring.

Then he crashed his lips back to mine. He kissed me thoroughly—darkly. Exactly how I imagined he would prefer it. His lips were cool to the touch, tasting of starlight and velvet shadows. Of a cold breath of night air. I would drown in the taste if I could, every bit as starved for him as he was for me. He curled one hand in my hair while the other was at my spine, drawing me closer.

After a moment, he leaned back. The shadows in his eyes simmered, taunting.

"I'm a monster," he rasped.

"You're anything but," I shot back, shaking my head.

"You saw what I am capable of," he insisted. "What I *did*. I summoned those demons, Esmer. They crawled from the Nocturne as if I were a god bent on destroying the world."

"The man I met at the Revel didn't want to destroy the world. He wanted to heal it." I kissed him again, if only to rip that look of sorrow and dread from his eyes. He could mock, twist, and taunt all he wanted, but his eyes betrayed him. I went on: "You need to surrender. Let go of your guilt, your resentment, your doubt—everything." I shook my head, shuddering. "If anyone is a monster, it's me. Everything I've done, everyone I've hurt—" I cut myself off, a sob threatening to burst from my chest.

Slowly, his eyes softened.

"If I'm not a monster, then neither are you," he said seriously, searching my face. "You are not responsible for your family's deaths, nor are you at fault for leaving Elliot behind. You have done everything you could. You are strong, and you are brave. We both did what we could. What we knew."

"I don't want to call you 'Shadow Bringer' any longer," I said in a rush, cupping his face. I was so close to breaking, but I held firm. I needed him to understand how I felt. I did not see him as a monster now, but as a man, and I had felt that way for longer than I'd even realized. "It's not who you are. You have a name, an entire life lived. Friends, family. Years of service to a Realm that once respected you. You aren't a monster to me, and I want to honor that... *Erebus.*"

He pulled back, lips a breath from my own. I waited, but he did not correct me.

"Erebus," I said again, twining a hand through his hair as he shivered. My face burned, knowing I could affect him like that. It was intoxicating. "Can I call you that?"

A pause as we both looked at each other, chests heaving.

"Yes," he finally breathed. "Yes, you can call me by my name."

"Good." I traced a hand across the shadows forming patterns over his exposed chest. His skin was cool to the touch; smooth, flawless, and a pale contrast to his raven hair. "If our shadows can somehow right some of our kingdom's darkness, then I want to walk with you. Wherever you go, I will go, too. I'm not afraid anymore."

"Then I will gladly welcome you," he murmured, lips warming as he brushed them against my temple. "And I won't be afraid, either."

He didn't hesitate after that.

Erebus brought his mouth to mine, tangling his fist in my hair and pulling me close. Pressed against him this tightly, and with nothing between us but the thin fabric of our robes, I could feel every smooth, hard plane of him. Every lean muscle. The power in his arms as he held me. The shifting of his thighs as he brought me closer still. We made it to the bed, somehow—he stumbled backward, sitting on the edge, and I moved to his lap, all too aware of how our robes had spilled open. His had slipped off a shoulder; mine had fallen open at the chest. He gently tugged my hair back, exposing my throat, and I felt both shadow and teeth graze my neck, tantalizingly slow, before he returned his attention to my mouth. I burned to do the same. To kiss him there, as he had done to me.

He groaned, completely unbound, the moment my lips met his neck.

I dragged my mouth leisurely down his skin, pausing at the curve of his shoulder and the hollow of his throat. When I next looked at him, his eyes were clear—bright and filled with wonder. And when we finally settled into his bed, curling into each other as if we could shield ourselves from the encroaching dark, we didn't just feel anger, fear, or helplessness.

We felt, for perhaps the first time, a wild, reckless hope.

36

Eyes of molten silver, spinning slowly with shadows and starlight, met mine.

Erebus.

We woke in his bed at the castle, no longer at Citadel Evernight, but for a moment, we chose to ignore it. It was a mutually understood commitment to delaying the inevitable, but I didn't mind. A minute longer, draped in velvet and silk as Erebus held me against his chest—*that* was what I craved. Even if our time was nearly out, I would burn this into my memory. I ran my fingertips down the side of his face, admiring his features that were no longer hidden by a helmet. His hair, no longer black but his usual moon white, curled over his brow and tapered just above his shoulders in a tantalizing sweep.

"Your white hair is back," I whispered, brushing it from his temples. He shivered at the touch, leaning into my hand. "It suits you."

"Most would say it makes me look like a ghost. Some bloodless, foul creature not meant to exist under the sun." He lifted part of my hair from where it rested behind my shoulders, rolling it between his fingertips. "I'm not sure when the pigment faded from my hair and my skin. Maybe it happened the moment I stopped believing I might one day walk free."

But while his hair had returned to what I knew it to be, his eyes seemed different. They were deeper, somehow, and absolutely radiant.

"And your eyes—"

"Are no longer the only ones with shadows in them," he finished, releasing my hair before guiding my hand to his lips. "Look at yourself."

A smooth, glass-like surface appeared in front of me, lifted by tendrils of his power, and I peered at my reflection. Sure enough, my eyes were now the same as his: silver and churning with shadows and stars. They would truly make us seem united in power and intent. If ever I encountered his enemies, they would discern my connection to him right away.

But I didn't mind.

In fact, I very much *wanted* to be associated with this haunted man made of shadows and stars. For so long, I'd sought nothing more than to run from the darkness—to escape Norhavellis and carve out a future for myself somewhere else. I'd dreamed of how wonderful it would be to live a life of normalcy and safety. Once, I'd even dreamed of killing this man who lay before me, pressing his mouth to the inside of my wrist.

But a life without hardships would never produce a girl able to fight Corruption.

An ordinary girl wouldn't be able to traverse the Dream Realm, learn its disquieting secrets, and emerge stronger through it all.

I needed to fight. I needed to face my purpose with my chin held high, even if the future was uncertain. I needed to fight for Elliot, for my mother and father, and for Eden, too.

As soon as I shifted my attention back to Erebus, admiring his mouth and the way his hair fell over the hollows of his cheeks, the mirror retreated to somewhere else in the room. He held my stare, even as he uncurled my hand and interlaced our fingers, and by his next breath, our hands were covered past the wrist in matching black leather. They were a stark contrast underneath the delicate sleeves of our night robes.

I flexed my fingers, unused to the sensation of my hands being so thoroughly covered. "I'm assuming these are for protection to 'remind us we aren't in reality'?"

"You're catching on," he remarked, a brief smile lifting his expression and sending a warm, tingling sensation to my stomach. Then he murmured, almost as an afterthought, "But perhaps that is no longer the worst of fates."

His chambers were eerily quiet; there were no demons screaming for their release, no Weavers waiting to interrogate us, no stars falling out of the sky. His castle was, for all it could be, still standing. It was just us, our spinning shadows, and a faint breeze drifting in from his balcony. But we couldn't hide here forever, no matter how good it felt to be alone in the world, together.

"We aren't in the Beyond, so let's see if we can escape before the domain finishes shattering," I said, beginning to sit up. *Maker*, this man was distracting. "I'm thinking we should try the main entrance—"

Shadows roped around my wrists, catching me off-balance and pulling me into a pile of velvet pillows. Erebus leaned over me, quickly replacing the shadows with his hands, and kissed me.

There was no softness or patience in his kiss.

It was all fire, teeth, and tongue—and the aching sense it might be our last.

"Not yet," he murmured, covering my body with his. My robe hitched up at the movement, and one of his thighs pressed between mine, pinning me in place. "I say we remain as we are."

My body responded to his heat, instinctively arching toward his hips as his mouth played possessively against mine. His attention drifted lower, trailing scorching kisses down my throat. When I was certain he was perfectly distracted at my neck, I threw the shadows back around him, yanking him out of bed by his shoulders.

"Stop kissing me like it's our last," I accused, standing to face him.

His eyes shuttered, betraying raw, desperate emotions clawing for attention. "I'm not."

I shook my head. "You *are*. And because of that, we're getting out of your bedroom and leaving this castle. Immediately. We can come back to this"—I gave him a searing kiss of my own—"later. When we're free."

He thrashed, but the shadows held firm.

"Don't make me drag you downstairs. It's a long way down."

He laughed, the sound deliciously rich and mirthful. It made my face burn. The shadows slid from his shoulders, drifting to his feet. "I'd like to see you try."

Erebus willed the shadows away as if they were as insubstantial as smoke, storming toward the door to his bedchamber. His robe slipped away as he walked, quickly replaced by his usual armor of liquid night and overlapping scales. He looked back at me, expectant, as an onyx crown slid into place, threading into his hair.

"What?" he asked, mouth twitching up into a half grin. "I wasn't about to face our fate in a robe. Unless that's what you'd prefer."

I decided I quite liked him like this—smiling, irritatingly beautiful, and *alive*.

I did my best to mirror him, willing my robe to change into a dark, flowing dress with scales like his and a crown to match. Adding a slit to the front gave my legs greater range, partially exposing a pair of slim boots, pointed and sharp, which swept up my calves like a second skin. The only things I didn't like were the gloves he'd attired us with. I formed a new pair over the old, their clawlike fingertips reminiscent of the ones he used to wear.

Catching him looking at me, I clicked the taloned fingers together. "I wanted to feel what it was like to be sharp and untouchable. I think I like it."

Identical claws stretched from his gloves as he reached for me. As soon as our hands made contact, the metal covering our palms shifted into black leather. This was surprisingly pleasant; even with the harsh metal on top, I could feel the shape of his palm and the length of every finger.

"What a pair we make," he murmured. Shadows spun around us in a slow dance. "Claws, scales, and onyx crowns. A wicked king and queen who can perhaps use their darkness for good."

The castle vestibule was as I had remembered it, candelabras twinkling from their grooves in the walls and extravagant furniture beckoning from the shadows. Claw marks still gouged the walls, and most of the tapestries and paintings were hanging loosely in snakelike tendrils, but beauty remained. The castle was surely a ghost of Erebus's original creation, but pockets of wonder and artistic intent were apparent. The iron doors were as I remembered, too; colossal and brimming with hundreds of meticulously carved figures.

We stopped just shy of the castle doors, silent as the weight of what we were about to attempt slid over us. The Light Bringer had forbidden me from doing what I was about to do, but what power did his warning truly hold? The "monstrous" Shadow Bringer wasn't a monster after all—and the demons had already escaped, rendering my initial promise useless. I'd deal with Mithras and the repercussions of my actions later. I had no other choice; this *was* the path forward.

So long as the doors opened.

"Go first," Erebus directed, taking a step back. "You should have no trouble stepping free of this place."

"No. You have every right to go first. Or we should go together," I told him.

Erebus made no motion to move, arms stiff at his sides. "Please. I insist."

His uncertainty unnerved me. If the curse hadn't lifted, then what hope did we have? I steeled myself, taking a deep breath. If he couldn't leave, I'd have to carry on by myself.

There is no other path forward.

"Fine," I said, quickly grabbing the handles and trying to hide my fear. The metal was cool underneath my palms, and the carvings, though shadows curled over their forms, were eerily still. "But I'm taking you with me the second I make it over the threshold."

I pulled.

Surprisingly, it was as effortless as pushing aside a curtain—one fluid motion, silent and smooth as the doors slid across the stone. Then, before I could dwell on what happened to Erebus when he temporarily left the boundaries of his castle, I took a quick step over the threshold.

No burning, no melting armor. No skin peeling from my bones. Nothing.

"Come on," I beckoned, immediately turning back toward the castle and holding out my hand. Erebus was still partially hidden in the shadows, firmly rooted in place. "I'm not leaving here without you, Erebus."

He took a step forward, the toes of his boots dusting the threshold. They did not smolder or catch flame; still, when he grabbed hold of my hand, his was shaking. An ugly, unwanted part of my mind screamed at me, a violent, desperate warning. It hissed at me to drop his hand—to push him back inside the castle and slam the door. But I shoved the voice away, pulling him toward me instead.

I wanted him to be free. I *needed* him to be free.

Erebus flinched, silver eyes narrowing, but he allowed himself to be guided forward. And, most importantly of all...

He didn't burn.

After five hundred years of torment, Erebus was *free*.

It was night, as it always was, but stars dappled the sky, illuminating the surrounding forest with its iridescent leaves and a courtyard filled with sculptures, sapphire vases, and stone fountains with star-flecked water. His domain had been restored.

He fell to his knees.

I rushed forward, holding him close. He held my waist tightly, pressing his face into my stomach as a heavy breath rushed out of him. A surge of overwhelming emotion filled my chest, almost too much to bear. I needed him to be safe. I needed him to be happy. And then, in a flash of clarity that nearly buckled me, I realized—I *knew*—I needed him as my friend, my partner, my *lover*. I needed him now as I'd need him always. Wind ruffled his hair, meandering through what remained of a few shadows atop his shoulders.

A sharp *crack* from somewhere in the trees snapped us to attention.

What had been silent and motionless a breath before was now pure chaos; demons swarmed at us from beneath the trees, screeching and howling in a desperate, hideous plea. Some ran, some crawled, some limped, but they all moved as quickly as their distorted limbs allowed. Erebus and I brandished our swords at the same time, and shadows rushed from the sky, the ground, and the castle itself to form a protective surge around us.

We didn't have time to do anything—breathe, think, move.

So we held our ground.

Surprisingly, the demons stopped just before the lowest stair, leaving Erebus and me towering over even the tallest of the horde. Eyes burned from within skulls, and teeth gnashed from bleeding lips as they beheld us, making way for two familiar figures: the tall, gray-faced demon with the mottled cape and the coal-eyed demon with the sharp tongue and judgmental stare. The two demons who had kept me company—if that was what it could be called—when I was alone in the castle.

When they reached the bottom of the stairs, they each gave a quick bow.

"These two seem familiar," Erebus said quietly, laying a protective hand against my back.

"The gray-faced one led me to your castle; I wouldn't have found you without its guidance." I tightened my grip on my sword. The coppery tang of old blood, hot breath, and unwashed fur was close to making me gag. "And they both found me when I was alone. They spoke to me from the woods whenever I was on your balcony."

"What do you want from us?" Erebus asked, eyes sharp and assessing. The demons stilled, listening. "You're all free now. Unless you're back to demand your end—in which case, Esmer and I can gladly oblige."

A chill swept down my spine, brutal and sharp. Erebus and me against hundreds of demons was foolish—an impossibility. But there was no other way out. The sword in my hands seemed to sense my desperation; it hummed, faintly warming my grip.

The gray-faced demon's lips twisted into a deformed smile. "We aren't free yet. But soon we will be."

The coal-eyed demon nodded, expression solemn. "Free us. Cleanse us. Only you know how."

The demons rose at the same time, a fiery, demanding hunger burning in their eyes.

And then they charged.

Erebus roared, bringing the surge of shadows down like a scythe. The force slammed the first wave of demons into the stairs with a brutal *crack* that sent stones flying and hurled dozens more back into the woods. In the middle of the chaos—among bleeding mouths, snarling teeth, and desperate lunges for our feet—Erebus threw us backward into a doorway-sized shadow.

It felt like slipping into a cold, icy pit. As though ice were sliding through my veins and a wind were pouring through the inner workings of my heart and plucking out anything dark or broken. It felt painful, briefly—but then it became a deep, comforting relief. Something that held on to my soul and poured water through its cracks, setting it free.

We stumbled from the doorway of shadow, now on the other side of the castle's sprawling courtyard.

"What *was* that?" I quickly asked. The demons hadn't noticed us, but it would only be a matter of seconds before they did. "It felt like my entire being was being cleansed. Or judged."

Erebus's jaw tensed. "I could feel the shadows working to pull something out of you. To examine—as you said—your very being. Your soul, perhaps. I've never felt anything like it before. Something is different, Esmer." He looked at me briefly, eyes flashing in concern. "Did it hurt you?"

"No," I said, giving a firm shake of my head. "The opposite, really. Like a cold bath after a long journey in the sun."

Some of his concern ebbed, but not all. "Good."

A realization dawned over me at his admission. *Something is different,* he'd said. But what? If we worked together, could we purify the demons in the courtyard as we purified the woman at Evernight? Perhaps something had changed in us now that we were back in the present and no longer divided.

"Would you be able to create something like that again? A gate big enough that all the demons could fit?" The demons noticed us; they roared in frustration, hurling themselves from the stairs and the trees. "If the shadows can quell or purify the demons, that might be our only chance at stopping them."

Erebus's mouth tightened. "Yes. But while I'm doing that, I'll need your help containing them. A wall"—the demons were nearly upon us, crashing through the central fountain— "or a tunnel. Now—*hurry.*"

I shoved my fear aside and focused on the shadows; if I couldn't manipulate them, we'd be lost. They felt like a web around me, a web with strings I could pull and shape. I mentally pulled one, two—*that's not enough*—then grasped for fistfuls and armfuls, forcing them into a tunnel that the demons began to surge through.

Not enough.

I squeezed the shadows narrower and narrower, resisting every part of me that wanted to scream or run. The tunnel was as large as I could make it; I had no more to give.

It has to be enough.

The first demons to reach us lunged for our throats. I flinched, losing my grip on all the threads—and they crashed over the demons like a wave, merging with a pitch-black gateway that Erebus hurled down the tunnel in a frantic sweep. I could feel the shadows pulling at the demons, plucking out every broken, terrible thing.

For a brief moment, all was dark.

And then...

It was as if the shadows had been pulled from the sky itself, rendering the stars as brilliant as I'd ever seen them. The castle and its courtyard were washed in silver, revealing hundreds of demons losing fur, teeth, claws, skulls, wings—hundreds of broken, distorted creatures transforming before our eyes into adults and children. They were human.

All of them.

The gray-faced demon had become an equally tall man with dark, honey-brown hair, and the coal-eyed demon was now a pale, lithe man with sharp features and black hair that framed his jaw in a smooth sweep. I recognized them instantly—they were the two men who had entered the coliseum with Erebus at Evernight.

"Ceveon—Sorren," Erebus choked out. "All this time, you were both here?"

"Always," Ceveon said weakly, attempting a small but roguish smile. A few tears began to slide down his light brown face, but he brushed them away before they could reach his jaw. "With you, always. Though your domain got to feel a bit stifling, I'll admit. Especially when you can't communicate properly inside its bounds."

"Stifling? That's putting it lightly," Sorren muttered, scowling at Ceveon. But when he turned to behold Erebus and me, his face settled into something that nearly resembled relief. His eyes, like Ceveon's, were glittering, but he did not cry. "Fortunately, five centuries pass in a blink when your mind is tethered to that of a demon. Now the curse is broken and the real work can begin."

My eyes swept the dreamers, heart racing at the thought of finding Eden or my parents. My throat tightened as I braced for what I might see. But when they didn't appear, a painful blend of disappointment and relief washed over me. If they weren't here, then surely that meant they were somewhere better—with the Maker in paradise. Still, the unexpected hope of hugging them one last time nearly shattered me.

"Esmer, what—" Erebus began, noting my distress, but was sharply cut off.

"How curious," a new voice interrupted, its silky pitch threading through the courtyard, "that the demons in your castle weren't demons at all. Merely locked-up souls, just as the tales declare. But you broke that narrative when you set them free today."

Somnus slid from the trees, hair covering his robes in inky tendrils. He didn't look at all surprised to find us; in fact, I sensed he had been watching the scene unfold from the very beginning. Around the castle courtyard, dreamers struggled into sitting or kneeling positions. Hundreds of dreamers, some sobbing, some groaning, some staring silently at the stars. Ceveon and Sorren staggered forward, flanking Erebus and me.

"Somnus," Erebus bit out. "You knew. You *knew* that these humans were locked inside the bodies of demons. All this time—*all this time.*"

"You should be grateful," Somnus said lowly, scarcely touching the ground as he strode toward us. "Aren't you pleased I led them back to you?"

"I'd be pleased to have known freedom five centuries ago. For myself, and all these innocent dreamers."

"Impossible," Somnus said with a dismissive shrug. "Your entire domain was locked, shielded from outside interference until you tricked Esmer into taking your place. Whom, by the way, you wouldn't have had the pleasure of meeting had you been freed five hundred years ago. You really should thank her, considering—"

"Erebus shouldn't have to thank *anyone* for being set free, me included," I countered vehemently. "And don't imply that his suffering was valuable just because he met me. There is never nobility in suffering. If there's anyone to thank, thank the Maker I found Erebus when I did."

I found Erebus's hand and squeezed it. Shadows left over from the dreamers' cleansing drifted around our bodies, winding through our fingers and clinging to our feet as if they wished to protect us.

"And find him you did. Curious," Somnus murmured, leveling us with a withering stare. "Either way, I saved you the hassle of collecting all these poor, lost souls. They scattered like mindless beasts the moment they broke free from your castle. Fortunately, leaving the castle allowed them to speak and have a somewhat-functioning sense of logic. Otherwise, my task would have been a bit more complicated."

I shook my head. "But they're not mindless at all. They're *human*. All of them."

"That depends on your definition of 'human.' Their mortal bodies have already perished, but their souls remain intact. That will be something to deal with when you begin commanding them, I'm afraid." He added, muttering darkly, "If they will even listen, that is."

"What do you mean, 'deal with'?" Erebus bit out, face paling.

Somnus swept his arms wide. "You have a Corruptive curse to break, a half-dead army to train, and a red-eyed demon thirsting for your souls. Quite the mess on your hands."

A serpentine smile slid across his lips.

"Best get started, Shadow Weavers."

EPILOGUE

Citadel Firstlight had never felt like such a tomb.

Mithras jammed his fingers under his cloak, warming them as best he could. He wasn't sure why he felt so cold. Someone had left a window open, or perhaps a guard had dawdled at their post exchange too long, allowing the night air in as they spoke with their replacement.

Damn them, he thought, channeling his rage at no one in particular.

But his anger was wasted. There was no *them* in these halls tonight. There was no open window or door. No one to blame, condemn, or lash out at.

But damn them, anyway.

Because the more he could focus on a *them*, the more easily he could forget that the cold was coming from *him*. He could feel it working through his veins. The bitter otherness of the thing that swelled within him. It would soon worm up his throat, stiffening his jaw and chilling his breath.

Hurry.

It hurt to breathe. His feet felt sluggish and dull.

Hurry.

He slammed his shoulder into the nearest door, stumbling inside and leaning heavily against it after it shut.

The third-floor chapel.

How fitting.

He locked the doors behind him, staggering to one of the seven mirrors that towered over the altar. They were designed to reflect the congregation; designed to honor the Maker and the seven Weavers who saw all. Tonight, they would reflect only Mithras.

Him and the spirit of another.

When he was ready, or near enough to it, he looked up. The red eyes that met him in the mirror were not his own. He watched, disgusted and helpless as his mouth opened and closed.

"You are running out of time, Mithras," the demon inside him hissed.

He regained control of himself just long enough to speak. "We've found a suitable host," Mithras gasped. A few breaths, if that, were all he was given in these conversations. "As soon as he is ready, I will bring you to him."

Mithras's skin itched. The vile thing inside him wanted *out.*

"I will be the judge of his suitability."

"You always are, my lord," Mithras answered, lowering his chin.

"Hmm," the creature rumbled. Mithras's hand began to move, and his head tilted down to behold it. He shoved down the overwhelming urge to recoil. The demon had never exercised this degree of puppetry before. "The longer I am here, the more I enjoy *this* body."

"I am glad it serves," Mithras said weakly.

"Perhaps you are more of a fit than I realized." There was that hand again. Moving without his will. It moved higher, connecting with the muscles and ligaments of his arm, and traced part of his reflection. "Would you deny me your mortal coil?"

Mithras swallowed and shook his head. It was all he could manage in response.

"No, you are too weak. My powers are forced to manifest through your anger and your shame. A god does not belong in the body of a cow-ard and a fool." The demon drew his hand away. Mithras's eyes—his own, but not—gleamed in the chapel's blue light, glowing crimson red and smoking as if they were aflame. "A god deserves the body of one who commands the dark and makes it bend." His eyes smoldered; smoke rose from them in horrible rivulets, burning his skin. "I think you are hiding them from me, Mithras. I think you are hiding them—and I will devour their souls and wear their skins before you can stop me."

And in another breath, the demon left him.

Mithras fell to his knees, retching violently as he dug his fingers into the stone and tried to keep himself from screaming. He trembled as he clawed his fingernails down, down, down, trying to ground himself in his body again. It was harder this time. It was harder every time. It used to take him a few minutes—seconds, even—to feel like himself.

Now it sometimes took days.

He did not recognize the tears as they fell. They curved down his frozen face and dripped onto the stone. Some wet the tops of his hands, but he couldn't feel them. He was afraid to think. Afraid to speak. So he wept in silence.

"I'm sorry," he finally whispered, fingers digging into the floor. It was a pathetic plea to everyone he'd ever hurt, betrayed, or tried to pro-tect. Everyone he'd tried so desperately to save from the monster within him. Esmer. Elliot. Silas. Erebus. *All of them.* He was about to break—shatter into dust. "I'm sorry."

ACKNOWLEDGMENTS

Once upon a time, there was a little girl who dared to dream big.

This book is for her as much as it is for anyone else: the one who first believed in the magic of books and the power of her imagination. That girl would grow up to become a college student who spent her midnight hours writing a story of a prince trapped in a nightmare, and a high school English teacher who finished what would become her debut novel between planning lessons and grading essays.

As someone who still believes in the beauty of their dreams and that everything really does happen for a reason, I first and foremost need to thank God for paving this path and for giving me the strength to pursue my purpose in life. Without my faith, there would be no story to tell.

And although *Dream by the Shadows* sat in my imagination for many years, publishing a book requires a team of incredible, passionate professionals to bring that vision to life. I am extremely fortunate to have such a talented team around me, and it is an honor to thank them here.

To my incredible UK agent, Ciara Finan. When you fell in love with my *The Phantom of the Opera*–inspired manuscript, you changed my life. I'll never forget when I first received your editorial notes; you found the heart of my story and made it sing. Thank you for being my first champion. You're a rock star.

I also owe so much to my spectacular US agent, Gwen Beal. I truly wouldn't be able to live out this dream without you and your relentless support, and I am so grateful for your expertise. You saw the potential in my work and fought for it. Thank you for all you do.

To the marvelous, genius, spins-words-into-*magic* US editor, Jessica Anderson: The stars aligned when *Dream by the Shadows* found its home with you. Thank you for believing in this book and in me, and for making my publishing journey something out of a fairy tale. From the first manuscript to the final pages, you have shaped this story with such enthusiasm, care, and brilliance. You are a dream to work with, and I am so lucky. Thank you.

Thank you to the outstanding team at Christy Ottaviano Books and Little, Brown Books for Young Readers who brought this book to life: VP and Publisher Christy Ottaviano, Art Director and Designer Karina Granda, Production Editor Lindsay Walter-Greaney, VP and Executive Director of Marketing Emilie Polster, editorial intern Nadja Anderson-Oberman, Marketing Coordinator Andie Divelbiss, Senior Digital Marketing Manager Savannah Kennelly, Associate Director of Publicity Cheryl Lew, Associate Publicist Melanie Rapoport, Senior Production Manager Jonathan Lopes, School and Library Marketing Director Victoria Stapleton, copyeditor Kerianne Okie Steinberg, and proofreader Tracy Koontz. Your dedication and expertise made this dream possible, and I am so fortunate to have such a talented team behind me.

Thank you to my cover artist, Andrew Davis. The Shadow Bringer's gothic castle looming in the background; the sweeping purple sky; our heroine, Esmer, preparing to embark on the adventure of a lifetime... it's everything I could have hoped for and more.

Thank you to my UK editor, Sophie Keefe, and the entire team at Headline: Marketer Ana Carter, Press Officer Federica Trogu, Sales Director Becky Bader, International Sales and Product Director Eleanor Wood, International Sales and Product Executive Ellie Walker, Divisional Director—Digital & Online Sales Sinead White, Senior Audio Manager Ellie Wheeldon, Production Controller Victoria Lord, and Picture Researcher Kate Brunt. Your early support and expertise have been invaluable in bringing this story to a wider audience, and I am truly grateful for this book to be in your expert hands.

I am immensely grateful for the authors who excitedly read *Dream by the Shadows* early: Kate Golden, Elly Blake, R. M. Gray, and Lyndall Clipstone. Thank you for your beautiful words and for diving into this dark and dreamy story of mine without hesitation.

To Meg Smitherman, specifically: You have been a source of encouragement and humor throughout this entire journey, and I am so grateful. I'm not sure what I did to deserve your friendship, but I can't wait to keep dreaming big and obsessing over fictional characters alongside you.

Thank you also to authors Hazel McBride, Lacey Lehotzky, Lyndall Clipstone, Shelby Nicole, Kate Golden, R. M. Gray, Lydia Gregovic, Stephanie Blair, Rebecca Kenney, Jordan Gray, Bea Northwick, Kara Douglas, and many others for being a source of knowledge, advice, and positivity at all stages in my writing journey.

Next, to my family, my unshakable foundation: to my husband, for being my anchor through every storm and light in every shadow; to my two boys, whose joy and laughter remind me why we chase dreams in the first place; to my mom and dad, for nurturing the imaginative child who spent her days drawing and writing, and for encouraging me to follow my passion for literature in both my collegiate studies and career; and to my brother, who helped me act out stories when we were kids—you were my first cocreator, and those adventures are still some of my favorites. Thank you all, not only for fostering my love for reading and writing but for instilling in me an unshakeable courage in myself and my dreams, too.

Thank you to the miscellaneous "extras" that inspired me to write this book: iced coffee; a nighttime breeze through an open window; long car rides with only music to daydream to; the songs "Mausoleum" by Rafferty, "Contagious" by Night Riots, and "Out of the Darkness" by Matthew and the Atlas; Erik from *The Phantom of the Opera*; all the beautiful character art of Esmer and the Shadow Bringer; and my own magnificently strange lucid dreams.

Thank you to the early indie supporters of this book. You stepped into the shadows with me and dreamed alongside this story, and your belief in its magic has been a guiding light. Thank you.

Finally, thank *you* for reading this book. I hope you enjoyed your time in the Dream Realm, and I hope it encouraged you to weave beauty and purpose out of the darkest shadows. Pursue your dreams relentlessly; they are waiting for you.

GLOSSARY

ABSOLVERS: People given an allowance by the sovereign of Noctis to distribute and regulate the kingdom's elixir supply.

CORRUPTION: A deadly affliction caused by the Shadow Bringer and his demons. A human can become Corrupt after a demon claims them in the Dream Realm. The only cure is a "purification" ritual performed by the Light Bringer. The soul will be saved, but the mortal body will perish.

DEMONS: Monsters that haunt humanity's dreams and plague the Shadow Bringer.

DOMAINS: Separate "kingdoms" within the Dream Realm that each host a Weaver. Dream scholars and acolytes are given small domains in which to practice and hone their skills.

ELIXIR: The only known substance to control Corruption. When consumed, it prevents the user from dreaming. However, it is extremely costly.

LIGHT BRINGER: As the esteemed sovereign of Noctis and leader of the Light Legion, Mithras Atrelle Tethebrum seeks to purify the kingdom's Corrupt. However, something twisted lurks behind his golden eyes.

LIGHT LEGION: Led by Mithras, the Light Bringer, the Light Legion travels the kingdom of Noctis to purify its Corrupt.

MAKER: The central deity of Noctis, who manages the Dream Realm and communicates to humanity through the Weavers.

SHADOW BRINGER: A monster said to have unleashed Corruption upon humankind. Though locked in a tomb five hundred years ago, the Shadow Bringer still lives, sealed in with the demons only he can contain.

WEAVERS: Immortal, powerful, and anointed by the Maker, Weavers manage, monitor, and protect the Dream Realm. They mysteriously vanished after demons, heralded by the Shadow Bringer, overran the Realm.

WEAVER OF THE PAST: Somnus

WEAVER OF THE PRESENT: Xander

WEAVER OF THE FUTURE: Theia

WEAVER OF FIRE: Fenrir

WEAVER OF WATER: Nephthys

WEAVER OF EARTH: Ceres

WEAVER OF AIR: Lelantos

LOCATIONS

BEYOND: The Beyond is the Dream Realm's equivalent of hell. A horrific, unfathomable place of darkness.

CITADEL EVERNIGHT: Located in the Dream Realm, Evernight once served as a lavish gathering place for dreamers and an academy for dream scholars and the Weavers' acolytes.

CITADEL FIRSTLIGHT: Located in Istralla, Citadel Firstlight is where Weavers once communicated with earthly rulers. It is also where they slumber in immortal sleep. Now it is where Mithras and his Light Legion operate from in their quest to cleanse Noctis of Corruption.

DREAM REALM: The Realm is where the seven Weavers once ruled, managing humanity's dreams and bringing divine inspiration to the masses. Now the Realm is dying and infested by the demons that were unleashed upon it.

ISTRALLA: The wealthy seaside capital of Noctis.

NOCTIS: A kingdom governed by the Light Bringer. Corruption festers in its shadows.

NOCTURNE: An ancient sea in the Dream Realm that holds humanity's dreams. Demons infiltrated its waters, rendering it a poisonous sea of nightmares and decay.

NORHAVELLIS: The small, Corrupt-ridden village where Esmer and Elliot grew up.

TOMB OF THE DEVOURER: A cave-like structure where the living body of the Shadow Bringer is held.

VISSTILL: A large forest that surrounds Norhavellis and holds the Tomb of the Devourer.

LOGAN KARLIE

holds a master's degree in English literature from the University of Arkansas. She loves writing stories brimming with gothic themes, atmospheric worlds, and characters who fight to overcome the shadows that haunt them. She lives with her family in Illinois, where she also taught high school English. She invites you to visit her on Instagram and TikTok @authorlogankarlie.

The Dream Realm

Domain of Ceres

Domain of Lelantos

Domain of Nephthys

CITADEL EVERNIGHT

The Nocturne,

Domain of Fenrir